KU-019-507

FORGOTTEN CHILD

Kitty Neale was raised in South London and this working-class area became the inspiration for her novels. In the 1980s she moved to Surrey with her husband and two children, but in 1998 there was a catalyst in her life when her son died, aged just 27. After joining other bereaved parents in a support group, Kitty was inspired to take up writing and her books have been *Sunday Times* bestsellers.

Kitty now lives in Spain with her husband.

To find out more about Kitty go to
www.kittyneale.co.uk.

By the same author:

KITTY NEALE

Forgotten Child

AVON

This novel is entirely a work of fiction.
The names, characters and incidents portrayed in it are
the work of the author's imagination. Any resemblance to
actual persons, living or dead, events or localities is
entirely coincidental.

AVON

A division of HarperCollins*Publishers*
77–85 Fulham Palace Road,
London W6 8JB

www.harpercollins.co.uk

A Paperback Original 2009

1

First published in Great Britain by
HarperCollins*Publishers* 2010

Copyright © Kitty Neale 2010

Kitty Neale asserts the moral right to
be identified as the author of this work

A catalogue record for this book is
available from the British Library

ISBN: 978-0-00792-597-1

Set in Minion by Palimpsest Book Production Limited,
Falkirk, Stirlingshire

Printed and bound in Great Britain by Clays Ltd, St Ives plc

MIX
Paper from
responsible sources

FSC
www.fsc.org   **FSC® C007454**

FSC is a non-profit international organisation established to promote the
responsible management of the world's forests. Products carrying the FSC
label are independently certified to assure consumers that they come
from forests that are managed to meet the social, economic and
ecological needs of present and future generations.

Find out more about HarperCollins and the environment at
www.harpercollins.co.uk/green

In memory of William (Bill) Goodbody, a dear friend who is sorely missed.

Prologue

The argument had raged for two days, but the man couldn't give in – wouldn't give in. His wife had to agree, and once again he urged, 'We've got to do something. All right, I know they were distant relatives, but it was still a shock to hear they died.'

'You've never mentioned them before.'

He sighed – he'd been through this, told her all this, but nevertheless he tried to remain calm. 'I told you, I haven't seen them since my childhood; lost touch with them when my parents died, but nevertheless we're the only family she has left now.'

'*You're* her only family,' his wife snapped.

'Like it or not, by marrying me they became your relatives. If this was someone in your family, I wouldn't think twice.'

'That's easy for you to say, but something like this wouldn't have happened in *my* family.'

'There's no need for the high and mighty attitude. We've no idea what happened to her – how she came to be in such a dreadful place, and I for one am not going to judge her.'

'I don't care. I can't do it. I've been unwell and you're asking too much of me.'

'And if you expect me to just walk away, you're asking too much of me. I'd never be able to forgive myself – or you.'

'Now you're using emotional blackmail.'

'If you had an ounce of compassion I wouldn't need to.'

'That isn't fair. I do feel sorry for what happened to her, really I do, but . . . but . . .'

The man saw the strain on his wife's face, but couldn't stop now. He had to convince her. His voice softened, trying honey this time. 'I'm sorry, darling, that was cruel of me. Of course you're compassionate, in fact it's one of the things I love about you. I think that's why I've been taken aback by your attitude. I somehow thought that, like me, you wouldn't be able to just walk away.'

'Please, please, we've been arguing about this for so long and my head is splitting. Let me think. I need time to think.'

He could tell she was weakening and felt a surge of triumph – sure that at last, one final push would do it. He stood up, bent to kiss her and before leaving the room said, 'All right, darling, I'll leave you to think. You're a wonderful woman, a kind, caring woman, and I feel sure you'll come to the right decision.'

It was another two hours before he got his answer. His wife had agreed, but only in part. She'd been adamant, and he'd been unable to bend her any further.

There was only one thing he could do now, but he dreaded it.

Chapter One

Wimbledon, South London, June 1971

It was home, a redbrick facade draped with wisteria, bay windows and an oak front door that appeared welcoming; yet as Jennifer Lavender pulled out her key, she knew there'd be no welcome inside. If her father was at home things would be different, but he was away again, his job often involving long periods of absence.

With a fixed smile on her face, Jenny walked into the drawing room. She had learned to be careful of her mother's moods, and said quietly, 'Hello, I'm home.'

'I can see that,' Delia Lavender said dismissively before turning her attention back to her son. She was a tall woman, slim, with immaculately groomed auburn hair and hazel eyes that were now showing concern as she asked him, 'Do you think you can manage to eat something, darling? I could make a shepherd's pie.'

'Yes, all right,' Robin said.

Her brother didn't look ill to Jenny, but as usual Robin avoided meeting her eyes. At seventeen years old he had the same colouring as their mother. He had come home from college the previous day complaining of a sore throat and headache and as always he was being mollycoddled. At that moment, her mother spoke and Jenny snapped to attention.

'Don't just stand there. Get changed and then peel the potatoes.'

Jenny ran upstairs, anxious as ever to please her mother. From an early age she'd been taught to do housework, but it had to be up to her mother's high standards or she would be made to do it again. Yet no matter how hard she tried, Jenny was aware of the gulf between them, a gulf that widened even further if she showed the least disobedience. It wasn't that her mother was physically cruel. Her punishments tended to be more mental than physical and worse when there were just the two of them at home. On those occasions, depending on her mother's mood, Jenny would either be made to scrub the kitchen floor over and over again, or be sent to her room and told to stay there.

At times Jenny felt her mother actually hated her, and for a moment she looked at her reflection in the mirror, wondering what she had done; what it was about her that was so unlovable. At nearly sixteen years old, she favoured her father in looks, yet lacked his height. Her friends told her she was pretty, but all Jenny saw was pale skin, blonde hair and light blue eyes: a face devoid of colour.

She was confused by her brother's recent attitude towards her too. As small children they had played together and Robin had been the one she ran to when upset. Nowadays though, he had grown as distant as her mother, until Jenny felt as if her presence was unwanted by either of them.

As so often happened, a wave of loneliness washed over her, but it was something Jenny didn't really understand. She had friends, a family, yet there was this feeling of something missing in her life – something inexplicable.

She heard the telephone ring, followed by the murmur of her mother's voice. It must have been a short call as only moments later Delia's voice rang up the stairs. 'Jennifer, do get a move on!'

'Coming,' she called back, hurrying to change out of her school uniform.

'It's about time too,' her mother complained when Jenny appeared.

'I got good marks in English today,' Jenny said, hoping to please her mother as she made a start on the potatoes.

'It's a bit late to do well now. If you hadn't failed your eleven plus exam you'd have gone on to grammar school. Instead you're only destined for some sort of menial work.'

'I've done well at typing and could get a job in an office.'

'A typist,' Delia said derisively. 'That's hardly something I can brag about at the tennis club.'

Jenny felt the sting of tears. She knew how important appearances were to her mother, how much she valued her social standing, and had always felt the pressure. So much so that when the exam papers had been put in front of her she had frozen, her mind refusing to work.

'Stop sniffing, it isn't ladylike. I sometimes regret that we didn't send you to a private school, but we have enough expense in funding Robin's education and his is more important.'

'I'm thirsty,' Robin said as he walked in to pour himself a glass of water.

'You should have called me, darling.'

'Stop fussing, Mother, there's nothing wrong with my legs,' he said, gulping the water and then asking, 'Who was that on the telephone?'

'Your father. He'll be home this weekend.'

'When is he arriving?' Jenny asked eagerly.

'Either late tonight or early tomorrow morning.'

Jenny's unhappiness faded to be replaced with joy. Her daddy would be home soon and she couldn't wait to see him.

Edward Lavender's eyes were rimmed with tiredness, the strain of such a long drive showing as he at last pulled into the drive. It was after eleven, but the light was on in the drawing room so he knew that Delia was still up.

It had taken a long time to set up another branch for the insurance company he worked for, to get a decent manager and sales team in place. Eight weeks away from home . . . yet he wasn't looking forward to seeing his wife.

Their marriage had been fine at first, a son born on their third wedding anniversary, but eighteen months later, from the moment Jennifer had been placed in Delia's arms, she had changed from a loving wife to a highly strung, moody and demanding one.

Delia now bore no resemblance to the young woman he'd fallen in love with, one who had lost her parents and seemed so vulnerable, so alone when they met. She'd had money though, and they had used her inheritance to buy their first house, but Edward had worked like a dog since then to provide all she wanted, gaining promotion after promotion until they were able to purchase one bigger house after another, until Delia was finally satisfied. It was large, detached – perfect, she said. Yet it wasn't a home, it was a showplace, with never a thing out of place or a smidgen of dust to be seen anywhere.

There had been times when Edward had been tempted to walk out on Delia, yet he could never leave his children, especially Jenny. Instead he found his needs elsewhere, brief encounters that he now paid for. It was less complicated that way.

Edward climbed out of the car and stretched his cramped muscles. He knew there would be a cold atmosphere to greet him, but nevertheless he made an effort, saying pleasantly as he went into the drawing room, 'Hello, my dear.'

'So you're back. I wasn't really expecting you until morning.'

'I made good time and it was pointless stopping somewhere overnight when I was so close to home.'

'I hope you're not expecting dinner at this time of night.'

'Just a sandwich will do, and perhaps a cup of cocoa.'

Delia exhaled loudly, showing her exasperation, but nevertheless went to the kitchen. Edward had barely sat down when his daughter rushed in, her face alight with happiness.

'Daddy, Daddy!'

'Hello, darling,' he said, rising quickly and hugging Jenny to him, thinking as always that she made coming home worthwhile. He'd get some sort of welcome from Robin, but his son was now a product of his mother, his manner tightly reserved. Thankfully, however, Robin showed no sign of Delia's so-called nerves, a condition Edward suspected his wife feigned to get her own way.

'How long will you be here?' Jenny asked eagerly.

'Just for the weekend, I'm afraid.'

'Jennifer, what are you doing up at this time of night?' Delia asked sharply as she stormed into the room.

'I was excited that Daddy was coming home and couldn't sleep.'

'Go back to bed, *now*!'

'Jenny, do as your mother says,' Edward urged softly. 'I'll still be here in the morning.'

For just a brief moment Jenny looked mutinous, but then she nodded. 'All right. Good night, Dad.'

'Good night, darling.'

Delia just stood there, tight-lipped, but when Jenny left the room she swung round too, heading back to the kitchen. Edward knew what this meant – another row – and once again he regretted coming home.

Delia slammed a small saucepan of milk onto the cooker. It was always the same. Edward had arrived home after two months away, but he was no sooner in the door than Jennifer got his attention and affection. She would punish him, Delia decided, just as she'd always punished him; something she had sworn to do from the moment another baby had been forced upon her. She didn't want another child and Edward had known that.

She fought to regain her poise as she took a loaf of bread, cutting two slices, but her mind still raged. Oh, she had tried to love Jennifer, but her resentment had been strong, so was it any wonder that the maternal instincts she had felt for Robin had been absent from the start?

Of course it hadn't helped that Jennifer had been a difficult and demanding baby, taking up so much of her time that she had felt she was neglecting her son. Then, at eighteen months old, Robin had been walking, a little unsteady on his feet, and into everything. He had needed her attention but, with the new burden of Jennifer and the demands of keeping up with the housework, it was something she'd no longer had time to give him. Of course she had made up for it since, her son developing into a wonderful young man who would go far, but Edward would continue to pay dearly for causing his early neglect and her own unhappiness.

'Thank you, dear, and I can see you're pleased to see me as usual,' Edward drawled sarcastically when she took a tray through to the drawing room.

'What do you expect? Unlike Jennifer, I didn't even get a kiss on the cheek.'

'Had I tried, you'd have rebuffed me as usual.'

'You don't know that.'

'Delia, I'm not playing your games. You're fond of giving me hope, but then withdrawing it. I'm not falling for it again. I'm content with the wonderful welcome I received from Jenny.'

'Yes, I'm sure you are. As always, you put her before me.'

'For goodness' sake, Delia, this jealousy is ridiculous. Is it any wonder that Jenny runs to me for affection? She certainly doesn't get any from you!'

'I am *not* jealous. As for my lack of affection, you're to blame for that.'

'I don't know what you're talking about, Delia.'

Delia knew she was fighting a losing battle; Edward was sure to deny it as usual. Still, there was more than one way to skin a cat.

'How many times do I have to tell you that a *jenny* is a female donkey? *Jennifer*, as we christened her, will be sixteen soon, old enough to leave home and it's time to tell her the truth – though of course not all of it.'

'No, Delia, I don't think there is any need.'

'Of course there is. She has a right to know and if you don't tell her, I will.'

'You'll do no such thing! It's unnecessary and I won't stand for it.'

Delia's jaws ground. Edward didn't know it, but she wasn't finished yet and he'd soon find that out. 'I'm going to bed. Please don't disturb me when you come up.'

'Don't worry, Delia, I know better than to come into your room.'

Without another word, she stalked out. Long ago Edward had given her the power to get her own way and she had made the most of it, insisting on separate bedrooms, among other things. She still had that power and intended to use it.

It was time for the truth to come out – time to stop living in a house of secrets.

Chapter Two

When Robin awoke the next morning, he could hear the sound of raised voices. It was always the same when his father was home, the atmosphere rotten until he left again.

There was a soft tap on his bedroom door and moments later Jenny poked her head into the room, hissing softly, 'Robin, are you awake?'

'Yes.'

'Mummy and Daddy are arguing.'

'I know.'

'I heard my name mentioned and think it's about me. Have I done something to upset her?'

'I haven't got a clue. Now just bugger off, Jenny.'

'But—'

'Just go!' Robin snapped, relieved when his sister did as she was told. Yes, his parents were rowing, but it was nothing unusual. He blamed his father for his mother's unhappiness, and it was odd that they slept in separate rooms. There had to be a reason, a problem, perhaps his father's, and Robin wondered if it was something that could explain his own disgusting feelings. Had he inherited some sort of deviant sexual tendencies from his father?

Yes, he knew about sex now, but the knowledge brought him agony. What he felt wasn't right – what he wanted wasn't right – yet night after night he lay awake, so aware that Jenny was only in the next room. She was his sister, and all he should feel for her was brotherly love, but from the moment he'd seen her small, burgeoning breasts, his feelings had begun to change.

If anyone found out they'd be horrified, sickened, so the only way Robin could deal with it was by pretending indifference, hiding his feelings behind the same facade his mother portrayed. He knew it confused Jenny, probably hurt her, but it was the only way to keep her at a distance – a safe distance.

Despite that, the temptation was always there and Robin knew he couldn't stand much more. He'd be finished at college next year and hoped to get the A level results he needed to go on to university. He had to be away from this house . . . away from Jenny.

Annoyed at the interruption when the milkman knocked, Delia impatiently rummaged in her purse, saying as she opened the front door, 'I think this is the right money, but I hate this new decimal currency. I'll never get used to it and why we had to change from good old pounds, shillings and pence is beyond me.'

'That's what most of my customers say,' the milkman said. Once satisfied that it was the correct amount, he licked his pencil before ticking off the payment in his book. 'See you next week, Mrs Lavender.'

Delia barely acknowledged the man before closing the door again. The argument with Edward had been raging for half an hour, yet still the issue was un-resolved. She returned to the kitchen, ready to take up where they'd left off, only to be thwarted moments later when Jennifer appeared.

'Good morning, dear,' Edward said, smiling warmly at his daughter.

Jennifer went to sit next to him, her manner subdued. 'Hello, Dad.'

'Why the long face?' he asked.

'I heard you having an argument. Was it about me?'

'Of course not, and anyway, it was just a heated discussion. Now cheer up. It's a lovely day and after breakfast I thought we could all go out for a drive.'

'You can count me out,' Delia snapped. 'I haven't got time for gallivanting. I've got housework to do.'

'Can't you leave it for once?'

'No, I can't. Look at this kitchen, it's filthy. Jennifer was supposed to have cleaned it, but as you can see it hasn't been done properly.'

'Filthy? Delia, it's immaculate as usual, as is the

17

rest of the house. Come on, let's all four of us go out together. It'll make a nice change.'

'What will make a nice change?' Robin asked as he walked into the room.

'Your father wants us all to go out for a drive.'

Robin frowned and then said, 'No can do, Dad. I've missed two days at college and will have to study all weekend to catch up. If I want to pass my A levels next year I've got to get my head down.'

'Why were you home for two days?' Edward asked.

'I had a bit of a fever and sore throat, though I'm fine now.'

'That's good, but as I've been away for a while I'd like to see something of you. Surely you can spare a few hours this morning?'

'If Robin wants to study it's to be commended,' said Delia, 'and I for one am proud of his dedication.'

'I'm proud of him too, Delia.'

'You don't show it. Jennifer is the only one you praise.'

'Look, if you two are going to start rowing again, I'm going back to my room.'

'Don't be silly, Robin, we aren't rowing,' Delia said quickly. 'Now sit down and I'll cook breakfast. What would you like?'

'A boiled egg would be nice.'

'Yes, I'll have the same,' Edward said.

'Do you want me to help, Mum?'

'Of course I do, and don't use that term. It sounds

18

so lower class and goodness knows what my friends would think if they heard you. I'm Mother, or Mummy. Your father may not object to being called Dad, but I have higher standards. Now lay the table and then butter some bread.'

'Yes, Mummy.'

Delia saw the look Edward threw her, the disapproval in his eyes, but ignored it. Jennifer wasn't a child and should earn her keep, help around the house and with the laundry, something she insisted on, whether Edward liked it or not. What he'd forced on her all those years ago had ruined their marriage and if it hadn't been for her need to maintain her social standing she'd have left Edward years ago. Divorce, however, had been unheard of in their social circle and back then the women at the tennis club would have shunned her, let alone the ladies in the Women's Institute.

And so she had stayed and played her role, but not any more. The time had at last come when she could get rid of Jennifer and she wasn't going to let Edward stand in her way. She just had to bring up the subject again and this time she would force the issue whether Edward liked it or not.

Edward hated the way Delia spoke to Jenny; how she was often as cold towards their daughter as she was to him. Delia had been a reluctant mother. She had done what was necessary when Jennifer was a baby, saw that she was clean and fed, but that had been all, any shows of affection brief. Jenny had been a beautiful baby, so easy to love, but instead Delia had rejected her.

'Daddy, will you be home again for my birthday?' Jenny asked.

'I've got three branch inspections scheduled, but I'll do my best.'

'Edward, if you aren't here,' Delia warned, 'I'll go ahead with what we've been discussing without you.'

'You'll do no such thing.'

'If you aren't here, how are you going to stop me?'

'Stop you doing what, Mother?' asked Robin.

Edward found he was holding his breath, but his fear of Delia blurting it out also forced him to a decision. With no guarantee that he'd be home for Jenny's birthday, Delia might just carry out her threat. He couldn't risk it. He'd have to tell his daughter now; at least coming from him the blow might be softened.

'All right, Delia, you've got your own way as usual. However, *I* will be the one to tell her.'

'When?'

'After breakfast,' Edward said, unable to miss the look of triumph that crossed his wife's face.

'Dad, are you talking about me?' Jenny asked.

'Yes, darling, but don't look so worried.'

'Tell me what?'

'Let's eat and then we'll talk,' he said, glad of even this small delay.

'Jennifer, do get a move on,' Delia urged. 'I want to get this meal over with.'

When his egg was put in front of him, Edward took off the top while his mind searched for the right words – the easiest and gentlest way to tell Jenny. She had always been a daddy's girl, but what he was being forced to do now could change their relationship for ever. Would he lose his daughter? God, he hoped not.

If he could reveal the *whole* truth it might help, but Edward knew that was impossible. After all, even Delia wasn't privy to it and, despite her accusations, she never would be.

Chapter Three

Jenny barely touched her breakfast. The atmosphere was tense, and something was obviously wrong, yet it seemed she hadn't been the cause of their argument. What was her father going to tell her? She'd known for some time that things weren't right between her parents, that theirs wasn't a happy marriage, and now an awful thought crossed Jenny's mind. Divorce! That must be it. Her parents were getting a divorce.

Jenny looked at Robin, but her brother seemed unconcerned as he mopped up the last of his yolk. Unlike her, Robin seemed unaware of the tension in the air and now pushed back his chair, saying, 'Right, I'd better get on with some studying.'

'No, Robin, stay where you are. What I have to say concerns you too.'

Her father's words added to Jenny's fear. If Robin was going to be told too it *must* be a divorce. Her stomach churned. Did it mean her father would move out of the house? Would she see even less of him than she did now? Unable to help it, Jenny blurted out, 'You're going to leave, aren't you? You and Mummy are getting a divorce.'

'Of course we aren't,' her father answered. 'Whatever gave you that idea?'

'I . . . I thought, well, the row . . . then you saying you were going to tell me something, Robin too.'

'Yes I am, but it's got nothing to do with divorce. You see . . . er . . . er . . .' Edward stammered, running both hands over his face, unable to find the words.

'Oh, do get on with it, Edward.'

'I'm doing my best, Delia, but this isn't easy.'

'I'll tell her then.'

'No, leave this to me,' he insisted. With a strained look on his face, he turned to Jenny again. 'I think it might be best if I start at the beginning. You see, many years ago, some distant relatives of mine in Ireland were killed when their cottage caught fire. They left one daughter, er . . . Mary . . . and with her parents' death she was left entirely alone. I was contacted by the home she was placed in, but by the time I got there she had tragically died too.'

'Oh, Daddy, that's awful. Was she badly burned?'

'No, it was nothing like that. Mary was pregnant and died in childbirth.'

For a moment he paused, his eyes pained, but nothing could have prepared Jenny for his next words.

'She had a baby girl, one who was left without a

mother or anyone to care for her. That's where we stepped in, darling. That baby girl was you and I brought you home. Your mother and I adopted you, made you our own daughter and one whom we love very much.'

Jenny stiffened in shock. Adopted! As she glanced at her mother, the feelings she always had of not being wanted, of something missing in her life, suddenly made sense. She wasn't her mother! Someone called Mary was her mother, but . . . but she had died. Jenny's eyes now darted to her father – but he wasn't really her father either.

'What . . . what happened to my real father?'

'I'm afraid we don't know, darling. Mary died without telling anyone his name.'

'Bloody hell,' Robin murmured.

'There's no need for bad language, Robin,' came the gentle rebuke.

'Sorry, Mother, but this has come as a bit of a shock.'

'I think it's more of a shock for your sister,' his father chided.

'Yes,' Robin said, smiling now, 'but Jennifer isn't really my sister, is she? Just how distant was this relative, Dad?'

'Mary's mother was a third cousin on my father's side of the family.'

'Wow! That means that Jenny and I are so distantly related that there's hardly a link at all.'

Jenny's head was reeling. Robin wasn't her brother either, instead just a very distant cousin. Not only that, he actually looked pleased about it. She couldn't stand any more, couldn't listen to any more, and, flinging back her chair, Jenny fled the room.

Edward reared to his feet.

'Did you have to be so indelicate, Robin? It was enough for Jenny to take in without you adding to her confusion.'

'Robin was only trying to make sense of it all, Edward,' snapped Delia. 'There's no need to shout at him.'

'Didn't you see his face? He looked delighted to hear that Jenny isn't his sister.'

'What do you expect? Robin knows what a trial that girl has been to me.'

'*That girl* is our daughter.'

'I have never accepted her as that.'

'Yes, you've made that obvious. You've treated her more like a servant. Nevertheless, legally Jenny is our daughter, our responsibility and this is her home.'

'For now,' Delia murmured, her head down as she began to clear the table.

'I won't have you driving her out.'

'What!' Robin exclaimed. 'Mother, surely you don't want Jennifer to leave home?'

'She'll be sixteen next month and leaving school soon after to find employment. That makes her perfectly capable of looking after herself.'

'And just where is she supposed to live?' Robin asked.

'She can get one of those bedsit things.'

Robin now reared to his feet too, and Edward witnessed a change in his son. Like a worm turning, he glared at his mother with an expression of disgust.

'Despite what you say, Mother, from what I've seen Jenny has never been a trial to you. She doesn't deserve this and if you force her out I'm going too.'

Delia's face was a picture, her expression registering both shock and bewilderment. 'Don't be silly, Robin.'

'Silly, am I? No, I don't think so. If Jenny leaves just watch me walk out behind her.' With this threat hanging in the air, Robin stormed from the kitchen.

Delia looked stunned, her jaw agape; before departing the room too, Edward couldn't stop himself from commenting, 'Well, Delia, that didn't go down quite as you expected.'

Jenny was still unable to process her thoughts into coherent order. She had no feelings of self. She wasn't Jennifer Lavender, daughter of Edward and Delia, but instead her mother had been Irish, and her father unknown. There were so many questions tumbling around in her mind that she felt relieved in a way when the man she had thought of as her father knocked softly on her bedroom door.

'I'm sorry, Jennifer. That must have been an awful shock for you.'

'I . . . I don't know who I am any more.'

'You're still the same person. You're our little girl, and you'll always be that.'

'But I'm not. I . . . I'm some sort of distant cousin.'

'No, Jennifer. When we adopted you, your mother and I became your parents.'

'I've always known that Mummy . . . no, Delia . . . has never really loved me. I thought it was me, that I'm unlovable, but now . . . What was she like, Dad?'

'Your mother had a difficult birth with Robin and it took her a long time to recover, but she was as keen as me to adopt you.'

'I'm not talking about her. I meant my real mother.'

'Oh, I see. Well, darling, I'm afraid there's very little I can tell you. As I said, they were very distant relatives and I hadn't seen them since my childhood. I . . . I never saw their daughter, Mary.'

Jenny felt a sudden pull to Ireland, a need to see what it was like, where her mother had lived. At that instant, she vowed that one day she'd go there.

'What was her last name?'

'Murphy. She was Mary Ann Murphy.'

'It . . . it's a lovely name, I like it. So my name should really be Jennifer Murphy.'

'Oh, sweetheart, don't say that. Your mother and I chose the name Jennifer, and as we legally adopted you, your name is Jennifer Lavender.'

'You . . . you said that you were the only family she had left. Does that mean I haven't got any relatives at all in Ireland? Isn't there anyone who could tell me more about my real mother?'

'I'm afraid not, darling.'

'You also said she didn't name my father, but I don't understand. Why didn't they know who he was? Why didn't he claim me?'

There was a pause, a sigh, and then he said, 'Jennifer, the home your mother was placed in was one for unmarried mothers.'

'Unmarried!' Jenny gasped. Earlier, when told that she was adopted, her mind had almost frozen, but now the truth sank in. 'That . . . that means I . . . I'm a basta—'

'Don't say it,' her father quickly interrupted. 'We have no idea what Mary went through, how she ended up in such a place, but one thing I'm sure of – had she lived, your mother would have loved you very much.'

Tears came then and began to run unchecked down Jenny's cheeks. She had never known a mother's love. All she had ever known was rejection, a feeling of being unwanted and in the way. She felt the bed dip as her father sat down next to her, and though he wasn't her real father Jenny had always felt close to him — always felt that at least *he* loved her. His arms reached out to her and, sobbing, Jenny fell into them.

Chapter Four

Robin knew Jenny was upset, but he was over the moon at the news that she was adopted. Jenny wasn't his sister, she was only a very distant cousin, and it meant that what he felt for her wasn't wrong, incestuous or sick.

Relief had flooded through him when he had heard, but Robin could have kicked himself for allowing his pleasure to show. Was it any wonder that Jenny had looked stricken as she fled the room? Yet what followed her departure had left Robin stunned. His mother's callousness had shocked him and the last thing he wanted was for Jenny to leave home. He just hoped that his threat to do the same would work.

Robin knew he had to speak to Jenny, to find an excuse for his behaviour. He couldn't tell her the truth yet. It would shock her; maybe frighten her off, so for now he would have to tread softly.

It was some time before Robin came up with something that might sound convincing. The timing was a bit out but, hopefully, with the shock of what she'd been told, Jenny wouldn't remember.

At last Robin heard his father going back downstairs. He went along to Jenny's room, asking as he opened the door, 'Can I come in?'

Her face was blotchy from crying, but thankfully she nodded.

'Jenny, I know I looked pleased when Dad told us you're adopted, but I think you got hold of the wrong end of the stick.'

'You *were* pleased.'

'No, Jenny. It was more relief than pleasure.'

'Relief? Why?'

'I've seen how unhappy Mother has been, heard the rows, and I thought Dad was going to tell us they're getting a divorce.'

'Yes, I thought the same at first. So you aren't pleased that I'm adopted?'

'Why should I be? After all, it won't make any difference and doesn't change anything. They're legally as much your parents as they are mine and our lives will go on as normal.'

'Yes, for you, but my life in this house has never been normal.'

'I know Mother can be difficult,' Robin placated, 'but she suffers with her nerves, gets depressed, and you have to make allowances.'

'Since you started college, you've been as bad, hardly speaking to me, shutting me out.'

31

'Have I? I didn't realise,' Robin lied, unable to come up with a better excuse quickly enough. 'I've been hard at it, Jenny, keen to get good exam results for university.'

'If you say so. But please, my head is splitting and I want to be on my own for a while.'

'All right, but if you need me I'll be in my room,' Robin said, hoping he had done enough to cover his behaviour.

Robin had always known his mother didn't show Jenny much affection, and the fact that she was adopted now explained it. He was simply happy that he no longer had to think of Jenny as his sister, and went back to his studies with a smile on his face.

Delia's mind was raging. Edward was right; Robin turning on her like that was indeed the last thing she'd expected. She and her son shared a special bond, one that didn't include Jennifer, so why he had acted like that on the girl's behalf was beyond her comprehension. She had planned this moment for so long, a time when she could finally get rid of Jennifer, but instead she now stood to lose her son too. No, no, that couldn't happen. Yes, she would miss Robin when he went to university next year, but they wouldn't have been estranged. He would come home every weekend and that would have fitted perfectly into her plans, but now . . .

Oh, *that girl*. As usual Jennifer had spoiled every-thing, forced her to rethink, and Delia began to quietly fume. She had to do something to bring Robin round . . . but what?

At last, though she was unhappy about it, by the time Edward had come back downstairs, Delia had decided what she had to do. If she didn't want to lose Robin it was her only choice – but one day, no matter what, she would make Edward pay for this.

Jenny stayed in her room for over an hour, trying to come to terms with the fact that she'd been adopted. She would never think of Delia as her real mother again, but Jenny couldn't feel the same about her father, and was deeply upset that she wasn't really his daughter. Edward loved her, she was sure of it, really loved her, and though they were only distantly related, at least that was some kind of link.

She clutched her pillow, trying to imagine what her real mother had been like, what her own life would have been like had she lived. It was half an hour later when thirst drove Jenny out of her room, only to find that Robin was leaving his at the same time.

'Hi, Jen, how are you feeling now?'

'I was just going to get a glass of water,' she said. Robin walked behind her as she went downstairs.

'Jennifer, there you are,' Delia said, smiling warmly. 'I know you've had a dreadful shock and I felt it best to leave you alone for a while. Are you feeling a little better now?'

'Er . . . yes,' Jenny said as she poured a glass of water and gulped it down. Delia was being nice, but as usual she was modifying her behaviour because Robin was around. However, she got a shock when he spoke.

'Mother, don't pretend that you care about Jenny's feelings.'

'But I do . . .'

'You could have fooled me,' he said.

Jenny had no idea what had caused Robin to turn on his mother, and feared being blamed for it, but then her father came in from the garden, smiling when he saw her.

'Jenny, I was about to see if I could persuade you to come downstairs.'

'I was too,' Delia said. 'I wanted to talk to you, Jennifer, to assure you that though you now know you're adopted, it won't make any difference. We are still your parents and this is your home.'

Robin made a snorting sound and left the room, leaving Jenny still feeling bewildered at his sudden change of attitude towards his mother.

Delia continued to be pleasant for the rest of the day, yet it didn't fool Jenny and she guessed it was her usual act put on for Robin and her father's sake. She avoided being alone with her, keeping close to her father; dreading him leaving when the weekend was over.

Chapter Five

All too soon it was Monday morning, and Jenny woke early. Her father would be leaving shortly and she was already close to tears. He might not have been her real father, but she loved him dearly and treasured the closeness they shared. She dressed hurriedly and crept downstairs.

'I might have guessed,' Edward said, smiling. 'It's so early, but here you are, the only one up to see me off.'

'I wish you didn't have to go.'

'So do I, darling,' he said, rising to his feet and hugging her. 'I know it's been a difficult weekend for you, but I promise that, no matter what, I'll be back for your birthday.'

Jenny didn't want him to go and clung to him. Her birthday was on the seventeenth of July, in about five weeks, but to her it felt more like five years as he pulled away. She watched, fighting tears as he picked up his briefcase, and then, with a quick kiss on her cheek and a whispered goodbye, he was gone.

Delia was annoyed to be disturbed by the sound of Jennifer getting up to see her father off at the crack of dawn. As far as Delia was concerned, she was glad that Edward was leaving. After all, it was Jennifer who got all his attention when he was here. To punish him she decided she would remain in bed.

She was still angry at being unable to get rid of Jennifer as planned, and at a loss to understand her son's change of allegiance. One minute Robin had been on her side, happy to leave Jennifer out in the cold, but then, at the mere mention of her moving into a bedsit, he had turned. Delia had been kind to Jennifer all weekend but it hadn't helped, and Robin was still giving her the cold shoulder.

Still puzzled by her son's behaviour, Delia continued to mull on it, wondering if it was sympathy that Robin had felt for Jennifer. Perhaps her son was soft and more like his father than she had realised. If that was the case, the only way to get Robin back on her side would be to turn the tables and become the damsel in distress.

With an idea coming to mind, Delia pondered on it. Robin was no longer a child; he was a young man and surely old enough to be spoken to as an adult. Yes, of course he was, though she daren't tell him everything.

At last, satisfied that what she'd come up with could work, Delia managed to doze off again until her alarm sounded at seven. She then got up to follow her usual routine. There would be no making an appearance downstairs until she was bathed, dressed, her make-up applied and hair immaculately in place. It was a standard that had been set by her late mother, one Delia always adhered too, and she ensured that both Robin and Jennifer followed her example.

Ready now, Delia went along to her son's room. Opening the door, she called, 'Robin, it's time to get up.'

'Yes, I know. I'm awake.'

Delia was surprised. Robin was usually difficult to rouse, the last one to make an appearance every morning, but for once he sounded fully awake and alert. She wanted to speak to him out of Jennifer's hearing and now made the most of this opportunity.

'Robin, I'm so unhappy and desperately need to talk to you.'

'Not now, Mother.'

'Please, Robin, it won't take long. It's just that I need to get this off my chest.'

'Can't it wait until we're downstairs?'

'No, darling, I'm afraid it can't,' Delia said, moving further into the room to sit at Robin's desk. Books were strewn over it, some still open, notes written, some crumbled up and tossed aside, but for once Delia's fastidiousness was put to one side as she composed her face to one of sadness. 'Robin, I was against adopting Jenny, but your father virtually forced me into it.'

'From what he said, we were her only family.'

'We were so distantly connected that I'd hardly call us that. Your father hadn't seen them since his childhood, so of course I had never met them. We already had you, and with so many childless couples desperate to adopt, I felt it would be kinder if Jennifer went to one of them. Your father didn't agree and I suppose I was full of resentment, but despite that I did my best when we adopted Jennifer and grew fond of her. I tried to love her, really I did, but she was such a difficult baby and I'm afraid one can't love to order.'

'I don't remember her being difficult.'

'You wouldn't, darling. You were just a toddler then,' Delia said, forcing tears into her eyes as she changed the subject. 'Oh, Robin, a few months ago it was my fortieth birthday and all I've ever been is a wife and mother. With you leaving home to go to university next year and Jennifer almost grown up too, I've been feeling lost, as though I won't have a role any more. I'll be redundant as a mother, with nothing to do but rattle around in this large, empty house.'

For a moment Robin looked a little sympathetic,

but then said, 'If that's the case and you're fond of Jenny, why would you want her to leave home too?'

'All right, I'll try to explain. As I said, I was beginning to feel lost, but then a woman at the tennis club, Marcia Bateman, made me look at things differently. When Marcia's children left the nest she saw it as *her* time, a chance to be something more than just a wife and mother. She studied interior design and then started up a very successful business. I admire Marcia, and it made me realise that when you go to university there 's nothing to stop me from doing something similar.' Delia paused to bite her lip, eyes lowered for effect.

'Yes, well, I suppose you could.'

'Robin, there's a lot of work involved in setting up a new business, and though this is going to sound dreadful, in truth I wanted the freedom to work as many hours as necessary without feeling I have to rush home to look after Jennifer. It was selfish of me and I realise that now. Until Jennifer is older this will remain her home, and I'll just have to rethink my business plan.'

At last Robin smiled. 'If that's the case I'd hardly call you selfish, but I don't think you need to change your plans. Jenny will be at work too, and she's quite capable of looking after herself until you come home. Now, why don't you tell me about this business venture?

'With so many large houses in this area needing domestic staff, I'm thinking of setting up an agency to provide them, along with catering services. However, I'm not going to do anything until you leave for university, and so for now I'd rather you didn't mention my ideas to your father.'

'Why? Do you think he'll be against it?'

'Yes, I do. You see your father wasn't well off when we married and I had to use my inheritance to buy our first house.'

'I didn't know that. I knew he'd lost his parents during the war and was brought up by his aunt, but I still don't see why he'd be against you starting up a business.'

'Your father is old-fashioned and I think it wounded his pride when I paid for our first home. So much so that from then on he insisted on being the provider while I stayed at home.'

'I see, but that was a long time ago and surely he'd feel differently now?'

'I hope so, because I'd love to be a successful businesswoman like Marcia.'

'And I'm sure you will.'

'I doubt your father thinks I'm capable of anything other than being a housewife, and oh, Robin, what if I fail?' Delia cried, pulling out her handkerchief and pretending to dab tears from her eyes. 'What if I prove him right?'

'Please, Mummy, don't get upset. I'm sure you'll

be fine, but if you want to chew your idea over with me, perhaps go over the setting-up costs and things like that, I'd be happy to help. I've no experience in such things, but as I'm going to study economics at university at least I'm good with figures. I should be able to work out the initial costs and even some profit projections.'

'Robin, that would be wonderful . . . but I don't want to take you away from your studies.'

'I've caught up now. Actually, it would make a marvellous project and something I'd look forward to getting my teeth into. How about we make a start this coming weekend?'

'Yes, I'd like that, but for now I'd better leave you to get ready for college,' Delia said, smiling as she left her son's room. Robin had been sympathetic, had offered to help, and that was a start.

Jenny had been sitting alone, still upset at her father's departure. Even though he'd promised to come home for her birthday, she guessed that it would only be for a weekend again. His job involved a lot of travelling, but now Jenny wondered if he preferred to be away – if he avoided coming home. Though she didn't like the thought, deep down Jenny couldn't blame him: this was an unhappy house, unwelcoming, full of tension, and laughter was a rare thing.

She heard her mother's footsteps on the stairs and tensed. What sort of mood was she going to be in? Jenny didn't know if she could bear it if it was a bad one. She felt a longing to escape this house, to run from all the unhappiness contained within these walls and to never come back.

'Jennifer, I do not appreciate being woken at the crack of dawn.'

'I . . . I'm sorry, I didn't mean to disturb you.'

'Don't just sit there, make a fresh pot of tea.'

Jenny did her bidding, relieved when Robin appeared, smiling at her as he said, 'Morning, Jen.'

'What would you like for breakfast, darling?' Delia asked him.

'How about scrambled eggs on toast?'

'Would you like the same, Jennifer?'

'Yes . . . yes please. Do you want me to make the toast?'

'Yes, and thank you, dear,' she said, smiling warmly. 'I know you're upset that your father has gone, but I'm sure he'll keep his promise and be home for your birthday.'

Jenny wasn't fooled. She knew that this sudden kind manner was all for Robin's benefit and it seemed to be working as Robin now grinned at his mother and said, 'When he rings, you'll just have to nag him, Mother.'

'Yes, and you can be sure I will.'

Jenny just wanted to get breakfast over with, to

go to school and get out of her mother's way. Twenty minutes later, she picked up her empty plate to take it to the sink.

'I . . . I'm off now, but I'll be a little late home as I have to see the careers adviser after school.'

'Oh goodness, Jennifer,' said Delia. 'I'm so sorry, I'd forgotten. Still, don't worry, I'll be there.'

Jenny's eyes widened with surprise. 'You're coming?'

'Of course I am. This is an important time for you and I want to make sure you're given the best opportunities for when you leave school.'

'But . . . but when I gave you the letter you said that . . .'

'I said I would be there,' Delia interrupted firmly.

Jenny saw the warning look and knew better than to argue, yet she remembered well that when she'd been given the letter, her mother had carelessly thrown it to one side, saying that seeing a careers adviser was a waste of time for someone fit only for menial employment. Now it seemed she had changed her mind . . . but why? Was it another show put on for Robin's benefit?

'Off you go now, or you'll be late for school,' her mother now said, and though her voice sounded soft, there was hardness in her eyes.

'Yes, all right. Bye,' Jenny croaked.

'See you later, Jen,' Robin called, clearly oblivious to the undertones.

Jenny hurried out, just wanting to be away from the house, her mother, and wishing she never had to come back.

Chapter Six

When Jenny left, Robin lingered at the table, his eyes on his mother. He could understand why she wanted to start up a business, to achieve something in her own right, but there was something in her explanation of not wanting to neglect Jenny that hadn't rung true.

As a small child he'd taken his mother's love and affection for granted, had hardly questioned why Jenny had been left out in the cold. His mother favoured him, while his father favoured Jenny, and he'd assumed it was the same in all households. Of course it wasn't, and he had eventually learned that, but at least now he knew why. Jenny was adopted, and because of her resentment his mother had been unable to love her. Robin felt he could understand that, and at least his mother had said she was fond of Jenny, though she hardly showed it.

'Robin, if you don't get a move on you'll be late too.'

'I'll be off in a minute,' he said. 'I'll be interested to hear how Jenny got on with the careers adviser when I come home.'

'I intend to see that she's given the best advice but, let's face it, Jennifer has never been as bright as you. Nonetheless, I'd like to see her with some sort of career, and I'll make sure she isn't fobbed off with some sort of dead-end job.'

'Jobs that offer a career usually start out with low pay.'

'If she's given the opportunity for advancement, the opening salary is irrelevant. After all, living at home, Jennifer won't have to worry about her earnings.'

'Right, I'd best be off,' Robin said, relieved that it was likely that Jenny wouldn't be earning enough to leave home for some time yet.

'Bye, darling,' Delia called.

Robin happily went off to college, content in the knowledge that Jenny would still be there, at least until he hopefully left for university next year. A year, Robin thought. He'd leave it for a year, but then he'd make his move.

Jenny had left Castle Close, hoping to meet up with Tina Hammond on the way to school. She knew her mother disapproved of their friendship, and she wasn't allowed to invite Tina to the house, but nevertheless they remained constant friends, albeit behind

Delia's back. Jenny preferred to have one special friend, a best friend rather than a group, and Tina partly fulfilled something she felt missing in her life – a sort of kinship. Though they occasionally chatted to other girls, for the most part the two of them were inseparable. Physically, they were very different, Jenny blonde and pale, Tina dark, her eyes brown and her skin olive toned. They both wanted to swap their colouring for each other's, and had laughed when they had first found this out.

Tina and her family lived in Princes Way, an area that had changed so radically in recent years that it had become something else for her mother to carp about. It had started with the building of a block of council flats, and had progressed to the development of what were now purpose-built estates of houses and maisonettes. A few large houses remained, set behind high walls, and though their proximity to Wimbledon Common still made them desirable, her mother said that because they were now surrounded by council property, they had depreciated greatly in value.

Tina's family didn't own one of these big houses. They rented a council flat and of course Jenny knew this was why her mother disapproved of their friendship. Unlike them, the Hammonds weren't well off, but Jenny hated her mother's snobbishness and would have swapped places with her friend like a shot. Tina's mum was kind, didn't suffer from nerves and wasn't obsessed with housework. She was a short, tubby woman who was full of laughter, her welcome always so warm that over the years Jenny had often found the cramped flat a much-needed escape from the coldness of her own home life.

'Jenny! Jenny, over here!'

Jenny dashed across the road to join her friend.

'Where have you been?' asked Tina. 'I waited in on Saturday but you didn't come round.'

'I'm sorry, but my father came home for the weekend.'

'That explains it then. Thankfully mine didn't show his face.'

'What do you mean? Your dad's nice,' Jenny protested. Tina's father was a long-distance lorry driver who was rarely in when she called round, but from what she'd seen he was full of affection for both Tina and her older sister.

'Huh, so he's fooled you too. Oh, I don't want to talk about my dad. Change the subject, Jenny.'

Jenny was puzzled, but nevertheless did as Tina asked. 'I'm sorry I couldn't come round, but you didn't wait in all day for me, did you?'

'No, I gave up by one o'clock and went to buy a new record. T-Rex has got two in the charts now, but I only had enough money for one. Ooh, I just love Marc Bolan.'

'Yes, I know,' Jenny said, smiling ruefully. 'You hardly talk about anything else.'

'Well, he is gorgeous.'

Jenny wasn't going to argue. Tina was absolutely mad about Marc Bolan and her bedroom walls were festooned with his posters. However, even had Jenny had an idol, she would never have been allowed to decorate her room with pictures of them. It was another thing that emphasised the many differences between Tina's home life and her own.

'I got a shock this morning,' Jenny said. 'My mother's coming with me to see the careers adviser.'

'Is she? Mine isn't.'

This was the last thing Jenny expected to hear. 'I thought your mummy would insist on being there.'

'Mummy! Gawd, you'd think I'd be used to the way you talk by now, but sometimes it still sounds so funny and posh. Anyway, as for my *mum*, all she did was to offer a bit of advice. She said to forget Germaine Greer and the feminist movement because it's all nonsense. Instead I should take anything on offer with decent pay and it'll do until the right man comes along.'

'And will you?'

'I'll take anything that pays well, but not for those reasons. What about you? What sort of job are you looking for?'

'I'm not sure, but one day I'd like to earn enough money to rent a place of my own.'

'Do you really mean that, Jen? If you do, I wouldn't mind sharing it with you.'

'Why would you want to leave home?'

''Cos my sister's said she's moving out soon. That'll just leave me for him to start on.'

Jenny didn't have a clue what Tina was talking about and asked, 'Who'll start on you? And start what?'

'I . . . I can't tell you. He . . . he'll kill me.'

'Tina, I'm your friend, your best friend, and there's nothing you can't tell me. If you want me to keep it to myself, I will, and you know that.'

At these words, as though a dam had burst, Tina haltingly told her. Jenny's stomach lurched in horror. She had envied her friend, had thought of her home as a haven, but now realised it was all an illusion. It was horrific to hear, dreadful, and as Tina continued to talk, Jenny felt the last vestiges of her childhood, of her innocence, being stripped away.

'Oh, Tina, we've been friends for all this time and I had no idea. Why didn't you tell me before?'

'Because the sick thing is, I grew up thinking it's normal, something that all dads do to their daughters. By the time I realised it wasn't, I was too scared of me dad to open me mouth. Oh Gawd, Jen, I shouldn't have told you. Don't tell anyone! Promise me you won't tell anyone!'

Jenny's heart went out to Tina and she reached out to clutch her friend's hand. 'I promise, but surely there's something you and Mandy can do to stop him? Why don't you tell the police?'

'He'd deny it and he's clever. He's made sure there's no proof.'

51

'What do you mean?'

'He hasn't, you know . . . gone all the way. He . . . he makes us use our mouths.'

'But what about your mum? Haven't you told her?'

'Jenny,' Tina said, her voice strangled with pain. 'She already knows.'

Bile rose in Jenny's throat. How could she? How could Tina's mother allow it to happen?

'If Mandy's moving out, why don't you go with her?'

'I asked, begged, but she won't take me. She wants to start a new life, to forget, and said I'd just be a constant reminder.'

'I can't believe she's leaving you behind,' Jenny said angrily, her mind turning. 'But listen, you could still leave home.'

'My dad won't let me. Even if I wait until he's away my mum would stop me. I'd have to do a runner.'

'You'll be sixteen soon and then they can't stop you. Anyway, just let them try,' Jenny said, ready to fight for her friend. It was as though her fear for Tina had brought about a change in her personality. Instead of her customary meekness she now felt strength, along with determination. Somehow she'd help her friend to get away.

'I wish I could leave, Jenny, but where would I live? At sixteen I'd only earn peanuts and I don't know how much it costs to rent a bedsit. I suppose

I could try getting into an empty place, you know, a squat, but I . . . I'd be scared to do something like that on me own.'

Jenny knew what she had to do. She hadn't suffered like Tina, but she was unhappy at home and wanted to get away too.

'You won't be alone, Tina. I'm coming with you. With two wage packets we're bound to be able to afford a bedsit.'

'Oh, Jenny, do you really mean it?'

'Of course I do,' Jenny insisted. Yes, they'd get away; start a new life, one that they'd be in charge of. From then on, nobody, neither man nor woman, was going to mess with them again – not with their minds, or their bodies.

Chapter Seven

That afternoon, Delia dressed carefully in a navy blue designer suit, and then put on her diamond stud earrings. She had never shown any interest in Jennifer's education before and had no idea what the girl was capable of, but now, to placate her son, she knew that getting rid of Jennifer would have to be delayed. It was something she hadn't anticipated, and for that reason Delia dressed to impress. Appearances mattered, and she wanted to show this careers adviser that the girl came from a good home, a superior family, and was therefore not suited to some sort of menial work. If she could persuade the man to place Jennifer in an office, if only on the first rung of some sort of career, it would at least be something she wouldn't be ashamed to tell her acquaintances at the WI and tennis club.

Delia picked up her leather handbag, knowing that within Robin's hearing she would have to continue to be nice to Jennifer. She would have to wait, keep up the act, but when the time was right she'd strike. Of course it would have to appear that she'd played no part in it, that Jennifer left of her own accord; but this time, no matter what, she wouldn't be thwarted.

It was a lovely day and rather than get her car out of the garage Delia decided to walk. As she left the drive a vehicle pulled up and she saw a fellow member of the WI behind the wheel.

'Mrs Lavender, Delia, I can see you're on your way out, but I'm glad I caught you,' Penelope Grainger said as she wound down her window. 'As you know we're having a fundraiser next week, but Mrs Brunswick has had to bow out. Could I put you down to take her place on the cake stall?'

'Yes, of course,' nodded Delia.

'Will you still be contributing some of your lovely walnut cakes? They always go down so well.'

'Yes, I'm making a half a dozen.'

'Wonderful, but I must go. You know how it is, things to do and all that.'

'Yes, I know what you mean. I'm just on my way to my daughter's school.'

'Oh dear, is there a problem?'

'No, it's an appointment with a careers adviser.'

'My daughter, Fiona, was determined to follow her father into medicine, and though it's jolly hard work, she loves it. Does your daughter have a career in mind?'

Delia swallowed, once again cursing the fact that

she had no idea what Jennifer was capable of. Penelope Grainger's husband was a consultant, and her daughter had attended a private school. In fact, other than seeing the woman at WI meetings, they didn't mix socially. Of course in this instance that could work in her favour – hopefully the woman unaware that Jennifer attended a state secondary school. Delia would have given anything to join Penelope's social circle, but her aspirations had come to nothing as yet.

'I think she's interested in law,' Delia lied, 'but if you'll excuse me I really must go now.'

'Righto, I'll see you next week,' Penelope said, giving a small wave before driving off.

Delia glanced at her watch. Only a few minutes had passed and she still had plenty of time, but nevertheless her pace was brisk as she continued her journey. Law! It had been the only thing that had popped into her head, and now sounded idiotic, especially as she doubted if Jennifer was capable of anything other than cleaning the chambers.

Jenny and Tina were waiting to see the careers adviser when Tina hissed, 'Jenny, I know you said my parents can't stop me, but when we leave I'm still gonna do a runner.'

'All right, but we'll need to find a bedsit. Have you got an area in mind?'

'Not really, but somewhere that's got a bit of life. How about Chelsea?'

'It isn't a huge distance away, but if you want to move there it's fine with me.'

There was silence for a moment, then Tina said sadly, 'It'll be ages before we can save enough to leave. Any landlord will want about a month's rent in advance, but my mum will want me to stump up at least half of what I earn.'

'Tina, we'll look for somewhere to live as soon as term's over – we've got to get you away from your father as soon as possible. Thanks to my dad I've got some savings, enough to pay the rent for at least a month, maybe more. Mind you, if you still want to do a runner, you'll have to pretend that nothing has changed until we leave. If the careers adviser arranges a job interview then go, otherwise your parents will guess that something's up.'

'Yeah, good thinking,' Tina agreed. 'As for the rent, I'll pay you back as soon as I can, honest I will.'

'Don't worry about it. You're my best friend, and that's what matters, not money.'

'You're more than a friend to me, Jenny. You're more like a sister, and a better one than Mandy.'

Jenny felt a surge of pleasure. It was nice to think that Tina saw them as sisters.

'Jennifer, there you are,' her mother said as she walked up to them, looking immaculate but slightly harassed. 'I was held up twice but thankfully it seems I've arrived in time.'

'I haven't been in yet, but I'm next.'

'Please have the courtesy to move along so I can sit down,' her mother then said, looking haughtily at Tina.

As the door opened beside her and a girl came out, Jenny reared to her feet and said sharply, 'There's no need to sit down, Mother. It's my turn now.'

'Very well, come on then, let's get this over with.'

'Good luck, Jenny.'

'Thanks, Tina,' Jenny said, ignoring her mother's disapproving look as they walked in to see the careers adviser.

Delia looked disdainfully at the weedy little man behind his desk. When invited to sit down, she inspected the chair before flicking it fastidiously with her handkerchief.

The man didn't seem intimidated by her actions. With a pair of round glasses perched on the end of his nose, he perused a folder in front of him until they were both seated. When he did finally look up, his eyes went to Jennifer, his smile warm.

'I see from this report that your work has been exceptional, with standards that your teachers feel would have been good enough for grammar school.'

'As she failed her eleven plus, I don't see how,' Delia said huffily.

'There are many intelligent children who fail the examination for one reason or another, and from this report it seems your daughter may well have been one of them.'

'Well, yes, I always knew she was bright,' Delia blustered now, blushing at the lie.

The man ignored her reply, instead pulling a card from an index file and focusing on Jennifer again. 'With your knowledge and interest in literature, I think I have a position that may appeal to you.'

Delia was startled. This was news to her, but then again she had barely looked at Jennifer's school reports.

'What sort of position?' she asked abruptly.

'It's in local government, as a local junior librarian.'

'Surely she needs qualifications?'

'The CILIP, that is the Chartered Institute of Libraries and Information Professionals, offer rewards for in-house experience and with training they can offer certification. This of course can eventually lead to managerial advancement, or work in other important sectors, such as museums, archives—'

Impatiently Delia interrupted the man, 'Yes, yes, I understand, but do you really think Jennifer has a chance of obtaining the position?'

'Yes, I do,' he said abruptly. 'However, it depends of course on whether your daughter is interested in this kind of work.'

Delia was annoyed to see that Jennifer was just staring at the man, her mouth agape. Far from appearing bright, the girl looked like an imbecile, and

Delia snapped, 'For goodness' sake, Jennifer, buck up and answer the man.'

'I . . . I'm sorry. It . . . it's just so unexpected . . . but yes, I'd love to train as a librarian. It would be like a dream come true.'

'Very well, I'll arrange an interview and you'll be notified in writing of the date and time.'

Still looking dazed, Jennifer rose to her feet. 'Tha . . . thank you.'

'Yes, thank you,' Delia echoed, feeling a little heady too as they left the room. She didn't know what she'd expected; perhaps a junior position in an office at the most, but this outcome was far better. For once, when Delia smiled at Jennifer, it was with genuine warmth.

'That went well,' she commented. 'Now we'll just have to ensure that you're successful at the interview.'

Jennifer ignored her, instead turning to talk to Tina, who was waiting her turn, 'You can go in now. I'll wait for you.'

'Great, see you soon,' the girl said, hurrying in to see the adviser.

Delia was annoyed. Jennifer knew she didn't approve of Tina Hammond. 'You'll do no such thing,' she said sharply. 'There's a stack of ironing waiting for you and you'll walk home with me.'

'I'm not a child. I've made my way home from school without escort for years so it's a bit late to start now.'

Delia heard the ring of sarcasm in Jennifer's tone

and bristled, her voice rising. 'How dare you use that tone with me. Now come on, we're leaving.'

'No, Mother. I'll do the ironing as soon as I get there, but I'll be walking home with Tina.'

A few heads turned, curious parents looking their way. Aware that they were causing a scene, Delia hissed, 'Right, I'm going, but I'll deal with you later and there'll be more than ironing waiting for you.'

'Yes, I'm sure there will,' Jennifer said, sounding, for the first time, unafraid.

Delia couldn't believe her ears, but she wasn't going to continue this here. Though she was inwardly fuming, she haughtily walked away, her dignity intact as she left the building. It was as though Jennifer had transformed in front of her eyes, changing from a compliant child who always tried to please to an assured young woman. Not only that, an argumentative one, and Delia knew that unless she could reassert herself, this new development would make living with Jennifer intolerable. It was bad enough that she'd been forced to look at the girl for nearly sixteen years, but at least she had been able to feel that in her coldness towards Jennifer she was punishing Edward too.

As Delia continued on her way home, her mouth was set in a tight line of annoyance. She had wanted rid of Jennifer as soon as possible, had planned for that, but then had been forced to put it off. Now, however, she set her mind to the problem again.

At last, Delia came to realise that she could use

this change in Jennifer's attitude to her advantage. She had told Robin that Jennifer was a difficult baby, but now she could extend that period. If she set the trap carefully and it worked, Robin would see Jennifer in a new light.

Delia expected to find her son home from college, and composed her face to one of sadness in readiness. Her new plan to get rid of Jennifer *had* to work. She would drive the girl out – but this time Robin wouldn't threaten to leave home too. He'd be on her side, and Delia looked forward to going into battle now.

Jennifer was no match for her and the girl would soon find that out.

Chapter Eight

Jenny was amazed that she'd stood up to her mother like that, but knew she'd suffer for it later. There'd be more than ironing to face – probably floors to scrub and other menial tasks lined up. Yet as she waited for Tina, she found her thoughts drifting back to her own interview with the careers adviser. If she could have chosen any job, it would have been in a library. She loved books, the smell of them, the feel of them in her hand and the anticipation of being enthralled by a story as she turned the first page. Many had taken her away from her un-happiness at home to another place and sometimes to another time. When would she hear about the interview? Would she be successful? But then Jenny's bubble burst. A local library, the careers adviser had said, and she now saw the job slipping away. Tina wanted to move out of this area and she'd agreed. Oh, but to work in a library! For a moment Jenny wondered if she should change her mind, stay at home, at least until she'd completed her training.

It didn't take Jenny long to dismiss the idea. It wasn't just that she wanted to get away from her mother, there was Tina to consider too. Her friend needed her and she couldn't let her down.

'Right, I'm done. Let's go,' Tina said.

'How did you get on?'

'I was offered a job in a department store and pretended I was keen. What about you?'

'A trainee librarian.'

'Blimey, I wouldn't fancy that. Talk about boring. With your posh voice and typing speeds I'm surprised you weren't offered something in an office.'

'It doesn't matter. We'll be moving from this area and finding our own jobs.'

'I know, and I can't wait,' Tina said, smiling happily as they left the building.

Jenny felt the same. She knew what would be waiting for her when she arrived home, but the thought of leaving gave her courage. She was sick of being punished for no reason, of being treated like a servant, and now all the years of hurt, of degradation, culminated in Jenny's mind.

She wouldn't be meek any more, and her mother was soon going to find that out.

When his mother came in, Robin saw that she was upset, surreptitiously wiping tears from her eyes.

'Mother, what's wrong?'

'Nothing, it's nothing,' Delia said.

Robin saw that her hands were shaking, her nerves obviously playing up again, and asked, 'Has something upset you?'

'Yes, but it doesn't matter.'

'You're crying, so of course it matters.'

'Please, Robin, just let it go. You wouldn't believe me anyway.'

'Of course I would.'

'It . . . it was Jennifer's behaviour. She was so rude to me and caused a dreadful scene at the careers office.'

'Jenny! I can't believe it.'

'I knew you'd say that,' Delia cried, tears filling her eyes again.

'Mother, I've never heard Jenny being rude to you.'

'Of course you haven't and Jennifer has made sure of that. What with the clubs you joined and now your studies, you're hardly around to see or hear anything, but let me tell you that since childhood Jennifer had been jealous of you, of my feelings for you. You see me as hard, cold towards her, but to maintain control I've had to be.'

'If that's the case, why haven't you said anything before?'

'I tried to tell your father, but he'd have none of it. In the end I gave up and you were my compensation, but it almost broke my heart when you turned on me too and threatened to leave home.'

Tears fell in earnest now and Robin rushed to his mother's side, placing an arm around her. He had never seen her as bad as this; her whole body was shaking as she turned into him, sobbing.

'Take no notice of my threat,' he said quickly. 'Of course I'm not leaving home. Well, not until I go to university, but then I'll be back every weekend.'

'I can't tell you how much that means to me . . . I should be used to Jennifer's behaviour by now. It . . . it just became a bit too much for me today, and I feel as though I'm losing control of her. Don't worry, I . . . I'm all right now.'

'Are you sure?'

'Yes, I'm fine,' Delia said with a brave little smile.

His mother looked so vulnerable and Robin felt awful for threatening to leave home. At least he'd put her mind at rest, yet he was still worried. When his mother had come to his room that morning she'd been a bit tearful, but it had been nothing in comparison to the emotional distress he'd just witnessed.

Robin now began to wonder if she could cope with running a business, with the stress it could cause her, and chewed worriedly on his lower lip. Not only that, he was still unable to believe the things she had said about Jenny. He'd never seen his sister behaving badly, yet something must have caused his mother to break down like this. Usually it happened only when his father was home, the rows affecting her nerves. Maybe that was it – perhaps she was still upset from his latest visit, and that was causing her to magnify things out of all proportion.

Thankfully Robin saw that his mother was looking a little calmer now, but he knew he'd have to keep an eye on her to ensure that she wasn't unnecessarily distressed. He'd have a word with Jenny when she arrived home, explain things, but if his mother got in such a dreadful state again, perhaps he should persuade her to see a doctor.

Delia moved away from Robin, pleased that things had gone so well. He had looked shocked to see her in such a state, and she was glad of her acting abilities. As a child her own mother had called her a drama queen, saying she was destined for the stage, though of course if Delia had suggested actually ever going to a stage school, both her parents would have been scandalised.

She had loved her calm, staid father, and been heartbroken when he had died suddenly of a heart attack at just fifty. She had been thirteen at the time and her older sister, Beatrice, seventeen. Though Delia had wanted to cling to both her mother and sister, emotions were never displayed and tears never shown in public. They had set her a wonderful example and she had grown up emulating their proud upright and dignified manner.

At twenty, Beatrice had married well to a diplomat who was posted abroad. It had been heartbreaking to see her sister leave, especially when just three years later her mother, also young at forty-six, had become seriously ill. Before her mother had died, she'd encouraged Delia to emulate Beatrice in marrying well. With her sister able to return from abroad only for the funeral, Delia had been left feeling totally alone.

He may not have been perfect, but Delia had married the first man who asked her – Edward. *That* side of marriage had shocked her, however. She wasn't used to being held or kissed, and on her wedding night, when things had gone further, she had been horrified. She didn't like it, found it messy, distasteful, and though she had never wanted to adopt Jennifer, it had at least given her the perfect ammunition to stop much further sexual activity. That, along with her nerves, had ensured that she always managed to get her own way, which was no more than Edward deserved.

Delia expected Jennifer home soon and now turned her mind to her plans. By being rude, by defying her, the stupid girl had played right into her hands. All she had to do now was to lay a trap – and in such a way that it would arouse the same response from Jennifer in Robin's hearing.

'That sounds like Jenny coming in,' he said.

As Robin was still looking at her worriedly, Delia decided there was no time like the present. She pretended to sway a little before sitting down.

'I feel a little dizzy and my throat is parched,' she said. As the girl walked into the room she added tremulously, 'Jennifer, there you are. I'm still upset about your behaviour, but before we talk about it please make me a cup of tea.'

'You said there's ironing waiting to be done and as I'm not an octopus, or your servant, you can make your own tea. I'm going upstairs to change.'

'See, Robin, I told you,' Delia wailed as Jennifer stalked off. 'That was nothing in comparison to how she usually talks to me. It's usually worse than that, much worse.'

'Please, Mummy, calm down. I'll make you a drink and then I'll have a few words to say to Jenny.'

Delia slumped, holding both hands over her face to hide her true feelings. She'd hardly had to make any effort at all before Jennifer had reacted – and in just the way she had wanted.

Jenny was pleased that she'd stood up to her mother again, but had only just changed out of her school clothes when her bedroom door was flung open and Robin stormed into the room.

'If I hadn't heard it with my own ears, I'd never have believed it. You were rude to Mother and now she's in a dreadful state.'

'I only told her to make her own tea. That's hardly reason to get into a state.'

'From what she told me it isn't the first time you've been rude to her. In fact you've been making her life hell.'

'Robin, all I did was to refuse to walk home with her after we'd seen the careers adviser.'

'There must be more to it than that. Mother is at the end of her tether, her nerves so bad that I fear she might be having a nervous breakdown.'

'If she is, it's got nothing to do with me,' Jenny protested.

'I doubt that, and from now on I don't want her upset. I want you to come downstairs and apologise, but be warned, Jenny. If she isn't better by the time Dad comes home I intend to tell him what you've been up to.'

'But I haven't been up to anything!' she called, but Robin had already marched out and her door slammed behind him.

Jenny slumped onto the side of her bed. Today had been the first time she had defied her mother and surely that wasn't enough to cause a nervous breakdown? She had wanted to stand up for herself, but somehow it had backfired, and instead something was going on – something Jenny couldn't grasp. She longed to escape all this, but she couldn't leave home yet, had to wait until she was sixteen, followed by two more weeks at school before the end of term.

Worried and confused by Robin's threat to tell her father, Jenny realised that her newfound courage had already deserted her.

Chapter Nine

Robin was thankful that an uneasy truce had now been formed. He kept a careful watch on both his mother and Jenny, at first not knowing whom to believe. Jenny insisted that she'd never been rude before, while his mother said the opposite, that it had been going on for years. Jenny said that she had always been treated badly when he wasn't around, almost like a slave, but his mother again said the opposite.

However, his mother was still a bundle of nerves, so to keep her happy Robin kept his promise, the two of them calculating the starting up costs and profit projections for the new business. He had his concerns, especially about the initial costs, but his mother had told him there was no need to worry – that if her savings were insufficient she would go to the bank for a loan. He didn't like this idea, suggesting instead that she approached his father for funding, but she would have none of it and, rather than upset her, Robin had said no more.

Five weeks had now passed and he hadn't heard his mother being anything other than kind to Jenny. On the other hand, though she wasn't actually rude, Jenny was barely polite. She'd be sixteen tomorrow, and Robin was wrapping her present.

'I wasn't sure what to get Jenny for her birthday, so settled on a book as usual. What about you?'

'Your father is buying her a record player and it will be from both of us. Talk of the devil,' she said as the telephone rang. 'That's probably him now. He usually rings to let me know when to expect him.'

Robin had finished wrapping the book and, intending to put it in his room until tomorrow morning, he followed his mother into the hall, pausing to listen to the one-sided conversation. He gleaned enough to realise there was a problem, but then there was a flurry of activity overhead and he quickly hid his present behind his back as Jenny appeared.

His mother had just replaced the receiver and, leaning over the banister, Jenny said, 'I heard the telephone. Was it Daddy? When is he arriving?'

Delia's reply was short. 'He isn't coming home.'

'But . . . but he promised,' Jenny cried.

'Work always comes first with your father and you should have learned that by now. He obviously feels it's more important than your birthday.'

Jenny looked stricken and fled back to her room.

'That was a bit harsh, Mother,' Robin said.

'I don't see why. I only told her the truth.' Then her voice cracked. 'Oh, I'm sorry, Robin. I was annoyed that your father broke his promise and spoke without thinking. It's always the same. He causes upset, but it's me who's shown in a bad light.'

Robin was alarmed that his mother was still so fragile, so easily upset. 'You aren't to blame and I'm sure Jenny knows that. I'll go and have a word with her.'

'I . . . I should do it,' Delia said, but tears began to come in earnest now.

Robin put an arm around her, leading her back into the drawing room. His mother needed him and Jenny would have to wait.

Jenny was unable to deny the truth of her mother's words. Her father *had* put his work first, so much so that it was more important than his promise to be there for her birthday. He hadn't even asked to speak to her, to offer any explanation, and Jenny couldn't help wondering if it was because she wasn't his real daughter. Perhaps it wasn't possible to really love a child who wasn't your own – that had certainly proved to be the case with Delia.

Jenny hadn't been able to stand up to her, not with Robin so sure that she had caused this so-called bout of bad nerves, and no matter how much she protested, told him that it was all an act that their mother dropped when he wasn't around, Robin didn't seem to believe her.

All Jenny thought about now was getting out of this house, and she was counting the days to the end of term. Tomorrow, on her birthday, she had planned to tell her parents that she was leaving home – that she and Tina were going to look for a flat together as soon as they left school. She had been worried about her father's reaction, but wasn't worried any longer. He wouldn't care. Once again Jenny was swamped with a familiar feeling, one of loneliness, of something missing in her life. She was alone, without real parents, or anyone else who cared about her.

But wait, she did have someone; she had Tina, who saw them as sisters, and at this thought Jenny came to a swift decision. Of course, she would have to speak to Tina, but she doubted her friend would take any persuasion. Only moments later Jenny went downstairs, saying shortly as she poked her head into the drawing room, 'I'm going out for a walk.'

She didn't wait for a response before heading outside. So intent was she on speaking to Tina that her face was gleaming with perspiration by the time she reached Princes Way.

As Jenny entered the block of flats she hoped that Tina's father was away, the thought of even looking at the man making her stomach churn. She took the lift to the fifth floor and, fingers crossed, she stepped out to knock on Tina's door. She was thankful that it was her friend who opened it.

'Tina, can you come out for a while?'

'You look all hot and bothered. What's wrong?'

'I need to talk to you.'

'Come on in,' Tina offered.

'No, we need to be on our own.'

'Oh, right. Hang on then. I'll just grab my shoes.'

'Tina! Who's that at the door?'

'It's Jenny. We're just going out for a while, Mum,' Tina called back. She winked, disappeared for a moment, and then reappeared, hopping on one foot as she put on her other shoe. 'Right, let's go.'

Jenny said nothing until the lift doors closed behind them, and then drew in a deep breath. 'Tina, instead of waiting, I want to leave home now.'

'What! Blimey, we've still got a week till the end of term. What's brought this on?'

'I've just had enough. You were sixteen last week, and as it's my birthday tomorrow I can't see the school kicking up a fuss if we don't go back.'

'Yeah, I suppose you're right. When do you want us to leave?'

'Tomorrow.'

'Gawd, that soon?' Tina said, as they stepped out of the lift, but then she grinned. 'Yeah, well, as far as I'm concerned it couldn't have come at a better time. My dad's due home on Sunday and you know what that means.'

'Oh Tina, yes, we've got to get you out of there. We could pack tonight and leave in the morning.'

'Yeah, that could work. With the old man arriving, mum is sure to go out to get in a bit of shopping. I could sneak out then, but I won't be able to say for sure what time it will be.'

'Don't worry. I'll have to draw some money from my post office savings book, and after that I'll wait for you in that café on the corner of the High Street.'

Tina linked arms with Jenny. 'It all feels like a dream, and I can hardly believe we're really leaving.'

'Well we are. I just hope that when we get to Chelsea we'll be able to find somewhere to stay.'

'It'll be a doddle,' Tina said with assurance. 'We just need to buy the local paper and there's sure to be rooms advertised.'

'Yes, but will they let us move in straightaway?'

'I dunno, but fingers crossed. If the worst comes to the worst, I suppose there's always a hotel.'

'That would soon swallow up my savings,' Jenny said worriedly.

'Now you sound like you're changing your mind.'

'No, I'm not,' Jenny insisted.

'Thank goodness for that. It'll be great, Jenny, you and me in a place of our own, and in Chelsea too. I wouldn't mind a job in a boutique on the King's Road, and at least you won't be stuck in a boring library.'

Jenny knew that leaving the opportunity of the

library job behind would be her only regret and doubted she'd get such a chance again. For a moment she was saddened but then again staying at home would be far worse. Perhaps she'd be able to find a job in a bookshop and that would be some compensation. Cheered by the thought she said, 'Right then, I'm off home to sort out what clothes I'm taking. I'll see you in the morning.'

The two of them retraced their steps and parted outside the flats. Jenny continued on her way, undecided whether to tell her mother she was leaving when she got home or wait until she was packed and ready to go in the morning.

Chapter Ten

Delia was upstairs, just leaving the bathroom when Jennifer returned from her walk. She hadn't wanted to overplay her hand and so had shown nothing but kindness recently towards Jennifer. However, the girl would be sixteen tomorrow and it was time to bait her again – time to strike.

She followed Jennifer into her bedroom but, not having had a chance to rehearse her words, Delia had to think quickly.

'Jennifer, I'm not happy that you went out without telling me where you were going. I know you were upset, and Robin thinks I was harsh with you, but I'm not prepared to make excuses for your father. He isn't coming home, accept that and pull yourself together.'

'I . . . I just went out for a walk, that was all.'

'It was more like you went off in a sulk. You are not a child now and I suggest you stop behaving like one. You're sixteen tomorrow and thankfully can leave home if you want to.'

'Thankfully? It sounds like you want me to go.'

Delia smiled sardonically, deciding to move this forward. Going out to the hall she raised her voice to a loud wail. 'I can't stand this again. I really can't. Your behaviour is just too much . . . too much . . .'

As Delia had hoped, Robin came running upstairs. 'Mother, what's the matter?'

'I tried to apologise, to explain why I was so harsh, but now Jennifer seems to think I want her to leave home. I don't, Robin, but . . . but she was so nasty . . . so . . . so rude to me.'

'Mummy, calm down and let me take you downstairs,' Robin urged, and then shouted at Jennifer, 'As for you, I'll deal with you later.'

Delia clutched her son's arm as they went into the drawing room. He was making a fuss of her and she enjoyed it, letting him think he had managed to soothe her.

'If you're all right now, Mummy, I intend to see that Jenny apologises for her behaviour.'

'Thank you, darling,' Delia said, glad that once again Jennifer had proved no match for her. The girl was too young and innocent to work out what was really going on, and Robin was the same, easily fooled.

While Robin went to get Jennifer, Delia composed her expression to one of wounded hurt. When the girl appeared, Delia waited for the apology. It didn't come. Instead when Jennifer spoke it was with defiance.

'I know you planned all this,' she said, 'but you needn't have bothered.'

'What is that supposed to mean?'

'That I'd already decided to leave home.'

'But you can't, Jenny,' Robin protested.

'Oh yes I can. It's just what your mother wants.'

'Don't be silly. She did once suggest it and had her reasons, but then we agreed that you're too young. Mother, tell her,' Robin urged.

'If Jennifer wants to go there's nothing I can do to stop her,' Delia said. Then, seeing the expression on her son's face, she could have bitten off her tongue. She quickly back-pedalled. 'Of course I would prefer her to stay, and hope we can persuade her to do just that.'

'If you believe that, Robin, you'll believe anything,' Jennifer told him. 'I've never made her life a misery. In fact it's the reverse and I've told you how she treats me when you're not here.'

Delia knew that she had to stop this, and wailed, 'It's you who's telling lies. You've always been jealous of my relationship with my son and now you're trying to come between us. Oh, Robin . . . please, I can't take any more of this.'

Just as Delia had hoped, Robin rushed to her side, and over his shoulder she saw the look of disgust Jennifer threw at her before she marched out. For a moment Delia was annoyed at her audacity, but then realised that it didn't really matter. The girl was leaving, and now all she had to do was to convince Robin that she'd played no part in her decision.

At last her torment was over and she would never have to look at that face again – the tears Delia shed now, ones of relief.

Robin was angry with Jenny for upsetting his mother again, but hated the thought of her leaving home. He would have to talk to her, but with his mother in this state it would have to wait.

'Jennifer really was telling lies, but I don't know how to convince you of that.'

'I'm not sure you have to. I've seen for myself now what Jennifer has been putting you through. I just wish you'd told me before and then I'd have understood why you always seemed rather cold and distant towards her.'

'I didn't want you upset; I tried to shield you.'

'I'm not a child, Mother.'

'You were when you took your eleven plus exams, followed by grammar school with more to face. I was so proud when you passed and went on to college, but what I feared is now happening. Instead of concentrating on your studies, you're distracted and worried about me because of Jennifer.'

'I'm still on course to pass my A levels.'

'That's good,' Delia said, but then she started to

sob again. 'I dread to think what your father will say. He'll blame me, I . . . I know he will.'

'Mother, don't worry. When he comes home again, I'll put him straight.'

'I doubt you'll convince him. Jennifer can do no wrong in his eyes.'

'I must admit I found it hard to believe at first, but I'm sorry now for doubting you.'

'There's no need to apologise, darling, but oh dear, with all this emotional upset I'm so tired,' she said, placing a hand over her mouth and yawning. 'I have an awful headache and think I'll go to bed.'

'Yes, do that, and don't worry. I'll see that everything is shipshape and the doors are all locked.'

'You're such a comfort to me. Good night, darling.'

Robin saw how emotionally drained his mother looked as she rose to her feet. It was *his* turn to protect her now, to shield her from any more distress, and to do that he'd have to make sure she remained calm in the morning. They would both talk to Jenny, persuade her to stay, and hopefully things would get back to normal.

After he checked all the windows and made sure the back and front doors were secure, Robin went upstairs. The house was strangely silent and his room hot and stuffy as he lay on his bed, his mind twisting and turning.

Despite the fact that he'd been blind to Jenny's

faults, she was in his system, and he hoped they could talk her round. Yet if there was another scene he doubted his mother could cope. She was already at the end of her tether, and he dreaded the thought of her breaking down again, of having to call the doctor, who might well have her hospitalised. Anger towards Jenny flared once more and Robin began to wonder if it might be for the best if she did leave home, though the thought still had the power to make his stomach churn. Where would she go?

Wait! Jenny said she had planned to go, and that must mean she had somewhere lined up. She must have broken into her savings to rent a room, but as the job she was starting was a local one, it wouldn't be far away.

At last, realising that all this could work out to his advantage, Robin smiled. Jenny would be living alone, and would perhaps be so lonely that she'd welcome his company. When he called round to see her, there'd be just the two of them and as his imagination took over, Robin groaned, his hand snaking downwards as he sought release.

Jenny packed, stuffing all that she could into an old rucksack that she had once used for a Guides camping trip, and then finally climbed into bed.

She thought over all that had happened recently. Thanks to Robin blurting it out, everything made more sense. Out of her hearing, her mother must have suggested that she leave home, but Robin, and perhaps her father, had been against it.

How clever her mother had been, pretending to agree that she was too young, pretending that she cared, convincing Robin that she didn't want her to go, yet all the time planning a way to drive her out.

Oh, what did it matter? She'd be gone in the morning, her only regret that she wasn't able to say goodbye to her father. Yet he wasn't really her father. If he had been he wouldn't have broken his promise. Feeling the threat of tears, Jenny blinked rapidly.

No, she wouldn't cry. She was being childish and by acting childishly she had played right into her mother's hands. It was time to grow up. Tomorrow was going to be the start of a new chapter in her life, one she couldn't wait to begin.

Chapter Eleven

Edward arrived home at eleven in the morning, two weeks after Jenny's birthday. He had wanted to be there, had promised to be there for her big day, but when he hadn't been able to make it he'd rung Delia to explain why. She'd have told Jenny about the fix he'd been in, that in those circumstances it had been impossible to make it home.

He pulled the belated present from the boot of his car, berating himself. He should have at least rung Jenny on her birthday, but he'd been so tied up with sorting things out he hadn't given it a thought. Delia was right in some things, Edward admitted to himself. He could be thoughtless and his work became his whole focus when he was away from home.

Of course, that hadn't been the case on Jenny's birthday, but nevertheless Edward intended to make it up to her this weekend. He'd book a restaurant, they'd all go out for a slap-up meal, and then he'd give her the extra present he had tucked away in his pocket, a lovely little gold pendant she was sure to love.

With a smile on his face in anticipation of his daughter's welcome, he went inside, calling, 'Where's my girl?'

There was no response, the house strangely silent. Puzzled, Edward looked in the drawing room but found it empty, and so he went into the kitchen. Empty again. Where was everyone?

Having expected an excited welcome from Jenny, Edward felt a strong sense of anticlimax as he placed the parcel on the kitchen table before heading for the stairs. At the top he called, 'Is anyone home?'

Robin came out of his room, saying quietly, 'Hello, Dad.'

'Where is everyone?'

'Mum's gone shopping, but she should be home soon.'

'What about Jenny?'

'Er . . . you're not going to like this, Dad, but Jenny's gone. She left home.'

'What!' Edward thundered. 'When?'

'She left on her birthday.'

'But why?' Edward asked, but then he heard Delia coming in. 'Oh, don't tell me, I can guess.' Turning away from his son, he hurried downstairs to confront his wife. 'So you've done it. While I was away you got rid of Jenny.'

'I . . . I did no such thing. She left of her own accord.'

'Don't give me that!'

'It's true, Dad,' said Robin, who had followed Edward downstairs.

'I don't believe it!' Edward snapped, dismissing his son as he focused on Delia. 'Tell me where Jenny is. Whether you like it or not I'm bringing her home.'

Delia's face drained of colour and Robin went to her side. 'We don't know where Jenny is,' he said.

Edward's fury mounted as he glared at Delia. 'Jenny's a child and you let her leave home with no idea of where she was going? Are you mad, woman?'

'Stop it! Please stop shouting,' Delia begged.

'Have you told the police? Have you reported her missing?'

'What would be the point of that? She's sixteen and free to leave home if she wants to.'

'She's a child! You . . . you . . . ' he ground out, so furious that he could have throttled her. 'I'll never forgive you for this!'

'Dad, stop it. None of this is Mummy's fault. Jenny's behaviour over the years had been abominable, and just lately she almost caused Mummy to have a nervous breakdown.'

'Don't talk rubbish!'

'See, Robin, I told you,' Delia cried. 'I said your father would blame me.'

'Leave this to me,' soothed Robin. 'Take one of

your pills. I know they make you feel groggy but it'll calm you.'

As Robin walked towards him, Edward noticed for the first time that his son no longer looked like a boy. He looked like a young man and a determined one at that.

'Dad, come on,' he said, grasping his arm. 'Mother really is ill and we need to talk.'

'Ill my foot,' Edward snapped, convinced that Delia was hiding behind her so-called nerves as usual. He'd get nothing out of her, but at least his son might be able to shed some light on the matter, a clue as to where Jenny had gone. If Robin could suggest somewhere, as a starting point, it would be something. He had to find Jenny. He just had to.

Robin was relieved when his father agreed to accompany him to the drawing room. His mother had tried to stop Jenny from leaving – they had both tried. There had been a tug of war when he tried to grab her rucksack, but Jenny had fought like a tiger, verbally attacking both him and his mother.

She had fled then, leaving his mother sobbing and in such a state that he'd had to call the doctor. She was now on medication, which was helping, but would it be enough to shield her from his father's anger?

'I need a drink,' his dad said, taking a decanter and pouring a large measure of whisky.

Robin waited until he had gulped it down, and

then said, 'There are things you should know about Jenny.'

'Don't bother. I know my daughter.'

'No, Dad, you don't. Mother told me that Jenny has made her life a misery for years, but I didn't believe her until I saw it with my own eyes,' Robin told him, going on to tell his father all that had happened since he was last here.

'That doesn't sound like Jenny,' Edward said. 'But if what you say is true, your mother must have driven her to behave like that.'

'She did not!' Robin insisted. 'If you had been here you'd have seen that for yourself, but of course you're always away. Not only that, if you hadn't put your work first, you'd have been here for Jenny's birthday and perhaps able to stop her from leaving. We certainly couldn't.'

'What are you talking about? I was driving home when my car broke down. I rang your mother to tell her why I couldn't make it and asked her to explain things to Jenny. Didn't she pass on my message?'

Robin could remember the phone call and frowned. His mother hadn't said anything about the car. Confused, he was about to tell his father that, but then bit back the words. It would anger him again, cause another confrontation, and his mother was upset enough as it was.

'Yes, of . . . of course she did,' he stuttered, hating having to lie. He knew that there had to be an explanation for his mother's behaviour but now, recalling how upset Jenny had been when Delia told her that dad's work came first, doubts crossed his mind. What else had his mother lied about?

'I had to find a garage, sort out repairs, but forget that for now. Jenny is my main concern and I need to find her. Where do I start? Have you got any idea?'

'I've been looking, asked around, and found out that her best friend left home at the same time. I think that means they're together, but as Jenny starts work at the local library on Monday, they're probably still in this area.'

A look of relief crossed his father's face. 'Well done, son, that should make it a lot easier. If I can't find Jenny before then, I'll just have to be outside the library when she turns up for work. Right, I'm going to have a quick bite to eat and then I'll make a start.'

Privately, Robin doubted that Jenny would agree to come home even if his father did find her, but he didn't say anything. They returned to the kitchen together to find his mother sitting at the table, her face slack, the pill she had taken making her groggy. Once again he wondered why she had lied about the telephone call, deciding to ask her as soon as his father went out.

However, as soon as Delia saw them, she rose tiredly to her feet. 'I . . . I'm going upstairs to lie down for a while.'

'Yes, all right, Mother,' Robin agreed, aware that his father was looking at her scathingly as she left the room. He felt protective of her and as soon as she was out of sight he sprang to her defence. 'I told you what happened and you can't blame Mother for this. Jenny really did leave of her own accord.'

'You're supposed to have a brain. Use it,' his father snapped. 'You said Jenny's been making your mother's life a misery, but don't you think it's odd that you've only just seen it for yourself?'

'Mother said Jenny's clever, that she only behaved badly when I wasn't around.'

'Right, let's think about that. From what I've gathered, she told you this so-called bad behaviour has been going on for years. How many years?'

'I don't know for sure, but since our childhood. Mother mentioned my eleven plus so it must have been before that.'

His father's laugh was derisive as he slapped a piece of ham between two slices of bread. 'So you're telling me that Jenny, who would have been around nine years old then, was wily enough at that age to make your mother's life hell without you seeing or hearing a thing? We didn't, and still don't, live in a mansion, and as this has supposedly been going on for at least seven years, I doubt that hiding it for that long is possible.'

'I . . . I hadn't thought of that . . . but I *have* seen it now, Dad.'

'So you say, but don't you think it's strange that after so many years of so-called concealing her bad behaviour, Jenny has suddenly come out into the open?'

Robin frowned as he thought it over. 'Well, yes, it is a bit odd.'

'As I said, use your head. I suspect what you saw was Jenny rebelling against *her* treatment for all these years. You've seen how cold your mother can be, how at times she speaks to Jenny like a servant, and I just wish I'd done more to put a stop to it. Now I'm going to find my daughter,' he said, not pausing to wrap the sandwich. 'I'll eat this in the car.'

Robin was left floundering, but it took only a few seconds for him to realise that his father was right. 'Hold on, Dad. I'm coming with you.'

'Fine,' said Edward. 'Two pairs of eyes are better than one. Though as your mother is supposed to be ill, aren't you worried about leaving her on her own?'

'No, Dad. Let's go and find Jenny.'

Delia didn't need pills. She wasn't in a nervous state or depressed. She'd been ecstatic that Jennifer had left home, but then Edward had turned up and now her happiness was replaced by worry. Delia hadn't gone to bed; instead she'd stood on the stairs listening, and had been horrified by what she'd heard. Blast Edward. Blast him for putting doubt in her son's mind.

Now, alone in the silent house, Delia cursed her own stupidity. She'd overplayed her hand by putting Jennifer at too young an age to be that clever – but there had to be a way to turn things round. Setting her mind to the problem, she at last realised that there was only one thing she could do. There was no choice. She hadn't wanted to play this hand yet though, had planned to wait until she was self-sufficient and able to tell Edward that their marriage was over.

It was the only option left to her, Delia decided – and at least she'd be entitled to the house, as well as a decent settlement until Robin finished his education.

Chapter Twelve

With no idea of the drama that was unfolding in Wimbledon, Jenny and Tina were in Chelsea, arms linked as they walked along the King's Road.

Jenny had found Chelsea nerve-racking at first. Unable to find a flat or rooms at such short notice, the two girls had spent that first night in a seedy hotel. Jenny had hardly slept for worrying that they'd made a huge mistake, but nothing had seemed to faze Tina, and her friend had snored gently all night.

The next morning they had begun their search again, but flats or even bedsits where the rent wasn't exorbitant proved impossible to find. Footsore and weary, they had finally stumbled across a rundown area at the far end of the King's Road called the World's End. The two-roomed pokey flat they at last found was thanks to a card in a shop window and the landlord had asked no questions when he pocketed the rent and deposit. Part of a tall, scruffy terraced house, it wasn't much, but once they had settled in, Jenny at last found herself happy.

Except for one thing, she thought, and that was her worry that they'd never find jobs. Her hopes of working in a bookshop hadn't come to fruition, having tried a few without success, including one that was tucked down an alley and specialised in antique books. Tina had thought her mad for wanting to work in what she called a dark, dusty, musty hole, but Jenny would have loved it.

They had tried boutiques, department stores, cafés and restaurants, growing increasingly desperate when it was always their age or lack of experience that let them down. With such a large chunk of her savings gone on securing the flat, Jenny feared that if they didn't soon find work, her money would run out.

'Come on, Jenny, step up the pace,' Tina urged. 'We don't want to be late.'

'There's no chance of that,' Jenny said, keeping her fingers crossed that they'd be lucky this time. Surely it had been a good omen that, just as they were passing a newly refurbished café-cum-restaurant, a sign had appeared in the window for staff. They'd been told the new owner would be conducting interviews at eleven today and they had left the flat with plenty of time to spare, determined to be first in line.

'Right, shoulders back and look confident,' Tina advised when they arrived.

They stepped inside to find several other

hopefuls waiting and were told to sit with them. It was over half an hour before their turn came. Jenny was called before Tina and nervously approached the man conducting the interviews.

He eyed her sceptically, his first question: 'How old are you?'

'I'm sixteen.'

'Is that so?' he said, a small smile playing around his mouth.

He wasn't young, but a bit of a dish, Jenny thought, with olive skin and dark hair, Italian or Greek perhaps, she decided, though he had no trace of an accent. She was shaking inwardly but did her best to hide it as she said firmly, 'Yes, I told you, I'm sixteen.'

'What's your name and where do you live?'

'Jennifer. Jennifer Lavender and I recently moved to Chelsea from Wimbledon.'

'I'm looking for waitresses. Have you any experience?'

'Er . . . no,' she said. Thinking on her feet, she added, 'But I'm a fast learner.'

Once again a look of amusement crossed his face and for a moment Jenny began to hope. It was short-lived, as he said, 'I want trained staff. However . . .'

As he paused, Jenny blurted out, 'I'll do anything, any job.'

'The only thing I can offer you is kitchen work, cleaning, washing up, that sort of thing.'

Without a thought, Jenny said hurriedly, 'I'll take it.'

'So without asking me about the hours, the pay, you'll take it?'

'Well . . . no . . . but . . .'

'But you're desperate,' he interrupted. 'Yes, I thought so, and I also doubt you're sixteen. What are you, a runaway?'

'Of course not.'

'Do you live with your parents?'

'Not now. I share a flat with my friend. She's over there,' Jenny said, nodding towards Tina.

His eyes narrowed, scrutinising Tina, then he crooked a finger to beckon her over. 'I suppose you're going to tell me that you're sixteen too?'

'Yeah, that's right.'

'And, like your friend, you'll take any job on offer?'

'I don't know about that. It depends what's on offer and the pay.'

'Have *you* any experience?'

'Look, we both left school recently so the answer is no, and we never will have unless someone gives us a chance.'

Jenny hid a smile. Unlike her, Tina didn't seem nervous or browbeaten as she looked the man in the eye. He shrugged, then said, 'As I told your friend, all I can offer is kitchen work. It's eight-hour shifts, six days a week, and the weekly pay is eleven pounds.'

'Eleven quid! Is that all?'

'Take it or leave it.'

'We'll take it,' Jenny said quickly.

'Hold on, Jenny. That's crap pay.'

'Tina, it's a job and we need the money.'

'Yeah, yeah, all right, I won't turn it down.'

Jenny sighed with relief. 'Thank you for giving us a chance, Mr ... Mr ... er ...'

'Mr Cane.'

'Cane,' Jenny said, surprised, 'but I thought ...'

'My mother's Italian,' he said dismissively, as though used to this reaction to his looks. 'You can both start your first shift on Monday morning, eight o'clock sharp when we will be serving breakfast and ending at four. Every four weeks your shift will change and you'll be working from four until midnight.'

Jenny was about to thank him again, but he was already looking at the next person in line, his voice strident as he called, 'Next!'

Tina waited until they were outside before she spoke, her tone scathing. 'Eleven soddin' quid a week and kitchen work! We must be mad. I know I'm not posh like you, but we could both do better than that.'

'I think he offered us employment because he felt sorry for us. I know it isn't much, but it's better than nothing.'

'Sorry for us! Don't make me laugh. I saw the way he was looking at you and it wasn't with pity.'

'What! Don't be silly.'

'Whatever you say, but there's something not right about him. He was trying to sound posh, but unlike you, it was false. Still, come on, however shitty they are, we've got jobs and should celebrate,' Tina said, trying to cast off her bad mood. 'If you don't mind stumping up again, we could go for a snack in Boris's sandwich shop. Susan said that he's had some famous customers, including Mick Jagger, John Lennon and Yoko. You never know, we might spot a famous face.'

'Yes, all right,' Jenny agreed.

Since moving into their flat they had got to know Susan, who lived in the studio flat below them. Susan was older than them, in her mid-twenties and she had taken them under her wing. Her style was hippie: maxi dresses, or skirts with peasant blouses and strings of beads. Tall and slim, with long brown hair, Sue completed the look with flat sandals instead of high heels. It wasn't a look that Tina felt she could pull off though, and as they passed a boutique she paused to look at a lovely mini-dress in the window.

'Jenny, look at that.'

'It's lovely,' Jenny agreed, her eyes flicking around as they walked on. 'Look at everyone, Tina. They're all dressed in a mixture of styles from hippie to rock and here's me in clothes chosen by my mother. I feel gauche, out of place . . . I wish I could afford a new look.'

'Yeah, me too,' Tina agreed, her tummy rumbling

as they reached Boris's. She felt rotten that Jenny had to pay for everything – the rent, their food – but at least she'd be able to put her share in soon. Eleven quid a week, Tina thought again disgustedly, but knew she'd have to stick it out until she found something better.

'I've been thinking,' Jenny said. 'After we've had something to eat, I wouldn't mind looking in that shop at our end, the one called Paradise Garage.'

'What for?' Tina asked. 'From what Susan said they sell American gear, second-hand denim jeans, along with Hawaiian shirts, some retro rock, and boiler suits or dungarees.'

'If it's second-hand it'll be cheap.'

Tina laughed. 'Oh yeah, I can just see you in a boiler suit.'

'Still, it might be worth a look.'

'It's weird enough on the outside, what with that 1950s petrol pump and the tiger-striped car, a Mustang, Sue said, sometimes parked close by. I'm game though. It might be fun to take a look inside.'

They had a quick snack but saw no sign of any famous faces, so they then headed off for Paradise Garage. They had often passed the shop, which was painted from top to toe in what looked like green bamboo but was in fact corrugated iron.

The Mustang wasn't outside today, but the interior had their eyes widening in amazement. There were caged lovebirds, an American jukebox playing rock and roll, and even a tiny dance floor. However, a quick look at the clothes on offer was enough for Jenny to see that they just weren't for either of them. She picked out a boiler suit, holding it against her, and they both giggled.

'Very fetching,' Tina told her.

'You've got to admit it's been worth a look, if only for the fun factor.'

'Yeah, but come on, you daft moo, let's go,' Tina urged. She was still putting on a front, pretending that she didn't have a care in the world, but in reality her stomach was churning. She really had seen the way that Mr Cane had looked at Jenny, a look she'd seen many times before in her father's eyes. Tina shivered, regretting that they had taken the jobs and wished she'd made more of a protest. Her lip curled into a scowl. If the bloke made one move – said one thing out of place – she'd get Jenny out of there.

Chapter Thirteen

In Wimbledon, the telephone continued to ring. Unable to ignore it any longer, Delia at last answered it.

Edward's sentences were short and clipped. 'Delia, there's been an accident. I'm at the Nelson Hospital, in casualty with Robin. He's been injured. You'd better get down here.'

'*What?* Oh no! Is he all right?'

'He's with the doctor. I've got to get back.'

'Wait!' Delia cried, but was left listening to the dialling tone.

For a moment Delia was frozen to the spot, but then she came back to life, grabbed her car keys and dashed out of the house. She made good progress at first but once on the main road the traffic increased and her speed slowed. The last thing she'd expected when Robin had gone out with his father was such a phone call. All she'd been concerned about was her plan to bring Edward down.

The traffic lights turned to red and Delia almost screamed with impatience. She had to get to the hospital – had to find out if Robin was all right. What if his injuries were so bad that he ... he ... No, she wouldn't – couldn't – think about that.

Delia's heart was thumping with anxiety when at last she arrived. After a frantic enquiry at reception she was directed to another room where a nurse led her to a cubicle and pulled back the curtain.

'Robin ... Robin,' she cried, horrified to see that her son was deathly pale and that his arm was in a splint.

The only response was a groan. Stricken, she looked at Edward. 'Is ... is he going to be all right?'

'I don't know what's going on; only that he's going to theatre. They're worried he may have internal injuries, and he's got a compound fracture of his lower arm.'

Delia burst into tears. Edward stood up and led her to the vacant chair beside Robin, urging her to sit down as she gasped, 'Wh ... what happened?'

'A bloody fool of a driver shot out of a side street at speed without checking the road was clear. He slammed into the passenger side and Robin took the brunt of the collision.'

'Oh, darling,' Delia said, reaching out to stroke Robin's hair.

He groaned again and Edward said worriedly, 'I

don't know why there's a hold-up. Where's that bloody doctor?'

For the first time in many, many years, Delia felt a common bond with her husband. Just then the curtain was drawn back and a doctor and nurse appeared.

'Right, young man, nurse here is going to prep you for surgery.'

Delia stood up, asking anxiously, 'He's going to be all right, isn't he?'

'He'll be in good hands,' said the doctor calmly.

'How . . . how long will he be in theatre?'

'It depends on what the surgeon finds, on the extent of the damage, but I should think for several hours.'

Delia didn't find this answer reassuring and swayed. She felt Edward's arm around her, offering support.

'Perhaps you should take your wife to the waiting room,' the doctor suggested.

'Yes, come on, Delia.'

She was reluctant to leave Robin but, having no choice, she allowed herself to be led away. Her mind twisted and turned as they sat in the stark waiting room. If Jennifer hadn't left home, her son wouldn't have gone out with his father to look for her. Jennifer had caused this. Yes, it was that girl's fault, yet even as she tried to shift the blame, Delia knew she couldn't. She was the one who had driven Jennifer out – and if the worst happened, if she lost her son, Delia knew she would never forgive herself.

Delia then found herself inwardly bargaining with God. *Please, let my son live and I'll change. I shouldn't have taken my anger out on Jennifer for so long and I realise that now. It was Edward's fault, not hers. Jenny is the innocent one in all of it and what I deprived her of is unforgivable. When she comes home, though some things can never be put right, I'll try to make it up to her, really I will.*

Delia felt no relief from her anxiety. She was no longer a regular attender at church and hadn't been for many years. Not only that, she didn't deserve God's ear. Nevertheless, Delia continued to pray, repeating the same liturgy again and again until at last, many hours later, the surgeon appeared.

Edward reared to his feet. 'How is he?'

'The surgery went well and your son should make a complete recovery.'

'Can . . . can we see him?' Delia asked, she too on her feet now.

'Just for a few minutes,' the man said, and a nurse appeared to lead them to the recovery ward.

Robin was groggy from the anaesthetic and hardly knew they were there, but Delia was so relieved that she found herself thanking God for listening to her plea. It was time to keep to her side of the bargain . . . but could she do it? Could she really bear to have Jennifer home again – to look at her face, one that had always served as a constant reminder? Somehow she had to make the effort.

However, Jennifer was one matter, but Edward was quite another. Until she no longer needed him, her husband's punishment would continue.

Edward now took the keys from Delia and drove her car home, his wife sitting stiffly beside him. His mind had been hopping between Robin and Jenny, but now, having been told that his son's prognosis was good, his daughter became his main concern again. Where was she? Did she have somewhere to stay? God, he hoped so; the thought of her roaming the streets and sleeping rough was horrendous. Jenny was just an innocent kid and anything could have happened to her!

Edward scanned the road as he drove along, looking out for the slim, familiar figure of his daughter. Again, his anger mounted towards Delia for having driven Jenny out. The sole consolation was that if he didn't find her before then, at least he had only to wait until Monday when she started work at the library.

'We have to find Jennifer,' said Delia suddenly. 'Bring her home.'

'What!' Edward said, incredulous.

'I know I treated her badly.'

'So you're admitting it at last.'

'Yes, Edward, I'm being honest at last, which is more than can be said for you.'

'Not this again? I'm just about sick of it, Delia.'

Delia huffed derisively and fell silent for the rest of the journey home. That suited Edward. He'd been listening to her accusation for years, but would never admit to it. Why should he? He had no need to, he was completely safe, and as far as he was concerned, what his wife had forced him to do was just as unforgivable.

Between searching unsuccessfully for Jenny and visiting his son in hospital, the weekend passed. It was now Monday morning and Edward had rung the office. They had offered him another company vehicle while his car was being repaired, but he'd insisted on a week's leave, despite the short notice.

'Right, Delia,' he now said. 'I'm off. I want to be at the library before it opens; catch Jenny when she arrives.'

'I'll come with you.'

'There's no need.'

'Jennifer won't come back unless I apologise and assure her that things will be different.'

'I'll tell her that.'

'No, Edward, she won't believe it unless it comes from me.'

Impatient to leave, Edward nodded in acquiescence, and soon they were in Delia's car, heading for the library. With his wife driving he used the opportunity to keep his eyes peeled, but so far there was no sign of Jenny. Perhaps his daughter had approached the library from another direction, he thought.

As Delia pulled up outside, Edward felt a surge of relief. This was it, he'd see Jenny again, and between him and Delia, she was sure to agree to come home.

They waited for a while, looking in both directions, until Delia said, 'I can't understand it. They opened ten minutes ago. Where is she?'

'If I knew that we wouldn't be standing here.'

Another fifteen minutes passed and impatiently Edward said, 'Perhaps we missed her. Let's go inside.'

Jenny wasn't there, however, and the head librarian was displeased that she hadn't arrived yet. Edward and Delia left and stood outside again, waiting on the wide steps for another half-hour, but by then Edward knew they were clutching at straws. Jenny wouldn't have been this late on her first day at work.

'Come on, Delia, she's not going to show. We might as well go home.'

'But Jennifer was so excited about working in the library. I don't understand. Why didn't she turn up?'

'I should think it's obvious. She doesn't want to be found.'

'There must be some way of tracing her.'

'How, Delia?' snapped Edward. 'She's probably in another area, or perhaps has even left London. Unless Jenny gets in touch with us, we don't stand a chance.'

Delia was quiet as they drove home and Edward's mind was churning. Surely Jenny would know how worried he was and he would hear from her soon?

Edward clung to that thought, unaware that it would be a long, long time before he had any news of his daughter . . . or that it would come from an unexpected source.

Chapter Fourteen

Summer passed and it was now close to Christmas, the weather outside cold, though in the café Jenny was hot and perspiring as she worked. She was up to her elbows in soapy water, her hair damp, stringy and clinging to her face. She glanced across at Tina to see that her friend wasn't faring any better.

Tina became aware that Jenny was looking at her, and hissed, 'We've stuck it out since August, but I ain't taking much more of this.'

'I feel the same, but we have to find new jobs first.'

'That's easier said than done. Look at the pair of us. We look like bleedin' ragamuffins and no wonder we ain't fit to be seen out front.'

Jenny knew Tina was right. They were scruffy, their hair a mess and faces bare of make-up. What they still needed was a new look, but what with paying the rent along with feeding the gas and electric meters, there was little left over from their small wage. At least they got a meal when they were working, and Jenny had developed a taste for Italian food as a consequence. The chef was temperamental though, and everyone knew when he was in a mood, all keeping their heads down.

If they wanted to find new jobs, Jenny knew there was only one thing to do, but she was loath to break into what was left of her savings. Even if she did, it wouldn't stretch far, but now, thinking about Susan, she had an idea. Their downstairs neighbour was a mine of useful information about the Chelsea scene and it was worth a shot.

'Tina, let's have a word with Sue when we finish our shift. She might be able to help.'

'With what?'

'She may be able to point us in the direction of some decent second-hand clothes shops.'

'Gawd, we weren't well off when I lived at home, but at least I didn't have to wear other people's cast-offs.'

'I know, but if we can just smarten ourselves up enough to go for interviews, we'd stand a better chance of finding decent jobs.'

'I don't pay you to chit-chat. Get on with your work!'

Jenny's face flamed, hoping Mr Cane hadn't heard their conversation. It was rare that they saw him, for he usually left the restaurant in the hands of a manager, but trust him to turn up just when they had been talking.

'Sorry, Mr Cane,' she said, turning swiftly back to her work.

She was aware of him walking up behind her and tensed as she felt his breath on her neck. Jenny knew she was mad, but on the rare occasions she saw him her body responded in a way that left her breathless. There was something exciting about him, something magnetic that drew her, and it took all her will not to turn around.

It was madness, Jenny told herself again as he moved away. What would a man like him want with someone like her? To him she was just a kid, and a scruffy, sweaty one at that.

Tina surreptitiously watched Mr Cane, almost daring him to lay a hand on Jenny. It was the way he stood behind her, almost like an animal sniffing her scent, and she was sure the day would come when he'd make his move. Thankfully this time he moved away, but he was yet another reason why Tina wanted to get them out of there, to find new jobs. Now, while she loathed the thought of wearing second-hand clothes, Tina knew it was their only option.

By the time their shift came to an end they were like wet rags and the cold air outside was welcome after the hot and steamy atmosphere of the kitchen. Shop windows looked festive, cheering the gloom and, unbidden, Tina's thoughts turned to her family. She knew that most people looked forward to celebrating Christmas at home – but not her. Because of her father it was the last place she wanted to be. She and Jenny might not be well off, and their Christmas celebrations would be Spartan, but for Tina it would be like heaven. There would be no cringing in bed, dreading the sound of his footsteps coming towards her door, then it opening, his silhouette framed from the light behind him before he closed it and advanced into her room.

Never again, Tina vowed as she glanced at Jenny. Sometimes she felt years older than her friend, her innocence long gone, and now she felt a twinge of worry. Jenny might not feel the same way she did. She might want to see her family again.

'Jenny, I know you haven't been in touch with your parents, but it's nearly Christmas. Are you going to see them or, failing that, send them a card?'

'I don't want to see my mother again, though Delia wasn't really my mother and she certainly won't want to see me. I miss my dad at times, but he isn't really my father either and sometimes I feel that I was just a distant relative who he felt obliged to adopt. I might send him a card though, just in case he's worried, but he might be in touch with your parents so I won't give him our address.'

'Good thinking,' Tina said. Her thoughts now turned to happier things. Susan was sure to have some ideas for their new look and in this classy area, especially Sloane Square, the second-hand shops might even have some designer gear on offer.

After having a bath and changing out of their damp clothes, both girls went downstairs to see Susan. As always, Jenny looked around her large studio room, loving the decor. There was a pink satin throw on the sofa, that doubled as a bed, tossed with red velvet cushions that should have clashed but somehow looked great. Colourful beads hung from lamps and picture frames, and an Indian-style patterned rug covered part of the lino.

'Sue, we're looking for a new look but we haven't much money,' Jenny said as she flopped onto the sofa. 'We thought that maybe second-hand clothes would be our best bet and wondered if you know of any shops in the area.'

'Yes, a few, but what sort of look are you after? It can be cheap and easy to find clothes like mine, or perhaps you'd prefer the Biba style?'

'Biba! I wish. When we looked in the boutique most of the dresses were around seven pounds.'

'That's not a problem. You could buy material, copy the cut and knock it on up on my sewing machine for a fraction of that.'

'I wouldn't know where to start.'

'No problem. I'll show you how to do it.'

'That's great! I can't thank you enough . . . though I'm still not sure what look to go for.'

Susan stood back to study Jenny. 'You've got a look of Twiggy about you. If you had your hair cut, I reckon you'd be a dead ringer.'

'Twiggy! Me! You must be joking.'

'I'm not, and you'll see for yourself if you let me sort out your hair.'

'You could do it? Cut it?'

'Jenny, I'm a hairdresser.'

'You are? But you told us you work in a pub.'

'I do now, but I trained at Vidal Sassoon's school.'

Tina looked amazed at this, jumping in to say, 'Blimey, why did you pack it in?'

'I got fed up with the long hours and always working on Saturdays. There's more to life than that and I prefer it behind the bar. But just in case I want to go back to hairdressing one day, I like to keep my hand in and cut friends' hair now and then. I'll do yours too, Tina, if you like.'

'Wow, thanks, but I'm not sure I can afford it. How much do you charge?'

'I know you're both struggling so it's free. I took a beauty course too and can show both of you how to make the best of yourselves with make-up.'

'Thanks and yes please,' both girls chorused almost in unison.

Susan got her kit, and soon, as her locks began to

fall to the floor, Jenny prayed that she hadn't made a big mistake. What if she didn't suit short hair? But it was too late to turn back now . . .

Over an hour later Jenny was looking at her reflection, blue eyes wide with amazement.

'I can't believe it. You've even managed to make it look as though I've got some colour in my cheeks.'

'That was easy with a bit of blusher.'

Tina was stunned too and said, 'Blimey, Sue's right. You do look like Twiggy.'

'I can see a bit of a resemblance, but I'm not as pretty as her.'

'You're just as lovely,' Susan insisted, then turned to smile at Tina. 'Right, it's your turn now.'

Tina was eager for a makeover and gave herself up to Sue's skilled hands. After another hour had passed, she noticed Jenny looking at her, mouth agape.

'What's wrong?' she asked worriedly. 'Do I look funny?'

'Funny! You must be kidding. You look incredible.'

Tina stood up to gaze in the mirror. She was hardly able to believe she was looking at herself. Susan had cut her straight dark hair to jaw-length into what looked like a shiny sheath with a full, straight fringe. Her eyes had been lined with black and the shadow on her lids was smoky. Red lipstick completed the look and for Tina it was as if she'd been transformed into an exotic stranger.

'Tina, you look sort of Egyptian, mysterious, and so much older,' Jenny said.

'I think you both look wonderful,' smiled Sue. 'One so dark, one so fair, and I think you're going to turn a few heads when you go out and about.'

Tina wasn't sure how she felt about that. She might feign interest in boys, her pretend idol Marc Bolan, but she'd seen enough and experienced enough at the hands of her father to last her a lifetime. She didn't want to be touched again.

Yet as she continued to look in the mirror, a thought crossed Tina's mind. She wasn't a child now, she was a woman and, instead of being abused, she could become the abuser. Men would be just like her father, all after her body, but from now on none would ever get near her. If they tried she'd empty their pockets before dumping them, and not give them a thing in return. They might want more, but they wouldn't get it.

Tina now smiled. She was looking forward to getting her own back on the male sex.

Chapter Fifteen

In Wimbledon there had been changes too. Contrary to Delia's expectations, she and Edward had grown closer in their shared concern about Robin. Edward had been a strong shoulder to lean on and Delia had gladly taken advantage of it. Despite the excellent surgeon, an infection had set in soon after Robin's operation and for a while they had feared he would lose his arm. That fear became terror when the infection threatened his life. Delia had been near to collapse, Edward giving her strength, but, just when they had almost given up hope, Robin had responded to the treatment and begun to recover.

Delia busied herself with a batch of mince pies, at last able to look forward to Christmas. Edward was watching for the post again, hoping for a card from Jennifer, but so far his hopes had come to nothing. It was strange to have him home after so many years of working away, but there was no doubting the change in her husband. He still worked for the same insurance company, but he was now a branch manager. It was a position that incurred a drop in salary, but at least it meant he was based locally.

Edward's concern for Robin and Jennifer had aged him and worry lines now ravaged his face. Delia knew that the last few months had taken their toll on her as well. Of course her worry had been for Robin and in truth, though she would never have admitted it to Edward, Jennifer had barely crossed her mind.

It was only when Delia thought about her bargain with God that she shivered. But if they couldn't find Jennifer, how was she supposed to make amends? Not only that, without the girl in the house and Robin home from hospital, she was happier than she'd been in years. Maybe she should attend church again, volunteer for some sort of good works – perhaps that would be enough to honour the pact.

'They smell good,' Edward said, sniffing the air.

'I've still got the cake to finish, but it can wait until tomorrow.'

'What can wait?' Robin asked as he came into the room.

'Icing the Christmas cake.'

'The icing on the cake would be to have Jenny home again.'

'I know, Robin, but you never know, we might still hear from her,' Delia said, wishing for a change of subject. Her relationship with Robin was still fragile and it was only thanks to Edward's intervention that her son was at last talking to her. Despite Robin being so ill, she'd borne months of silence, with barely a word passing between them, her son ignoring her in favour of his father.

It had almost broken her heart, but as soon as Robin was in recovery and stronger, Edward had spoken to him on her behalf. He may not have listened to her, but he listened to his father. Edward had been able to convince Robin that his mother really was sorry and wanted Jennifer to come home. Yet in her innermost thoughts, Delia knew it wasn't true, that her happiness would come to an end if they ever found Jennifer again.

Robin sat opposite his father and saw the strain etched on his face. There'd been nothing from Jenny, not a phone call, nor a letter and, like his dad, he was beginning to give up hope. When he glanced at his mother, he couldn't fail to see the contrast. She was happy, and though it was said to be because of his recovery, Robin suspected there was more to it than that. His mother was supposed to be sorry, to want Jenny home again, but was it real, or another one of her acts?

What a blind fool he'd been, Robin thought . . . yet how could he judge his mother when he was no better? He had been living a lie, pretending brotherly concern, but now the thought of what he'd really wanted sickened him. If he was anything to go by there'd be other sick bastards out there after her body too. Jenny was so innocent that she'd be helpless against them.

'How does your arm feel?' asked Edward.

'What? Sorry, Dad, I was miles away.'

'I asked about your arm.'

'It still feels a bit weak, but the physiotherapy helps.'

'That's good. You should be able to go back to college for the new term in January.'

'I've missed so much, and with A levels to sit in June I doubt I'll pass.'

'Don't worry, son, we'll get you some extra tuition.'

'Thanks, Dad. I just hope it works.'

'Of course it will, darling,' his mother said. 'There's no need to fret, you'll be fine.'

Yes, possibly, Robin thought, but what about Jenny? She was prey to so many dangers, and his only consolation was that Tina Hammond was probably with her. Had they found somewhere to live? Had they found work by now, or were they half-starved and penniless? And if that were the case, would it force them to come home? God, he hoped so.

Edward could see that his son was worried. Was it college on his mind or was he fretting about Jenny too? If only she would get in touch, he thought sadly. Though he'd been able to partly forgive Delia at last, it was hard to forget that his daughter had left home because of her.

Yes, he'd forgiven his wife in part because, during the many hours he'd sat by his son's bed, Edward had looked at himself and not liked what he saw. He had been a bastard in the past, had lied to Delia and then blamed her for the choice she'd forced him to make. He hadn't been able to stand the guilt and had left her with a new baby and toddler son to look after while he drowned his misery in work.

The telephone rang, snapping him out of his thoughts. For a moment Edward froze but then he was on his feet and rushing out to the hall to answer it.

'Hello,' he said eagerly.

'It's Bert Hammond. I'm calling again to see if you've heard from your daughter.'

'No, have you? Has Tina been in touch?'

'Nah, not a word.'

In his search for Jenny, Edward had found out where the Hammonds lived and been to see them. They soon established that the girls had probably run away together and now Bert or his wife rang every week. They were a bit rough around the edges but they were a nice couple, and while he could accept that Jenny had good reason for not wanting to get in touch with them, surely Tina had no need to feel the same about her own family?

'Let's hope we hear from them soon.'

'Yeah, fingers crossed, mate,' agreed Bert. 'I'll keep in touch. Bye for now.'

Edward murmured his goodbyes, aware then that Robin was at his shoulder. He too looked disappointed that it wasn't good news. They returned to the kitchen.

'Who was it?' Delia asked.

'Bert Hammond, but he hasn't heard from Tina.'

'I'm glad you answered the telephone. I hate talking to him, his wife too. They sound so common.'

'Delia, like us, they're worried sick about their daughter.'

'I didn't approve of their friendship and, if you ask me, it was Tina who encouraged Jenny to leave home.'

'Don't push the blame onto Tina,' Robin snapped.

'I'm sorry. I shouldn't have said that, but sometimes it's easier to find a scapegoat than to look at ourselves. It was my fault, of course, and I know that now.'

Robin looked surprised, but then approving as he smiled at his mother. Edward was relieved. Yes, Delia could be a snob, could say the wrong things, but at least she'd been quick to apologise in this instance.

He wanted Delia's relationship with their son to return to normal – at least that would help to assuage some of his guilt. Of course there were other things to torment himself with too, things that he would never be free of. Could he ever really forgive Delia for putting him through that?

Somehow Edward doubted it.

Chapter Sixteen

It was now the summer of 1973 and small cracks had begun to form in Jenny and Tina's friendship, the first of these appearing when they were both offered promotion. Tina had turned down Mr Cane's offer, saying he was an old letch, and had left to find another job. Jenny, though, had stayed. To her, a man in his thirties wasn't old. Mr Cane was vibrant, exciting, and the thought of leaving the restaurant, of never seeing him again, wasn't one she liked.

Jenny was waiting to take Table Four's order. These days she was confident in her abilities as a waitress; in fact, having done the job for sixteen months now she was becoming rather fed up with it. If it hadn't been for Marcos – yes, Marcos now, not Mr Cane – she'd have left ages ago.

Their relationship had developed slowly at first. Marcos had been impressed with her new look, his eyes darkening with something that made Jenny thrill with delight, but it had been another seven months before he had asked her out, coinciding with her seventeenth birthday.

It hurt Jenny that nowadays Tina seemed to prefer Sue's company to hers, and the closeness they had once shared had become a thing of the past as the gulf between them widened. Tina didn't approve of Marcos, but she was wrong of course – Marcos was the perfect gentleman. On their first date he had treated Jenny like a princess, taking her to the theatre to see a play called *Voyage Around My Father*, starring Alec Guinness, that she had loved. Afterwards Marcos had driven her home in his beautiful Jaguar and walked her to the door. He had only kissed her hand, but that had been enough to make her melt. If he had held out his arms she would have fallen into them, but it had been several more dates before that had happened.

As they continued to go out together, Jenny's feelings for Marcos grew but, despite the longing for something more that overwhelmed her when she was in his arms, he never took things any further.

At last the customers on Table Four made up their minds and Jenny forced a smile, which turned to a genuine one as Marcos walked into the restaurant. Oh, he was gorgeous, his dark good looks never failing to strike her. As she passed on the order to the kitchen, he came to her side and whispered, 'Are you free tonight?'

'As you told the manger to put me on permanent day shifts, you know I am.'

'I'll pick you up at eight.'

'Lovely,' she breathed, but then Marcos was gone, leaving as swiftly as he'd entered. He was a busy man, the restaurant, he'd told her, just one of his many enterprises. Only two more hours to go and then her eight in the morning until four in the afternoon shift would be over.

In contrast, Tina was in the shop that had once been called *Paradise Garage*, but which had now been taken over by a young woman called Vivienne Westwood and her partner Malcolm McLaren. At first they had renamed it, *Let it Rock*, stocking clothes and memorabilia that attracted long-standing teddy boys to the area. However, earlier this year it had metamorphosed again and was now called *Too Fast to Live, Too Young to Die*.

Tina was like a magpie, attracted to anything that glittered, and she wandered around looking at what was on offer. There were slogan-printed T-shirts, zoot suits, and styles she hadn't seen before that sported zips in odd places along with chains. They weren't for her. Tina's style now was glam and she loved wearing platform shoes with wide, flared trousers. She'd been unable to find a target yesterday, however, so she was short of money until she got paid that night.

Feet aching, Tina walked home and, instead of

going upstairs, she tapped on Susan's door. As it opened she sniffed the air knowingly. As usual, Sue was smoking cannabis, and Tina walked in eagerly.

'I've had a look around loads of shops and saw a few things but, for now, I'm skint.'

'If you keep on buying new clothes you always will be. Are you working tonight?'

'Yeah, and tomorrow lunchtime.'

'I still don't know how you managed to get taken on in a pub.'

'I blagged it, said I'm eighteen, and as I was wearing a low-cut top the landlord's eyes were hanging out on stalks. It was a doddle. He pays me cash in hand and that suits both of us.'

Susan took a drag on her joint and then held it out. 'Here, as Jenny isn't around you can have a few puffs.'

'I don't give a sod if she's around or not. She ain't my keeper.'

'What's going on with you two?'

Tina shrugged. 'We've grown apart since she started courting. How she can stand that old man touching her is beyond me.'

'You've told me about Marcos and I'd hardly call a man in his thirties old.'

'He ain't right for Jenny.'

'She obviously doesn't agree, and from what I've seen of her, she looks happy.'

'For now, but things will change. Blokes only want

one thing and Jenny will soon find that out,' Tina said, handing the joint back to Susan.

Sue took a puff and then asked, 'What happened to you, Tina?'

'Nuffin'. I'm fine.'

'I doubt that. You're only seventeen but already you sound like a man-hater. Someone must have hurt you badly.'

'Nah, it's me that does the hurting,' Tina insisted, not liking the way this conversation was going. She reluctantly stood up; Susan hadn't finished the joint yet and she might have been offered a few more drags, but her past and her father were a closed book. 'I'm off to get ready for work.'

'It's a bit early.'

'Jenny usually sees Marcos on Friday nights and that means she'll hog the bathroom when she finishes work. I need to get in first.'

'I was thinking we could throw a bit of a party. It'll give me a chance to meet Marcos.'

'Thanks all the same, but if he's gonna be there you can count me out.'

Susan shook her head and looked ready to argue, but Tina didn't give her the chance as she called goodbye and scooted upstairs. She didn't care what Jenny said: however how much she waxed lyrical about Marcos, he would always make Tina cringe. It wasn't just that he was at least twenty years older than Jenny. There was something else that worried Tina, something about him that was dodgy and shifty. But, without proof, she'd never be able to convince daft, besotted Jenny of that.

Marcos was heading for home, recalling the first time he'd seen Jenny and heard her voice. She may have looked a mess, yet she'd sounded classy, which stood out in complete contrast to her mouthy friend. He'd had enough of Tina's type – loud, pushy women whose voices grated on his nerves – but things were set to change. Soon the two women he hated would be out of his life and he'd be glad to see the back of them.

He smiled, thinking about Jenny again. When he'd first seen her new look it had bowled him over. Yet despite being drop-dead gorgeous, she still looked so innocent, untouched, and Marcos was determined to keep her that way – exclusively his.

It had been an added bonus to discover that Jenny was estranged from the couple who'd adopted her and that meant there were no relatives to worry about. There'd be nobody to ask questions, nobody to probe into his life, or to stand in his way.

Marcos smiled in anticipation. He was almost ready, having put the fronts in place and sorted the bank accounts. That left just one last thing to take care of before he could make his move. He pulled up outside his home in Battersea, a good-sized yet fairly modest house in Mysore Road, and only his closest associates knew why he chose to live there. It would be unnecessary soon but, for now, if Marcos didn't want to spook anyone he'd have to play the game.

Of course he wasn't really worried. Just like every stunt he pulled, when the time came to make his move, Marcos knew he'd get away with it. He always did.

Chapter Seventeen

Tina had seen an expensive pair of shoes she just had to have, but it was Jenny's birthday in a couple of days and she'd need to buy her a present. It would have to be something nice, something to match the great handbag Jenny had given her last week for her own eighteenth birthday.

What she needed, Tina decided, was a few extra bob on top of her wages again and her eyes scanned the punters for a soft touch. It would be easy, it always was, and with only forty minutes to go before last orders, her eyes searched for a customer who'd had too much to drink. It was Friday night and most of the customers would have just been paid. Even better, Eddy, the landlord, was upstairs feeling under the weather, and so she was alone in the bar.

Old Bill Clement would be a doddle, but she'd done him over a few times now and he might just cotton on if she wasn't careful. Thankfully she didn't have to wait long for another mug to come along, another regular looking decidedly tipsy as he headed for the bar.

Tina fixed a smile on her face and asked, 'What can I get you, darlin', another shot of whisky?'

'Yesh, a double,' he slurred.

Tina went to the optic and returned, almost scowling when the bloke put coins onto the counter. What she had wanted was a large note. She took the coins to the till, thankful that at least he hadn't tried to chat her up, something that was a common occurrence since she had started work behind the bar.

She didn't want to go out with blokes, hated the thought of their wandering hands, and it was even worse when old geezers tried to chat her up. She'd intended to pack in the job, but then, by sheer chance, she had discovered how stupid drunks could be. It was easy to short-change the bleary-eyed idiots and she often gave them a quid short, or more on those occasions when big money was flowing.

Just then the door opened and a late customer walked in. Tina blinked as she found herself gazing into the bluest eyes she'd ever seen. She judged the bloke to be in his mid to late twenties and he was a looker. His Afghan coat was open and she could see a large-collared shirt and a wide tie, though his short blond hair was out of fashion, unlike the rest of his appearance. What sickened Tina was that she found herself attracted to him.

'When you've finished giving me the once over, I'll have a pint of bitter.'

Tina flushed, but was quick with a reply. 'Don't kid yourself, mate. I was looking *through* you, not at you.'

He grinned. 'If you say so, but to be honest I can't take my eyes off you either. My name's Paul. What's yours? Cleopatra?'

'Don't be daft. It's Tina,' she said, face still pink as she served him.

'Do you live locally?'

'Yeah, I share a flat with a friend. Not that it's any of your business.'

'No chance of getting you alone then?'

'You cheeky bugger,' Tina snapped, angry at his innuendo and moving further away along the bar. He was just another bloke, another pig who wanted to maul her, yet even so her eyes kept returning to him. He smiled again, winked, and then raised his glass in a toast.

Thankfully a regular now asked for another drink and, remembering Jenny's birthday, Tina hoped this would be her chance. She was in luck, the man paying with a ten-pound note but, unsure how drunk he was, Tina knew it was going to be a bit risky. Still, she wanted those shoes too and, with so little time left, she flirted with the man to distract him while handing over his change.

He shook his head. 'This ain't right, Tina. I gave you ten quid.'

'No, Jack, it was a fiver. Look, I'll show you,' she said, quickly opening the till again to pull one out.

'I'm telling you it was a tenner. I know that because it's the wife's housekeeping money and I hadn't intended to break into it.'

Tina felt her stomach flip, but knew she had to stand her ground. 'And I'm telling you I didn't make a mistake.'

'I ain't having this. Where's Eddy? He'll sort this out.'

Tina didn't want the landlord involved. 'He's sick and won't take kindly to being 'isturbed.'

'I don't give a shit. I want that till checked.'

'It'd be a waste of time, mate,' said Paul, moving closer. 'I was watching and you gave her a five-pound note.'

Puzzled, but grateful, Tina hoped that would shut Jack up, but he would have none of it.

'I did not! Now give me the rest of my change, Tina, or else!'

'It sounds like you're threatening this young lady,' Paul said, pulling out his warrant card.

Oh no! Tina thought. A soddin' plod! But wait, he was on her side and now she'd be able to defuse the situation. Jack was always flying close to the wind, flogging dodgy gear, and he'd be quaking in his boots at the sight of a copper.

'It's all right, constable,' she said, smiling sweetly. 'I'm sure Jack didn't mean it. He's upset and in the circumstances it's understandable. He was just mistaken, that's all. Isn't that right, Jack?'

'Yeah, I suppose so,' he said reluctantly.

'Right then,' said Paul. 'I suggest you apologise to this young lady and leave.'

'Sorry,' Jack said abruptly before scuttling off, though not before throwing Tina a look of disgust. She chewed worriedly on her lower lip. Jack was a regular, knew the landlord well, and she doubted he'd let it go. If the landlord became suspicious he'd start watching her, and that meant her chances of making a few extra bob in future were gone. Paul spoke, startling Tina back to attention.

'To be honest I didn't see how much money changed hands, but I gave you the benefit of the doubt.'

'Thanks for stepping in.'

'Did he really give you a five-pound note?'

'Of course,' she said, feigning indignation. 'If I had made a mistake I'd have owned up to it, but I didn't. It was definitely a fiver.'

'That's good. Have I earned enough Brownie points to take you out one night?'

'Don't you mean Scouts? Brownie points are for girls.'

'Scouts then . . . but seriously, can I take you out?'

Tina shook her head. He was a copper and the last thing she needed in her life. His smile was appealing, his gorgeous blue eyes earnest, but it didn't touch her.

'Sorry, I'm already seeing someone,' she lied, turning away to ring the bell. 'Last orders, please.'

As she served customers, Tina avoided looking at Paul again. He was a man and she knew that they were all the same – predators, with one thing on their minds. She hated them . . . hated them all.

Paul Ryman was cursing his luck as he left the pub. He'd just found the girl of his dreams, but she was already taken. Of course with looks like that it was hardly surprising and his only hope was that the relationship she was in wasn't serious.

Sure that the attraction had been mutual, Paul wasn't going to give up, and if Tina became available he wanted to be around when it happened, the first to step in before anyone else got the chance. He hadn't been in the *Nag's Head* for a long time, but with Tina behind the bar, he now intended to become a regular.

Of course, when working nights it would be impossible, which meant next week was out. That only gave him tomorrow night and Sunday . . . but he'd be there, watching and waiting. A flashy car turned the corner in front of him, and now Paul's mind snapped to attention. He was sure it belonged to one of the crew the CID had been after for years, although this one seemed to have gone legit. Paul didn't believe it, sure that this particular leopard would never change its spots. He'd surface again and, when he did, Paul wanted to be involved in nailing him.

He wanted promotion, wanted out of uniform and to be involved in the action and with his application to CID already made he was hoping for good news. If he was successful and made it to CID, it was sure to impress Tina, he thought, and the extra money would be great, plenty to support a wife.

Wife! What was the matter with him? Marriage had been the last thing on his mind. But then again, he mused, with someone like Tina it wouldn't be a bad idea.

Paul continued on his way, wondering what it would be like to come home to Tina after every shift, to have the feel of her next to him in bed. As his imagination took over, he had to fight an erection. Perfect, he decided, she'd be just perfect, and now all he wanted was the chance to take her out.

Chapter Eighteen

It was Jenny's eighteenth birthday, and Marcos had hinted that he'd planned something special. The problem was that, without knowing where they were going, Jenny wasn't sure what to wear. Marcos liked the theatre, or sometimes clubs, but it was a problem finding suitable clothes that weren't enormously expensive. She did her best, buying things to mix and match, and was thankful that so far she had just about managed to appear presentable. Of course, Marcos always complimented her no matter what she wore, yet Jenny was all too aware that her clothes couldn't measure up to the glamorous outfits she saw other women wearing at some of the venues.

'What do you think of this?' she asked Tina, holding up a short, dusky-pink dress with a square neckline.

'Yeah, it's fine,' Tina said shortly.

Jenny longed for things to get back to the way they

used to be between the two of them, but felt she was fighting a losing battle. So much for Tina saying they were like sisters, Jenny thought sadly, knowing that if it hadn't been for Marcos she'd feel so alone again. Yet even Marcos couldn't fill that gap, the feeling that something was missing in her life, and for a while only her feelings of kinship with Tina had been able to do that.

Jenny picked up her present again, holding the necklace against the dress. The tiny pink-tinged beads that looked like pearls were perfect, giving the dress just the lift it needed.

'Look, Tina, they're just right. Thanks again. I love them.'

'You're welcome. Speaking of new things, what do you think of my shoes?'

Jenny looked at the yellow slingback platform shoes, wondering as always how Tina could afford to buy so many new things. Surely bar work wasn't that well paid, yet Tina's wardrobe was bulging.

'They're great.'

'Yeah, they ain't bad, are they?' grinned Tina. 'I'm off to work now. Happy birthday again and I'll see you later.'

Jenny waved goodbye. With her working days and Tina evenings, they didn't see that much of each other nowadays, but she was pleased that things seemed a little easier between them. She just hoped it would last, but now turned her attention to getting ready to go out, wondering if her outfit would be nice enough to please Marcos.

The last thing on Marcos's mind was Jenny's appearance. He hoped he wasn't rushing her, but he couldn't wait any longer. The restaurant offered privacy along with intimacy, soft music in the background adding a romantic touch. He'd ordered champagne and was now waiting for it to arrive, rehearsing his words in his mind. Jenny would be expecting a present, of course, and this one was certain to outshine all her expectations. It should do, Marcos thought, and though from a certain source it had still cost him a pretty penny.

The champagne arrived and Jenny took a sip, her nose wrinkling delightfully. She giggled and Marcos smiled. He adored everything about Jenny, but mostly it was her lack of worldliness, of hardness, that so appealed to him. There was nothing grasping about her and Marcos wanted to keep her that way, gentle and unspoiled. He'd do it now, ask her now. Taking the box out of his pocket, he opened it to show it to Jenny.

'Happy birthday, my darling. Would you do me the honour of becoming my wife?'

Jenny gasped, her eyes wide in wonder as she looked from the large diamond solitaire to him. 'Oh, Marcos . . .'

'I know I'm a lot older than you, twenty-one years

in fact, but I promise you won't regret it. I'll look after you, cherish you. Please, Jenny, say yes.'

'Oh . . . oh . . . yes, of course yes.'

Marcos took Jenny's hand, kissed her palm, and then took the ring from the box to place on her finger.

'You've made me the happiest man in the world,' he said, snapping his finger for the waiter. 'We have a lot to talk about but, for now, let's order our meal.' He looked up at the waiter. 'We'll have soup to start, followed by fillet steaks, rare.'

'That sounds lovely,' Jenny said.

She was always happy to let him order for her, and as the waiter left Marcos took her hand again.

'I don't want a long engagement, so how do you feel about a December wedding? Perhaps just before Christmas, and then we can celebrate the festive season together.'

Startled, Jenny's eyes widened, but she husked, 'I . . . I'd love that.'

'Darling, there's one other thing. As you know, I lost my parents many years ago, and as an only child I've only distant relatives. I don't want to disappoint you, but would you mind a small wedding, perhaps in a registry office?'

Jenny was quiet for a while and Marcos held his breath, but then she said, 'I suppose every girl dreams of a big, white wedding, yet without any real relatives either I'd have few people to invite.'

'What about the family who adopted you?'

'I doubt Delia would come and to be honest I don't think I'd want her there. My father, maybe, but I can't send an invitation solely to him.'

Secretly, Marcos was pleased at Jenny's estrangement from her family. 'Well, then, in that case let's do something wildly romantic, something just for us. We'll have a quiet wedding, but afterwards go abroad to somewhere special for our honeymoon. How does that sound?'

'It sounds wonderful.'

'Have you got a passport?'

'No, and I haven't got a clue how to get one.'

'It's all right, darling. Leave it to me. Just give me your birth certificate and I'll sort the forms out. All you'll have to do is sign them.'

'Yes, all right, and I'm glad now that I remembered to pack my adoption certificate when I left home.'

Only one more thing to worry about, thought Marcos. Still, he'd work something out, a way to keep everyone – most importantly, Jenny – in the dark.

Jenny was so thrilled she could hardly eat, though she was saddened at the thought that her father wouldn't be at her wedding. Yet he wasn't her real father, she reflected, and so was it any wonder that he couldn't really love her as his true daughter? Robin wasn't her brother either, and by now his life would have moved on. He'd be well into his time at university and probably hardly spared her a thought. That left only Tina and Susan but, knowing how Tina felt about Marcos, it was doubtful that she'd want to come to her wedding anyway. Sadly, Jenny realised that she didn't really have anyone, no real family.

'What's wrong, my darling?' Marcos asked breaking into her thoughts. 'One minute you looked so happy, but now you're sad. Please, don't tell me you've changed your mind.'

'No, of course not. It . . . it's just that I have so few people to invite to our wedding and I feel sort of, well, alone.'

'You have me, Jenny, you'll always have me. We'll have children too, many children, and you'll never be alone again.'

Jenny looked across the table at Marcos and felt tears well in her eyes. Yes, she had Marcos, and the thought of having children filled her with joy.

'Oh, Marcos, I love you so much.'

'And I love you,' he said, picking up his glass to raise it in a toast. 'To us.'

'Yes, to us,' Jenny agreed as they clinked glasses.

'I know you have never asked, but I'm quite a wealthy man and I'll see that you want for nothing. We will live in a beautiful house, and you will never have to work in my restaurant again, or anywhere else.'

'I . . . I won't?'

'Of course not. You will be my wife, the mother of my children, and treasured.'

145

Jenny smiled. Marcos sounded so masterful, yet his dark eyes were soft with emotion as they gazed at each other. Treasured, she thought, that sounded nice, and now that a new future stretched ahead of her, it was one she was sure would bring her true happiness at last.

Tina had been in for twenty minutes when Jenny arrived home. Something had happened, the look of Jenny's face enough to tell Tina that, but she was nonetheless completely unprepared for her friend's words.

'Oh, Tina, you're not going to believe this. Marcos has asked me to marry him.'

'Don't tell me you said yes!'

'Of course I did. Look,' Jenny said, holding out her hand to show off her engagement ring.

'Impressive, but you must be mad to want to marry that slimy git. I mean, how can you bear to let him touch you?'

'I love being in his arms, and he is *not* slimy. I'd thank you not to talk about him like that.'

'Ooh, I do beg your pardon, your ladyship,' Tina said, mimicking Jenny's posh voice. 'He talks like a toff too, though it's all put on if you ask me.'

'Please, can't you just be happy for me?'

'How can I be when you're making the biggest mistake of your life?'

'I'm not, Tina, I love him.'

'Don't make me laugh. Like me, you're only eighteen and as he's the only bloke you've been out with, how can you possibly know it's love? If you ask me it's more like some sort of daft infatuation. Not only that, you know nothing about him.'

'Yes I do.'

'All right then, so tell me where does he live? Has he got a family? Is he taking you to meet them? And more importantly, has he been married before, 'cos if he has, he might have kids.'

'Tina, if that was the case Marcos would have told me. And as for his parents, they both passed away so he can't take me to meet them.'

'So when it comes down to it, all you know about him is that he owns a restaurant. You've never been invited to his home – come to that, have you even met any of his friends?'

'Well, no, not yet, but I'm sure I will. Marcos is a very busy man and with other business interests I don't think it leaves him much time for socialising.'

'What other business interests?'

'Oh, Tina, I don't know, but he once mentioned something to do with cars and he told me he's rather well off.'

'Is he now? But other than a vague reference to cars, he hasn't said where his money comes from? I dunno, Jenny. He's too much of a closed book and I don't like it.'

'You've never liked Marcos and I think you're just looking for problems that don't exist,' Jenny said crossly. 'We're getting married just before Christmas, and no matter what you say I'm not going to change my mind.'

'But that's only five months away!' Tina gasped. 'Why so soon?'

'Marcos doesn't want a long engagement.'

'He may not, but what about you?'

'I feel the same and can't wait to marry him. Please, Tina, please be happy for me.'

Tina looked at Jenny's face, seeing the appeal there, but despite that, she shook her head. 'I wish I could, but I still think you're making a big mistake.'

'Well, I don't, and I'd like you to come to my wedding.'

'No thanks,' Tina said. Just then an awful thought crossed her mind – this would mean that Jenny would get in touch with her parents. She'd want them at her wedding, she'd need her father to give her away, and they would learn of this address. 'I suppose you'll be sending an invitation to your family?'

'There's no point in contacting them. Delia wouldn't come to my wedding and, as I told Marcos, I don't want her there anyway. That only leaves you and Sue. Please, Tina, please come.'

Relieved that she was still safe from her father, Tina said, 'I'll think about it.'

'Thanks,' Jenny said, then yawned. 'Gosh, I'm tired.

I'm off to bed, but I'm so excited that I may not be able to sleep.'

Soppy cow, Tina thought. She had no intention of going to the wedding, of watching Jenny being led like a lamb to the slaughter, but had refrained from telling her that. Jenny could stew, Tina decided. She had herself to think about now.

Once married, Jenny would move out of the flat, and Tina wondered how she was supposed to pay the rent without her, let alone the bills? She couldn't even fiddle a few extra bob now, not when it had become obvious during her weekend shifts that Jack had had a word with the landlord. Eddy had taken to watching her and after dwelling on it for a while, Tina decided that if she wanted to keep this flat she'd better start looking for another job, one where a bit of fiddling might be possible.

However, as she continued to consider the matter, Tina realised that it wouldn't be easy to find another landlord like Eddy, one who paid cash in hand with no questions asked. She was eighteen now so working behind a bar was legal, but another landlord would take her National Insurance payments, plus income tax and that would leave her wages seriously depleted. Her heart sinking, Tina realised that she'd gain nothing by leaving her present job, but she hated the thought of having bugger all left over once the rent and bills were paid. No, she wouldn't go back to that. She'd find a way of making a few extra bob somehow, and if it couldn't come from punters, it would have to come from somewhere else.

Her mind drifted back to Jenny. It was all right for her, she was marrying Marcos, and it seemed he had a few bob. Jenny would be living in clover while she'd be left scraping for every penny. If it hadn't been for the sickening thought of sleeping with Marcos, she might have been green with envy.

Tina scowled. All she had ever known was living in a council flat and then this pokey place, whereas Jenny had lived in a big posh house with her parents. Yeah, Jenny's parents were well off – and at that thought, Tina paused. They had money, probably lots of it, and now an idea began to form in her mind, one that changed Tina's scowl to a grin of satisfaction.

Yes, why not? She didn't have to stay in Chelsea and a good few bob would go a long way in giving her a fresh start. In fact, with any luck, it would be enough to keep her in clover too for a long, long time.

Chapter Nineteen

Tina posted the letter on the way to work, satisfied that she had given him enough time. Of course there was always the risk that he'd blab, but in such a public place she'd be able to make sure that her instructions had been carried out before showing herself. If he wasn't alone she'd scarper, Tina thought, shivering at the thought of discovery.

Serving behind the bar, Tina's mind was on her other plans and so she didn't notice Paul coming up to the bar until he asked for a drink.

'Sorry, what was that?'

'A pint of bitter and a chat if you've got time.'

As always, Tina found herself drawn to Paul, but her feelings sickened her. He hadn't been in for a while, and it was annoying that he'd turned up again.

'A chat about what?' she asked, handing him his pint.

'Oh, you know, this and that. How's the boyfriend?'

'What boyfriend?' Tina asked, then flushed. He'd

caught her off guard and now she'd given the game away.

'So, you're footloose and fancy free again? Does that mean I can take you out?'

Tina was about to say no but then, for some inexplicable reason, she changed her mind. It would be a first date and surely he wouldn't try anything on? Mind you, if he did she'd kick him where it hurt. Yes, let Paul spend a few bob, take her somewhere nice. At least it would stop her from fretting about the next stage of her plan.

'Yeah, all right,' she said, 'you can take me out on Friday, but make it somewhere special.'

His blue eyes lit up, his smile wide. 'In that case I'll have to put my thinking cap on. What do you fancy, a nice meal, or perhaps the theatre?'

'Both,' Tina said haughtily.

'Do you like murder mysteries?'

'I dunno. I've never seen one.'

'Right, I'll take you to see *The Mousetrap*. It's been running for years so it must be good.'

'Just make sure you get decent seats. I don't want to be stuck up in the gods.'

'Yes, your majesty,' Paul agreed, smiling as he gave a small bow. 'With expensive tastes like yours, it's just as well I'm up for promotion.'

Tina picked up a glass and began to dry it. So far she hadn't had the money to indulge in expensive luxuries, but that was set to change. Yes, Paul could treat her on Friday night, and if he behaved himself she might see him again. After that, hopefully she'd be off, with her pockets bulging for the first time in her life.

Marcos locked the door behind him, smiling in anticipation of Jenny's reaction when she saw their first home. It was perfect, a bit pretentious perhaps, but there was no reason to hide his wealth now. He'd show Jenny the house soon and she was sure to be delighted. After all, what girl wouldn't be?

Marcos smiled wryly. Oh, he knew one, in fact two, who were never satisfied, but Jenny was totally different, a breath of fresh air after years of putting up with ear-bending purgatory. He couldn't wait to tell them, and what it was going to cost him would be worth it just to see their faces. There wouldn't be any protests, they wouldn't dare, for they both knew him too well to risk that. Also, to keep his largesse they would have to keep their mouths well and truly shut, and he'd make sure they understood that too. The threat of what he'd do to them if they didn't was sure to be enough.

Marcos locked the gates at the end of the drive now and drove off. There were a few people he needed to talk to, ones who had to be told of his plans, and now was as good a time as any. Of course he had nothing to fear from them, but they too would need to keep their lips zipped. However,

Marcos was confident that again his reputation would be enough to ensure that they did just that.

The small members' club was down a flight of stairs and the musty air in the basement was masked by the smell of booze, smoke, and the Jeyes fluid that Denis, the owner, was fond of using liberally to clean the floor and toilets. They were at their usual table playing cards, Bernie shuffling the deck and a fag hanging from the corner of his mouth.

'All right, boss?' came his mumbled greeting.

'Leave the cards, we need to talk,' Marcos ordered, pulling out a chair. All four of them looked at him expectantly, but to start with Marcos threw a note on the table, 'Steve, get the drinks in, and chasers.'

He waited until the newest recruit was out of earshot and then filled the others in, leaning back nonchalantly when he'd finished.

Bernie was the only one who had the nerve to comment, 'Are you sure about this, Marcos? When they find out, all hell will break loose.'

'No, Bernie, it won't. I'll see to that. While I'm away you'll be in charge, and if anyone comes sniffing around, make sure everyone keeps their mouths shut.'

'Yeah, don't worry.'

'I'm not, but I still want Steve kept in the dark where business is concerned. He asks too many questions and I'm not sure about him yet.'

'Steve's all right,' Liam argued.

Marcos narrowed his eyes. That was enough to

make Liam cower, and he added hastily, 'Still, whatever you say. You're the boss.'

'Yes, and don't forget it,' Marcos warned as Steve returned with the drinks.

'What's going on? Have I missed something?' Steve asked, dishing the glasses out.

'Nothing that concerns you,' Marcos drawled, noting the look of annoyance that flashed across Steve's face. The others had been with him for years and he'd trust them with his life, but Steve had a long way to go yet.

He wasn't the only one who would need to be kept in the dark: Jenny would be too. But, unlike Steve, who could gain entrance one day, she would never be allowed into the inner sanctum.

Chapter Twenty

It had been over two years since Jennifer had left, and Delia felt that she was living in some sort of limbo. Robin was at university in Birmingham, which meant he was rarely home. It left Delia with too much time for retrospection and the past often came back to haunt her.

Housework failed to fill her days, and anyway, what did this house matter now? It was just an empty shell, a mostly silent one until Edward came home from work, and even during the weekends he spent hours in the garden. Her attendance at church helped, along with her voluntary work visiting hospital patients who had no family or friends to come to see them.

It was midday when Delia arrived at the hospital, her first call to see an elderly patient she had visited on several occasions.

'Hello, Mrs Milton. How are you?' she asked softly. 'I cut these this morning and thought you might like them.'

'Roses, no, please, take them away,' Mrs Milton begged, her voice reedy with age and her rheumy eyes beginning to brim with tears.

'Oh dear, I'm sorry, I didn't mean to upset you,' Delia said worriedly.

'It isn't you, it's the flowers. They . . . they remind me of Rose, my daughter.' As though she had a desperate need to talk about it, the words began to tumble out. 'I drove her away, you see, I favoured my son.'

Delia hastily put the flowers out of sight and sat down, listening as the old lady spilled it all out. She found that Mrs Milton's story resonated with her own, except that the daughter Mrs Milton had driven away had been her own flesh and blood. Delia took the woman's hand, holding it gently and feeling an affinity.

'It might help you to know that you aren't the only one. I did the same thing.'

'You did?'

Delia hadn't spoken of it before – not to the vicar, not to her friends at the WI – yet now, at last, she opened up, telling Mrs Milton about Robin's accident, her pact with God, and her fear that her son would suffer punishment in some way if she didn't put things right with Jennifer.

'I know I have to make amends, vowed I would, but in all honesty I can't bear the thought of her turning up again. I joined the church, do voluntary work, but because of how I really feel, I fear it isn't enough.'

157

'Voluntary work is all very commendable,' the old lady said, 'but I think you're doing it for the wrong reasons, to appease a God you seem to think is harsh. I don't think He is, my dear, nor do I fear retribution. I think He's a loving father, and forgiving.'

Delia gazed at Mrs Milton and it was as if the truth of her words resonated within her. She felt as though a huge weight had been lifted from her shoulders, yet something still puzzled her.

'But . . . but you seem so upset about your daughter.'

'Yes, but that's because I can't forgive myself.'

Delia gently squeezed Mrs Milton's hand, her heart going out to the elderly lady. 'I wish you could because I feel so better since talking to you.'

'Good, I'm glad to hear it,' the old lady said, 'and knowing that I've helped you has made me a little better about myself.'

Delia continued to sit beside Mrs Milton, enjoying the affinity she now felt with her and they continued to talk for a while. It was with reluctance that Delia eventually left but she had other patients to visit and didn't want to let them down. It was only later, on her way home, that she found an old ambition resurfacing.

Thanks to Mrs Milton, it was time to move on – to at last come out of limbo.

The following morning, Edward was the first up, unaware that Delia had spent hours lying in bed, thinking about her plans. He heard the rattle of the letterbox as the post was thrust through, but didn't rush to see what had been delivered. It had been so long now since Jenny had left home that any hope of hearing from her had diminished.

It was still hell, never knowing if Jenny was all right, if she was safe, and his fears for his daughter were never far from his mind. Though only in his late forties, Edward sometimes felt like an old man these days, his travelling days over and his life now staid and centred on his newfound interest in gardening.

Two envelopes lay on the mat, and as Edward picked them up he saw that one was a bill and the other a letter addressed to him in unfamiliar writing. Puzzled, he tore the envelope open to find a single page inside, the letter short but taking his breath away. It was brief, mainly comprising of a list of instructions with no signature or clue as to who sent it.

He heard Delia coming downstairs and quickly stuffed the letter in his pocket. 'Tell nobody' had been one of the instructions, and if this wasn't a hoax, if it gave him the smallest chance of finding his daughter again, Edward would carry out each and every one of them to the letter.

'Good morning,' he said, hoping his face didn't give anything away.

'Is that the post?' Delia asked.

'Just a bill.'

They both went to the kitchen; Edward relieved that Delia didn't notice how his hands trembled with excitement as he filled the kettle.

'I'll make a pot of tea,' he offered.

'All right. What do you want for breakfast?'

'Toast will do, and perhaps some of that lovely marmalade.'

'Marjory Ellington's jams and marmalade always sell well,' Delia said, sighing as she added, 'and I'm known for my cakes, though I'd hardly call that an achievement.'

'You sound a bit fed up. What's the matter?'

'You'll think I'm silly.'

'Of course I won't. Now come on, tell me what's troubling you.'

'I . . . I just feel that I've done nothing with my life, that I'm capable of more and once wanted to prove it. With all that happened, I let it drift, but I now feel the need to look at my ideas again.'

'Delia, I'm sure you could do anything you put your mind to.'

'Even running a business?'

'You don't need to work, Delia.'

'I know that, but you see, I want to.'

'What sort of business are we talking about?'

'I did a little research and found there's a niche that needs filling, a demand for domestic staff. I want to set up an agency to provide them.'

Edward baulked. If Delia had been exploring

possibilities already this was clearly no whim. She was serious about this and he wasn't sure how to respond. He didn't like the idea and doubted his wife had the capabilities or the business acumen to make it a success. Maybe if he gently probed she would see that.

'Have you looked into the setting-up costs?'

'Yes, office space, advertising and so on, along with projected profit margins. However, my figures are out of date and I'd have to reassess my initial outlay.'

'From what you've told me any profit would be commission-based. I can't see that amounting to much.'

'That would only be a part of the services my agency would offer. I also want to employ women for office cleaning, and for landlords who want a property made ready for new tenants. There are other options too, and I could even expand into catering.'

Edward found himself looking at his wife in a new light, unable to believe that Delia had it all worked out. He had never seen her as anything other than a housewife and mother, and the idea of her being a businesswoman was impossible for him to grasp.

'Let me think about it, Delia. Starting up a business can be very stressful and I'm not sure you'd cope.'

'Edward, don't patronise me,' she snapped. 'I don't

need you to think about it, nor do I need your permission. I'm quite capable of making my own decisions and if I want to open an agency I will.'

His temper rising in response, Edward's reply was equally sharp. 'If that's your attitude, fine, but don't expect me to fund this ridiculous venture.'

'Did I ask you to?'

'Delia, talk sense. It's going to cost a lot of money to set up and you won't be able to do it without my financial help.'

'Yes I will. I have savings and I can apply for a bank loan.'

'I doubt that, not without some sort of security, and if you're thinking about using my house, forget it.'

'*Your* house! I see . . . but be careful, Edward, because if that's what you're saying I'm sure a divorce lawyer would see it differently. I think you'll find I'd be entitled to half.'

'For goodness' sake! How have we gone from you setting up an agency to a divorce?'

'What do you expect? All I've ever been is a wife and mother, but now I want to achieve something for myself – to prove I'm capable of more. And instead of supporting me as I'd hoped, you're throwing obstacles in my way!'

Edward drew in a deep, calming breath. In the past he had used Delia for his own ends, and because of that he had been forced to stay, though he'd wanted to leave her on many occasions. But did he want a divorce now? No, not when he thought about what he'd lose financially. He'd have to start up again, live alone without a woman to see to his needs and that certainly didn't appeal to him. They had both lost their tempers, and Edward decided he needed to defuse the situation now, to talk rationally.

'Delia, I'm just worried that you won't be able to cope.'

'How will I know unless I try?' she argued.

He glanced at his watch. 'I've got to leave for the office shortly, but we'll discuss it again this evening.'

'You won't talk me out of it.'

'I don't intend to. I just want to make sure, for your sake, that the business would be viable.'

Delia smiled then, and for a moment Edward saw a trace of the carefree young woman he'd married. It was his fault she'd changed. He'd pushed her too far ... but she had caused him torment too. Of course Delia had no idea just how much torment, she'd never be privy to that, and feeling a surge of familiar guilt, Edward shifted uncomfortably in his seat.

He heard the slight rustle of the letter in his pocket, and his stomach churned again. His thoughts had been distracted from it for a short while, but now he left the second slice of toast Delia had made for him in the rack as he considered the instructions again. Once again, Edward dreaded that it was all some kind of sick hoax. Was it real? Did someone really know where Jenny was? But if so, why had the letter been unsigned? Why the secrecy?

The questions ran staccato through Edward's mind, but he knew that, until Saturday, they'd remain unanswered.

Chapter Twenty-One

With no idea that Edward had received news of Jennifer, Delia was self-absorbed as she cleared the breakfast table. She was fuming that Edward had tried to dismiss her ambitions, and had meant it when she had threatened divorce. She would be fine on her own, and would soon give up her voluntary work. In the meantime, it was thanks to Mrs Milton that she had come out of limbo and she was looking forward to going to see her again later that day.

For now Delia got out all the old figures she had for starting up the business, ones that Robin had helped her with. She had a go at reworking them, but nothing seemed to balance and she was soon feeling out of her depth. Could she really do this? Could she really set up her own business and run it successfully? For the first time, Delia found herself unsure, her confidence wavering. Yes, she could run a home, make nice cakes for the WI, but with Edward paying all the household bills she'd never had to worry about money, budgets and such. With her head beginning to ache, Delia pushed her figures to one side, still undecided as she got ready to visit Mrs Milton.

It was a beautiful day, the sun shining, but when she arrived at the hospital it seemed gloomy in the ward after the brightness outside. Mrs Milton smiled when she saw her, but Delia didn't think the smile reached her eyes.

'Hello,' she said, smiling warmly and hoping to cheer the old lady up. 'It's a lovely day today.'

'Is it?' Mrs Milton said, her voice lacklustre. 'I hadn't noticed.'

'Would you like to go outside for a while? I could ask one of the nurses for a wheelchair.'

'Yes . . . yes, all right.'

It took some time to sort out, but at last Delia was pushing Mrs Milton into the grounds, the sun blazing overhead. She found the chair difficult to manoeuvre and Mrs Milton's answers monosyllabic whenever she spoke to her. After a while, feeling very hot, Delia spotted a bench under the shade of a tree.

'Do you mind if we stop for a while?'

'I think a little shade would be welcome.'

As they settled themselves, Delia noticed a man nearby who seemed to be watching them both. She found it a relief to sit down and took a handkerchief from her handbag to delicately dab the perspiration from her top lip.

'I spoke to my husband this morning, told him I'd like to start up my own business.'

Mrs Milton didn't seem interested, only saying, 'My ulcerated leg has improved. I'm being discharged soon, going back to the residential home.'

'You must be pleased.'

'No, I'm not. I hate the place, hated giving up my home, but with nobody to care for me I had no choice.'

'I'm so sorry.'

'Don't be. It's my own fault and perhaps another lesson for you.'

'What do you mean?'

'Starting up a business is all very well, but there are more important things in life, and by that I mean your family. Like you, I didn't value my daughter, but there's an old adage that goes something like this: a son's a son till he gets a wife, but a daughter's a daughter for all of her life.'

'Yes, I've heard it.'

'Then, unlike me, learn from it. I favoured my son too, but then he married a girl I didn't approve of. It caused a rift, one that has never been healed, especially as they then immigrated to Australia without so much as a goodbye.'

'Didn't he write?'

'Yes, in the early days, but my silly, stubborn pride got in the way and I didn't reply. When I had to give up my home, I did write to tell him, but it's been so many years and I don't even know if he was at the same address.'

'There must be a way to find him.'

'Perhaps, but I fear it's too late.'

'What about your daughter?' Delia gently asked. 'Can't you get in touch with her?'

Tears welled in Mrs Milton's eyes. 'You can't send letters to heaven.'

'You . . . you don't mean . . . ?'

'Rose died many years ago.'

'Oh, Mrs Milton, I'm so sorry.'

'Life has a way of teaching us lessons, but I made the same mistake over and over again before learning mine. I drove everyone who loved me away, my daughter, my son, and though we lived in the same house, my husband too. I didn't appreciate him until he died, but by then it was too late, and I was left a sad, lonely old woman. It's my own fault of course and I deserve to be alone.'

'You aren't alone, Mother.'

Delia was startled by the voice. It was the man she had seen nearby who had now come to stand beside them. However, her shock was nothing compared to Mrs Milton's reaction.

'William . . . oh, William,' she gasped, struggling to stand up.

He helped her, supporting her in his arms, the two of them locked in an embrace as sobs racked Mrs Milton's frail body.

'It's all right, I'm here now,' he soothed.

'How . . . how did you find me?'

'I went to the house and was told by a neighbour that you had moved into a residential home. I went there and they directed me here.'

It was such an emotional scene that Delia too felt close to tears. She remained seated for a while but then, feeling that her presence was an intrusion, she touched William on the shoulder.

'If you don't mind, I'll leave now.'

'Yes . . . and don't worry. I'll take care of her.'

As Delia then slipped quietly away, she found her emotions all over the place. She was doing the same thing Mrs Milton had done, driving everyone away. Jennifer had gone, been forced out, and Robin no longer seemed to need her. Delia hadn't really thought about it before, but now realised that one day her son would get married, move away, and when he did that left only Edward.

It was a wonder her coldness hadn't driven him out years ago, Delia decided, and only that morning she had threatened divorce. If she didn't want to end up a sad, lonely old woman, she would have to make changes, and to start with Delia knew she would have to overcome the sickening thought of sleeping with her husband again. Other women found enjoyment in sex, and perhaps she could too; yet even if it was impossible, Delia knew she'd have to pretend otherwise.

Like it or not, it was time she became a proper wife, to accept now that keeping the house immaculate and cooking perfect meals couldn't make up for the fact that she had kept Edward out of her bed. Her marriage had to come first and so for now she would have to put aside her ideas for starting up her own business.

Chapter Twenty-Two

Marcos wanted her to stop work, had offered to continue to pay her wage until they were married, but Jenny refused. It didn't feel right, and not only that, with Tina still surly she was glad to get out of the flat.

Over two weeks had passed since their argument over Marcos's proposal, and now, arriving home after her shift on Tuesday, Jenny felt a reluctance to go upstairs. Instead she knocked on Susan's door, deciding that she'd stay there until Tina left for work. It would be nicer than the atmosphere she'd have to face upstairs and, as she wasn't seeing Marcos that evening, it would be a refuge for a while.

'Come on in,' Sue invited when she opened the door, her eyes heavy, and tone drowsy.

Jenny stepped inside to find the air thick with smoke and to see Tina sprawled out on the sofa. 'Sorry, I'll go.'

'Well, well, if it ain't the blushing bride to be,' Tina drawled.

'Shut up, Tina,' said Sue. 'Sit down, Jenny, you don't have to leave.'

Jenny didn't need to be told what was going on, she could smell the drugs in the air and shook her head. 'No, it's all right, I'd rather go.'

'Yeah, bugger off, Miss Goody Two Shoes.'

'No, stay, join us,' Sue urged. 'I hardly see you these days and I'd love to hear about the wedding.'

'Sod that,' Tina said. 'I'm off.'

'I don't know why she had to behave like that,' Sue said when the door closed behind Tina.

'She doesn't like Marcos.'

'I know, but he's your choice and Tina has to accept that. Now come on, cheer up and tell me about the wedding.'

'With so few people to invite, Marcos wanted to make it something different, something special that we'd never forget.'

'How nice, he sounds so romantic.'

'He is, and he told me yesterday that just the two of us are going to Scotland, to Gretna Green, to get married. We're going to stay in a cosy little inn, though in separate rooms until after the service. Then we're off on our honeymoon.'

'That sounds wonderful and certainly different. Where are you going for your honeymoon?'

'I don't know, Marcos said it's a surprise. I'm sorry,

Sue, but it means I can't invite you or Tina to the wedding now.'

'Don't be silly. I'm just happy for you, and I'm sure that when Tina gets used to the idea, she will be too.'

Jenny hoped Sue was right, but somehow, sadly, she doubted it. 'I feel awful about moving out of the flat, and I don't know how Tina will manage the rent and bills on her own. I tried to talk to her, suggested she find something smaller, but Tina insists she'll be fine. How though, Sue? She only works in a bar and I can't believe the pay's that good.'

'I live alone and work in a pub, but I manage,' Sue said. 'Tina can take on extra shifts, work lunchtimes and cut down on the amount of money she spends on clothes.'

'But your rent must be a lot less than ours.'

'Jenny, stop worrying about Tina. She's resourceful, wily, and quite capable of taking care of herself.'

'Do you really think so?'

'Yes, I do, and, let's face it, you're getting married, not emigrating. You can still see Tina, visit her, and vice versa.'

'Yes, of course I can,' Jenny said, smiling at the thought. They would stay in touch and still see each other; but then Jenny's face sobered. Tina was so against Marcos and the marriage that she might not want that.

'Where will you be living, Jenny? In Chelsea?'

'I . . . I don't know yet. Marcos is buying a house, another surprise, but he hasn't said where.'

Sue frowned. 'Surely you should have some input, a choice in the matter? What if you don't like it?'

'I'm sure I will.'

'I hope so, because from what you've told me Marcos has decided where you're getting married, chosen the honeymoon, along with the area you'll live in and a house, all without consulting you. He seems rather controlling, Jenny.'

'Now you sound like Tina, but as I told her, Marcos isn't like that,' Jenny insisted. 'He just likes to take care of things, of me, and I trust his judgement.'

'I should have kept my nose out – I didn't mean to upset you. If you're happy with Marcos making decisions for you, that's fine.'

With Tina and Sue saying the same thing, a shadow of doubt crossed Jenny's mind. Was she happy to let Marcos make decisions for her? Well, yes, to a certain extent, but what if she didn't like the house, or the area? She'd have to talk to him, ask to see it before the sale was finalised, and surely he'd be happy to let her do that? Yes, of course he would, so why was she feeling this frisson of doubt?

Tina had been pleased to see Paul when he turned up unexpectedly close to the end of her shift. She was now holding his hand as he walked her home. She hadn't told Jenny or Sue about him, not when she had intended simply to use him by letting him pay for just one expensive night out. The trouble was, another date had followed, then another, and now her feelings were all over the place.

So far Paul hadn't even tried to kiss her but, as they neared her front door, Tina tensed. Would he try it on this time? Did she want him to? Yes, yes, she did, but her stomach now lurched with self-disgust. This would be the last time she saw Paul, and as she was feeling this way it was just as well.

They stopped outside the house, Paul still gripping her hand as he said, 'Can I see you over the weekend? After that I'm on nights for a fortnight.'

'I'm working, lunchtimes and evenings,' Tina lied.

'You'll have a few hours off between shifts. How about Sunday? We could go out for a drive.'

'Yeah, yeah, all right,' Tina agreed, knowing that by then, as long as everything went as planned, she'd be long gone.

Paul's head bent towards her, and though Tina hated herself, she couldn't resist as she let his lips touch hers. It was as though a bolt of electricity shot through her and she quickly stepped back. No, no, it was disgusting, and turning she hurried to the front door, fumbling to put her key in the lock.

'Tina, what's wrong?'

'Nothing . . . nothing,' she stammered. 'I . . . I'll see you on Sunday.'

'I'll pick you up after your lunchtime shift.'

'Yeah, great,' she called over her shoulder, relieved to step inside and close the door. For a moment Tina leaned against it, stomach churning, and then, hand over her mouth, she ran upstairs and was violently sick in the toilet.

It was some time later before Tina was able to pull herself together, to force her emotions to one side. She was leaving tomorrow and nothing was going to stand in her way.

Jenny was asleep when Tina crept into the bedroom and, climbing into bed, she closed her eyes, fighting to push away a picture of Paul's handsome face as it rose in her mind. She had to forget him – and she was going far enough away to do just that.

Chapter Twenty-Three

The following morning Tina was well in control of her emotions again; in fact she felt almost numb as she sneaked out in the early morning while Jenny was still asleep. She hadn't even looked at her friend, her mind set only on what she was now going to do.

With time to kill when she arrived at the station, Tina had to hang around. She had only seen Jenny's father once or twice and was now worried that she wouldn't recognise him. As she fought to conjure up his face in her mind, he appeared in reality, alone as she'd instructed. Yes, it was him, Tina was sure of it, but to be on the safe side she kept out of sight, her eyes darting this way and that for signs of deception.

After fifteen minutes she hesitantly moved towards him, but his eyes flicked past her, not recognising her as he too nervously scanned the throng of people buzzing around the busy mainline station. Tina hadn't wanted to leave any clues if this went wrong and had chosen King's Cross because it offered many potential avenues of escape. She could leave by several exits, or run down to the tube and hop on the first underground train that drew in.

'Mr Lavender?'

'Yes,' Edward said, puzzled now as he focused on her.

'I can see you don't remember me. I'm Tina, a friend of your daughter.'

'Tina? Tina Hammond?'

'Yes, that's right.'

'My God, your parents have been ringing me on and off since you left. They're desperate to find you.'

'I hope you didn't tell them about this, that you were coming here to meet me!'

'How could I? You didn't sign the letter and I had no idea who sent it.'

In that moment of fear Tina had forgotten for a second that she'd kept her identity a secret, and now felt foolish. She didn't like that, felt she was losing control of the situation and, seeking to reassert herself, she said abruptly, 'I can tell you where Jenny is, where we live, but first we need to talk.'

'Where is she? Where is my daughter?'

'Come on, there's a café over there and you can buy me a bottle of Coke.'

Edward looked annoyed, but reluctantly followed as Tina led him across the crowded station. He went to the counter and got her a Coke, but then said as he sat down, 'What's going on? You wrote to me, told me that you know where Jenny is, but now for some reason you're stalling. Where is she?'

'That bit of information is going to cost you, and I ain't talking peanuts.'

'Money! You want money! But you're Jenny's friend.'

'What's that got to do with anything? Jenny is doing all right, but I need money to make a fresh start. This is just a bit of business and if you want my information, you'll have to pay for it.'

Edward's eyes hardened as they locked with hers, but Tina kept her gaze steady.

'All right, how much?' he finally asked, reaching into his inside pocket to pull out a chequebook.

'Five grand, but I want cash.'

'What? You must be joking.'

'No, I'm not.'

'I don't have that kind of money.'

'Leave it out. You live in that big, posh house, and your car must have cost a pretty penny too.'

'Any money I have is tied up in the house, and it's a company car. On top of that, my son is at university and I have to fund his education.'

Tina scowled. She'd have to bargain a bit, lower her price. 'Right, what can you offer me then?'

'Five hundred pounds?'

'You must be kidding,' Tina spat, rising as though to leave.

'No, wait! A thousand then, but I promise you that's my limit.'

It was a lot less than Tina wanted, but if Edward Lavender was telling the truth he wasn't as well off as she'd thought. She sat down to test the water again. 'All right then, make it three grand.'

'I'd have to ask my bank for a loan. It will take some time to arrange.'

Tina was starting to feel desperate. If she had to wait for him to arrange a sodding loan, it would also give him the chance to contact her parents! She wasn't going to risk that and had no choice but to drop her price.

'Twelve hundred quid, today, and you've got a deal.'

He hesitated for a moment but then said, 'Very well.'

'As I said, I want cash.'

'Yes, all right, but I'll have to go to my building society.'

'Yeah, I guessed that, but I'm only gonna wait an hour. If you ain't back by then, I'm off.'

'I'll have to find a branch. Now give me Jenny's address?'

'Don't take me for a mug. You'll get it when I get me money, but no funny business. If I get a sniff of trouble I'll disappear, along with any chance you've got of finding Jenny.'

'Don't worry, finding my daughter means everything to me and I'm not going to jeopardise that.'

'Right, see you soon,' Tina nodded, watching him leave. Twelve hundred pounds still sounded like a small fortune to her, and at least this way she was safe. She had already worked it out that even if Edward Lavender went straight to a telephone box to ring her parents, there was no way they could get here within the hour.

Behind Jenny's back, Tina had had also packed most of her clothes and her suitcase was now in a locker at another London station, Victoria. From there she'd buy a ticket to Brighton, her chosen destination.

She wouldn't be around when Jenny opened the door to see her father standing there, and even if Edward did tell her own parents, she'd be long gone before they turned up. Tina shivered. Over two years might have passed, yet the thought of seeing her father again still had the power to strike fear in her heart.

Tina finished her Coke, left the café, and as she waited around for Edward's return, she found herself thinking about Paul. He'd had that disgusting effect on her – yet Tina knew that if she'd remained in Chelsea, she wouldn't have been able to resist seeing him again. Once again a feeling of self-loathing clenched her stomach. It was just as well she was going and, anyway, the die was cast . . . her new life set to begin.

Edward was searching for a branch of his building society, anxious to find one before closing time. It was just past mid-August, the day hot, and he was perspiring. Tina Hammond's audacious demand for money had shocked him, knocking him off balance, but at least he'd recovered his equilibrium enough to bargain for a lower price.

Of course, what Tina hadn't known was that he would have paid anything to find Jenny, even to the extent of selling his house, but annoyed at being virtually blackmailed by his daughter's so-called friend, his years of sales experience had come to the fore.

Yes, it felt like blackmail, Edward thought, but it would probably be a waste of time reporting it to the police. Jenny wasn't being held against her will and, as far as he knew, asking money for information wasn't illegal.

He'd been shocked by Tina's appearance. She was only eighteen, but looked much older, hardened, and, as his anger abated, Edward wondered if she was in some sort of trouble. He'd have to ring her parents, but it would have to wait as he didn't have their telephone number with him. Still, from what Tina had said, she and Jenny lived at the same address, and once he had that he'd pass it on to her parents. For now though, Jenny was his main priority and, at last finding a building society, Edward hurried inside. Tina had said that Jenny was doing all right, and that was a little reassuring, but was she telling the truth?

Though Edward was back at King's Cross with five minutes to spare, there was no sign of Tina and he began to panic. Minutes later he saw her walking towards him, her eyes darting left and right, then over her shoulder. Tina was nervous. No, it was more than that, Edward decided. She actually looked frightened.

'Tina, are you in some sort of trouble?'

She ignored his question, just saying abruptly, 'Have you got the money?'

'Yes, but is Jenny in trouble too?'

'Look, I don't know what you're on about. I'm fine, Jenny's fine. Now give me the money or I'm off.'

Edward took the bulky envelope from his inside pocket, briefly lifting the flap to show Tina the contents. 'It's all there, and now I want Jenny's address.'

Tina took a scrap of paper from her handbag, holding it out with one hand while reaching for the envelope with the other. 'It's flat number two.'

Edward momentarily held onto the envelope, saying, 'Tina, if you're in trouble, I'm sure your father would help you.'

'What! No, no,' she said frantically. 'I don't want to see him.'

The money was snatched from his grasp and Tina

ran off as though chased by demons. Edward clutched the scrap of paper, frowning, wondering why Tina had reacted like that. Maybe he should go after her, but it was too late, the girl already out of sight.

Edward now looked at the address, his heart lifting at last. Chelsea, not too far away. With an urgent need to see Jenny, to make sure that she was all right, he strode quickly from the station to find a taxi.

Chapter Twenty-Four

Jenny was tidying up, still surprised that Tina had already gone out by the time she had woken up that morning. She must have dressed in a hurry, for there was a discarded skirt on the floor, but it looked clean and so Jenny had picked it up. Going over to Tina's wardrobe, however, she found it almost empty, the hangers bare. It took a moment before the ramifications of what she was seeing sank in.

Tina had gone, left, moved out without saying a word! All right, they hadn't been getting on lately but surely there was no need for this? Bewildered, Jenny wondered if Sue knew anything about it and went downstairs to talk to her.

'Tina's gone. Did you know she was moving out?'

'Goodness, I had no idea,' Sue said as she beckoned Jenny inside.

'I can't believe she left without saying a word. Do you know why, Sue?'

'I haven't got a clue. Have you had a row or something?'

'We had a few tiffs about Marcos, but surely that isn't why she's moved out?'

'Perhaps Tina felt the rent would be too much on her own. She may have found a smaller flat or something.'

'I'm not getting married for months yet, and anyway, why move out without telling me?'

'Search me, but she'll probably be working tonight and you can talk to her then.'

Jenny was angry, upset, and shook her head. 'To leave like this Tina obviously doesn't want to talk to me and I'm not chasing after her. We've been friends for years, like sisters, but if this is the way she wants it that's fine with me.'

'You don't mean that, Jenny. You're just hurt and it's your pride talking.'

'Yes, I'm hurt,' Jenny admitted, feeling close to tears now. She croaked an excuse to leave Sue's flat. 'I . . . I must go. I . . . I've got things to do.'

Jenny knew it sounded weak, but bolted, tears now overflowing as she ran back upstairs. Sue had mentioned hurt and pride, but it was more than that. Tina had left without any explanation, uncaring, and to Jenny that signalled that their years of friendship had meant nothing to her.

* * *

As the taxi pulled up outside a tall, rather dilapidated terraced house, Edward climbed out. He paid the fare, hardly aware of the vehicle driving off as he checked the address again. Yes, this was it, and tensely he pressed the appropriate doorbell. He stood there for what felt like ages, his heart sinking. Jenny might be out, or worse, Tina might have sent him on a wild-goose chase.

He was about to ring the bell again when the door opened, and his heart skipped a beat. Jenny! She looked older, her eyes puffy as though she'd been crying, but it was her, his Jenny.

'At last,' he choked.

'Dad! How did you . . . ?'

'Tina gave me your address,' he interrupted, wanting nothing more than to pull her into his arms.

'Tina!' Jenny squeaked. 'How did you find her?'

'I didn't. She wrote to me, but Jenny, do we have to talk on the doorstep? Aren't you going to invite me in?'

She looked bewildered, but nodded and Edward followed her up a flight of stairs into a dingy room. The furniture was old, scratched, the lino worn, and the rug threadbare. It was clean though and an attempt had been made to brighten it up with posters on the walls and a colourful throw on the sofa.

'Why did Tina write to you?'

'Let's sit down,' Edward suggested, then told Jenny about Tina.

He saw the changing expressions on her face, moving from hurt to anger, and when he'd finished she said, 'So Tina used, me, sold this address to you for money?'

'I think she was desperate, Jenny. If you're in trouble too, let me help.'

'I'm fine.'

'But Tina seemed so frightened and when I suggested her father could help she ran off. What is it, Jenny? What are you so afraid of?'

'Nothing, Dad, and the only thing Tina's afraid of is her father.'

'There's no need for that. All he wants is to find her.'

'That's the last thing Tina wants. He . . . he interfered with her, made her do things to him.'

'*What!* No, I don't believe it.'

'It's the truth! It's why Tina ran away.'

'My God! I was going to tell him I've found her.'

'You haven't, Dad, and it sounds like Tina had it all worked out. She's got money now, her things have gone, and that means she won't be coming back here.'

Edward was sickened by the thought of Bert Hammond abusing his daughter. 'The man should be locked up and no wonder she ran away. But Jenny, the same can't be said for you. You had no need to just disappear like that. Didn't it occur to you that I'd be worried sick?'

'I was little more than a kid when I left home

and too centred on my own pain to think about anyone else. That first Christmas away from home I considered sending you a card, but didn't – I think because I still wanted to punish you. Your work always came first and you were hardly home. If you'd been there, you would have seen what she was up to, how she just wanted rid of me.'

'Jenny, I'm sorry, and I can understand that you wanted to punish me, but things are different now and I no longer travel. Your mother is sorry too, deeply sorry for the way she treated you. All she wants is reconciliation, a chance to make amends, and I do too. Please, darling, come home.'

'No, Dad, I'll never come back, nor do I want to see her. You may think she's changed, but I don't believe it.'

'At least give her a chance.'

Jenny's face hardened. 'No, Dad, and I don't see why I should.'

Edward was worried that he was pushing Jenny too hard and the last thing he wanted was to alienate her. He'd found his daughter, and surely given time he'd be able to persuade her to come home. In the meantime, he could at least do something to help her. 'All right, you won't come home, but look at this place, Jenny. At least let me help you financially.'

'There's no need, Dad, I'm fine. I'm getting married at the end of the year.'

'Married! You're getting married?' Edward exclaimed, struggling to come to terms with the enormity of what Jenny had just told him.

'Yes, to Marcos . . . Marcos Cane, on the 22nd of December.'

'Marcos,' Edward parroted.

'He's used to that reaction. His mother was Italian.'

Edward just couldn't take it in. 'I can't believe this. You're getting married in four months and this is the first I've heard of it. Just when were you going to tell us?'

'I didn't intend to.'

Agonised, Edward ran a hand over his face. 'Jenny, I know you were badly hurt, but please, don't cut us out of your life like this. We're your parents and if you have children, they'll be our grandchildren.'

'No, they won't. Delia won't be interested in them, and as for you, they'll be even more of a distant relative than I am.'

She sounded so hard, so bitter, her hurt still deep.

'Jenny, don't say that. I see you only as my daughter, and I will love your children, my grandchildren, just as much as I love you.'

'Oh . . . oh . . . Dad,' she said, her eyes flooding with tears.

Edward felt that he'd broken through her barriers at last and joyfully pulled his daughter into his arms. 'Yes, I'm your dad, and don't you forget it. In fact, I intend to give this fiancé of yours the once over.'

Jenny pulled back, her eyes still watery but bright. 'You'll like him, Dad. I work in his restaurant, well, until we get married.'

'Oh, so he owns a restaurant?'

'Yes, and he has other business interests too.'

Edward still wasn't happy that Jenny was getting married, but at least it sounded like the chap was well set up. He'd reserve judgement until he met him. 'Right then, when do I get to meet Marcos?'

'We'll have to work something out,' Jenny said, snuggling into her father again. 'Oh, Dad, I didn't realise it until now, but I've missed you so much.'

'I've missed you too,' Edward said, his arms tight around her. There was still so much to talk about, so much to sort out, but for now, Edward found that holding his daughter again was enough.

Chapter Twenty-Five

Marcos dressed with his usual care, though as he thought back over recent events, his lips were set in a tight line. It was down to Tina that Jenny's father had turned up and if the bitch hadn't scarpered he'd have throttled her. He had endured yesterday evening, when all Jenny had wanted to talk about was her father, and had agreed to meet the man the following weekend, but the last thing he wanted was any interference.

Of course he'd have to tread carefully, Marcos thought, allay any suspicions by playing the role of the perfect fiancé and have a ready answer for any questions thrown at him. At least he had a week to prepare, but for now it was a lovely Sunday morning, the day all his and Jenny's. He was taking her to see the house and anticipating the look on her face, Marcos smiled at last.

When ready, and without a word of goodbye, Marcos strode to his car, his thoughts still on Jenny.

It had been hell keeping his hands off her, but he was determined to wait. He wanted everything to be perfect this time, Jenny untouched on their wedding night.

He had just got out of the car when she appeared on her doorstep, fresh and pretty, despite the cheap skirt and blouse. He wanted to buy Jenny beautiful clothes, to dress her like a princess, but so far she'd refused to let him take her shopping. It annoyed him, yet contrarily it was also one of the things he loved about her. Unlike the others, Jenny wasn't grasping.

'I was looking out for you,' she said, closing the street door behind her.

Jenny rarely invited him in, but Marcos was happy with that. He hated her flat, the dinginess of the decor, and was keen to drive her to the new house, which he knew she would see as a palace in comparison.

'In you get,' he invited, opening the passenger door.

'Here's my adoption certificate,' she said.

'Good, and now I'll see about getting the passport forms.'

'Where are we going?'

'I haven't booked our honeymoon yet.'

'I meant, where are we going today?'

'You'll see,' Marcos said, moving round the car and climbing in behind the wheel.

'Why the secrecy?' Jenny asked as they drove off.

'I want it to be a surprise. One I hope you'll love.'

'I'm not sure I can cope with any more surprises.

It was enough that Tina left yesterday and then my father turned up.'

'This will be a pleasant one.'

Jenny was quiet for a moment, but then said, 'Once I got over the shock, it really was nice to see my father.'

'From what you told me, I thought you wanted to sever all ties with your adoptive parents.'

'I did, but seeing my father again made me realise how much I'd missed him. I'm still not sure I want to see Delia though, and I'll never again think of her as my mother.'

This was good news to Marcos and he struck. 'Does that mean you're still happy about going to Scotland to get married?'

'Yes, of course I am.'

'Your father may want you to marry here, to have a church wedding?'

'With Delia there! No thanks.'

'Are you sure, Jenny? I've already put arrangements in place, such as finding stand-ins to register us as living in Scotland, something you need to do before you can marry there, but if you're going to change your mind I'll have to cancel everything.'

'I won't change my mind.'

Despite Jenny's reassurance, Marcos was still worried. He had no idea how persuasive Jenny's father might be, and getting married here was the last thing he wanted. It would be too risky and he'd have to back off, to scupper his plans. No, he didn't want that and had to do something! Quick-thinking as always, Marcos had an idea. He'd bring things forward, make it another surprise, and before there was any chance of Jenny's father talking her out of it.

'When are you going to tell me where we're going?' Jenny asked, breaking into his thoughts.

'I'm not saying a word till we get there,' he said, turning his head to give her a brief smile.

'Oh you,' she said, but her smile was warm, and blue eyes sparkling.

As usual Marcos was struck by how young and innocent she looked. It was an innocence he cherished. He would have preferred her blonde hair long, and he intended to insist that she grow it once they were married.

There'd be no mistakes this time. He'd mould Jenny into the perfect wife. She might be in touch with her father again, but once Marcos had put a wedding band on her finger, he'd see that there was no interference from him in their lives. Once again Marcos turned his head to glance at Jenny, smiling in satisfaction, unaware that he was heading in entirely the wrong direction to achieve what he wanted.

Jenny was starting to feel tense as their journey progressed, a tension that turned to panic as they drew closer. Surely this wasn't the surprise? No, no, she didn't want this! She was about to yell out against it when common sense took over. She was being silly. With no knowledge of her parents' address, it would have been impossible for Marcos to arrange.

They were only three streets away when Marcos took a right turn. As he pulled up outside a property, she wondered why he had brought her here. Perhaps he was going to introduce her to his friends at last – but what a coincidence that they lived so near to Castle Close.

The house and grounds were hidden by large trees and Marcos got out of the car, using keys to open the double gates. Puzzled, Jenny watched him, ready to ask questions when he got back into the car but, as though in anticipation, he said, 'All in good time, let's get inside first.'

Tall trees bordered all sides of the large front grounds, the drive long and curving before the house came into view. The property was impressive, obviously the home of someone who was wealthy. Gulping, Jenny looked down at her outfit, at the creases in her skirt, feeling inadequately dressed as she at last got out of the car. Her parents' home was large, but nothing in comparison to this.

'Come on,' Marcos urged, using the same set of keys to open the front door and ushering her inside with a flourish.

She saw a large hall, wood panelling, a sweeping

staircase, and nervously whispered, 'Why have you got the keys? Who . . . who lives here?'

'This is my house, Jenny, empty as yet, but once we're married it will be our home. I hope you'll love it as much as I do.'

'Oh, Marcos,' she gasped. She had intended to ask him about the house, where it would be, and now wished she'd spoken up before this. 'Let me show you this floor first,' Marcos said, leading her from one room to another, extolling the beauty of each and every one of them until they ended up in a large, modernised kitchen. 'Well, darling, I knew you'd love it, but I didn't expect you to be dumbstruck. I've ordered most of the furniture, choice antiques, pieces that will fit perfectly.'

'You . . . you have?' Jenny said distractedly, not sure that she liked the thought of living so close to Delia. He must have seen something in her expression, but misinterpreted it. 'Oh darling, I hope you don't mind. Of course if you dislike anything I've chosen it can be changed, and I've left the choice of all the soft furnishings to you.'

'Marcos, I grew up in this area and my parents live just three streets away from here.'

'What!' Marcos exclaimed as his expression changed to one of anger. 'Oh perfect, Jenny. Fucking perfect!'

Jenny's eyes widened, shocked by this mercurial change in his character. 'I . . . I don't understand.'

'No, no, of course you don't. Forgive me, darling,

I didn't mean to swear,' he said apologetically, the change in his manner swift again. 'It's just that the area I grew up in was very different to this, very poor with mean little terraced houses and everyone living on top of each other. The door was always open, people walking in and out, and everyone knew each other's business.'

'Marcos, I had no idea. This is the first time you've talked about your past.'

'Yes, well, it's hardly something to brag about and I've come a long way since then. The problem is that living in those conditions did something to me, Jenny. I felt stifled and it made me value my privacy. The last thing I want is to live like that again, your parents calling round whenever they feel like it, interfering in our lives. God, Jenny, I love this house and thought it was perfect – not too far from my various businesses, large grounds, surrounded by trees, making it feel totally secluded. It would have been the perfect haven, but now . . . well, I'll just have to sell it.'

Jenny would have been happy for Marcos to do just that, but she could see how much he loved this house and hated to see him so upset. 'You don't have to sell it. My parents aren't the type to call round without invitation, and anyway, as for my mother – no, not my mother – Delia, it's the last thing I'd want.'

Marcos looked at her, his eyes brightening. 'All

right, darling, I suppose we could give it a try. I just hope our privacy isn't invaded. If it is, I'll just have to put this house on the market again.'

Jenny still wasn't keen on the idea of living so close to Delia, but with Marcos looking so happy again as he pulled her into his arms, she had to be content with that.

Chapter Twenty-Six

Unaware that Jennifer was currently looking at a house just three streets away, Delia was still trying to come to terms with the fact that Edward had found her.

'Why didn't you tell me about the letter?'

'I didn't want to raise your hopes. I wasn't sure if it was genuine or some sort of sick hoax.'

'I find it appalling that Tina Hammond demanded money for Jennifer's address. You should have refused.'

'Tina didn't get as much as she wanted, and anyway, it was worth every penny to find Jenny.'

'Yes . . . yes, I suppose so,' Delia agreed, yet in truth she wasn't happy that Jennifer was going to be back in their lives. So many things had altered since the girl left, not least the relationship between her and Edward. Now that they shared a bed again, they were closer than they'd ever been. She still didn't enjoy the sexual side of it, but managed to put up with it, and it was worth it to see the affection she now saw in her husband's eyes – affection aimed solely at her.

If Jennifer came home it would change all that, his precious daughter becoming Edward's whole focus again. Yes, Delia admitted to herself, she was jealous, had always been jealous of the relationship Edward and Jennifer shared. And she had just cause. More than just, and though Delia knew that she had played a part in what had happened too, it was nothing in comparison to what Edward had done.

'Delia, there's something else,' said Edward. 'I should have mentioned it when I came home yesterday, but you were overwhelmed enough and I felt it could wait. Jenny's engaged and very soon to be married.'

'Really? My goodness, I can't believe it,' Delia said, unable to help a surge of relief as the ramifications of this sank in. Even if Edward was able to persuade Jennifer to come home, it wouldn't be for long.

'From what Jenny said, her fiancé sounds well set up.'

'When is she getting married?'

'In December, on the 22nd.'

'That soon?' Delia said, delighted, but then the telephone rang and Edward went to answer it. Shortly after she heard him shouting and, puzzled, she went to the hall. She was appalled by what she overheard.

'Now listen, you sick bastard,' Edward was yelling. 'Even if I knew where your daughter was, I wouldn't tell you. Perverts like you should rot behind bars.' And with that he slammed down the receiver.

'Edward, your language,' Delia complained. 'What on earth was all that about?'

'That was Bert Hammond and what I found out about him is enough to make a saint swear. He was sexually abusing Tina. That's why she ran away from home.'

'No! Oh, Edward, that's dreadful. Are you sure?'

'Yes, there's no doubt,' he said darkly. 'The poor girl looked terrified when I mentioned him, and Jenny told me why.'

'At least the money gave Tina the opportunity to get away from him again and I suppose that's some compensation.'

'Yes, it is,' Edward agreed, 'though I doubt that anything can truly compensate for that sort of abuse.'

The subject soon returned to Jennifer and Delia was glad when at last Edward did what he always did on Sundays: he went out to the garden and, secateurs from the shed in hand, began to prune dead blooms from the roses.

Edward was over the moon that he'd found Jennifer, but though she'd pretended to feel the same, pretended to feel unhappiness that Jennifer didn't want to see her or to come home, in truth that suited Delia just fine.

Paul Ryman was at the pub again on Sunday evening, but there was still no sign of Tina. The landlord had said she'd rung in sick on Saturday, and he was disappointed that they'd missed their date that afternoon.

'No Tina again?' he said casually to the landlord.

'Nah, and this time she hasn't rang in. I ain't too happy about it.'

Paul pursed his lips, wondering when Tina would return to work. They'd had several dates, but there was a reserve about Tina, a sort of hands-off attitude, and he wondered if she was upset that he'd kissed her. Tina wasn't easy to get close to, that was for sure, and he doubted she'd appreciate it if he called round to see her without an invitation.

It was ten thirty before Paul left the pub, a little unsteady on his feet and smiling wryly that he'd drowned his sorrows in drink. He didn't turn towards home and instead walked to Tina's street where he stood looking up at her window. He was a daft sod, Paul told himself, but the drink had lowered his inhibitions. He needed an excuse to ring Tina's bell, and as she was under the weather he could say he'd called round to see if she was all right. Yes, that would do it, Paul decided, placing his finger on the doorbell.

There was only the dim light from a streetlamp a little further along the street, and Paul strained to see who had opened the street door by just a crack. It wasn't Tina but a young blonde girl who was peering back at him.

'What do you want?' she asked nervously.

'I'm a friend of Tina's. She didn't turn up for work. Is she all right?'

'She's gone. She doesn't live here any more.'

'Gone! Gone where?'

'I don't know, and I don't care,' the girl said, about to close the door.

'Hold on, are you Tina's friend, Jenny? She once mentioned you.'

She just nodded and, annoyed now, Paul said, 'If you're her friend there's no need for that attitude.'

'Believe me, there is. Now please go away.'

With the door firmly closed this time, Paul was left floundering. What was going on? Tina had left the flat and now it seemed her job too. Why? And where had she gone?

With no answers he walked away, yet determined to return. He was sure that Jenny knew more and somehow he'd get his answers.

Chapter Twenty-Seven

By the time the weekend came around again, Jenny had almost forgotten the young man who had called looking for Tina. She had a lot on her mind – her father, but mostly Marcos. When they had been viewing the house, his swift anger had allowed her to see another side of his character. She'd also seen what Sue had warned her about – Marcos *was* controlling.

Insidious doubts wormed into her mind, ones Jenny fought by making excuses for him. Yes, Marcos had chosen the house, but he was a successful businessman who was used to making his own decisions. He wasn't used to consulting anyone, so hadn't realised it was inconsiderate. He had, surely, just wanted to please her.

His apology for his anger had been equally swift, and after hearing about his background she could understand his need for privacy. Marcos had so many wonderful qualities, Jenny decided, and those were the ones she should focus on. He was kind, caring and wanted to look after her, and she felt loved, cherished. She loved him too, so very much.

Jenny glanced at the clock. It was Saturday morning and her father would be here soon. Not only that, Marcos had agreed to meet him. When the doorbell rang she looked quickly in the mirror to check her appearance before running downstairs. The last time her father had seen her she'd been blotchy-faced with tears, but this time her smile was bright as she opened the door.

'Hello, Dad.'

Edward stepped inside to hug her. 'I know it's only been a week, but I've missed you.'

'Same here, but come on up. Marcos should be here to meet you shortly.'

'I'm looking forward to meeting him.'

'Sit down, Dad. Can I get you anything?'

'No thanks,' he said, taking a seat on the sofa. 'Jenny, I know you're getting married soon, but won't you come home until then? You're mother is longing to see you and she really does want to make amends.'

'No, Dad, I told you.'

'But—'

'That'll be Marcos,' Jenny said when the doorbell rang, relieved at the interruption as she ran downstairs again to let him in.

'Is your father here?' Marcos asked after kissing her.

'Yes, and looking forward to meeting you.'

Her father looked a little surprised when he saw Marcos, but recovered well, standing up to hold out his hand. 'Hello, I'm pleased to meet you.'

'Good morning, Mr Lavender,' Marcos returned, shaking it.

'There's no need for formality. Call me Edward.'

'Thank you.'

They both looked so stiff, Jenny thought, like two businessmen, dressed in immaculate suits and wearing ties despite the hot weather.

'Dad, Marcos, sit down,' she urged, hoping that the ice would soon break.

They sat, her father the first to speak. 'So, Marcos, you're going to marry my daughter?'

'Yes, sir, with your permission of course.'

'It's a bit late for that, don't you think?'

'Well, yes, Jenny has already agreed to marry me, but I am sure she would want your blessing.'

'Tell me a little about yourself, Marcos. Jenny said you have a restaurant, and other business interests.'

'Yes, that's right, though the restaurant was a new venture for me. I'm involved in import and export, mainly cars, and have showrooms along with garages.'

'I see, and your family?'

'Unfortunately, my parents have passed away.'

'I'm sorry to hear that, but tell me . . .'

'Dad, stop it,' Jenny protested. 'This is beginning to sound like an inquisition.'

'No, it's all right, darling. Your father is looking after your best interests and I respect that.'

'Thank you, Marcos. However, I was only going to ask you both about the wedding arrangements. Jenny, I realise that any plans you've made won't have included your mother and me, but they can be changed. And, Marcos, as Jenny's father, I will of course pay for everything.'

'Dad, we're getting married in Scotland, in a registry office, and I don't intend to change anything, including the fact that there'll be no guests.'

'No guests! Oh, Jenny, please have a proper wedding and at least allow me the honour and pleasure of walking my daughter down the aisle.'

'Oh . . . Dad . . .'

'I'm sorry,' Marcos cut in, 'but I'm afraid it's too late for that. The arrangements are already in place and, as Jenny said, she doesn't want to change them. Now, darling, have you told your father about the house?'

'Er . . . no . . . not yet,' she said, floundering at the abrupt change of subject.

'I've just purchased a property, Edward, close to yours in Almond Crescent, and we'll be moving in when we return from our honeymoon.'

'That's marvellous and it'll be lovely to have my daughter living close by, but I'm still disappointed about the wedding and my wife will be too. I know she wants to meet you, Marcos, so can I persuade you both to come to dinner tomorrow?'

'What do you think, darling? It's up to you.'

In that one moment any doubts Jenny had harboured about Marcos being too controlling were swept away. He had deferred to her, and as she knew he didn't want any interference from her parents, and that she certainly didn't want to see Delia, she said firmly, 'Sorry, Dad, but the answer is no.'

'Jenny, please, I know you were treated badly, but if you come to dinner you'll see that your mother really has changed.'

'I said no, Dad.'

'Marcos, can't you talk some sense into her? As I said, my wife wants to meet you.'

Marcos thought about it for a moment, and then said, 'Jenny, it will make me appear rude if I don't meet your mother, and preferably before we're married.'

Jenny was not only confused, she felt chastened. 'All right, Marcos, we'll go to dinner.'

'Jenny, that's marvellous,' her father said, smiling with delight. 'Thank you, Marcos. Shall we say around two tomorrow? Is that all right for you?'

'That's fine. There will be just enough time for me to meet your wife before Jenny and I go on our trip.'

Startled, Jenny said, 'Trip? What trip?'

'I've been very busy, but things are a little quieter now and it's the ideal time to take a holiday.'

'Where are we going?'

'It's a surprise and I don't want to spoil it.'

'When are you leaving?' asked Edward.

'On Monday.'

'That soon!' Jenny exclaimed. 'But I haven't booked any time off work.'

'Don't worry, it's done and I've covered your shifts,' Marcos said, then turned to her father. 'Please be assured that I've booked separate rooms.'

'I'm glad to hear that. How long will you be away?'

'I'm not sure yet, a week, maybe longer. It depends if business calls me back.'

'I see. Well then, Jenny, I'm so pleased you've agreed to come to dinner before you go and I think I'd best be off. Your mother is going to be so happy and she'll want everything to be perfect, which means of course giving her advance warning.'

Jenny's head was reeling. A holiday sounded wonderful, but it was such short notice. She'd need time to sort out her wardrobe and pack, but instead they were going to Wimbledon tomorrow and she would be seeing *her* again, the woman she now refused to call her mother. Memories of the last time they'd been face to face surfaced – the yelling, the shouting, fighting with Robin to wrench her rucksack from his hand.

Now, already regretting her decision to go, Jenny wondered if she could so much as look at the woman again without all the bitterness she still felt inside spilling out.

* * *

Edward shook Marcos's hand again, hugged his daughter and then left. His feelings about Marcos were mixed. He'd expected someone younger, more Jenny's age, but there was no getting away from the fact that with several business interests, the man would be well able to take care of his daughter. A restaurant, show-rooms, garages . . . Marcos had done well for a man who looked to be in his late thirties.

It made Edward wonder how Delia would have fared if she had started up her own business, but for some reason she had changed her mind of late and the subject was no longer mentioned. He doubted that Delia could have coped, that she had the experience or acumen needed for success in the business world. That thought brought Edward back to Marcos. He had wanted to find out more about his background, but Jenny had put a stop to that, his questions cut off.

There was no trace of an Italian accent, instead Marcos's tones were those of an upper-class and well-educated Englishman. Of course with Jenny living close by, Edward knew he'd be able to keep an eye on her, yet in reality he didn't think it would be neces-sary. Marcos was a gentleman with the wherewithal to afford a house in Almond Crescent, and he obvi-ously came from a very good background.

As Edward drove home, he thought about the wedding, feeling upset that he couldn't give his daughter away. It rankled that Marcos had insisted that the arrangements had already been made. Surely a registry office affair in Scotland could be cancelled and a proper wedding arranged? He didn't know what Delia was going to say about it, though at least he'd be able to tell her that they were both coming to dinner tomorrow. Perhaps between them they could talk both Jenny and Marcos round, persuade them to change their plans. After all, a man had the right to walk his daughter down the aisle, and Marcos had seemed a reasonable sort of chap.

Edward arrived home, pleased to be able to pass the good news on to Delia.

'Well, Delia, it went really well. I met Marcos, Jenny's fiancé, and he's a gentleman, a wealthy one at that, so much so that he's bought a house in Almond Crescent.'

'What! But that's the most exclusive place in this area. Penelope Grainger lives there and her husband's a consultant. There's a judge too, a merchant banker, and now you're telling me that Jennifer is going to be living there? Oh, wait until I tell Penelope Grainger, she's sure to be impressed.'

Edward had to smile. He didn't feel the same, yet knew how much importance Delia placed on her social standing, that she coveted getting into that particular circle, and now it seemed that Jenny had given her an opening.

'That isn't all, Delia. Jenny and Marcos are coming here for dinner tomorrow.'

'They are?' Delia squeaked, her expression then changing to one of anxiety. 'Oh goodness, there's so much to do and I'm not sure our small joint of meat will stretch to four. I'll dash to the butcher's . . . and vegetables, I'll need more . . .'

'Delia, calm down, there's plenty of time.'

'Of course there isn't. On top of the shopping there's the housework and . . .'

'What housework? Everything looks fine.'

'No it doesn't. I *must* polish the furniture, the best cutlery, clean the bathroom . . .'

'All right, tell me what you want from the shops and I'll go, but before that I could do with a cup of tea.'

'Tea! What now?'

'Yes, and for goodness' sake, take a deep breath,' he said, urging his wife into the kitchen. 'They'll be here for dinner tomorrow, not today, and between us I'm sure we'll get everything done.'

Delia made the drinks, calmer now as she said, 'If Marcos comes from a wealthy background I should think the wedding is going to be very grand.'

'I'm afraid not,' he said and saw the shock on Delia's face when he told her about Scotland.

'But if he's so well off, why have such a mean little wedding?'

'I don't know, but Marcos has lost both parents so that may be it.'

'What a shame. I'm sure all girls dream of a

fairytale wedding, but Scotland, and no guests! Poor Jennifer.'

'I asked her to change her mind, and thought for a moment that she was wavering, but Marcos insisted it was too late to change their plans now.'

'Nonsense. Though it would be jolly rushed, an off-the-peg dress, I'm sure I could organise a dream wedding for Jennifer.'

'In that case, when they come to dinner tomorrow, maybe between us we can persuade her to let you do just that.'

'Oh, yes, and it would be the perfect way to show her that I want to make amends.'

Edward reached across the table to grasp Delia's hand. She wanted to help Jenny, to arrange the perfect wedding for her, and it proved how much she cared. Soon, Jenny would see that for herself.

Chapter Twenty-Eight

Paul Ryman was back, and in uniform. This time it wasn't late in the evening, but one o'clock in the afternoon, though once again on a Sunday. He knew it was out of order, that this wasn't an official enquiry, but Paul was desperate enough to risk it. He doubted Jenny would recognise him as it had been dark the last time he'd called, and now he rang the doorbell.

As most people did when they saw a policeman on their step, Jenny paled. 'Is something wrong?'

Paul quickly flashed his warrant card. 'It's nothing to worry about, miss. I'd just like to ask you a few questions concerning Tina Hammond.'

'Tina . . . but she's gone.'

'Do you have a forwarding address?'

'No, but can you tell me what this is about?'

'All I can say is that Miss Hammond is part of an ongoing enquiry,' Paul lied, hoping that sounded official enough to discourage any more questions.

'Is it about the money she took from my father?'

Paul was startled, but recovered quickly. 'What money is this, miss?'

Jenny hesitated, bit on her lower lip, and then said, 'It's nothing really . . . er . . . just money my father gave her for a fresh start.'

'So Miss Hammond didn't "take" it. Your father gave it to her?'

'Yes . . . yes that's right.'

'I see, and does *he* have a forwarding address for her?'

'No, I'm afraid not.'

It all sounded a bit fishy, Paul thought, and he persisted, 'Didn't Miss Hammond give any indication of where she was going?'

'No, none.'

'But surely you expect to hear from her?'

Once again there was a hesitation, followed by a floundering answer. 'No . . . well, maybe. I . . . I don't know.'

'If you hear from her I want to know,' Paul said, pulling out his pad to quickly write down his phone number. 'You can reach me on that.'

She took it, but her eyes failed to meet his as she said, 'Yes, all right. Now is that all?'

Paul still felt there was something fishy going on, but with no other choice he said, 'Yes, miss, but as I said, if you hear from Miss Hammond, ring me.'

She nodded and closed the door. Tight-lipped with

frustration at what had been a fruitless interview, Paul walked away.

With no information, no clue as to Tina's whereabouts, he was stumped. Of course if he got into CID a great deal more resources would be open to him, ones he could use to find Tina. Now more than ever he hoped that his application for promotion would be successful.

Jenny had been shocked to see the policeman, and bewildered too. He'd said something about an ongoing enquiry, but what had Tina done? If the police were involved it must have been something illegal – probably that was the reason why she'd left so suddenly.

It might also explain why Tina had been so desperate for money that she'd used a form of blackmail to get it, but somehow Jenny had refrained from telling the constable that. She hadn't told Sue about it either, because, in spite of what Tina had done, she still cared about her and didn't want to blacken her name. Worried now that Sue might have seen the policeman from her window and come into the hall to ask questions, Jenny scurried upstairs to avoid her.

Back in her flat, she crumpled the piece of paper the policeman had given her before throwing it into the bin. Only moments later the doorbell rang again and Jenny looked out of the window to see Marcos's car. She grabbed her handbag and ran downstairs.

'Hello, darling,' Marcos said as she climbed in, leaning over to kiss her.

Jenny returned the kiss, then said, 'A policeman has just been round looking for Tina.'

'The police! Why?'

'I don't know, but it probably explains why she left.'

Marcos nodded, saying only, 'Yes, probably,' before he started the engine and drove off.

'I know you feel you should meet Delia,' Jenny complained, 'but I'm not looking forward to this.'

'I had my reasons, Jenny. For one, your mother needs to see that you're an adult now, and as such she no longer has any influence over you. You know now how much I value my privacy and I don't want her interfering in our lives, especially when we move into our house.'

'I don't want that either, and though my dad insists that she's changed she's probably fooled him just like she fooled Robin. In fact, she'll probably take you in too and you'll think she's charming.'

'I doubt that.'

Jenny wasn't so sure but, as Marcos said, she was an adult now, ready for Delia's wiles. She had dressed carefully, her make-up skilfully applied and, yes, Delia would see that she was an adult now. Marcos looked wonderful too, so handsome and Italian, dressed in light grey trousers with a white silk shirt and tie. His suit jacket was hanging on a hook in the back of the car, and though it was a hot day he would probably put it on when they arrived.

'I don't want to stay too long anyway, I've still got packing to do for our holiday. Are you going to tell me where we're going now?'

'No, darling. I don't want to spoil the surprise.'

Surprises, Jenny thought, she was beginning to hate them . . . but surely a surprise holiday was nothing to worry about?

Marcos wasn't looking forward to dinner with Jenny's parents either, but he wanted to test the waters, to see what he was up against. He didn't want to sell the house, it was perfect, but neither did he want her parents poking around, asking questions, and so one way or another he'd need to find a way to put a stop to it. Her father was already trying to interfere with the wedding plans, but it wouldn't work; Marcos had already had the forethought to scupper any chance of that.

Edward Lavender had no idea who he was dealing with, Marcos thought, smiling wryly, but if the man continued to get in his way, he'd soon find out. Other women whose husbands had dared to challenge him had become widows, and if her husband became a constant nuisance, Delia Lavender might well join them. It would be simple enough, easily arranged . . . but of course it might not be necessary, and Marcos had decided to bide his time for now.

Yes, he'd keep up the facade and it might be that he'd find an easier way to put a spoke in the relationship between Jenny and her parents.

'Nearly there, darling,' he said, briefly taking his eyes off the road to look at Jenny. 'You'll just have to direct me to your parents' house.'

'It's the next turning on the left,' she said.

Nice, Marcos mused, as he drove into Castle Close, but not a patch on Almond Crescent. It was a bit too close for comfort, but not to worry, Marcos thought confidently. If Edward Lavender continued to interfere, he'd soon find out who he was up against.

Chapter Twenty-Nine

Delia was on the telephone to Robin, pleased that he was doing so well at university, but as always, missing him. 'Yes, Jenny and Marcos will be here soon. Darling, of course I'll tell her that you wanted to be here.' They spoke a little longer, but then Delia reluctantly ended the call. She had finished laying the dining room table, using her best cutlery and linen, but still had to fold the napkins. This just done when she heard a car pull into the drive.

'Edward, they're here,' she called. 'You let them in. I'll wait in the drawing room.'

'Yes, your ladyship,' he said, though he was smiling.

Delia managed a small smile in return. She wanted this to go well, for Edward to continue to believe that she wanted to make amends to Jennifer. Not only that, but as Jennifer was going to be living in Almond Crescent she intended to use that to her advantage, as a way to get into Penelope Grainger's social circle. At least, she'd decided, it would be some compensation for having Jennifer back in their lives.

There was the murmur of voices, and then they walked in. Delia was momentarily stunned. This wasn't Jennifer – pale, wishy-washy Jennifer. This was a young woman and a stunning one at that.

'My dear,' she said. 'You look wonderful and I'm so pleased to see you.'

Jennifer's face was set, no hint of a smile as she made the introduction. 'This is Marcos, my fiancé.'

'Marcos, I'm delighted to meet you,' Delia gushed.

'Good afternoon, Mrs Lavender,' he said formally.

'Oh please, call me Delia, and do sit down,' she invited, 'both of you.'

'What can I get you to drink?' Edward asked. 'Marcos, there's wine, red or white, and sherry, or perhaps something stronger?'

'A glass of red wine would be nice,' he said as they sat on the sofa.

'What about you, Jenny?'

'I'll just have a soft drink.'

Delia sat down again, searching for something to say. 'Jennifer, what a lovely ring,' she said, impressed by the size of the diamond.

'Marcos chose it and I love it.'

'Who wouldn't? I've just been speaking to Robin and he asked me to tell you that he's sorry he couldn't be here. I'm afraid it was too short notice.'

'How is he?'

'Fine, but as he's in Birmingham we don't see much of him nowadays. He seems to be enjoying university though, and is sharing a flat with friends.'

'What is your son studying, Mrs Lavender?'

'Please. I told you to call me Delia. As for Robin, he's taking economics.'

'More wine, Marcos?' Edward asked.

'This is a lovely burgundy, but as I'm driving I'll refrain for now. Perhaps another glass with dinner?'

'Talking of dinner, if you'll excuse me,' Delia said, 'I'll just see to the vegetables and then we can eat.'

As Delia stood up, she saw that Marcos did too. He was obviously well bred, a lot older than Jennifer, but as far as Delia was concerned that didn't matter. What did matter was that Marcos was successful and handsome. She was impressed by him and that meant others would be too, particularly Penelope Grainger. A new social circle beckoned, one that Delia couldn't wait to get into.

Marcos took a seat at the dinner table, Jenny at his side and Delia opposite him. He knew that both Edward and his wife would want to know more about him and that the questions would begin soon, but he was prepared for them. It was a scorching hot day and he'd have preferred something lighter, but Delia had prepared a traditional Sunday roast.

'Thank you,' he said as Edward carved slices of lamb to put on his plate.

'Edward tells me that your mother was Italian,' Delia said. 'I wasn't sure what to serve you and hope this meal is to your taste.'

'My father was English, and I love both cuisines.'

'I'm sorry to hear that you lost your parents. How old where you when they died?'

This was just the opening Marcos wanted, a way to prevent further questions along this line. 'I was twenty-six and, before you ask, they died in a car accident. It was very painful for me, still is, and not something I wish to be reminded of.'

'Oh dear, I'm so sorry for bringing it up,' Delia said, looking stricken.

'Please, don't upset yourself,' Marcos said graciously. 'You weren't to know that any mention of my parents distresses me.'

'Would you like another glass of wine now?' Edward asked as he finished carving.

'Yes, please,' Marcos said, noting that Delia looked grateful for her husband's intervention.

She composed herself, then began to pass the vegetables around. 'Jennifer, I hear you're going to be married in Scotland.'

'That's right.'

'Your father is so disappointed, and I am too.'

'We've talked about it, Jenny,' Edward said, 'and

your mother doesn't think it's too late to change the arrangements.'

'Yes, Jennifer, and I'd love to help if you'd prefer a white wedding? Just imagine it, a fairytale dress, a beautiful cake, flowers, a wonderful day that you'd never forget.'

'Please, Jenny, say yes.' Edward urged. 'As I said yesterday, I'd love to walk you down the aisle.'

'Marcos . . .' Jenny said, eyes wide in appeal as she looked at him.

Marcos knew it was safe to stall them, but nevertheless took this opportunity to assert himself. 'Look, you're overwhelming Jenny. Leave if for now and we'll discuss it again when we return from our holiday.'

Edward nodded. 'Very well, and I suppose that gives us a bit of hope. Now pass the gravy boat around, Delia, and we can tuck in before this gets cold.'

'This is delicious, Delia,' Marcos said after a few mouthfuls. 'I hope you've passed your culinary skills on to Jenny.'

Delia didn't get a chance to answer, Jenny saying, 'No, she didn't, but don't worry, Marcos. I picked up a few things in your restaurant and I can take some lessons.'

'Jennifer, you used to help me in the kitchen,' Delia protested.

'Yes, but all I was fit for was scrubbing the floor

or peeling potatoes,' she said, then threw down her napkin. 'Excuse me. I . . . I need the bathroom.'

There was another awkward silence as Jenny left the room, which Edward quickly filled. 'I think you said the wrong thing, Delia.'

'I didn't mean to. I . . . I'll go and talk to her, apologise . . .'

'No, leave her,' Marcos ordered as Delia was about to stand up. 'Jenny needs a little time to calm down.'

'Oh, this is so difficult,' she said. 'I feel that I'm walking on eggshells.'

'Just think before you speak,' Edward warned. 'Now let's change the subject. We don't want Jenny to find us talking about her when she returns. Marcos, how's business?'

'Fine, thanks. I've been busy and now looking forward to taking a break.'

'Yes, this surprise holiday. Very nice too, but surely you can tell us where you're going?'

'Not when there's the risk of Jenny walking in.'

'Point taken,' Edward said, chuckling. 'Maybe we should think about a holiday, Delia. We haven't been away for years.'

Delia had been picking at her food and now laid down her cutlery. 'Yes, it might be nice.'

'Tell me, Marcos,' Edward asked, 'how did you get into the car business?'

Marcos had his story ready. 'My father had a garage, and as his only child he left it to me. I expanded it, took on my first dealership, and then added others.'

'The restaurant is a bit of a departure from that.'

'Yes, but it's turned out to be a good investment.'

'Do you specialise in Italian food?' Delia asked.

'I do, and I have a very good Italian chef.'

Jenny came back into the room again and took her seat, but made no attempt to finish her dinner. It was an awkward moment, but her father once again covered it. 'I like your hairstyle, Jenny.'

'Thanks. The girl who lives downstairs cuts it for me.'

'She . . . she does it beautifully,' Delia said hesitantly. When there was just a curt nod from Jenny in response, she rose to her feet. 'As everyone seems to have finished, I'll clear the plates.'

Edward stood to help and they both left the room. Once they were alone, Marcos turned to Jenny and said, 'Are you all right, darling?'

'Yes, and I'm sorry for behaving like that.'

'You have nothing to be sorry for.'

'She does seem different, but I just can't forget the past. I arrived with my back up, and it didn't take much to make me flip.'

'I'm not sure that leopards change their spots and, until you're sure of her, I suggest you take things very slowly.'

'Yes, yes, I'll do that.'

Marcos had found it easy to put doubt in Jenny's

mind about Delia, but her father was another matter. Marcos wasn't worried, however, he was sure that he'd find a way to come between them. He'd win. He always did.

Chapter Thirty

Jenny had been glad to leave after dinner. She'd been away from Delia for over two years, but time and distance hadn't softened her memories, and seeing her again had brought them back to the surface. When saying goodbye, Delia had put her arms around her and whispered what had sounded like a heartfelt apology, one that Jenny doubted she could trust. Marcos had warned her to take things slowly and she intended to do just that.

It was now Monday morning and Jenny was thankful that this holiday had served as an excuse to avoid making any firm arrangements for a return visit. Marcos had a few things to sort out before they could leave, but he was picking her up at twelve, so when the doorbell rang a few minutes before midday, she ran downstairs to throw open the street door.

'I'm ready,' she called. 'I just need to fetch my case.'

'I'll carry it down,' Marcos said, kissing her on the cheek.

Upstairs in the flat, Jenny pointed to her case. 'I wasn't sure if one will be enough.'

Marcos simply smiled as he picked it up and for a moment Jenny was exasperated. He didn't seem to understand that, with no idea where they were going or for how long, deciding what to pack had been a nightmare. She followed him out and locked the door, her face downcast as Marcos stowed her luggage and they climbed into the car.

He turned to look at her, saying softly, 'Jenny, there's no need to worry about small things, clothes and such. I have everything in hand, so just relax and enjoy the journey.'

His expression was so appealing that Jenny found it impossible to resist. 'All right, I'll try, but after what has happened lately I'm not really keen on surprises.'

He leaned across, kissed her, then put on his sunglasses and started the engine. 'In that case, we'll turn the journey into a game. There'll be clues on the way, and if you can work out our destination I promise that when we stop for the night, I'll tell you why we're going there.'

'I already know that. We're going on holiday.'

Before driving off, Marcos said, 'It could be more than a holiday, darling.'

'What do you mean?'

'Don't spoil the game. Work out the destination first.'

Marcos wouldn't be drawn any further and, given no other choice, Jenny began to enjoy the game as they picked up the A1. She soon worked out that they were going north, but as Marcos had mentioned stopping overnight she didn't make any suggestions until far-flung places began to appear on signposts.

'Leicester,' she suggested.

'No, try again.'

'Derby then?'

'No, darling, not there.'

'I've got it,' Jenny said some time later, 'Robin Hood. Sherwood Forest. We're going to Nottingham.'

'That wouldn't involve an overnight stop.'

Stumped for now, Jenny's eyelids began to droop and she fell into a light doze. The rumble of the tyres on the road became distant, and when she opened her eyes again it was to see another destination.

'Sheffield?' she asked sleepily.

'So you're awake, but I'm afraid you're wrong again. I don't know about you, but I could do with a break so we'll stop soon.'

'I'm thirsty, so yes please,' Jenny said, surprised to find they'd been on the road for over three hours. 'Where are we?'

'Close to one of your suggestions, Nottingham,' Marcos said, turning off the road and pulling up outside a village café shortly after.

Jenny was glad to get out of the car and her first call was to the toilets. After that she was soon sipping a Coke while they waited for their sandwiches to arrive.

'It's nice here,' she said. 'The countryside is so pretty.'

'Not as pretty as you,' Marcos said.

She smiled. 'Thank you. Are you going to tell me where we're going now?'

'No, the game is still on.'

Jenny sighed. She had no idea where to suggest next, but surely the next stretch of their journey would reveal the final clue?

Marcos bit into his sandwich. He hadn't wanted to reveal where they were going before now, worried that if he told Jenny she would mention it to her father at dinner yesterday and give the game away. Of course it was perfectly safe now and he could have told Jenny when they set out earlier, but after the pressure her parents had put her under he wasn't exactly confident that this would work. He'd decided to wait, to turn the journey into a game, hoping that at some point he'd find the perfect moment.

'It's such a lovely day,' Jenny said, bright sunlight

shining through the café window to gleam on her hair. 'I hope the weather doesn't change.'

'Are you too hot? Would you like to move away from the window?'

'No, I'm fine,' she said.

Marcos was fascinated by the way the sun high-lighted the natural blonde tones in Jenny's hair, and one side of her face was illuminated too, her skin perfect. She'd gone along with the game, hadn't carped or complained once on the journey, which made a refreshing change.

The others would have done nothing but moan, and in fact just telling them that he'd be away for a while had provoked a barrage of complaints. He had no idea why, especially as all that interested them was his wallet. It certainly wasn't his company – they had each other for that.

He'd shut them up by using his fists on one of them as usual, enjoyed it too, afterwards throwing them extra funds. Despite a black eye, he'd seen the avid greed but, if all went well, this very greed would ensure their silence.

Jenny had finished her sandwich and Coke by now so, draining the last of his coffee, Marcos said, 'Ready, darling?'

'Yes,' she said, dabbing her lips with a paper napkin.

The gesture reminded Marcos of Delia, and though he hated what the woman had put Jenny through, he knew that her mother's immaculate manners had been passed on. Delia was a woman of class, a class he aspired to, and in their new home Jenny would entertain with the same style and grace as her mother.

They continued their journey, Jenny spotting a signpost and asking 'Manchester . . . or Leeds?'

'Neither of those,' he said as they travelled further north, talking of other things: the house, the colour schemes for soft furnishing. Then Jenny mentioned cooking lessons again.

'If that's what you want to do, it's fine with me,' Marcos said, 'or failing that we could employ a cook.'

'Don't be silly,' Jenny said, giggling. 'I'm looking forward to learning how to prepare wonderful meals and I don't want another woman taking over my kitchen.'

'All right, darling, I'll just have to put up with burnt offerings until you've finished the course.'

'Now you're being silly again,' Jenny protested. 'I can cook simple things. It's just that I want to learn more. Look, that sign is pointing to Newcastle.'

'We'll be passing through it,' Marcos said, and nearly three hours after leaving Nottingham, they did just that. After taking a left turn, Marcos was unsurprised to hear Jenny's little squeal.

'We're going to Scotland!'

'Yes, I thought that rather than just seeing it briefly

in the winter, it might be nice to explore some of the area now, to see it in the summer, even if it is a bit late in the season.'

Jenny smiled with delight. 'I think that's a wonderful idea.'

They were close to the border now, but after so long on the road Marcos had had enough, glad that he'd had the foresight to plan an overnight stop. 'There's a hotel in Blaydon which isn't far from here and I've arranged two rooms for the night.'

'That's nice,' Jenny murmured.

Marcos glanced at Jenny, saw that she looked puzzled and wondered if she was working it out. If so, would she agree?

The hotel was lovely, her room too, and Jenny was enjoying relaxing in a bath. They'd be in Scotland again for their wedding in December, but Marcos was right, it would be lovely to see some of the area in the summer.

She soaked for a while, then washed and climbed out. Her tummy was rumbling and she was looking forward to dinner, thankful to find that the clothes she'd packed weren't creased. They were going to eat at seven thirty and, as if on cue, there was a soft knock on her door.

'I hope you're ready, darling,' Marcos said. 'I'm starving.'

'Yes, me too,' Jenny said, and taking his hand they

went down to the dining room. They were given a table for two, beautifully laid with fresh linen, and Marcos ordered their meal.

'Jenny, you agreed we wouldn't alter our wedding plans, but when your parents were pressuring you yesterday I thought you were wavering.'

'No, I wasn't, and I was glad when you stepped in to put a stop to it.'

'I doubt they'll give up,' Marcos said as their first course arrived, 'and I can't say I'm happy about it.'

Jenny found the slivers of smoked salmon suddenly unappetising. She looked at Marcos, saw he was toying with his food too, and said, 'Don't worry, I won't change my mind.'

Marcos looked deep in thought, but then said, 'I don't like the idea of you putting up with four months of pressure, and I think I've come up with the ideal solution. We don't have to wait until December to get married, we can bring the date forward. As we'll be in Scotland tomorrow, what's wrong with now?'

'Now! But how?'

'We aren't registered just yet, but we can do that straightaway, stay in the area for three weeks, and then we can be married. Think about it, Jenny. We could return as man and wife.'

Jenny did think about it, but it didn't take her long to reach a decision. Now, or in four months, what difference did it make? And Marcos was right, it was the ideal way to stop any further pressure from her father, something she suspected would be increasingly hard to resist.

'All right, Marcos, let's do it.'

'Darling, that's wonderful. Now come on, let's eat, and I'll order a bottle of champagne to celebrate.'

He looked so happy and, with her appetite now restored, Jenny began to tuck in. It was a wonderful meal, but by the time she had finished it, along with the champagne, Jenny was feeling a little tipsy. She was glad of Marcos's support when they went upstairs, and outside her bedroom door he kissed her. Jenny clung to him, her inhibitions dulled by champagne, and loving him so much that a need rose within.

'Oh, Marcos,' she husked.

'No, Jenny,' he said, gently pushing her away and unlocking the bedroom door. 'You've had too much to drink and I don't want to take advantage of you. Go to bed now, but soon, darling, soon you will be my wife.'

With a chaste kiss on her cheek, Marcos was gone, and feeling strangely let down Jenny threw off her clothes to climb into bed. She had never been with a man and didn't really know what to expect, but she loved Marcos so much and yearned to find out.

Jenny hugged the pillow and thought about his parting words. Yes, they'd be married soon. She'd be Mrs Jennifer Anne Cane . . . and children, they'd have children. A wonderful future beckoned, and, closing her eyes, Jenny fell asleep with a smile on her face.

Chapter Thirty-One

'There's nothing from Jenny again. Not even a post-card,' Edward said as he placed the morning post onto the table.

'Robin is keen to see her, and to meet Marcos. He was disappointed that they weren't back when he was here last weekend.'

'I didn't expect them to be away for so long.'

'Perhaps they've gone abroad,' Delia suggested as she rifled through the envelopes. She found a letter addressed to her and opened it eagerly. 'It's from Beatrice.'

Edward sat down. Delia was busy reading, but his mind was still on Marcos. He'd only met the man twice, and though his initial impression of him had been good, Edward now had a few niggling doubts. Marcos had been charming when they came to dinner, but while he'd told them a little about his business activities, along with his background,

Edward sensed that he'd disliked being questioned, especially when it came to his family.

'Edward, this is wonderful,' Delia said, glancing up from her letter. 'Beatrice is coming home.'

'That's nice,' he said automatically, still distracted by his thoughts. Marcos said that his parents had died when he was twenty-six, and as that must be well over ten years ago, his excuse that it distressed him to talk about them didn't quite ring true.

'Timothy has been given a post here and Beatrice hopes it's going to be permanent. Oh, Edward, wouldn't that be wonderful?'

'Yes, very nice,' he murmured.

'Edward! Are you listening to me?'

'Sorry. What did you say?'

'What's the matter with you? You're miles away. I said my sister and her husband are coming home and, not only that, Timothy has been given a post in London.'

At last Edward focused on Delia. 'When do they arrive?'

'In November,' Delia said, her eyes shining with delight.

Edward tried to arouse some enthusiasm. He hardly knew Beatrice or her husband, having only seen them about five times during the whole of his marriage to Delia. On those rare occasions he'd found Timothy pompous, and Beatrice an utter snob.

'So, they'll be here in a couple of months.'

'Yes, well in time for the wedding,' Delia enthused. 'I'm worried though, Edward, there's so little time to get all the arrangements in place. It was a stroke of luck that the Grand Hotel had a cancellation and that the vicar can do the service so close to Christmas. There's still a lot more to do – the invitations, the flowers, and Jenny's dress of course.'

'Delia, I told you to wait. I know Marcos said he'd discuss it when they return, but they may still decide to marry in Scotland.'

'He wouldn't have said we'd discuss it if that was the case. Marcos is on our side, Edward, I'm sure of it, and let's hope he's working on Jennifer while they're away.'

'If you say so, and of course I hope you prove to be right.'

'I will be, and as they are moving into Almond Crescent, I'm going to invite Penelope Grainger to the wedding. I'll be able to introduce her to Timothy and she's sure to be impressed that my brother-in-law is a diplomat.'

Edward had thought Beatrice a snob, but in reality Delia equalled her, judging people by their social position and wealth. He smiled wryly. It was just as well Jenny had met a man who was well set up, with the wherewithal to buy a house in Almond Crescent. If she'd chosen a dustman, goodness knows how Delia would have reacted.

'What about Marcos?' he asked. 'How will he be received?'

'Very well, I should think. Marcos is a successful businessman, as well as being handsome and charming.'

'We know so little about his past and he wasn't keen on enlightening us. In fact, all we know is that his father had a garage.'

'Yes, I must admit it's a little worrying. It hardly seems a wealthy background, but as Marcos avoids the subject it's unlikely anyone will find out.'

'I don't see why it would matter if they did.'

'Edward, you have no idea. One's breeding is so important.'

'He's not a racehorse.'

'Now you're being silly.'

'No, I'm not, Delia. You may want to hide it, but I want to know more about his background. Whether rich or poor, it doesn't concern me. What does is his aversion to talking about his past. It's almost as if he's got something to hide.'

'I didn't get that impression and as we hardly know Marcos your judgement seems a little premature. Like all fathers, I doubt you think any man would be good enough for your daughter, and as such I think you're just looking for faults.'

Edward was about to protest, but then paused to think. Jenny had been missing for over two years and it had been a joy to find her. He wanted her to come home, but instead she was getting married and it felt almost like she was lost to him again. Was Delia right? Did he resent the fact that Marcos was now the most important man in his daughter's life? *Was* it jealousy?

'You may be right, Delia,' Edward finally said.

'Don't worry, dear. I think where fathers are concerned it's perfectly normal.'

Yes, perhaps it was, Edward thought, yet even though Delia had come up with a plausible reason for his worries, they refused to go away.

Marcos glanced at Jenny, saw how she was twiddling her wedding ring and smiled. It had been wonderful, over three weeks in Scotland, culminating in their marriage yesterday on Friday, the twenty-eighth of September. Last night, their wedding night, Jenny's innocence had given him confidence, yet even so he'd feared losing it. He'd rushed it, lasting only minutes, but at least for the first time in years he'd managed a climax. Afterwards, and with no yardstick to judge him by, there'd been no derision from Jenny. It was just as he'd hoped, and now all he had to do was take the final step.

'Are you happy, darling?' he asked.

'Yes, very.'

'We're on the outskirts of London now and we'll soon be home.'

'I can't believe I started out with one suitcase, and I'm returning with three.'

'The weather is changing and you needed some autumn clothing. It's a shame there wasn't much to choose from, but never mind, once we're settled we'll sort out the rest of your wardrobe,' Marcos said automatically, well used to women wanting more clothes, jewellery or – lately – money.

'There's no need. You've already bought me so many lovely things.'

Marcos shot Jenny another glance. She actually meant it. She was unbelievable, wonderful, and deserved to be rewarded. 'Those few bits were nothing.'

'I don't need anything else,' she insisted. 'I know we're near London, but when are we moving into the house?'

'Now, of course.'

'But what about the furniture, and we haven't got things like china, bed linen, curtains . . .'

'Other than the curtains, everything's in place.'

'Already! But how did you manage that?'

'I put someone onto it, and we can use the shutters until you select the curtains,' Marcos said, but another quick glance at Jenny revealed she was frowning. 'Look, I told you before: if things aren't to your taste we'll change them.'

'I'm sure they'll be fine, but I'll have to go to my flat. I want to pick up the rest of my things, and of course tell the landlord I'm leaving.'

'It can wait until tomorrow,' Marcos said, heading for Wimbledon. He had things to do tomorrow too, the last strings to cut. They had a shock coming and he was looking forward to seeing their faces.

Jenny glanced at Marcos as they drove up East Hill, unable to push away the memory of last night – their wedding night. She'd been nervous, yet excited, yet all there had been was a sharp pain, followed by a frantic coupling that had left Marcos gasping, but her feeling bewildered. She had gone into marriage knowing virtually nothing . . . but was that it? Was that all there was to the sexual act? Tina had only ever spoken about it in a derogatory manner, but after the hateful experiences she'd been through it was hardly surprising. Sue, on the other hand had once laughingly said that a 'bit of nookie', as she called it, was great, but fearful of appearing childish in her lack of experience, Jenny had never found the courage to bring up the subject again.

'You're miles away,' Marcos said.

'I was just thinking that we should stop to buy food and other essentials,' Jenny fibbed. Though it was true, she realised: they would need some shopping.

'That's been taken care of too.'

'It has? How?'

'I rang ahead while you were in the bath this morning.'

'Goodness, is it being delivered?' Jenny asked.

'Yes, in a way . . . but look, Jenny, we're home,' Marcos said as he turned into Almond Crescent.

He stopped the car, opened the gates, and Jenny couldn't believe her eyes when they drove in. The trees had been pruned, the overgrown shrubbery cut back, and the house looked wonderful, the mullioned windows clean and sparkling as though in greeting. This was to be her home, and as Marcos parked the car she sat unmoving, unable to tear her eyes away from the facade.

'Come on,' Marcos said, smiling as he opened the passenger door. 'I can't wait to carry you over the threshold.'

Excited now, Jenny got out and Marcos picked her up to carry her inside. She blinked. There was the smell of lavender furniture polish, a large vase of flowers on the hall table, and her ears pricked when she heard sounds coming from the kitchen. Marcos kissed her before putting her down, and recovering her wits, Jenny asked in surprise, 'Is someone here?'

'Yes, but it's only Edna.'

'Edna?'

'Edna Moon, our cleaner.'

'But we don't need a cleaner!'

'This is a large house and I don't want to turn you into a drudge.'

'I don't mind housework.'

Marcos looked exasperated and his tone was firm. 'Nevertheless, Mrs Moon has been employed for two hours every morning to help you. She can take on the more arduous tasks while you, my darling,' he said, softening his voice again now, 'can concentrate on learning how to cook, along with making yourself beautiful to greet me when I come home.'

For the first time Jenny was beginning to realise how different her life was going to be. She'd been a dishwasher, then a waitress, but now she'd be living in this large house, with a cleaner no less. Goodness, she'd be living like a lady, and as Mrs Moon appeared, Jenny at last smiled. If she had pictured a daily, Edna Moon certainly fitted the bill. The woman was even wearing a cotton coverall, her round face, though plain, was pleasant, with rosy cheeks and twinkling brown eyes. Jenny loved her on sight.

'Mr Cane, you're back.'

'Yes, Edna, and this is my wife.'

'Hello, dearie, it's nice to meet you, and I hope you're happy with what I've done. The kitchen is stocked up and things stowed away, but if it's not to your liking you can change things round.'

Jenny smiled; she was already sure they'd get on. 'It's nice to meet you too, Mrs Moon, and I'm sure I'll be happy with everything.'

'Call me Edna,' she replied. Then, turning to Marcos, she said, 'Mr Cane, I did what you asked and there's a chicken casserole in the oven, but if it's all right with you, I'll be off now. My Tom will be home soon and looking for his dinner.'

'Tom?' Jenny said.

'Yeah, me son.'

'Of course you can go, Edna,' Marcos said. 'It was good of you to take on the extra work and hours. I'll see you're rewarded.'

'It was no trouble. I'll see yer in the morning, Mrs Cane. Bye for now.'

'Goodbye,' Jenny called, finding it strange to be addressed as Mrs Cane.

'Come on, darling,' Marcos said. 'Let's look around and then tuck into that casserole.'

'It seems you thought of everything,' Jenny said as she took his hand.

They went from room to room, Jenny unsure about the dark antique furniture, but Marcos seemed so pleased with everything that she said nothing. She'd brighten things up with soft furnishings, pretty ornaments and late flowers from the garden. For now though, the smell of chicken casserole was irresistible and soon they were seated in the dining room and eating their first meal together in their new home.

'I suppose we'll have to see your parents to break the news,' Marcos said.

'It can wait until tomorrow.'

'They're bound to want to see the house so we'll invite them round, get it over with. However, I don't want it to become a habit, Jenny.'

She was surprised by the hardness of his tone, which now turned to exasperation as he said, 'This casserole is oversalted.'

It tasted fine to Jenny, but Marcos was very particular, and she began to worry that nothing she cooked would be to his tastes. 'If you don't like this, I dread to think what you'll make of my efforts.'

'I know you want to take lessons, and in the meantime anything simple will be fine.'

Jenny began to clear their plates while making a mental list of things she could cook. It was woefully short, but hopefully a few recipe books would help. She carried the china to the kitchen, began to fill the sink with water, but then Marcos came to stand behind her and wrapped his arms around her waist.

'What are you doing?' he asked.

'I'm putting these things in water. I'll make coffee then wash up.'

'What do you think that is?' he asked and as her eyebrows rose he nodded. 'Yes, my sweet, a dishwasher.'

Jenny remembered the stacks of plates, saucepans and meat tins she used to have to tackle at the restaurant and said without thinking, 'When I was washing dishes in your restaurant I could have done with one of those, but not now.'

Marcos's face darkened. 'Jenny, you are my wife, and as such I do not expect you to criticise me.'

'But I'm not.'

'You're inferring that I treat my staff badly, that I treated *you* badly.'

'No, no, Marcos. I just meant that with two of us

there's hardly enough washing-up here to warrant loading the dishwasher.'

'I see,' he said, his face relaxing. 'Then I'm sorry for misjudging you.'

'That's all right,' Jenny said, though in truth she felt intimidated. There had been a few occasions in Scotland when Marcos had been volatile, usually because of what he saw as bad service, but his anger hadn't been aimed at her. Now, though, it seemed he was hypersensitive to what he perceived as criticism and in future she would have to choose her words carefully.

'I can see I've upset you, Jenny, but please don't take my outbursts seriously. I'm afraid I have my mother's temperament, swift to anger, yet swift to forgive too. I know I was in the wrong and, once again, I'm sorry.'

Jenny saw his contrition, his handsome appealing smile, and melted. She turned into his arms, her head resting on his chest. 'Oh, Marcos, I love you so much.'

He lifted her chin, kissed her and then said, 'And I love you too.'

Jenny was content. She'd get used to Marcos's temperament, one that might be passed on to their children. She wondered what they'd look like. Dark like Marcos or blonde like her? As he continued to hold her, Jenny felt that strange feeling again, a longing. Maybe it would happen tonight – maybe

their lovemaking would result in a baby. Jenny
felt a thrill of excitement. She couldn't wait to find
out.

Chapter Thirty-Two

Marcos awoke on Sunday morning and for a moment felt disorientated. He felt an arm snake around him, and as realisation crept into his foggy mind he smiled. This was no dream – this was real, his new life. Turning on his side, he said, 'Good morning, darling.'

Jenny's expression was dreamy as she snuggled closer. 'Marcos, wouldn't it be wonderful if I'm having a baby?'

'Yes, it certainly would,' he agreed, for a moment daring to hope it was possible, but then, as though she was in the room with them, hissing her venom in his ear, words his mother had once spoken curled insidiously into his brain. *You think yourself a man, but you are nothing. You can't even make babies, can't give me nipoti.* He cringed from the memory, and as Jenny spoke, his arms tightened around her.

'Marcos, what would you like for breakfast?'

'You, of course,' he said, determined to prove his mother wrong. With Jenny the miracle could happen, he could become a father, but one thing was certain, his mother would never know the joy of holding a grandchild in her arms.

'Oh, Marcos,' Jenny gasped when it was over and he was spent.

Unlike the others, Marcos knew Jenny wasn't pretending; she didn't have the wiles for that. She had climaxed this time and Marcos felt a surge of pure happiness. He'd been belittled so many times that he'd almost been made incapable, but then he'd found a way. He had paid for his pleasures elsewhere, and the toms hadn't dared to snigger.

'I need the bathroom,' Jenny said, unravelling the tangle of sheets to get out of bed.

'Me too, and coffee.'

'Give me a minute and then I'll set up the percolator.'

Marcos waited until the bathroom was free. After breakfast he'd drop Jenny off at her flat, and then make his way to Battersea. Though he had made a stupid promise to his father before he died, and guilt had made him keep that vow, he'd envisaged this confrontation so many times in his mind.

Now it was going to become a reality and Marcos was about to break the vow, to sever the ties that had bound him for so long. The leeches would be off his back, and if his old man came back to haunt him, so be it.

Jenny ran lightly downstairs. She loved the long silk robe she had on, one that Marcos had insisted on buying for her. It was pretty, rose pink, but of course Delia would have had a fit if she'd seen her downstairs in such a garment. Jenny sighed. For goodness' sake, what was the matter with her? She was married to Marcos, this was her home, and she was free to do as she pleased. In some ways the thought gave her courage. When they had been to dinner at her parents' house, her behaviour had been very far from that of an adult, and she had struggled under the pressure they'd put her under to change the wedding plans. Instead of speaking up for herself, she had appealed to Marcos and he had had to step in. It hadn't ended there – no, later she had let Delia get under her skin again and had childishly fled the table.

Why was she thinking about this now? Was it because they were home again and living just a short distance from her parents? Well, it wouldn't do, Jenny thought, getting on with the task in hand. Marcos would want his coffee shortly and he liked it strong, black and without sugar, something she had tried but found distasteful. From the kitchen window Jenny could see the huge rear garden. The lawn area was immaculate and a high wall ran alongside the wide flowerbeds, with the chrysanthemums and other late flowers still in bloom. It looked lovely, and she'd explore it later, maybe cut some flowers to brighten up the decor.

'That smells delicious,' Marcos said when a little later he appeared in the kitchen doorway, 'and you, darling, *look* delicious.'

Jenny sat down at the large kitchen table and poured two cups of coffee, adding milk and sugar to her own.

'What would you like for breakfast, Marcos?' she asked, turning pink at the memory of what had happened when she had posed the same question earlier.

'Jenny, you're blushing. I can guess why, but there's no need.'

Despite his words, Jenny lowered her eyes. Last night she had enjoyed making love, yet there had still been something missing, something just out of her reach. She had found out what it was that morning, had felt it rising within her until she lost control, screaming with delight at the wonderful sensations that ripped through her body.

'I . . . I didn't expect it to be so wonderful.'

'I'm glad you enjoyed it,' Marcos said, looking pleased and still standing as he picked up his cup of coffee. 'As for breakfast, I think I'll have a boiled egg. Bring it through to the dining room when it's ready.'

'Why don't we eat breakfast in here?'

'Jenny, this room is for preparing food, not eating it.'

'But my parents have breakfast in the kitchen.'

'That's their choice, but it isn't mine,' he said shortly, then walked out of the room.

Jenny sighed and rose to her feet. She knew that Marcos had high standards, something she would just have to get used to. She now hoped that she wouldn't ruin something as simple as a boiled egg.

Marcos was already feeling contrite as he waited for his breakfast. After such a wonderful start to the morning he'd been a bit short with Jenny, but this spacious house was the culmination of his dreams, a chance to live like a lord, and lords, he was sure, didn't eat in the kitchen.

The dining room was large and the long mahogany table perfect. He pictured it with every chair filled, he at the head of the table of course, magnanimous in entertaining his guests. Jenny would be the perfect hostess, gracious, and instead of feeling shame, he would be able to proudly show her off.

'I hope this is all right,' Jenny said as she carried in a tray. 'I know you hate it if the yolks are overcooked.'

'It seems our time in Scotland has revealed my little foibles. Don't look so worried, I'm sure it's fine, and it won't matter if it isn't. Where is yours?'

'I had a slice of bread and butter while waiting

for your egg to boil and now I want to get dressed. I know it's silly, but it doesn't seem right sitting down to eat in my dressing gown, especially in here.'

'So you just had a slice of bread and no doubt think I'm to blame for that.'

'No, Marcos,' Jenny said in surprise. 'It's just something I was brought up to. Delia never appeared downstairs before she was dressed and insisted that we follow her example.'

'I'm sorry, Jenny, I didn't mean to snap, it's just that I have rather a lot on my mind this morning,' Marcos said, hoping the excuse would serve. He had to stop this, refrain from expecting criticism where none was intended. 'Yes, get dressed, darling, and I must admit I admire your mother's standards. In fact I'll ring your parents shortly, invite them round this evening and we'll tell them then that we're married.'

'All right, but I dread to think how my father's going to take it.'

'How we chose to get married was our decision, not his.'

'Yes I know, but he's going to be unhappy,' Jenny said, kissing him on the cheek before going upstairs.

Marcos tucked into his egg, and though it was hard boiled, he ate it. What did it matter? Jenny would learn, and until she did he'd have to put up with it. However, that was all he would tolerate.

Jenny should concern herself with his feelings now, not those of her father, and once again Marcos was determined to find a way to put a spoke between them.

Chapter Thirty-Three

When Edward answered the telephone he straight-away recognised the voice as Marcos, who told him they'd returned from their holiday. He was puzzled by the invitation to the new house, asked a question and then accepted it, knowing full well that Delia would be thrilled at the prospect.

'That was Marcos,' Edward said, returning to the kitchen.

'They're back?'

'Yes.'

'Thank goodness for that. It's already the end of September and there's so much to do.'

'We've been invited round to Almond Crescent.'

'Really! When?'

'Today at six, but it's odd. I didn't know Marcos was living there. In fact I seem to remember him saying something about moving in after the wedding and honeymoon.'

'Perhaps he just wants to show it to us. Are they coming back here afterwards?'

'I don't know. I didn't think to ask.'

'Edward, I need time to talk to Jennifer about the arrangements I've made. I need her input on the flowers among other things.'

'You can talk to her at the house.'

'It'll be empty, probably cold, and I doubt we'll be there for long.'

'Then I'm sure they'll be happy to come here. I just hope you haven't jumped the gun and that Jenny appreciates all the arrangements you've put in place.'

'I'll have to change. You never know, we might bump into Penelope Grainger. When I last saw her at the WI, I told her that our daughter was going to be a neighbour of hers.'

Going along with it, Edward said, 'I suppose that means you'll want me to wear a suit.'

'Well, of course.'

He sighed. Yes, Delia was a snob, out to impress, but nowadays it was her only fault . . . and hopefully Jenny would soon see that.

As Marcos drove Jenny to Chelsea, a thought crossed his mind.

'Jenny, I'm sorry we haven't had a honeymoon. I'm too busy now, but maybe later.'

'We had three lovely weeks in Scotland.'

'Yes, but I've never heard of a honeymoon before the wedding.'

'Or one in separate rooms,' Jenny said, smiling now. 'It really doesn't matter though. I've got lots to do in the house, and perhaps next summer we can have another lovely holiday.'

'Yes, we'll do that and I'll make it even more special.'

'I think the one we just had will take some beating.'

'What about glorious sunshine, blue sea, palm trees?'

'That sounds wonderful, but wherever we go, our first holiday together, culminating in our marriage, will be one I'll never forget.'

'Nor me, darling, but here we are. I'll pick you up again in a couple of hours.'

Jenny leaned over to kiss his cheek. 'Don't get out, there's no need. I'll see you later.'

Marcos made the kiss a proper one, and when Jenny had gone inside he drove off. It wouldn't take too long to get to Battersea, and now he grinned. This was it.

The Sunday morning traffic was light and soon Marcos was pulling up outside the house. The two-faced bitches were both staunch Catholics, but he was there well before they went to the Sunday service. There was only one of them there to greet him and he asked abruptly, 'Where is she?'

'Uppa stairs, making my bed.'

'Upstairs, you old hag. Not uppa.'

'You should not speaka to me like that.'

'Yeah, she's right,' a voice drawled.

Marcos spun round and seeing the cigarette dangling from the corner of her mouth, he spat, 'Keep out of this or else. It's got nothing to do with you.'

'It's me who looks after her, and let me tell you she won't be able to make it upstairs soon. It's just as well you're back 'cos you'll need to turn the front room into a bedroom.'

'I'm not staying. I'm moving out. Permanently.'

'You can't do that!'

'Don't pretend you care, especially as you'll still be taken care of.'

'All right then, I don't give a shit,' she said, actually having the nerve to smile, but then a calculating gleam sparked. 'What about her? I ain't being lumbered. It's your job to look after her, not mine.'

Marcos wasn't fooled. He knew how close they were, in fact almost joined at the hip. They weren't twin sisters, far from it, but acted like ones and he knew this was just greed, a way to up the ante. He felt like laying into her, wiping that smug smile from her face, and his fists clenched.

As though aware of his feelings, she said, 'If you're thinking about giving me a smack, go ahead. After all these years I'm immune to it.'

'In that case I won't waste my energy,' Marcos

said, nonchalantly sitting down. 'And as for her, she stays with you, but don't worry, I'll make it worth your while.'

'You'll have to.'

'I don't *have* to do anything. In fact I could just get rid of the pair of you. Yes, why not? It would save me a packet,' he mused, loving the fear he saw on both their faces now. 'However, as long as you just take my money and keep your mouth shut, I'll leave you in peace. Now this is the way it's going to be from now on . . .'

Her expression when he'd finished was a picture. There was still fear, but mixed with greed too as she said, 'Yeah, yeah, don't worry. I'll go along with that.'

'What about you?' he asked turning cold eyes to the other one.

'I will say nothing. Go! Just go! You are dead to me.'

'Listen to yourself, after all these years you still sound like a wop. As for being dead to you, good, that's just how I want it. Just make sure I remain that way or the pair of you will end up in a coffin.'

With that final warning he left, slamming the door behind him. It was done.

Jenny had finished sorting her things out, and after carrying her cases downstairs she knocked on Sue's door.

'Jenny, come in. Goodness, you look wonderful.'

'Thanks. It's one of the new suits that Marcos brought me,' Jenny said, placing her cases on the floor.

'One of them?' Sue echoed, her brows rising. 'It must have cost a fortune.'

'Yes, I'm afraid it did, and . . . and while on holiday, we were married.'

'What! But I thought you said December?'

'I did, but we brought it forward.'

'You're not . . . well . . . you know, pregnant?'

'No, of course not!'

'Oops, sorry. I just wondered if that's why you brought the date forward.'

'It's nothing like that. We went to Scotland on holiday, and just thought, why wait?'

'I suppose you're moving out then?' Sue said, eyeing the cases.

'Yes, but the landlord isn't around. I wrote a note and put it through his letterbox, along with the keys. It should be all right. It's the end of the month and the rent was paid up to today. I know I haven't given any notice but my deposit should cover that.'

'I'm going to miss having you around, but congratulations, Jenny.'

'Thanks, but as Marcos isn't back yet, do you mind if I hang around for a while?'

'Not at all. I'll make us something to drink.'

Jenny settled on the sofa. She was leaving Chelsea, and that thought prompted a swift succession of memories of her arrival here with Tina. It had been fine at first, but somewhere along the line things had gone wrong between them. No, it wasn't something, it was someone – Marcos. Tina hadn't liked him from the start, but surely that couldn't justify what she had done? She had used their friendship, the knowledge that her father had a little money, to virtually blackmail him. Had Tina felt abandoned, was that it? Had Tina felt that Marcos had become more important to her than their friendship?

'It's only orange squash I'm afraid,' Sue said, holding out a tumbler.

'Thanks. I was just thinking about Tina. If I hadn't met Marcos, things might have been different.'

'But you did, and had the situation been reversed, if Tina had met someone, would you have acted in the same way?'

'No, I'd have been happy for Tina . . . But I feel now that I abandoned her.'

'You met Marcos, fell in love, and you have no reason to reproach yourself for that. You and Tina were different, not just in looks, but your personalities too, with little in common.'

'But to start with, we were like sisters.'

'I think that's because you needed each other at first. Though some friendships last, even grow, there are others that don't and we go our separate ways.'

Jenny found that despite everything she missed Tina – missed that brief feeling of kinship they'd shared. However, she said only, 'I suppose you're right.'

A car pulled up outside and, seeing it was Marcos, Jenny picked up her suitcases, said goodbye to Sue, while all the time wondering if she'd ever see Tina again.

On the drive home Jenny's mind turned to that evening and how her father was going to react to the news. She was looking forward to seeing him, but hoped he wouldn't be too upset. When her thoughts turned to Delia, however, Jenny's lips tightened. She wouldn't allow Delia to get under her skin this time. Things would be different, she would be in her own home, and Jenny was determined to assert herself.

Just a short while ago, as though their thoughts were in accord, Tina had been thinking about Jenny as she walked along the seafront. Others would expect her to feel guilty about what she'd done, Tina knew that, but she didn't feel a shred of guilt. Unlike her, Jenny hadn't really needed to leave home. She might not have got on with her mother, but it had been obvious that Edward Lavender was a normal caring father; so much so that he had opened his wallet wide to find out where his daughter was. In fact, Tina decided, Jenny should thank her for bringing about their reunion.

The sky was overcast, the call of the gulls a lament that emphasised how Tina was feeling. She had arrived well into the season and had loved Brighton at first, finding that staying in a hotel not far from the beach was like the holiday she'd never had. Tina reached her destination now and crossed the road to walk up to an ice cream stand. The woman in the booth smiled when she saw her, asking, 'Well, have you thought it over?'

'Yeah, but the summer season is over. If I take it on now I'd have nothing to show for my money until next year.'

'You'd be mad to turn it down. It's fully licensed and you won't get an offer like this again.'

The wind cut round the corner and Tina shivered. When she'd first seen the stand it had been busy, trade brisk, and she'd rather fancied the idea of selling ice creams. There had been people parading the front, all mostly jolly and some wearing silly hats, but now there were few left to be seen.

'No, sorry, it ain't for me.'

'Please yourself,' the woman said huffily.

Tina walked away, shoulders slumped. The seaside was nice in the summer, the holiday-makers friendly. There had been so many families too, happy ones, fathers playing with their kids, mothers smiling; normal family life, something she had never known. She'd felt lonely and apart from it all, and she hated what her father had done to her, what he'd turned her into. She wasn't fit for anyone now, not fit to be a mother.

Pebbles crunched underfoot and, startled, Tina realised she had been so deep in thought that she'd unintentionally strolled onto the beach. At last, staring at the waves, she came to a decision. She couldn't live like this any more, couldn't live with herself any more and wanted to reach out for help. Yet who could she turn to? There had only been Jenny, but as Tina knew she had destroyed their friendship, she couldn't go to her. Sue? No, Sue wouldn't understand. What she needed, Tina decided, was to talk to someone who wouldn't be shocked, who had heard something similar, maybe even worse.

Tina sighed and finally admitted where her thoughts were taking her. Paul Ryman, the only man she had ever felt safe with, the man she hadn't been able to forget.

Dare she go back? Now that Jenny had been reunited with her family, she had probably gone home, but that still left Marcos. Jenny was sure to have told him about the scam, and Tina didn't know what caused it, some sort of sixth sense perhaps, but the thought of bumping into him made her shiver with fear . . . Wait, as long as she kept away from the King's Road she'd be safe.

Now, with a new determination, Tina hurried back to the hotel. She was ready to pack.

Chapter Thirty-Four

When Marcos had picked Jenny back up from Chelsea, he had been in a very good mood and was feeling magnanimous. He'd pulled into a Berni Inn close to home and, though it wasn't exactly fine cuisine, they'd been served a decent enough Sunday roast. Jenny had been pleased, explaining that she'd been nervous about cooking a roast, and Marcos was happy to bask in her gratitude. She'd learn to cook soon enough, and in the meantime Marcos was feeling well satisfied with life. Things had gone well in Battersea and after all these years he'd finally got the hags off his back. It had been worth every penny, and he didn't feel guilty. He had at last shrugged off his promise to a dying man and now wished he'd done it years ago.

Jenny's parents would be here soon, Marcos thought as he walked into the drawing room. She'd been busy, one vase of chrysanthemums on the sideboard, and he'd already seen another one on the dining room table. He'd left the gates open, but it wasn't something he wanted to make a habit of. New ones were on order, the latest on offer, electric with an entry-phone system to ensure that nobody could gain access without permission. He glanced out of the window and saw a car pulling up behind his on the drive.

'Jenny, they're here,' he said, putting a proprietary arm around her waist. 'Let's let them in together.'

'Yes, all right,' she agreed, though she looked a little apprehensive.

Marcos had to hide a smile when he opened the door. Delia was dressed to the nines in a brown and white dress, wearing a matching hat with a wide brim as though she had come to some sort of formal reception.

'Edward, Delia, do come in.'

'Hello, you two,' Edward said, hugging Jenny and then Delia following suit.

'My goodness, this is lovely,' Delia enthused as her eyes swept the hall before coming to rest on the large crystal chandelier.

'Come on through to the drawing room,' Marcos invited.

'I'll make some tea.'

'All right, darling, and while you're doing that I'll show your parents around.'

Delia looked puzzled, Edward too, and he was the first to speak as they walked into the room. 'We expected the house to be empty.'

'No, I've furnished it. My study is next door and

there's another reception room on the other side of the hall, along with the dining room. Come, I'll show you.'

'It's all delightful,' Delia murmured as they wandered from room to room until they were back where they started.

'Please, sit down,' Marcos invited. 'I'll show you upstairs later, but here's Jenny with the tea.'

It was Delia who at last posed the question. 'Marcos, have you moved in?'

'Yes, we both have,' he said as Jenny placed a tray on a side table.

'What!' Edward exploded. 'But you aren't married yet.'

'Oh no, what will people think?' Delia gasped. 'Jennifer, you can't do this.'

'It's all right, Jenny, leave this to me,' Marcos said. 'Delia, Edward, there's no need for concern. Yes, we've moved in, but as a married couple. We moved the date forward.'

'But why?' Delia asked. 'Oh, Jennifer, you're not . . .'

'Pregnant,' Jenny finished for her. 'No, but you're the second person to jump to that conclusion.'

'Then why?' The question this time was from Edward.

'Dad, we were on holiday in Scotland, and . . . and as we were already there, we thought why wait until December.'

'Well, I can't say I'm happy about it, but it's done now and I suppose all that remains is to congratulate you both,' Edward said, face straight as he shook Marcos's hand. 'Congratulations and welcome to the family.'

'But Edward, I've booked the Grand Hotel for the reception, and the church.'

'Well, Delia, I did warn you not to jump the gun and now you'll just have to cancel them,' he said, moving to kiss Jenny on the cheek. 'Congratulations, darling. I suppose this calls for a toast.'

'Yes, your father's right,' agreed Marcos. 'Leave the tea, Jenny. I'll open a bottle of champagne.'

'That's more like it,' Edward said.

Once the champagne was poured and Jenny and Marcos were toasted, the atmosphere became lighter.

'There are some very influential people in this crescent, Marcos,' said Delia. 'I think they could perhaps be useful to you. In fact you're actually living next door to an acquaintance of mine, Penelope Grainger. If you'd like to celebrate your marriage in some way, perhaps with a small reception held here, I could invite Penelope and that might lead to other introductions.'

'I'm afraid I'm far too busy at the moment.'

'Oh, you need not concern yourself with the arrangements. You can leave all that to me.'

'If we wanted to hold a reception in our home, then I would arrange it,' Jenny said defensively. 'But for now it's out of the question. I want to finish the house, choose soft furnishings among other things.'

As though unaware of Jenny's chilly manner, Delia said, 'A delay wouldn't matter, in fact it could be perfect. Your Aunt Beatrice and her husband are coming back to England in November and I could invite them too. My sister is married to a diplomat, Marcos, and they too are very well connected.'

'I hardly know them,' Jenny said.

'We rarely saw them when you were growing up, but they're family and I'm sure you'll agree it will be lovely to see them.'

'They're *your* family, not mine.'

Marcos was pleased to see that Jenny was clearly still at odds with Delia, but he was looking for the same thing with her father too. He sat back, biding his time and hoping that an opportunity might arise.

'Jennifer, please, don't say that,' Delia appealed. 'I hurt you, and I really am sorry, but can't we make a fresh start? We could do things together, such as shopping, and I could help you to choose your drapes.'

'I'm perfectly capable of choosing them myself.'

'I didn't mean to imply that you couldn't. Oh ... oh dear, I feel like I'm walking on eggshells again.' And with that, tears filled her eyes.

'Delia, don't get upset,' Edward said worriedly, then turned to Jenny. 'Can't you see she's trying? Can't you at least give your mother a chance?'

'She *isn't* my mother,' Jenny snapped, and ran from the room.

'Delia, give her time. She just needs time,' Edward consoled.

Marcos saw the opportunity and seized it. 'Yes, he's right. Jenny needs time, but I fear you're pushing her again.'

'But . . . but I only suggested shopping.'

'I'm afraid that Jenny sees any suggestions you make as interference. In fact, I hate to tell you this, but when Jenny saw this house she was horrified and didn't want us to live here.'

'But why? It's a lovely house.'

'She didn't want to be this close to you.'

As Delia gasped, Edward threw an arm around her, and Marcos saw a flash of anger in the older man's eyes as he looked up at him.

'My wife is upset enough. Did you have to tell her that?'

'I'm sorry, but my concerns are for Jenny and what she's been through. I persuaded her to move in here, but now I'm starting to regret it. From what I've just seen it's obvious she isn't ready for a mother-daughter relationship – especially because, from what she's told me, they never had one in the past.'

'Now that's enough!'

'It's all right, Edward, and anyway, Marcos is right,' Delia said, dabbing her eyes. 'I just don't know what to do, how to build bridges.'

'May I make a few suggestions?' said Marcos.

'Yes, please do,' she said.

'Firstly, as your husband says, give Jenny time, take things very slowly. Now that you've found her again, I know you both want to see more of her, but remember it wasn't Jenny who came to you. She was happily living an independent life, and if you force yourself on her, or if she feels that you're interfering in any of her decisions, she'll just back away.'

'So what you're saying,' Edward said, his voice still tinged with anger, 'is that we should wait until Jenny comes to us?'

'I'm afraid so. Of course I'll do all I can to help,' Marcos lied. 'With no family of my own now I really appreciate that you've welcomed me into yours. But if you'll excuse me for a moment, I must see if Jenny is all right.'

Marcos left them, hoping he had said enough to ensure that Jenny's parents now kept their distance. He didn't want their interference and if it hadn't worked there were other options. Extreme ones, yes – but it would take them out of the picture.

Jenny was annoyed that she had let Delia get under her skin again. Instead of appearing poised and in control, she had reacted like a child. Delia hadn't changed, she was still devious, a consummate actress, and just as she'd done in the past, Jenny realised she'd played into her hands. Delia now appeared like the wronged one, the one who needed sympathy and, as she suspected, her father was falling for it, just as Robin had.

She gripped the kitchen sink, feeling powerless, and now regretted the day her father had found her. She'd been told that Delia wanted to make amends, but Jenny began to wonder what her real motives were. Delia had wanted rid of her, had planned and schemed to drive her out, so why pretend now that she wanted reconciliation?

Unable to work it out, Jenny felt arms wrap around her waist and then Marcos kissed the back of her neck.

'Are you all right, darling?'

Ashamed of her behaviour, Jenny turned into his arms. 'I'm sorry, Marcos. I ran from the room like a child.'

'It doesn't matter.'

'But it does. I was so on the defensive that I put myself in a bad light, upset her, and you saw how my father responded.'

'Yes, and I'm sorry, but I'm afraid it annoyed me. He knows what you've been through, but when I jumped to your defence and told Delia a few home truths he was angry with me for upsetting her again.'

Jenny found herself fuming on Marcos's behalf. Her father was obviously blind when it came to Delia and so he had turned on Marcos, but she wasn't going to stand for that. She had run away, leaving Marcos to speak up for her, but she didn't intend to put him in that position again. 'I'm going to tell them to leave.'

'Darling, there's no need for that. We've sorted it out and everything is fine now. Delia won't interfere again, and they both know that any invitation to see them again must come from you.'

'After this they'll be few and far between – if ever. I'm happier when it's just you and me,' Jenny said, clinging to Marcos, sure it was true. Her father and Delia had been out of her life for so long, and seeing them again had served only to dredge up bad memories, ones it seemed her father now expected her to simply forget.

'Are you feeling better now?' Marcos asked.

'Yes, thank you. Let's go back to the drawing room,' Jenny said, feeling stronger and more determined than ever to tell her parents to leave.

Edward stared at his daughter. She looked so cold, her voice icy as she told them to leave.

'Jenny, please, there's no need for this.'

'I think there is.'

Marcos put an arm around her waist. 'Jenny is still upset and it might be for the best.'

'But we've barely been here an hour.'

Delia came to his side. 'Come on, Marcos is right, Edward. We should leave.'

'So this was your idea, not Jenny's,' Edward snapped, eyes glaring hard at Marcos.

'No, it was mine,' Jenny snapped. 'And don't speak to my husband like that!'

'It's all right, darling,' Marcos cajoled. 'It doesn't matter and I think we should all calm down.'

'It matters to me.'

'All right, Jenny, I'm sorry,' Edward ground out.

'Why don't we all sit down?' Marcos suggested.

'No, I want them to go.'

Marcos sighed, his tone mellow. 'I'm sorry, but you heard Jenny and so I'm afraid I must join her in asking you to leave.'

'Jennifer, I truly am sorry that I upset you,' Delia said. 'We'll go now, so goodbye, my dear. I hope we'll see you again soon.'

'Don't hold your breath,' Jenny said derisively.

Edward couldn't believe that this was his daughter. He understood that Jenny had been hurt, that he and Delia had a lot to make up for, but they weren't being given a chance. Delia was trying so hard, but she was being met with only belligerence. 'Come on, let's go,' he said. 'Goodbye, Jenny.'

His daughter said nothing and it was Marcos who escorted them to the door. Delia said goodbye to him, but Edward's mind was still reeling.

'I'm sorry, Edward,' Delia said as they got into the car. 'I did my best.'

'I know you did.'

'Marcos was right. Jennifer isn't ready to forgive me yet, and . . . and I fear she never will.'

'I still don't like the way he spoke to you.'

'It doesn't matter.'

'It does to me, and if you ask me there was something fishy going on.'

'What do you mean?'

'When Jenny came back into the room she was so angry, and her anger was aimed at me. Marcos must have said something to her, something that caused it.'

'He wants to help us so I doubt that. You were rather short with him and as we don't know where Jenny went it may be that she overheard you.'

Edward pulled into the drive. Yes, that made sense and he'd give Marcos the benefit of the doubt.

'We'll have to trust the man to talk Jenny round, and in the meantime we'll just have to be patient.'

'Do you think they'll hold a reception?'

'Delia, I think that's the last thing we have to worry about.'

'I wanted Beatrice and her husband to meet Penelope Grainger.'

Edward sighed with impatience. 'I hardly think that matters.'

'Maybe not to you, but it does to me.'

'Is getting in with that crowd more important than establishing a relationship with Jenny?'

'No, of course not.'

'Well, I'm glad to hear it, because it didn't sound like that to me,' Edward said, getting out of the car. He was finding that his feelings were all over the place – one minute he was sympathising with Delia, the next with his daughter.

'I'm sorry, Edward, I know I can be shallow,' Delia said as she too got out of the car. 'I spoke without thinking.'

'We're both a bit fraught. I don't know about you, but I could do with a brandy.'

'Yes, me too,' she said, watery-eyed now.

'It may take a little longer than I expected, but Jenny will come round,' he said, hoping he was right and that he really could trust Marcos. A niggle of doubt arose, but Edward pushed it away. The man loved his daughter and, like him, he would only want her happiness, one that he must know included Jenny being part of her family again.

Delia was still going over what had happened as she lay in bed that night. At first she'd mistakenly thought that Jennifer and Marcos were living together, but then this had been followed by the news that they were married. They had brought the date forward and was it any wonder that she had jumped to the wrong conclusion? No, of course not, and Edward would understand that.

She had shown Edward that she was trying to build bridges, had been perfectly nice to Jennifer, and it wasn't her fault that the girl had been impossible. No, she had nothing to worry about; Edward was on her side, she was sure.

'Can't you sleep?' he asked.

'No, I can't stop thinking about Jennifer.'

'I'm the same. She was fine with me before this, but she's been against seeing you again from the start. It was obvious that nothing has changed and now I'm in her bad books too.'

'You can't blame me for that,' Delia protested.

'She still harbours bad feelings towards you and I realise now that her back was up from the start. When Marcos persuades her to see us again you'll need to make more of an effort, and for goodness' sake, watch what you say,' he said, rolling over so that his back was turned towards her. 'Now let's get some sleep.'

Delia was left stunned. These days she always fell asleep with Edward's arms around her. They had been so close, so happy until he'd found Jennifer again. The girl wasn't living at home any more, but seemingly that made no difference – as always, Edward cared more about his relationship with his daughter than he did about her.

'That isn't fair,' she said, choking back tears.

'I'm sorry,' he said, turning round again. 'I know you did your best and I can't blame you for what happened.'

'You're upset, we both are,' Delia said.

Edward kissed her, but it wasn't one of passion and, placing an arm around her, he closed his eyes. Delia closed hers too, but sleep still wouldn't come. Maybe it would be all right after all, she finally decided, and even if Marcos persuaded Jennifer to see them again, it wouldn't be a daily occurrence, just an occasional one. There was still the compensation that Jennifer was living in Almond Crescent and, if they did have a reception, one to which Penelope Grainger was invited, it could lead to what Delia had coveted for ages – a way into Penelope's social circle.

At last Delia drifted off to sleep . . . and now she had a small smile on her face.

Chapter Thirty-Five

It was Monday morning and Tina was back in London. She was in Pimlico, staying in a hotel in Ebury Street, far enough away from the King's Road to feel safe for now.

She had plenty of money left, but it wouldn't last for ever and a part of her regretted turning down the ice cream stand. It would've been nice to be her own boss and opportunities like that didn't come up every day. There'd be nothing to match it in London – well, perhaps a market stall, and the more Tina thought about it, the more appealing it sounded. She could sell just about anything from a market stall, but her first choice would be costume jewellery. Yes, stuff that was different, striking, and sure to attract trendy young punters. First things first though, Tina thought. She had to sort herself out before anything else, and so she now put the finishing touches to her make-up.

With no idea where Paul Ryman lived, she'd decided that the only way to find him would be to ask for him at the police station. Though nervous, Tina left the hotel and headed for Sloane Square. She'd tried to kid herself that she only wanted to see Paul to ask for help, but there was more to it than that. Unless she straightened herself out, however, she wasn't fit for a relationship with anyone.

Tina quickened her pace, keeping her fingers crossed that he'd be on duty, but it was a long walk before she reached Draycott Avenue. She entered the station and hesitantly approached the desk. At first the policeman on duty kept his head down, busy with some kind of paperwork, but at last he looked up.

'Yes, can I help you?'

'Could you tell me if Constable Paul Ryman is on duty?'

'What's this in connection with?'

'Er . . . er, it's a personal matter.'

The policeman went to a door behind him, opened it and called, 'Charlie, have you seen Paul Ryman? Is he around?'

'Search me. He's with CID now, joined them this morning. You could try there.'

Tina's ears pricked. So Paul was in plain clothes now, but was he still based in this station?

The man came back to the desk. 'I expect you heard that. Take a seat and I'll ring upstairs.'

Looking behind her, Tina saw a short row of shoddy-looking chairs and sat down. There were two other people waiting, both men; the younger looked at her with interest. Get lost, Tina thought, as the stale stench of sweat and booze from the other one cloyed her nostrils.

She kept her eyes ahead, fixed on the desk, listening to the one-sided conversation as the telephone was answered.

'I've got someone down here to see Paul Ryman,' the copper said. He paused, presumably waiting until another person came to the phone. 'Hello, yes, that's right. No, she said it's personal. Hold on a sec.'

He held the telephone away from his ear and Tina was beckoned forward. 'What's your name, miss?'

She told him, watching as he passed it on, and then he replaced the receiver. 'He's on his way down.'

Now that the moment had arrived, Tina suddenly had doubts. She couldn't talk to Paul here, there was no privacy, what with the desk sergeant and the pair of geezers watching. Thankfully another woman came into the station just then, walking up to the desk and causing a bit of distraction.

A voice spoke from behind her. 'Tina.'

She spun round. 'Hello, Paul.'

'What are you doing here?'

'I . . . I came to see you.'

'Why?' Paul asked, face straight.

'Is there somewhere we can talk in private?'

'Are you in some sort of trouble?'

'No . . . yes . . .'

He opened a door. 'We can talk in here, but make it quick. This is my first day with CID and a personal visit isn't making a good impression.'

Her heart sank as she walked ahead of him. He seemed so cold, as cold and impersonal as this small room.

'I'm sorry, I shouldn't have come.'

'Why did you bugger off without a word?'

'I . . . I was all mixed up and I wanted to get away, to make a fresh start, but . . .'

Paul interrupted, 'Get away from what, Tina? Me?'

'No . . . yes . . . ' she stammered. She had only told one other person, shame keeping her silent, but now she had to tell him, had to get help. The words caught in her throat but somehow she forced them out. 'It . . . it was because of my father, and what he did to me.'

'And what was that?' Paul asked, but his voice was softer.

'He . . . he interfered with me, you . . . you know, touched me.'

'You should have told me that he'd found you instead of running off. I'd have nailed the bastard,' Paul said venomously.

'He didn't find me,' Tina said, fumbling for words. 'I left because I was frightened of my feelings for you, how you made me feel.'

'Tina, you're not making any sense.'

'I . . . I wanted you to . . . to touch me . . . but it's disgusting.'

'No, Tina, it isn't.'

'I want to believe that, but . . . but I need help.'

'We'll sort something out and I'm glad you came back, Tina. I went looking for you, but your flat-mate told me her father had given you money to make a new start. I was angry that you'd left without a word, and felt sure that she had your address, but she wouldn't pass it on to me.'

Tina had to think quickly. 'I asked Jenny not to tell anyone where I was going.'

'Look, I've got to get back upstairs, but don't disappear on me again. We'll talk later, but for now where are you staying?'

She gave him the address of the hotel in Pimlico and they arranged to meet that evening. Paul then hurried off and Tina left the station feeling much lighter. He was going to help her, and if it worked, maybe, just maybe, they could have some sort of future together.

In Wimbledon Jenny had been looking at swatches of material. Marcos had told her there was no need to trawl the shops, that he'd arranged for someone to call, and the woman had just left. Jenny had settled on rich, antique gold silk brocade with pelmets to match. They were not the most expensive in the range, about midway, and she hoped

Marcos would approve of her choice. He was so generous, not only with the housekeeping allowance, but he'd also insisted on putting money in her bank account too. After having looked after her own finances it felt a bit strange, but Marcos had told her not to be silly. She was his wife now, he'd insisted and therefore he'd see that she wanted for nothing.

Edna Moon appeared in the doorway, a cheery smile on her face. 'I'll be off soon, but do you fancy a cup of tea before I go, Mrs Cane?'

'Yes, lovely, Edna, but I've told you earlier, you can call me Jenny.'

'I know you have, but I don't think Mr Cane would like that.'

'Marcos won't mind.'

'I think I should stick to his instructions.'

'When we came home on Saturday, I had the impression that you already knew Marcos before coming to work here.'

'Yeah, well, my Tommy works for him.'

'Really, goodness. In what capacity?'

'He . . . er . . . works in one of the garages.'

'Has he been there long?'

'Oh yeah, he and Marc . . . Mr Cane go back years,' she said, but then her eyes widened as though in fear. 'Oh Gawd, I shouldn't be telling you all this. Mr Cane will think I've been gossiping. Don't tell him! Please don't tell him!'

'Edna, what's wrong? You sound frightened, but why?

'No, no, I ain't frightened, it's not that,' Edna said quickly. 'It's just that I've lost jobs in the past because I spent too much time chatting and I don't want to lose this one.'

'Well, if that's all that's worrying you, I won't say a word to Marcos, and as he won't be here during the day, there's nothing to stop us having a little chat now and then.'

'Thanks, Mrs Cane,' said Edna, looking relieved and bustling off.

Jenny was left feeling puzzled. Edna's explanation made sense, but there was something underlying it . . . something akin to fear. Yet surely Edna had no need to fear Marcos? No, of course not, Jenny decided. Yet just below the surface of her mind, she was left with doubts.

It was nearly eight in the evening before Marcos arrived home. The legit stuff had all run smoothly in his absence, his choices of managers good ones. On the other side of things, Bernie had done well. The boys had brought cars in and they'd been turned round quickly before being sent out with new papers.

Bernie had made good money and the boys paid, but with so much high expenditure lately, Marcos felt his cash was running low. Yes, he had good money coming in from both sides, but he had a lot more expenses now and could do with replenishing his coffers in one big hit.

Still, time enough to think about that later, and for now Marcos just savoured the pleasure of turning into his own drive and seeing his house at the end of it. Yes, it was fit for a lord, Marcos thought as he got out of the car, and he had a lady waiting for him. There'd be no moaning, no hands held out, just Jenny's soft, relaxing voice.

'Hello, darling,' he said when she ran into the hall to greet him.

'I've missed you,' Jenny replied as her arms wrapped around him.

He sniffed the air. 'It's faint, but something smells good.'

'I've made a spaghetti sauce and just have to cook the pasta.'

'Nice,' he said, kissing her. 'While you do that, I'll get changed.'

Jenny smiled happily and headed back to the kitchen while Marcos went upstairs to their bedroom. This was the life, coming home to a beautiful woman, one who welcomed him, not only his homecoming, but in bed too.

In no time he was sitting in the dining room and Jenny was nervously dishing up the meal. 'I hope it's all right. I caught a bus to the local shops, but I'm afraid I couldn't get any garlic bread.'

'A bus,' Marcos said, frowning. 'Jenny, I must get you a car.'

'There's no need – I can't drive.'

'Then I'll arrange lessons.'

'Oh, Marcos, thank you.'

'I've been remiss and should have thought of it before this.'

'We've only just married and moved here, yet already you're going to arrange driving lessons for me. That's far from remiss.'

'Nevertheless, I'll get onto it in the morning.'

'I chose the material for our curtains today, antique gold. I hope you like them and that I didn't spend too much.'

Marcos smiled. Jenny was perfect, just perfect, completely ungrasping. Now all he wanted was to get her pregnant, to prove his mother wrong. He was a man, nobody crossed him, and already Jenny's father was finding that out.

Chapter Thirty-Six

In November, Tina made the final breakthrough. Thanks to Paul she was seeing the woman twice a week, but at first she'd been reluctant to talk. However, towards the end of her third session and just before her time was up, Tina had suddenly found herself spewing it all out. There had been so much locked inside, not just hatred for her father, but for her mother too, a woman who had stood back and allowed it to happen, instead of protecting her. A woman who had never shown Tina an ounce of genuine affection from the day she was born.

There was something else tucked safely in another compartment of Tina's mind, something she hadn't wanted to face, or admit, her guilt making it unsayable. Today the woman had opened that door and now Tina was crying as if her heart would break. It wasn't just her parents. She hated herself too and for so, so long, had been disgusted that there'd been occasions when she'd almost enjoyed the touch of her father's hands. It sickened her, filled her with self-loathing.

'How could I? It's disgusting.'

'Tina, you craved love, affection, and it would have been a natural response, your body simply reacting to stimulus. It's a response that men like your father use to justify what they do.'

'He's made me as bad as him, as sick as him.'

'No, Tina, far from it. Your father took your need for affection and abused it in the worst possible way.'

'I . . . I'm going out with a bloke now, but if he tries to hold me I back off. I'm frightened of getting those feelings again. It would be wrong . . . bad.'

'No, Tina, it would be perfectly natural. You see . . .'

Tina listened as the woman continued to speak, and it was as though a huge weight lifted from her. Until Paul came along she had thought she hated all men, had wanted to punish them by fiddling their change, blowing their money on clothes and luxuries. She now realised that in truth she had been punishing them for her own feelings too, for what her father had once aroused in her, for the poison of self-loathing that had crept into her mind. In betraying Jenny, had she unconsciously been punishing her too? Had she hated it that her friend had found happiness while she was still floundering in a pit of putrid self-loathing?

'I'm afraid our session is over now, Tina, but we've made tremendous progress. So much so that you may feel you won't need to see me again. Give yourself a day or two. See how you feel, and if necessary we can make another appointment.'

Tina felt drained as she rose to her feet, guessing she must look a mess. She had cried so much that her eyes probably looked dreadful and her make-up ruined, yet somehow it didn't matter.

'Yes, all right and . . . and thank you.'

It was cold outside, but Tina hardly noticed. She still had things on her mind, and had been tempted to confess the awful things she'd done since she got away from her father, but was now relieved that the session was over before she'd had the chance. It wouldn't change anything. What was done was done, but she would never do such things again. She felt free, liberated, as if the canker in her mind that had driven her had been cut out.

'Hey, gorgeous, do you want a lift?'

'Paul! What are you doing here?'

'I knew you'd be coming out around now and as I'm finished for the day we can go home.'

'But it's only four o'clock.'

'With all the hours I've put in lately I think my DI decided to cut me a bit of slack.'

She got into his car, smiling at him, but in return he frowned. 'Tina, you've been crying. Are you all right?'

'I'm fine, in fact more than fine. That may have been my last session.'

'That's terrific, though I still wish we could prove what your father did to you. I'd like to nail the sick pervert.'

'I know, but I just want to forget him now, to put it all behind me,' Tina said as they drove off. She meant it. How she felt now was thanks to Paul; in fact she had a lot to thank him for, not least the flat she now lived in, above his in Battersea that had somehow miraculously become available two weeks after she'd moved back to London. Paul said he'd had nothing to do with the previous tenant moving out but, as the man was a friend of his, Tina somehow doubted that.

'I'm bushed, and sick of living on sandwiches. We thought our inside man had a sniff of something, but after weeks of watching and waiting it came to nothing. We've got enough to do the bloke for stolen cars, stuff like that, but the DI wants him to go down for more than that, and for a lot longer.'

'What bloke?'

'Now, you know better than to ask me that. Sod it, forget work. How do you fancy going out for dinner tonight?' Paul asked, as usual taking nothing for granted.

Tina wasn't surprised that Paul was tired. He worked long hours, sometimes long into the night and it wasn't always possible to see much of each other. Yet when they did he never took liberties and she was growing ever more fond of him.

'How about staying in and I invite you up to my place for a meal?'

'What? Blimey, Tina, that's a first.'

'I know – but it doesn't mean it's a first time for anything else.'

'If you're saying what I think you are, you should know me better than that.'

'Yes, I do. Sorry,' Tina said. Yet maybe, just maybe, she thought, she was ready to take that next step. Paul was so hesitant around her, so frightened of scaring her off, but tonight she would try to let him hold her, kiss her. She had to move forward, to stop allowing what had happened in the past to ruin the rest of her life. With Paul, she was beginning to feel she could do just that.

On Saturday evening Marcos was sitting in the drawing room. A fire was glowing, the curtains drawn against the night, and he was admiring what Jenny had done with the room. He had of course given her free rein, and she hadn't disappointed him, the cushions toning perfectly, and tasteful ornaments strategically placed. None of those statues of the Madonna, crucifixes, lace tablecloths, and the other sickening paraphernalia that the hags had favoured.

Jenny had class, taste, and Marcos was pleasantly surprised that she was still refusing to see her parents. There'd been one big mistake with the telephone – they weren't ex-directory and so

Jenny's father had been able to find their number. Marcos had been furious and the bloke he'd instructed to sort out everything to do with the telephone line and utilities paid for his slip-up with a split lip. Of course if Jenny hadn't hung up as soon as she'd heard her father's voice, it could have been worse, the man getting more than just a split lip. It had driven the idiot to sort it out and very quickly; they had a new number now, this time ex-directory.

Jenny's father hadn't given up though, he'd been to the house, but it had been left to Marcos to tell the man that she didn't want to see him. Marcos had also told Edward that he was just making things worse, that he still needed time to talk Jenny round, and that until then it would be better to stay away. So far it had worked, but for how much longer?'

'Here's your coffee,' Jenny said as she placed it beside him.

'Thank you, darling, and that casserole was delicious.'

'The cookery course is starting to pay off, the driving lessons too. My instructor said that after a few more I should be ready to take my test.'

'In that case I'll see about getting you a car.'

'Don't you think you should wait to see if I pass first?'

'I'm sure you will,' Marcos said, pulling Jenny onto

his lap, 'but it doesn't matter if you have to take it again. In the meantime it will be an incentive to see your own car in the garage.'

'You spoil me,' Jenny said, kissing him.

Marcos felt a familiar stirring. He was still a very happy man who looked forward to taking his wife to bed, knowing that he pleased her. He wanted only one thing now, to hear Jenny say that she was pregnant, that he was going to be a father.

Obviously aware of what he was feeling, Jenny stood up, saying with a mischievous wink and a smile before she left the room again, 'Later.'

Marcos was content, but then his mellow mood was broken by the buzz of the new gate system. Who the hell was that? He wasn't expecting anyone. He went into the hall, finger on the intercom.

'Yes, who is it?'

'It's Robin. I've come to see my sister.'

Blast, Marcos thought. He could hardly deny him entry. 'Come on in.'

He waited until he heard the sound of a car engine and opened the door to see a ratty old Citroën pulling up.

'Nice motor,' he said sardonically as Robin climbed out.

'A present from Pater and preferable to travelling by train. I suppose you're Marcos.'

Pater, Marcos thought, what a pretentious twat, but he hid his thoughts with a smile. 'Yes, that's me, and it's nice to meet you. Come inside, I'm sure Jenny will be pleased to see you.'

Robin made no comment, but Marcos saw his eyes widen, even more so when they went into the drawing room.

Yes, he's impressed, Marcos thought, and he was pleased. 'Take a seat. I'll find Jenny,' he said, hating this invasion of his privacy.

Robin looked around at the room and then sat down on a sofa. His mother had told him about the house, but even so this was more than he'd expected. He'd arrived home last night, and though he'd already heard about it on the telephone, his mother told him again what had happened, his father saying that he couldn't understand why Jenny was still behaving like this towards them.

A vision now walked into the room and Robin blinked. This couldn't be Jenny, this glorious creature. Yes, she'd always been pretty, but now she was beautiful – perfectly dressed, perfect make-up, perfect hair. She was a woman now, no longer a child.

'Hello, Robin.'

'Jenny, you look fantastic,' he said, rising to his feet.

'Thanks. Are you home for the weekend?'

'Yes, but if I hadn't been told to wait, that you might refuse to see me, I'd have come before this.'

'Nonsense, I'm sure Jenny is very pleased to see

you,' Marcos said as he came to stand beside Jenny, an arm around her waist. 'Isn't that right, darling?'

'Of course, and do sit down again, Robin.'

Robin hadn't known what to expect, but found it awkward, as though his sister had become a formal stranger. 'It's been a long time, Jenny.'

'Yes, it has indeed. Can I get you anything? Tea? Coffee?'

'No, nothing thanks. I'm fine.'

At last Jenny sat down beside him, while Marcos took a chair by the fire, his dark brown eyes studying him. There was something in them, deep, unfathomable, and for some reason Robin felt intimidated. He'd come here for two reasons. One was to see his sister, the other to find out what the hell was going on, and he wasn't going to let some daft feelings he had about Marcos stop him.

'Jenny, I know you have good reason to feel the way you do, but I promise you, Mummy really is a different person now.'

'Robin, she may be your mother, but she isn't mine.'

'I know that, but she wants to be.'

'You might believe that, but I don't. You've always been blind, taken in by her act, and now Dad's the same. He's taken her side too.'

'Jenny, there are no sides, it's just that a lot happened when you left, including my accident, and it somehow drew them closer.'

'What accident?'

'That isn't important now; suffice to say that for a while they thought they were losing me.'

'Dad didn't mention it.'

Just then, the telephone rang. Robin thought he saw a look of annoyance cross Marcos's face as the man said, 'I'll have to get that.'

Robin watched him leave the room, and then spoke to Jenny again. 'My accident was a long time ago. Dad was so overwhelmed, so happy that he'd found you I doubt it crossed his mind. Now I don't know all the ins and outs of what happened the last time you saw them, but what went wrong, Jenny?'

'I wasn't taken in by *your* mother's act, and when I supposedly upset her she turned on the crocodile tears. Dad was annoyed with me, told me I should give her a chance.'

'Dad's right. You should give her a chance.'

'Oh, you're as bad as him.'

'Jenny, we both know exactly what Mummy did, how she drove you from home, but we were also there to see the change in her, her contrition, and believe me it was genuine.'

Marcos came back into the room and Robin fell silent.

'Who was that on the telephone?' asked Jenny.

'Just a business associate,' he said, sitting down again. 'Robin, you were saying something about an accident before we were interrupted.'

'Yes, a nasty blindside, broken bones, but thankfully no lasting effects.'

'I'm glad to hear it. Did Jenny tell you she's taking driving lessons?'

'No, we've been talking about my parents,' Robin said, determined to continue. 'Jenny, please, I know things went wrong, but won't you give them both another chance?'

Jenny was quiet again, but at last she spoke. 'Yes, all right, but I'd prefer them to come here. Is . . . is that all right with you, Marcos?'

'I suppose so,' he said.

'Perhaps dinner then . . . tomorrow,' she said a little hesitantly, looking at her husband.

'Jenny, that's great,' Robin said, elated. He couldn't wait to tell his parents the good news. He had told them he was coming here, knew they were hoping he could make a difference, and though he had other things to tell Jenny, not least about his girlfriend Julia, it could wait until tomorrow. 'I hope I'm included in the invitation?'

'Of course you are, silly.'

For a moment Robin saw a trace of how Jenny had looked at sixteen and remembered what he felt for her, what he had wanted. He flushed with shame. Those feelings had died now, but he felt a surge of affection as her playful punch brought back other childhood memories, games they'd played, Jenny always running to him for comfort when she had fallen over.

'Great, I'm off now,' he said, 'but I'll see you tomorrow.'

'Make it around two o'clock,' Jenny said.

It was Marcos who showed him out, but had Robin looked back he would have seen the worried look on Jenny's face. Neither did he notice that Marcos's face was etched with annoyance. Instead he drove home feeling pleased with himself, sure that everything was going to be fine now. After all, it had to be.

He hadn't told his parents of his own plans yet, and didn't want to until it was absolutely necessary – but when he left university he'd be leaving the country. Julia's father had already offered him a job with his company in South Africa and it was too good an opportunity to turn down.

Chapter Thirty-Seven

Marcos had known that Jenny's estrangement from her parents wouldn't last indefinitely, but he was still annoyed that she had invited them to dinner.

He had made his feelings plain, giving Jenny the cold shoulder last night in bed, and had hardly spoken to her since they had got up that morning.

'Marcos, please, I told you last night, I won't make inviting my parents round a regular occurrence. It's just that I felt I'd be more confident on my own ground.'

'If you feel like that, why bother to see them at all?'

'I . . . I miss my . . . dad.'

'Oh, so your father comes before me, does he?'

'No, of course not.'

'You know how hard I work during the week, hardly arriving home before seven and how much I therefore value having the weekends to ourselves. It seems you didn't give that a thought.'

'I'm sorry, really I am, and I promise it won't happen again.'

'See that it doesn't,' Marcos snapped, but then, seeing Jenny's eyes flooding with tears, he decided to relent. He'd said enough to ensure that she wouldn't make the same mistake again. 'It's all right, I forgive you, now come here and give me a kiss.'

Jenny was still feeling a little shaky. Marcos was usually wonderful – loving, generous and kind, if a little touchy at times. Now, though, she had become aware that there was another side to him, one that she feared, and it was as though the man she loved disappeared at times to be replaced by another.

Thankfully Marcos was acting normally now, charming her parents and Robin when they'd arrived. To her relief, dinner had turned out perfectly and, laying the meat platter on the dining room table, she now said, 'Marcos, would you carve while I fetch the vegetables?'

'Of course, darling.'

'Can I help, Jennifer?' Delia asked.

'It all right, I'll give her a hand,' Robin said, following Jenny to the kitchen. 'I wanted a chance to speak to you alone; to say thanks for this and to ask you to give Mummy a real chance this time.'

Jenny handed him a dish large dish of mixed fresh vegetables. 'I'll try to be open-minded.'

'Fair enough,' he said, smiling.

'Go on, take that through. I'll bring the gravy and mint sauce.'

'This is lovely, Jennifer,' Delia said.

'Smashing roast potatoes,' her father commented.

'I tried several ways of cooking them, but Edna's turned out to be best.'

'Is she a friend of yours, Jennifer?' Delia asked.

'No, she's our daily.'

'Goodness, a daily. Aren't you lucky?' Delia enthused.

'Jenny, did you have to tell us that?' her father said, chuckling. 'Your mother will want one now.'

'Marcos mentioned yesterday that you're learning to drive, Jenny,' said Robin. 'How's it going? Have you hit anything yet?'

'Trust you to ask that. But no, I haven't. I'm taking five lessons a week so hopefully it won't be long before I can take my test.'

'That's wonderful, Jennifer, well done,' Delia said. 'It took me ages to learn to drive. I don't suppose you need it, but if you feel like a bit of extra practice between lessons I'd be pleased to help. We could use my car.'

Delia's smile looked genuinely warm, her offer a kind one, and for the first time Jenny began to wonder if she really had changed. 'Er . . . thank you. I . . . I may take you up on that,' she said.

Robin lifted his eyes heavenward. 'God help us, Dad, another woman driver on the road.'

'Down to me, I'm afraid,' said Marcos. 'I suggested driving lessons.'

'Good for you,' Delia said, 'and Robin, I'll have you know I've never had an accident. There is nothing wrong with women drivers, and I'm sure Jennifer will be a good one too.'

Jenny was pleased with the vote of confidence and smiled at Delia, receiving a wink and a smile in return. She didn't know it then, but it was to be the start of a huge change in their relationship, one that would grow as time progressed.

Chapter Thirty-Eight

It was 1974 and a year had passed. Tina was lying quietly beside Paul, unable to believe that she'd actually done it.

'I suppose I'll have to marry you now,' he complained, yet he was smiling.

'Who said I want you to?'

'Now listen here, minx, it was you who demanded my body. What if this results in a baby?'

'Daft thing. Men can't have babies.'

He laughed, hugging her. 'Seriously, Tina, will you marry me?'

'I thought my first proposal would be sort of romantic, perhaps over a candlelit dinner.'

'First! How many do you expect?' Paul asked.

'I didn't expect that one, and anyway, you don't have to marry me. There won't be a baby. I've been taking the pill.'

'In advance? You planned this?'

'Not exactly planned, but we've been courting for

ages and . . . and I was scared you'd lose patience with me. I've been taking the pill, well, just in case, hoping I could pluck up the courage.'

'So you thought you *had* to go all the way.'

'Yes . . . no . . . well, sort of, but I'm glad I did.'

'There was no need. I'd have waited for as long as necessary. I . . . well, I love you.'

Tina's stomach flipped. Paul had never said that before, but she felt the same. 'I love you too.'

'I'm glad to hear it, but you can forget about the pill. I've heard about the side effects and no doubt it accounts for those headaches.'

'But what if I get pregnant?'

'There'll be no chance of that. In future I'll keep my hands to myself.'

'I'm not standing for that!' Tina said, feigning indignation. 'I rather liked it, and though another bloke might not be as good as you, I don't intend to turn into a nun.'

'What!'

Paul's face was a picture and, unable to hold it back, Tina burst out laughing.

He grinned. 'You had me going there for a while. Now come here. If you liked it so much we'll do it again, but only on condition that you agree to marry me.'

'Yes please, on both counts,' Tina said. She was so happy, couldn't remember a time when she'd ever been this happy, and it was all thanks to this man.

Since they'd been going out together there had been terrible things happening, IRA bomb blasts all over the place, both here and in Ireland. Parliament had been targeted, as well as the Tower of London and Brooks's Club in London. Just two days ago a bomb had gone off in a Birmingham pub and it seemed nowhere in England was safe.

Yet now, lying in Paul's arms, Tina felt cocooned and her heart swelled with love. They were getting married, she would be his wife, and she'd never have to fear anything again.

Jenny was in the drawing room, wondering about the men who had called to see Marcos. He'd barely introduced them and they were now ensconced in his study, the door closed. It was Saturday, and they rarely entertained, other than the occasions Marcos allowed her to invite her parents to dinner, usually about once every seven to eight weeks. Marcos usually worked late and, as he was keen to have their weekends undisturbed, it wasn't often they accepted a return invitation.

It was difficult because her dad wanted to see more of her, but Jenny had found it best to please her husband rather than her father. Marcos wanted her there when he was at home, which meant she was only free during the day, and her father was at work then.

What surprised Jenny was the growing relationship

she had with her mother. Their personalities were still miles apart, but on one occasion when her parents had been round for dinner, Jenny and Delia had found a shared interest in cooking. When her mother offered to teach her how to ice cakes, Jenny had taken her up on it, going for a lesson once a week. She was proficient now, but still called in to see her mother, the two of them now relaxed in each other's company.

Jenny glanced at the clock and saw that Marcos had been in the study for over an hour. Though drinks had been refused on arrival, she thought the men might want one now.

'Excuse me,' she said, going into the study, 'can I get you anything?'

'I wouldn't mind a beer,' one said, and Jenny struggled to remember his name. She saw something on the desk, a drawing of some sort, a building, but then her view was blocked as Marcos stood up in front of her.

He looked annoyed, his tone hard when he spoke. 'I'll see to their drinks, and *do not* disturb us again.'

'So . . . sorry,' Jenny stuttered.

He grabbed her arm, almost pushing her out of the room, and as the door began to close Jenny heard someone say, 'You jammy git, Marcos. She's a bit of all right and I can see why you left . . .'

The rest of the words were cut off as the door was firmly closed. Upset, Jenny returned to the drawing room. They had been married for over a year now, and there had been other occasions, like this one, when Marcos seemed a cold, hard stranger. Thankfully it didn't happen very often, and mostly Jenny told herself she was happy, except for the fact that she hadn't fallen for a baby. She was puzzled too by what she had overheard. What had Marcos left . . . or who?

'I haven't got beer, it'll have to be whisky,' Marcos said, pouring them all a drink.

'Well, I ain't complaining,' Liam said.

'Nor me,' Steve agreed, slugging it back as if it were nectar.

Marcos poured him another measure. During the past year he'd kept a wary eye on Steve but, having found nothing to arouse his suspicions, he'd finally let him into the inner circle. The man had proved useful in finding the perfect target, and then in casing the joint, but there was a lot more planning still to do before Marcos was ready to make a move. He'd come this far by careful, meticulous attention to detail and he wasn't about to start taking risks now.

He looked at the drawing again. Hatton Gardens, London's diamond quarter, usually impenetrable, but they had found an easy way into one of the shops.

'Steve, how can we be sure this man is going to cooperate?'

'For one he's a wimp, and, two, it'll be me holding his wife and kids.'

'I still don't like it, boss,' complained Bernie. 'We haven't done anything like this before. If we get nabbed the jury ain't gonna take it too kindly.'

'We won't get caught,' Marcos said, 'but if you want out, say so now.'

'No, no, I'm in, but I don't know why we can't just do it the old way.'

'Look, Bernie, we walk in, and then walk out again. No walls to break through, no alarms, and no safe to crack. It's perfect.'

'He's gonna know our faces,' said Liam.

'Not if they're covered up, you moron,' Marcos told him. Liam looked a bit peeved, but the other two were trying to suppress laughter. 'All right, I shouldn't have called you that, but you've got to admit you sound like an old woman. Here, have another drink.'

Mollified, Liam held out his glass. 'I'm just making sure nothing can go wrong, that's all.'

'Right then, let's go over the plans from start to finish again, and we'll need a few more meets after this one until we're sure the timing is perfect,' Marcos said. He'd chosen to bring them here, away from any chance of prying eyes, or ears. There'd been a time, about a year ago, when something had niggled, a feeling that had passed now, but he'd learned to trust his instincts. He felt safe here. Other than a chosen few, so far this house was unknown to anyone else and he intended to keep it that way.

'It's simple enough,' Steve said after they'd gone over it once more.

'Right, that's it for now,' Marcos said, 'but one for the road before you leave.'

Glasses filled, they drank the whisky and then Marcos escorted them out, and he was in a good mood afterwards when he walked into the drawing room. He'd been a bit short with Jenny, but now recalled that he hadn't told her not to disturb them. She looked at him nervously.

'It's all right, darling,' he said. 'My fault and I'm sorry if I upset you.'

Relied flooded her features. 'That's all right, but who were those men?'

'They work for me. I'm making a few changes to one of my premises. You probably spotted the plans.'

'Yes, I saw them briefly.'

He waited for more questions, pleased when they didn't come, and decided to reward her. 'Would you like to invite your parents to dinner tomorrow?'

'Yes, I'd love to.'

'Give them a ring then.'

Jenny looked happy as she went to the telephone, but she had a much bigger surprise coming, one he had thought long and hard about. As soon as they'd pulled off this job, he was going to sell up the lot – the businesses, this place – and with Jenny on his arm he'd move to Spain. It wasn't that there'd been any sign of trouble, in fact not a whisper from the hags, his money keeping them nicely quiet, but he was sick of forking it out. Once he was out of the country they could say what they liked, do what they liked, but they wouldn't be able to touch him.

Yes, a nice villa beckoned, and that left only one thing. It was about time Jenny fell pregnant. The words his mother had once said rose up to haunt him once more, but Marcos forced them, and her image, away. There was still time, lots of it, and in Spain he'd be completely relaxed, at ease, which was sure to make a difference.

Edward replaced the receiver. Late and short notice again, but Delia was sure to be pleased, as was he. He wanted to see more of his daughter, but at least Delia saw her regularly.

'That was Jenny. We've been invited to dinner tomorrow,' he said, returning to sit by the fire.

'Oh, good, but I suppose it will just be us again. I really don't understand Marcos. I've offered to introduce him to Penelope Grainger, and getting into that circle might be useful to him. He just isn't interested.'

'Delia, it's you who wants to get in with them, but you've just got to accept that Marcos is a man who values his privacy.'

'What about Jenny? They've been living in Almond Crescent for over a year, yet she hasn't made any attempt to meet her neighbours.'

'It's her choice and as long as she's happy, what does it matter?'

'She seems so isolated.'

'Of course she isn't. She passed her test ages ago, tootles about in her car and comes round here to see you every week.'

'But she hasn't got any friends.'

'Of course she has. What about the other young women she met in her cookery classes?'

'Well, yes, she has mentioned meeting them for lunch occasionally.'

'There you are then. Now stop worrying about Jenny. She's fine, Marcos adores her and she wants for nothing. What more could a girl want?'

'I know she wants a baby.'

'There's plenty of time,' Edward said, then he yawned. 'It was all right going to Kensington to see Beatrice and Tim, but I'm worn out.'

'Isn't their apartment lovely?'

'Yes, very nice,' he said, though he found it hard to sound enthusiastic about what he had considered over-the-top ostentation. The decor was all deep reds and golds, with dark wood furniture, high ceilings and chandeliers. As in Jenny's house, Edward had found it hard to relax.

'Did you notice the china? It must have cost a fortune.'

'No, not really,' he said, yawning again. They saw Beatrice and her husband about once a month and that was enough for him. He had little in common with Timothy, found the man a bore, and Beatrice's haughty manner was hard to swallow. Still, it made Delia happy to have her sister in the country again, and in her company they became like two peas in a pod, Delia always bragging about Jenny and Marcos, about their huge house and how well off they were, as if that gave her some sort of kudos just by association. Beatrice in turn talked about the fabulous parties she and Timothy went to, the influential people she met, including, it seemed, members of royalty. Yet, underlying this, there was no doubt the sisters were fond of each other.

'I'm hoping to persuade Marcos to invite them to dinner soon.'

'I don't think he particularly enjoyed it when we took them to Kensington. Jenny may have wanted to see her aunt, but I got the feeling that Marcos didn't.'

'Nonsense, he was charming and Beatrice was very impressed. It'll be Christmas soon and tomorrow I could hint that we all spend it together. They could invite Beatrice and Timothy and make it a lovely family Christmas.'

'Don't build your hopes up. Last year Marcos took Jenny to a hotel and he may be planning to do the same this year.'

'I doubt it. Jenny would have said something, and anyway, it was different then. Things were still a little strained between us, but everything is fine now.'

For Delia's sake, Edward hoped Marcos would agree to a family get-together, but he was difficult to read and he still hadn't got to the bottom of the man's character. Yes, he could be charming, the perfect host, but there was a reserve, a distance, as though they were having dinner with an acquaintance instead of their son-in-law. Still, he thought, give it time. Jenny was happy, and as long as she continued to be, that was all that mattered.

Chapter Thirty-Nine

The new year had come in with high January winds, the lawn now covered in leaves that the gardener would tackle, but with housework to do Jenny took off her engagement ring to put in her jewellery box. As always, when she looked inside, she was struck by Marcos's generosity. For their first Christmas together he had given her a Cartier watch among other things, then an emerald bracelet for her birthday. On their first wedding anniversary it had been a trip to Paris, and a diamond-encrusted heart-shaped locket.

They'd just had their second Christmas, a family one this time, and Marcos had given her pearls, along with the promise of another trip away soon. Jenny closed her jewellery box. So many wonderful presents, so many lovely things, but all Jenny really wanted was a baby.

The entry system buzzed and she hurried downstairs to let in Edna. It wasn't long before the woman was at the front door and Jenny smiled.

'Hello, Edna, did you have a nice Christmas and New Year?'

'Yes thanks, Mrs Cane,' she said.

Edna still called her Mrs Cane and Jenny sighed. She had tried, but had been unable to get past Edna's reserve. The woman was friendly enough, happy to chat, but only about mundane things, and Jenny had soon come to realise that talking about Marcos was strictly taboo.

'We had my parents here for Christmas dinner, along with my brother, aunt and uncle.'

'That's nice.'

'Yes, it was, though I don't think Marcos would agree. He'd have preferred it if we had spent Christmas alone.'

'Yeah, well, I'd best get on,' Edna said, heading for the kitchen.

Jenny followed her. She wasn't surprised that Marcos had found her aunt trying on Christmas Day, she'd felt the same, but worse, Penelope Grainger and her husband had called round later in the evening. That had been down to her mother taking it upon herself to invite them, and though Jenny had seen that Marcos was annoyed, he had managed to hide it well. She'd been so nervous, expecting him to go mad when everyone left, but instead, to her surprise, he had shrugged it off, saying that it hardly mattered.

'It was good of you to give me so much time off,' Edna said as she took off her coat.

'Nonsense, you've been with us for over a year and you've never missed a day.'

'I had a holiday in July.'

'Well, you deserved another one,' Jenny said.

'The time's flown past and now it's 1975. I hope it's going to be a good year.'

'Yes, me too,' Jenny agreed, the thought of having a baby once again springing to mind.

'Right then, I expect you'd like a cup of tea?'

Jenny smiled. This was Edna's routine, a cup of tea before she got down to any work. She had missed her presence in the morning, and was pleased to have her back.

'Yes, please, I'd love one.'

When the tea was made they chatted over it, but once again the subject of Marcos was avoided.

'How is your son, Edna?'

'Tom's all right, but if you ask me it's about time he found himself a decent woman and got married.'

'How old is he?'

'He'll be forty this year.'

'Marcos will be too.'

'Yeah, I know, they went to school together.'

'Did they? Goodness, I didn't know that.'

'There's a lot you don't know,' Edna said, but then her expression changed to one of horror. 'Gawd, I shouldn't have said that.'

'It's all right, Edna. You're right, I know hardly anything about Marcos's childhood. He did say once that he came from a poor background, but I'd love to hear more.'

'I can't tell you anything. I . . . I don't know anything.'

'You just said Marcos went to school with your son.'

'Please, you're a nice young woman, a kind young woman, so don't mention it to Mar . . . Mr Cane. He'll know it came from me.'

'Edna, I've noticed this before. You seem frightened of Marcos, but why?'

'No! No, I'm not. It's just that, well, er . . . some things in his past he doesn't like talked about.'

'Is it that something dreadful happened to him during his childhood?'

'I'm sorry, Mrs Cane, really I am, but if he wants you to know he'll tell you himself. Now . . . now I really must get some work done.'

Jenny knew she'd get nothing more from Edna, but felt she had a clue now. Poor Marcos, something really awful must have happened to him, something so dreadful that he didn't want it talked about. Perhaps that was why he avoided the subject, perhaps he hated the memories of his childhood; having bad ones of her own, she could understand that.

Marcos was sitting in a small office at one of his garages, going over the books, when Bernie walked in.

'Morning, boss.'

Marcos smiled. Bernie looked hung over but, reliable as ever, he'd still turned up for work. 'Rough night?'

'Nah, I'm still recovering from seeing in the New Year.'

'Close the door,' Marcos said.

Bernie did so, asking worriedly, 'What's up?'

'I've decided to schedule the job for the end of February. They'll have stocked up after Christmas sales and, even better, Steve's had a sniff of a huge diamond coming in. It's for someone famous who wants it made into a ring for his wife, and apparently it's worth a mint.'

'Sounds good to me, but what about selling the stuff on?'

'We'll use the Dutchman again. He knows better than to do us on price.'

'Yeah, but he . . .'

'We'll go over it later in the week,' Marcos interrupted, 'at my place.'

'Just the four of us?'

'There's no need to include Dan. He's just the driver and doesn't need to know the details of the job. I'll be using Tommy, but I'll pay his cut.'

'So you're gonna pull your usual stroke?'

'Yes, but that's strictly for your ears only. As far as the others are concerned, we're sticking together. When they see you've got the haul they won't argue.'

'Are you sure you can trust Tommy? You know what he's like with the booze.'

'We go back a long way, and yes, I trust him.'

'If you say so, boss.'

'I do,' Marcos said shortly, looking up and seeing a man looking over a car in the showroom. 'That's enough for now. You've got a customer.'

Bernie hurried out while Marcos sat back in his chair. The decision was made, with just a few tweaks left to sort out, but yes, he'd pull his usual stroke. If anything went wrong, the others would be the main focus of attention, while he slipped quietly away.

Edna Moon was thinking about Marcos as she changed the sheets. Jenny, as she wished she could call her instead of Mrs Cane, was lovely and if hadn't been for that bastard she'd have enjoyed working for her. It made her sick that the poor young woman didn't have a clue. She wanted to put her straight, to spill her guts out, but Marcos had warned her to keep her mouth shut. She'd wanted to refuse the job, but with Tom pouring anything he earned down his throat, the money had been too good to resist.

It was the break over Christmas that had done it, lowered her guard, and Edna had spoken without thinking. Now Mrs Cane wanted to know more, but she couldn't tell her, daren't tell her. Edna's nerves were jangling. Good money or not she wanted out, but would Marcos let her leave?

No, she thought, not without a bloody good excuse, but somehow she'd have to think of one. Her health perhaps, she could try that, but she doubted Tom would have the sense to keep his mouth shut. If Marcos asked how she was, the daft sod would say she was fine, and then what?

She wished God would strike Marcos down, but in her experience men like him always survived. The devil takes care of his own, they said, and Marcos was definitely in league with him.

At ten thirty Jenny answered the telephone.

'Good morning, Jennifer, it's Penelope. I've invited your mother round for coffee at eleven. She gave me your number and I'm ringing to see if you'd like to join us.'

'Er . . . well . . . yes, and thank you.'

'Wonderful. See you in half an hour then. Bye for now.'

Jenny was left listening to the dialling tone, her grip tight on the receiver, wishing now she'd had the wits to make an excuse. If this led to more, Marcos would hate it, but it was too late now. She'd accepted the invitation and Penelope Grainger was expecting her. Of course, this was down to her mother again, Jenny thought. She was probably champing at the bit to see the inside of Penelope's house.

With her hair brushed and a fresh coat of lipstick applied, Jenny was on her way back downstairs again when Edna came out of the kitchen with her coat on.

'I'm off now, Mrs Cane.'

'All right, Edna, and thanks.'

'You . . . you won't say anything to Mr Cane . . . you know, about what I told you earlier?'

'No, I won't say a word.'

'Thanks,' Edna said, looking relieved. 'I'll see you tomorrow.'

'Hang on a minute. I'm popping next door and instead of waiting to buzz you out, I'll come to the gate with you. This entry system is such a nuisance. I'll have to ask Marcos to give you a key.'

Edna said nothing as they walked along the drive, only calling goodbye as she hurried off. Jenny shook her head, still wondering why the woman was so reticent about Marcos, but then saw her mother pulling up outside Penelope Grainger's. Delia got out of her car, having chosen to drive rather than walk and Jenny could see why. Her mother was dressed up to the nines, complete with a hat, as though going for a formal lunch.

'Jenny, hello. Coffee with Penelope. Isn't it wonderful?'

'For you maybe, but I'm not so sure.'

'Nonsense. It's about time you became acquainted with your other neighbours and I'm hoping Penelope has invited a few of the wives along.'

Jenny was ushered down the drive, her mother prattling on as she rang the doorbell. 'You could have made more of an effort, Jennifer. That dress and cardigan are hardly suitable.'

'It's just coffee, Mummy,' she protested.

Penelope opened the door dressed in brown corduroy trousers and a thick, green, baggy crew-neck jumper, her hair dragged back untidily. Jennifer glanced at her mother, saw her shocked expression, and had to bite her lip to stop herself from bursting with laughter.

'Delia, Jennifer, come on in,' she said, 'and give me your coats.'

'Thank you, and thank you too for inviting us.'

Her mother sounded so formal, but Jenny just smiled at Penelope as they stepped inside. The entrance hall was a shamble of coats, wellington boots and umbrellas, and their coats were hooked precariously on top of a pile of others.

'Goodness, you look awfully smart, Delia.'

'This is just an old suit,' she blustered. 'I've had it for years.'

'And there's me still dressed for the stables.'

'Do you keep horses, Penelope?'

'Of course, in local stables. Don't you?'

'Er . . . no.'

'What about you, Jennifer? Do you ride?'

'No, it isn't something I've tried.'

'Goodness, how odd. My father put me on my

first horse before I could walk. Come on through,' Penelope then said, leading them to a drawing room that was clean, but dreadfully untidy. There were shabby leather sofas with cushions scattered haphazardly and side tables piled with magazines. 'Take a seat and I'll fetch the coffee.'

'This is nice, sort of cosy,' Jenny commented as she sat on a wing chair by the fire.

'It isn't what I expected.'

'No, I didn't think so.'

'Still, now I've looked around there are some wonderful pieces in here. That clock is marvellous, and that horse painting,' Delia said, pointing over towards the hearth. 'It looks like a Stubbs and if so I bet it's original.'

'Of course it is,' Penelope said, holding a tray. 'It was my father's and he gave it to us as a wedding present. I had the coffee ready, but excuse the mess. I've just lost another daily.'

Jenny saw that her mother was flushing, obviously flustered that she had been overheard, but Delia recovered quickly. 'Yes, staff can be very unreliable. Jennifer has a wonderful woman, though, and she's been with her for over a year.'

'Has she? Jennifer, do you think she'd work for me too?'

'I don't know, I could ask her.'

'Wonderful,' Penelope enthused, pouring the coffee. 'I'm having a small dinner party on Thursday night. You must come, Jennifer, your husband too of course.'

Just as she had feared, an invitation, one Marcos wouldn't like, and Jenny quickly sought an excuse. 'I'm afraid that won't be possible. Marcos is rather busy at the moment and he's rarely home before nine.'

'I can sympathise with that. When Freddie was training he worked so many hours that I hardly saw him. Of course that was many years ago. Sugar, Delia?'

'No, thank you.'

Jenny was thankful when the two of them began to chat, mostly about the WI, and she was happy to sit quietly. She had got out of the invitation this time, but for how much longer?

At last, after they had both refused another coffee, her mother said, 'We should go now, Penelope, but you must come to me next time, perhaps tomorrow?'

'Sorry, Delia, I've got something else on, lunch with friends and after that a frantically busy week.'

'I see, well, never mind,' Delia said, lips tight.

They left then, and as soon as the door shut behind them, her mother hissed, 'Did you hear what she said, Jennifer? Lunch with friends, but she didn't invite me, nor did she invite your father and me to dinner. That invitation only went to you and Marcos.'

'I shouldn't think Daddy will care about that.'

'Well, I do,' Delia said as they reached her car. 'When you moved into Almond Crescent – in a superior house to Penelope's, I might add – I hoped it would gain me entry into her set.'

Jenny frowned. 'I see, so what you're saying is that you saw me as a way in to what you deem a higher social circle?'

'Well, yes, but you make it sound awful.'

'What do you expect? I really thought you'd changed, but now I realise what all this mother-daughter stuff has been about. You just wanted to use me.'

'No, Jennifer, that isn't true. I've really come to enjoy the time we spend together, and you moving here just seemed opportune, that's all. In fact, why don't we spend more time together today? We could go for a look around the shops if you like.'

Jenny shivered, cold in just her cardigan, but her mother sounded sincere and she wanted to believe her. 'I'll have to get my coat.'

'Rather than getting yours out we might as well go in my car,' Delia said.

'All right,' Jenny agreed and after getting a jacket rather than a coat, she climbed into her mother's car.

'I don't know about you, Jennifer, but I'm a bit peckish. I thought Penelope would have at least offered us a biscuit with our coffee . . . and the way she was dressed. My goodness, she looked awful.'

'She'd just returned from the stables.'

'She could have changed.'

'Perhaps Penelope doesn't place as much import-ance on appearances as you do.'

'Obviously not, and I've been silly, Jennifer. I haven't got a thing in common with the woman, least of all horses, and no doubt the rest of her friends will be of a like mind. In future, I don't think I'll bother with Penelope. She really isn't my cup of tea.'

Jenny hid a smile. In reality the situation was the reverse, and it was her mother's pride talking. It had been nice though when her mother had said that she enjoyed their time together. They usually met once, sometimes twice a week. At other times Jenny had to admit that she was often lonely. She hadn't had a real friend for ages, not since Tina, and still found herself thinking about her now and then, wondering where she was and if she'd at least put her father's money to good use.

It still hurt to think about what Tina had done, and the experience had left Jenny slow to trust. It had meant that the young women of her own age that she had met at cookery classes remained just acquaintances, and these had now drifted away. She had Marcos and her parents, but what Jenny really wanted was a baby, something to fill the empty space she still felt in her life.

Jenny inadvertently touched her tummy, a small smile playing around her lips. It was possible, just possible.

Chapter Forty

The end of February found Jenny smiling in anticipation. She couldn't wait to see Marcos's face and just hoped he'd be home a little earlier than usual. She had been wondering what to get him for his birthday, and had eventually settled on a watch, giving it to him that morning. Now, however, she had something much better – the perfect gift.

Headlights lit up the curtains and she rose to her feet. It was only five o'clock but he was here. She wanted to fly out to the hall to welcome him, to blurt it out, but resisted. This was so special, so precious, and she wanted to savour the moment.

'Hello, darling,' Marcos said.

'I was hoping you wouldn't be late, but wasn't expecting you yet.'

'Is this a nice surprise then?'

'Yes, lovely.'

'Good, because I'm afraid I won't be home at all tomorrow night. I've been offered a garage in Wales and as sorting out a deal might drag on I've booked a hotel for the night."

'Oh, right,' Jenny said, hardly listening.

'You're not upset, are you? It's only one night.'

'No, no, it's fine,' she said. Then, unable to wait any longer: 'I . . . I went to see the doctor today.'

'The doctor! Why? Are you ill? What's wrong?'

Poor Marcos, he looked a little worried, and now Jenny smiled widely. 'There's nothing wrong. That's unless you consider pregnancy an illness.'

His eyes widened, his mouth opened, then closed again, and the next thing Jenny knew she was in his arms, lifted off her feet.

'You're having a baby!' he cried out joyfully. 'Jenny, you're having a baby!'

'Yes, I am,' she said as he put her down, though his arms remained around her.

'I can't believe it. A father. I'm going to be a father.'

'You certainly are, and our baby will be born in August.'

He was quiet for a moment, but then said, 'That means you're already three months gone. Why didn't you say something before this?'

'We've had false alarms, disappointments, and well, this time I wanted to be one hundred per cent sure.'

He released her, stepped back. 'What am I doing, Jenny? Sit down. Rest.'

'There's no need. I'm fine.'

'I'll have to see about getting you more help. We'll extend Edna Moon's hours.'

'Marcos, please, that isn't necessary.'

'All right, maybe not now, but in a few more months.'

He looked so worried and just to reassure him, Jenny said, 'We'll see, but there's no need to get in a tizzy. I'm only having a baby.'

'Only! Jenny, you have no idea how much this means to me.'

'Me too,' she said, moving back into his arms. Over the last month or so, she had dared to hope, but her monthlies had always been a bit irregular, and until the doctor had confirmed it she'd had doubts, especially as there'd been no sign of the symptoms she'd heard about, morning sickness being one of them.

'I wonder if it's a boy or girl?' Marcos said, standing back again to place his hand on her stomach.

'Do you mind?'

'No, but a boy would be nice. I can't believe I didn't notice before. You've actually got a little bulge.'

'It'll be a lot bigger than that soon.'

'You'll still be beautiful. You'll always be beautiful to me. Now then, time to be practical. No doubt babies need lots of things, and we'll have to kit out a nursery. I'll put more money into your account before I leave for Wales tomorrow, enough to cover everything.'

Jenny smiled. Yes, there were times when Marcos appeared different, cold, hard, but they were few and far between. Mostly he was like this, so loving, so generous, and he'd be a wonderful father too.

Marcos went upstairs to freshen up, his mind racing. As though she was in the room with him, he whispered, 'See, you old witch, you were wrong.'

Smirking, he shaved, something he had to do twice a day. A son, yes, he'd love a son, and his boy would never suffer as he had. His father had beat him, thrashed him with a belt, while his mother had stood by watching it happen, doing nothing to stop it. He knew why, of course, she had been too frightened that the old man would turn on her. Better to let her son suffer than for her to be at the receiving end of his blows.

He had grown up with hate in his heart and had hardened, determined that outside of his home nobody else would dare to lay a finger on him. He'd become the leader of a gang, and built a reputation for violence to any opposition. Still the beatings from his father had continued, until one day Marcos had turned, using his fists and more until the old man's face had looked like pulp. It was only then that Marcos realised he'd gone too far, and he had stupidly agreed to his father's dying words, made that vow that had held him for so long. What a mug he'd been then, but at least as he'd had the wits to cover his tracks well, disposing of the body so far from home that it had been weeks before it was found. Only the old witch had guessed, thought she knew, but she couldn't prove it, which was just as well or he'd have taken her out too.

Marcos didn't want to think about her now. He'd just had wonderful news. He was going to be a father and he swelled with pride. His child would want for nothing and it was just as well the job was on for tomorrow night to fill his coffers. Jenny was pregnant, but it didn't mean he had to change his plans. With the proceeds, along with everything else, they'd still go to Spain where his son, or perhaps his daughter, would be born.

Refreshed, Marcos went back downstairs and pulled Jenny into his arms again. 'Have you told your parents?'

'No, of course not. I wanted you to be the first to know.'

Marcos found that he wanted to share the news, to preen, to show he was a man. 'Come on then, let's go round to your parents' house now.'

'But what about dinner?'

'It's only six o'clock, and anyway, I think that after we've told them we should all go out to celebrate.'

'They're going to be grandparents and thrilled to bits,' Jenny said, her eyes shining as she went to get her coat.

Marcos hid a smile. By the time the baby was

born they'd be long gone, in Spain, and Jenny's parents would be well and truly out of the picture.

Delia was surprised to see Jennifer and Marcos, even more so when her son-in-law said, 'We're going out for dinner and wondered if you'd like to join us?'

'What, this evening?' she asked.

'Well, yes. You see, we have something to celebrate.'

Delia smiled as the penny dropped. 'Of course, your birthday.'

'And thank you for your card and present.'

'You're welcome and happy birthday,' Edward said.

'Thanks, but we've more than that to celebrate and I'm sure Jenny is itching to tell you. Go on, darling.'

With a radiant smile, she said, 'I'm having a baby.'

'What! Oh my God, that's wonderful,' Edward said, rushing forward to wrap Jennifer in his arms.

'My turn,' Delia said.

Edward vigorously pumped Marcos's hand. 'Well done and congratulations.'

'Thank you.'

'Edward, we're going to be grandparents.'

'Though smashing news, it makes me feel a bit old.'

'Nonsense, Marcos isn't that much younger than us,' Delia said, but then flushed. Trust her to say the wrong thing, but thankfully Marcos was still smiling, Jennifer too. 'Of course, Marcos, we were a lot younger than you when we married, so that accounts for it . . . you know, that we're about to be grandparents when we're little older than you.'

'Delia, before you dig an even deeper hole,' Edward said, 'I think we should all have a drink to celebrate this wonderful news.'

'Yes, yes, of course,' she agreed, feeling hot and flustered. 'What can I get you, Marcos?'

'A whisky please.'

'Jennifer, what about you?'

'I think I'd better have something nonalcoholic.'

'I'll see to the whisky while you sort Jenny out,' Edward offered.

'I've told you so many times that a *jenny* is a female donkey, but I give up now. Come on, *Jennifer*, leave the men to their whisky and join me in the kitchen. I'll make you a nice cup of tea.'

'Lovely,' she said, 'but no sugar for me. I'm going to have to watch my weight.'

Delia made the tea, pleased for Jennifer that she was having a baby, though it was still impossible to think of her as a daughter, and it always would be. They did get on now though, jogged along nicely together, and Jennifer, just as she had hoped, had turned out to be useful at last.

'I've got a bit of news for you too, Jennifer. You're

not going to believe this, but Penelope Grainger has actually invited me out to lunch.'

'Has she now, and what brought that on?'

'I have to confess I manoeuvred it. You see, when she invited us for coffee, ages ago, I realised that on occasions I overdress, and that I can come over as too formal and pompous at times.'

'What you, Mummy? Never,' Jenny said, grinning.

'Now don't be cheeky,' Delia said, yet she was smiling too. 'You must have noticed that I changed my style.'

'Yes and I did from the start, but didn't like to say anything. You certainly dress less formally now.'

'I also stopped going out of my way to speak to Penelope when I saw her at the WI, but last week she approached me. It seems we now have something in common. Penelope has become acquainted with someone in the diplomatic service, and he, in turn, is acquainted with Beatrice and Timothy.'

'So that makes you acceptable now? It's so snobby, Mummy.'

'Of course it isn't, and I'm rather looking forward to joining Penelope for lunch. I'll also encourage Beatrice to hold a dinner party and, along with us, she can invite the Graingers and this mutual acquaintance of theirs too.'

'Keep us out of it. Marcos won't want to go.'

'Honestly, Jennifer, I just don't understand him.

It's like he wants to live in a castle and your security gates are the drawbridge.'

'I've told you so many times before, Marcos is very busy and tired when he comes home. He just likes to relax during the evening and cherishes his weekends off. He's only suggested going out to dinner now so we can celebrate the baby.'

Yes, the baby, Delia thought, and she found herself hoping it would be a boy, and a dark-haired one like Marcos. The last thing she needed was another blonde-haired girl, another reminder.

Delia doubted that she would ever be able to think of this coming baby as her grandchild. Of course Edward would adore it . . . but of course it was easy for him.

Chapter Forty-One

It had all gone to plan, and Marcos was smiling behind his balaclava at the size of the haul. Piece of cake, he thought. They'd be leaving the same way they came in, by the back door, where Dan was waiting in the car a few steps away in St Cross Street.

Careful not to use Liam's name, Marcos pointed. 'Take him, and when you get to the car shove him in the boot.'

'But . . . but I've done what you asked,' the man protested.

'Shut up!' Liam spat. 'You'll be released when we're clear.'

This was where they'd split up and going to the back door, Marcos opened it. He poked his head out and, seeing nothing to worry him, turned back to nod at Bernie.

'You take the haul, and you,' he said, looking at Liam, 'make sure you hold onto him. Now *go!*'

Bernie was first out, followed by Liam, intent on

holding the man as he dragged him towards the car. Marcos yanked off his balaclava, ran out, and was headed in the opposite direction towards Grenville Street when all hell broke loose. There were shouts, yells and when he saw rubbish bins, along with a stack of empty cartons just ahead, Marcos shot behind them. He ducked down, but felt trapped, his mind screaming to get out of there and in a burst of adrenaline Marcos did just that, keeping as close to the wall as he could, expecting to feel hands on him at any moment. He thought he'd never reach Grenville Street, but at last, just ahead, Marcos saw the car, the engine already revving. Tommy, you fucking saint, he thought, dragging open the door and jumping in.

With a scream of tyres Tom shot off towards Farringdon Street, and expecting to hear the sound of sirens, of a police chase, Marcos couldn't believe it when they actually made it that far.

'The bastards were waiting,' he ground out through clenched teeth as they took the corner, heading for the Thames and Blackfriars Bridge.

'It must have been a tip-off,' Tom said, keeping up the speed, his hands tight on the steering wheel.

At that time of night, in fact two in the morning, there wasn't much traffic, just the lights of a lorry coming towards them on the other side of the road. Marcos turned to look out of the back window. There was still no sign of anyone giving chase. Of course only Bernie knew about this part of the plan, and that probably accounted for it, but now his hands clenched into fists. He should have trusted his instincts, should have smelled the rat.

'Yes, and from Steve,' he spat.

Tom turned his head. 'What! You think it was him?'

The stench of his breath hit Marcos. 'For fuck's sake Tommy, have you been drinking?'

The car swerved. 'Watch out!' Marcos yelled, but it was too late, they were veering onto the other side of the road and into the path of the lorry.

There was a sickening crunch. It was the last sound Marcos heard.

Paul Ryman wasn't surprised that Steve looked gloomy. The ones they'd nabbed had been carted off to the station and the premises secured as Steve said, 'I can't believe Cane slipped away. He didn't say anything about that part of the plan.'

Paul felt sorry for him. Steve had been under-cover for ages, worming his way in, and unless they apprehended Cane it would have all been for nothing. 'We'll get him and in the meantime at least we've got the other two.'

'*Shit,*' Steve said angrily, Paul's words failing to console him. 'Cane fell for the lot, had no idea it was a setup, that Keith here wasn't really the jeweller and I wasn't holding his family hostage.'

'Come on, back to the station,' the DI ordered as he walked to their side. 'We've got those two to interview and a debriefing before we can call it a night.'

'Waste of time if you ask me,' Steve said, the two of them lagging behind the DI as they walked to the cars. 'They won't tell us where Cane is heading.'

'He won't get far,' Paul said, hoping to placate the man.

'He's a slippery bastard, and knowing him he'll have a contingency plan, probably one to get out of the country.'

'If he tries that, they'll get him at passport control.'

'Oh yeah, you think he'll take a normal route?' Steve said sarcastically. 'He'll have a small boat on standby somewhere, ready to slip across the Channel unnoticed.'

They reached the cars and were about to get in when a uniformed officer approached the DI. 'Excuse me, sir,' he said. 'You put out a warning to all units?'

'Yes, what is it?'

'It might be a coincidence, but we've just heard about a car crash on Farringdon Street, a nasty one.'

'You might as well check it out, Paul.'

'What about me, sir?' Steve asked.

'I doubt it's anything and therefore Paul can handle it.'

The DI obviously thought this was a waste of time, Paul thought, just sending him to check it out, but he nonetheless followed the patrol car to Farringdon Street.

As he approached, the lights of an ambulance were flashing, the fire brigade already there too. Paul got out of his car and found himself staring at the mangled remains of another. He moved closer, gagged, while the uniform beside him said stoically, 'They're not a pretty sight, sir.'

'Who is that in the ambulance?'

'The lorry driver,' said the policeman on the scene. The man in the ambulance was sitting up, a bandage wrapped around his head. He looked all right, Paul thought, but he certainly couldn't say the same for the men in the car.

'Both dead,' the policeman on the scene observed. 'They'll have to be cut out.'

'Have you found any ID?' Paul asked, again fighting nausea.

'Not yet, but it shouldn't take long,' he said as a fireman approached the car with cutters.

As the doors on the first ambulance were being closed, another turned up. 'No hurry, mate,' he heard the driver shout to the other. 'There's nothing anyone can do for them.'

'Did the lorry driver tell you what happened?' Paul asked.

'He said the car looked to be speeding when it

veered onto his side of the road. He didn't have a chance to do anything before they hit.'

Paul's brows furrowed. Speeding! Impatient now, he watched as the bodies were cut out, but with so much blood it was hard to see what was left of their mangled faces. It was the dark hair on one that did it and he leaned closer. Was it him? Shit, it could be. He raced to his car, got on the radio, and then slumped. There was nothing he could do now until Steve turned up. He'd been close to Cane, might be able to make a positive ID, and if it was him . . . Bloody hell, what a night!

Well over an hour later they were back at the station, celebrating and Paul saw that Steve couldn't keep the grin off his face.

'Even with that mangled mug I recognised him,' he said.

'Who was the other one?' Keith asked.

'Tommy Moon, small fry.'

'Dead fry now,' Keith observed.

'Sick,' Paul said in mirth.

'Yeah, I suppose it is really,' Steve agreed. 'Moon's mother is going to take it badly. She's on her own and he's all she has.'

'All she *had*,' Keith pointed out.

'Well, I hope it isn't down to me to tell her.'

The DI called order. 'You're right, their families need to be told, but you've done your bit, Steve.

Good work too. Now bugger off home and get some sleep, you deserve it.'

'Thanks, sir,' he said.

'You too, Keith.'

He chorused his thanks too, and as the two men left the DI spoke to Paul. 'Take a female uniform with you and go to Cane's house. I know it isn't a nice job, but she's got to be told.'

'Which house, sir?'

'You can go to the one in Wimbledon. Just tell her he was involved in a robbery, died while attempting to escape, and no more. Steve said the young woman had no idea, that she's innocent in all this, and she'll find out the rest soon enough. I'll send someone else to Battersea and when you've done your bit you can go home too.'

'Thanks, sir,' Paul said. This was the first time he'd had to do a job like this and he was dreading it, but at least he'd have a female uniform on hand if there were any hysterics.

Jenny opened her eyes, but then closed them again. There had been that noise again, one that had intruded into her dream, and for a moment she felt disorientated. The buzz sounded again, and awake enough now to realise that it was the entrance gate, she dazedly reached out to switch on her bedside lamp to look at the clock. Five in the morning! Who on earth was at the gate? Fear clutched her stomach, a dread. Had something happened to Marcos? Had there been an accident?

She flung back the blankets and grabbed her dressing gown, throwing it around her as barefoot she hurried downstairs. Frantically she pressed the intercom.

'Yes, who is it?'

'Police. Let us in please.'

Jenny pressed the button to allow entry. She then shoved her arms into her dressing gown, her heart beating like a drum in her chest as she fumbled to tie the cord. At last she managed it, and at the sound of car doors slamming she opened the door. It was dark and Jenny quickly turned on the outside light to see a man and a policewoman. Her legs trembled, and she almost caved, clutching the doorframe for support.

No, no, not Marcos! Please, not Marcos!

Hands supported her, and Jenny found herself staring up at the man. He looked vaguely familiar and she blinked, but then the policewoman said, 'By the look of her she needs to sit down.'

'Which way?' the man asked.

Jenny pointed to the drawing room, glad of his continued support, and soon, head swimming, she found herself sitting on the sofa. For a moment nobody spoke, but then the policewoman said, 'Would you like a glass of water?'

'No, no,' Jenny said, feebly shaking her head. She

dreaded the words, wanted to shut them out, but then the man spoke.

'I'm here to inform you that Marcos Cane was involved in a robbery.'

It wasn't what Jenny expected to hear and the first thing she felt was relief, swiftly followed by denial. 'That's impossible.'

As though she hadn't spoken, the man said, 'I'm afraid that while attempting to escape there was an accident.'

Jenny frowned, unable to make sense of any of this. Marcos wouldn't have been involved in a robbery. They had made a mistake, a dreadful one. 'Where was this accident?'

'In London, on Farringdon Street.'

Angrily she said, 'Marcos is in Wales! You come here, saying such dreadful things but you've obviously got him mixed up with someone else!'

'There's no mistake, he's been identified, and the accident was a bad one. He . . . he didn't survive.'

Jenny found herself staring up at the man, his words impossible to believe.

'No, I told you, it can't be Marcos. He's in Wales!'

The policewoman knelt in front of her. 'I'm sorry, but we haven't made a mistake. The ID was positive, and the man with him, his associate, has been identified too. Perhaps you know him. Thomas Moon?'

Jenny gasped. Tom, Edna's son! She saw pity in

the policewoman's eyes, compassion. She felt odd, sick, and the truth when it hit her was more than she could bear. Her vision blurred, the room dimmed. Sinking into darkness, Jenny knew no more.

Chapter Forty-Two

On Sunday morning, Delia was pacing in the kitchen. 'Edward, I don't know how to comfort Jennifer. She fell downstairs yesterday, lost the baby, and with Marcos gone too she's inconsolable.'

'What do you expect?'

'I know, I know, but she should have been admitted when she was taken to hospital.'

'Jenny refused and they couldn't force her to stay. If there are any complications we'll insist she goes back, but so far, with you to look after her, Jenny seems fine.

'I still think she should be in hospital.'

'Delia, she just wanted to grieve in private. She wouldn't be able to do that in a hospital ward.'

'Yes, I suppose so, but I feel so inadequate. All she said is that Marcos died in a car accident, but other than that I can't get a word out of her.'

'For goodness' sake, she's still in shock, and it's little wonder she doesn't want to talk.'

'I . . . I thought it might help.'

'I know, I know, dear,' Edward consoled.

'I'll try again. It's gone nine, I'll see if she'll eat a little breakfast.'

'I don't want anything,' said Jenny, suddenly appearing at the kitchen door.

'Jennifer, you shouldn't be up!'

'I can't stay in bed forever,' she said, taking a seat at the table.

'How are you feeling, darling?' Edward asked.

'I'm . . .'

Jenny was interrupted as the entry system buzzed. She didn't move, but Edward did. 'I'll see who it is.'

'I don't want to see anyone.'

'I know, darling,' he said.

'I know you don't want anything to eat, dear,' Delia said, 'but would you like a cup of tea? There's a fresh pot made.'

'Yes . . . yes please.'

Delia had only just poured it when she heard the sound of raised voices and moments later a woman stormed into the kitchen.

'Who are you?' she demanded. 'What do you want?'

'I tried to stop her,' Edward said, hurrying in behind her.

'He killed him! He killed my son!'

'Now look here . . .'

'It's all right, Mummy,' Jennifer said. 'This is Edna and her son died in the crash too.'

'It was down to Marcos,' the woman cried. 'He killed my Tommy.'

'Of course he didn't,' Delia said. 'It was a tragic accident.'

'My boy shouldn't have been there. You've seen the newspapers, but my Tommy wasn't like that. He wasn't like *him*.'

'Jennifer, what on earth is she talking about?'

There was no answer. Jennifer just placed both hands across her face and gave a groan of anguish, followed by a sob.

As though the wind was taken out of her sails, Edna said, 'The poor cow. She had no idea.'

Edward sat beside Jennifer now and quietly said, 'Please, darling, let us help. Talk to us.'

As though a dam had burst, she blurted, 'I . . . I can't believe it, Daddy. The police said that Marcos was involved in a robbery . . . that he died while trying to escape apprehension.'

'What! No, that's impossible,' Delia cried.

Edna snorted. 'You don't know the 'arf of it.'

'What do you mean?'

'I felt sorry for Jenny, and yes I can call her that now, not Mrs Cane. I knew she was being made a mug of, wanted to tell her, but Marcos warned me to keep me mouth shut.'

'Tell her what?'

'Look, when the other one turns up, and I doubt it'll be long before she arrives, Jenny's gonna find out anyway,' Edna said, moving to lay a hand on Jennifer's shoulder. 'I'm sorry, I . . . I just needed to let off steam, but I shouldn't have come. It ain't your fault and I know that. I feel sorry for you, I really do. You don't deserve this, but brace yourself, 'cos there's worse to come.'

With that, Edna walked out of the room and Delia hurried after her. They reached the front door and Delia asked, 'What did you mean about worse to come?'

Edna pushed the gate release and opened the front door to step outside before she answered, 'Your girl's had enough for now and I'm saying no more. She's gonna need you though so, like I told her, brace yourself.'

'Wait,' Delia called, but ignoring her, the woman hurried away.

Delia closed the door, her stomach churning. She felt sick. Marcos involved in a robbery! Oh God, what if it was in the newspapers? Since rushing to look after Jennifer they hadn't seen one, but if it was in the press everyone would know! But it had to be a mistake. Marcos wasn't a thief! He was a cultured, charming man. Yes, yes, that was it, obviously a case of mistaken identity, and that was what she'd tell everyone.

Of course there'd be a retraction in the newspapers

too, Delia thought, feeling slightly better as she returned to the kitchen. Her son-in-law involved in a robbery! It was absolutely ridiculous.

Jenny couldn't bear to talk about it any more and wandered into the drawing room. Unlike her mother, she'd accepted that the man she loved, the man she thought she knew, was involved in a robbery. Her mind twisted and turned, sure that for some reason Marcos had been driven to do it, and the only thing that made any sense was an urgent need for money. Something must have gone dreadfully wrong with his businesses, it had to be that. Perhaps fearing that he wouldn't be able to support her and the baby, Marcos had been driven to take such desperate measures.

Oh, Marcos, Marcos, if only he had told her. She would have said that she didn't care about money, only him, but it was too late. He was gone now, their baby too. She felt so lost, bereft, empty inside.

The telephone rang, but Jenny ignored it. She heard her father's voice and then he came into the drawing room. 'That was Robin, ringing to see how you are. He said he'll drive down to see you on Saturday.'

Jenny dashed the tears from her eyes. 'I'd rather he didn't.'

'He's your brother and he's worried about you.'

'I . . . I'm all right.'

'No, you're not. Look at you, you've been crying again.'

'I . . . I can't help it.'

'Of course you can't. You've been through hell this last couple of days.'

'Edward, who was that on the telephone?' asked Delia, entering the room.

'Robin, and he's driving down on Saturday.'

'That's nice. Did you tell him that we're staying here?'

'Er . . . no . . . I wasn't sure where we'd be by then.'

'You can go home. I'll be all right,' Jenny said.

'No, Jenny, we don't want to leave you on your own yet. It's too soon.'

'Daddy, I'll be fine by Saturday.'

'Jennifer, I hate to say this,' Delia said, 'but there are so many things to do, to arrange, the . . . the funeral, and of course we have to ensure that the press print a retraction.'

'I can handle all that, Delia.' Edward said.

'Yes, yes, but we have to think about Jennifer's financial position.'

'I doubt she'll have any concerns there. I'm sure Marcos will have left her well provided.'

Jenny couldn't listen to any more. She stood up, swaying for a moment, then fled the room.

'Jennifer, wait . . .'

'Leave her, Delia. She isn't ready for any of this yet.'

'It's got to be faced.'

Jenny didn't hear any more and back in the bedroom, she flung herself across the bed, clutching Marcos's pillow. She could smell him, the dressing he used on his hair, the thought of never seeing him again unbearable.

Why had he been driven to attempt a robbery? Not only that, Edna had said there was more to face. Jenny sobbed. She didn't care. Whatever it was, it couldn't be that bad, nothing in comparison to losing Marcos.

At last, exhausted after getting hardly any rest the previous night, Jenny fell asleep. She had no idea that soon she would wish she had never woken up.

Chapter Forty-Three

On Monday morning Tina was reading the newspaper yet again. She looked up, scowling. 'I knew he was dodgy, tried to warn Jenny, but she wouldn't have it.'

'Like I said, you could have knocked me down with a feather when I was sent to his place in Wimbledon. I had no idea until then that she was the bird Steve had talked about.'

'I'm not surprised she was in a right old state.'

Yes, Jenny had been, Paul thought, but she had just lost her meal ticket so it wasn't surprising. Steve had said that Jenny was an innocent in all this, but Paul had his doubts. Nobody could be that innocent, especially as he doubted Marcos Cane had been able to hide his true colours. He'd been a nasty piece of work – violent, making his money by intimidation and having a nice turnover in auto theft. There'd been other robberies too, ones he'd got away with, and CID had been trying to nail him for years.

'I ain't seen her for ages,' Tina said, 'not since we split up, but I feel sorry for her now.'

'I hope you're not thinking of going to see her? You could be tarred by association and it wouldn't look too good if it got back to my DI,' Paul warned. Not only that, he didn't want Tina mixing with Jenny's type, women who'd put up with anything for a man's money. Tina wasn't like that, she was honest through and through, and he was happy to think that in just five months she'd be his wife.

'Keep your hair on,' Tina said as she pushed the newspaper to one side. 'We've gone our separate ways now and I'm not in favour of going backwards. I don't want reminders of my past, and that's what Jenny would be. Look to the future, that's what I say, and mine is with you.'

'It certainly is,' Paul said, smiling with relief.

Tina reached out behind her to grab a holdall and unzipped it. 'I'd best get off to me stall, but before I go, what do you think of these samples? I'm thinking of adding them to my range.'

'Sorry, sweetheart, I know nothing about beads and things.'

'The other stuff I got from that warehouse sold well.'

'I don't know how you stick it on that stall all day.'

'As long as you wrap up warm it's all right.'

'Once we're married you can give it up.'

'I'm not sure I want to. I enjoy it.'

'You'll have to when a baby comes along.'

'You're jumping the gun. We ain't married yet, and anyway, I can always stick the pram next to my stall.'

'You must be kidding,' Paul protested.

'Yeah, course I am, silly,' she said, dropping onto his lap and demanding, 'now give me a kiss.'

'Yes, your ladyship,' he said, happy to obey. Tina had agreed to get married in the summer, and he couldn't wait. From day one he'd known she was the girl for him, and after losing her once he wanted to make sure it didn't happen again.

It was the commotion that woke Jenny that same morning, shouting, a loud raucous voice drowning out her mother's. She threw back the blankets and went to the top of the stairs to see a big, blousy woman in the hall yelling, 'Where is she?'

'I don't know who you mean.'

'That bitch! I want her out of my house!'

'This isn't your house!' Delia protested.

'Yes it is, lady, and you can bugger off too. Now get out of my way!'

Jenny saw the woman shove her mother aside and quickly went downstairs. 'Don't do that!' she shouted as she neared the last step. 'Leave my mother alone!'

The woman's eyes were like slits, narrowed in fury. '*You!* Yeah, it must be you!'

Jenny felt her knees shaking as she tried to reason

with her. 'You must have come to the wrong address. This isn't your house. It belongs to my husband, Marcos Cane.'

'*Your* husband, don't make me laugh. *I'm* Pat Cane! His wife!'

'No, no, we were married last year, in Scotland.'

'Jennifer, she must be mad,' said Delia. 'I'll call the police.'

'Go on then, but it won't do you any good,' the woman spat. 'As his *wife*, I know my rights. If this soppy cow married him, it was bigamous.'

Jenny stumbled then and her mother rushed forward to support her. 'My daughter has just suffered a miscarriage and as you can see, she's still weak.'

'*What!* You was having his baby! Well, well, with that tiny willy of his I didn't think it was possible. Still, think yourself lucky you lost it. It stopped you bringing another bastard like him into the world.'

'Please . . . please don't . . . don't say that,' Jenny gasped.

The fight seemed to go out of the woman at this and shaking her head, she said, 'You poor cow.'

It was the same thing that Edna had said, but even had she been able to brace herself, Jenny knew she could never have been prepared for this. Her knees went from under her again. The two women supported her now, but she wanted to throw one of them off. She was Marcos's wife, not this loud-mouthed woman. Too weak to fight, Jenny was taken to the drawing room.

'Bloody hell, look at this,' Pat said as she looked around. 'That git living like a lord while I was stuck with his mother in Battersea.'

'This confirms there's been a mistake,' Delia said as between them they lowered Jenny onto the sofa. 'Marcos told us that both his parents had passed away.'

'His dad, yes, but his mother has always suspected that Marcos killed him.'

Unable to speak, words frozen in her throat, Jenny shook her head. This woman, this awful woman was talking about someone else. She had to be.

'Yeah, I can see you're shocked,' Pat continued as she flopped onto a chair.

'You were *not* invited to sit down,' Delia said haughtily. 'Now please leave. I refuse to believe that my daughter's husband was a thief, and I certainly don't believe he was a murderer!'

'Believe it, lady, 'cos it's true.'

'My son-in-law was a cultured man, a businessman, and,' she said, lips curling with distaste, 'he'd hardly be associated with, let alone marry, the likes of you.'

'Watch your soddin' lip, you stuck-up cow. As for Marcos being cultured, don't make me laugh. It was all an act, good enough to pull the wool over your eyes, it seems, so take a pew too because I'm gonna put the pair of you straight.'

Mouth gaping, Delia sat down while Pat took something out of her handbag. 'Right then, as I said, I'm his wife, and here's me marriage lines to prove it. Course I regret the day I met him now, and to be honest I didn't give a shit when he told me he was going off with you. In fact . . .'

'Wait, are you saying you're divorced?'

'No, the git knew I wouldn't agree to that. Firstly I'm a Catholic, and secondly, I wasn't about to take some measly one-off settlement. He paid me well to keep my mouth shut, and anyway, I knew what the bastard would do to me if I didn't. I ain't got to keep it shut now though, so let me tell you more about this so-called cultured man . . .'

Jenny listened, wanting to scream, to shout against what she was hearing. By the time the woman had finished, she was reeling in shock. Marcos, Marcos the man she loved, had been a monster, a vicious, violent monster. She was barely aware that her mother had reared to her feet until she spoke, and Jenny cringed against her words.

'My God, no wonder he didn't want to talk about his past! It was bad enough when the newspapers reported the robbery, but now this! What if it gets out? What will people think? What will Beatrice and Penelope think? I'll never be able to live it down, never be able to hold my head up again. How could you do this to me, Jennifer?'

'I . . . I didn't know.'

'I can't believe you're that stupid. You're just a tart, Irish trash like your mother!' Delia yelled, then marching from the room.

Pat opened her handbag again, pulling out a packet of cigarettes and lighting one.

'Well, that wasn't very nice,' she said, blowing out a stream of smoke.

Jenny hadn't expected her mother to react like that, but it shouldn't have surprised her. 'She . . . she always put a high value on appearances and feels I've let her down.'

'It ain't your fault. As I said, Marcos well and truly pulled the wool over your eyes, hers too come to that. Still, we've got things to sort out and we'd best get down to it. Now, I hate to say this, girl, but as his wife I'm entitled to everything.'

'I . . . I . . .'

'It's no good arguing,' Pat broke in. 'Things might've been different if he'd left a will, but I know he hasn't. The bastard wouldn't make one, thought it'd jinx him. Huh, what a laugh . . . and now the last laugh's on him.'

Jenny hadn't been about to argue. After losing Marcos, her baby, and then being told all this, she didn't have an ounce of fight in her.

'I was going to say that I'll move out, that's all.'

'Oh, right, well that's all right then,' Pat said, then looking at Jenny intently. 'Gawd, you look rough, but after what you've just heard it ain't surprising. It's funny though. When I came here I was spitting feathers, expecting to find a right tart, not someone like you.'

Jenny started to stand up. 'I'll go and pack my things.'

Pat's arm came out, pushing her back down again. 'No, love, if you'd been some old tart it might have been different. But you ain't, and I feel sorry for you. I'll give you a few days – shall we say Thursday?'

'Th . . . thank you.'

'Make sure you only take your own stuff, clothes and things.'

'Wh . . . what about my car?'

'Take it, I don't want it. There's plenty more in the garages, and hopefully mostly legit ones. Right, I'm gonna have a look round, but then I'm off. Oh yeah, and I'll want a set of keys.'

'There's some over there, in the drawer,' Jenny said, indicating.

'Nice bit of stuff this,' Pat said, running her hand over the wood. She took the keys, turned, avidly taking in everything else in the room, then walked out.

Jenny slumped. Despite all she had heard, all the sickening things about Marcos, she still found it hard to equate it with the man she knew. He had been kind, loving, generous . . . but with that thought the position she was now in finally hit Jenny. She had to move out of this house, the one she had lived in thinking she was his wife. Marcos had lied to her, lied about everything!

She heard the front door close and the sound of footsteps. Her mother walked into the room, her face contrite.

'She's gone, Jennifer, but I heard what she said, that you've got to move out by Thursday. Goodness knows what your father will say, but no doubt he'll insist you move in with us.'

'Don't worry, I won't be doing that.'

'Where will you go then?'

'I don't know, somewhere, anywhere, as long as it's miles away from here,' Jenny said, standing up to walk past her mother.

'Well, for your father's sake, I suggest you keep in touch this time.'

'I see you haven't included yourself in that,' Jenny said bitterly. She couldn't cry, she had no tears left. All she could do was pack.

Chapter Forty-Four

'Mary came from Bray, on the coast in County Wicklow,' Edward said, thankful that a place had come to mind, 'but with so much going on, why are you asking me where your mother was born?'

'Because I want to go there.'

'Go there! But why?'

'Since . . . since all this happened I've had this strange feeling, as though something is calling me. And . . . and last night, I had this dream, saw this place, a beautiful place. Is it beautiful there, Daddy?'

'There are lots of beautiful places, darling, and I'm sure it was just that, a dream. You've had a terrible shock, that's all, and perhaps this is your mind's way of coping with it.'

'No, it was more than that. I've decided, I'm going to Ireland.'

'Don't be silly. You aren't fully recovered yet and I insist you come home.'

'No, Daddy.'

'Jenny, there's nothing in Ireland for you, nobody to look after you.'

'I can take care of myself. '

'Look, I know what this is about. It's your mother and how she reacted.'

'She doesn't care about me. All she cares about is her social standing.'

'That isn't true. Your mother realises now that she behaved badly. She wants to apologise, but you won't take her calls.'

'I will, Daddy, perhaps tomorrow.'

'Jenny, you shouldn't spend another night alone here. Come home with me now, this evening.'

'I can't leave yet. I've still got packing to do and I don't have to move out yet, in fact not until Thursday morning.'

'You won't want to be here when that woman turns up again. What about tomorrow evening? I could come round to give you a hand with your cases.'

'I can manage. I've got my car.'

'Yes, but you shouldn't lift heavy things yet.'

'All right then, you can give me a hand.'

'That's my girl and in that case I'll hang on to the keys. Now, if you're sure you'll be all right, I'll go now.'

'I'll be fine.'

'See you tomorrow then, darling,' Edward said, heaving a sigh of relief that Jenny had given up her silly idea of going to Ireland. She'd be coming home, and as they had grown so close of late, Delia would be pleased. He drove home now, looking forward to passing on the good news to his wife.

'Well, what did Jennifer say?' Delia asked as soon as her husband walked in the door. Delia knew that in the heat of the moment, she had behaved badly, that all she'd been concerned about was her social standing and desperately wanted to apologise for the terrible things she'd said to Jennifer.

'She was reluctant at first, but I managed to talk her into coming home. I'm going back tomorrow evening to help with her cases.'

'I'm surprised she agreed, but pleased.'

'Are you really, Delia?'

'Yes, of course I am, though for all our sakes I think we should move away from this area. The gossip is dreadful and will get worse. People already know about Marcos, about the robbery, and that's bad enough. When it gets out that Jennifer wasn't really his wife, that she was just living with him, our lives will be made a misery.'

'I can understand why you feel like that, and yes, it might be for the best. However, it won't happen overnight. We'll have to put this house on the market, wait for a buyer . . .'

Delia was just relieved that Edward had agreed and shut out the rest of his words. She had already been shunned. At the grocer's that day when she'd bumped into a member of the WI – the woman had looked at her with disgust, giving her the cold shoulder before walking out of the shop. It had been devastating and Delia was especially worried now about her son having to face the same kind of behaviour. She had rung Robin, and though he had wanted to come down to see Jennifer at the weekend, she had encouraged him to stay away for now.

Delia's thoughts now turned to her sister. Beatrice had been horrified, and had expressed her disgust that Marcos had brought this shame on their family. She had then offered a few words of comfort, but so far she hadn't been in touch again. Delia had tried to ring her on several occasions, but the telephone had not been answered. Perhaps Beatrice was worried that by association it could cause ramifications for Timothy, yet surely it wouldn't come to that? Delia was upset that Beatrice seemed to be distancing herself, felt it was unnecessary, and given time she was sure her sister would realise that.

'. . . in the meantime Jenny needs us, our support, and when she comes home tomorrow evening, we'll be able to give her just that,' Edward said, looking at Delia now as though waiting for her response.

'Yes, we will, but I still need to apologise and perhaps if I ring her in the morning she'll take my call now,' Delia said. She had thought long and hard about her behaviour, how in the heat of the moment she had turned on Jennifer, but in all reality none of this was really the poor girl's fault. Like her, Jennifer had been taken in by a man's lies, and instead of offering sympathy and understanding, she had called Jennifer and her mother Irish trash. She shouldn't have said that, it was awful. It was the men in all this who were to blame, not the women. When Jennifer came home, Delia was determined to make amends, unaware then that it would be a long time before she got the opportunity.

When her father left at seven thirty, Jenny went upstairs to finish packing. She'd lied to him, but he'd left her no choice. If she hadn't agreed to go home her father would have gone on and on at her, and at least the fib had made him stop. Alone again now, the same thoughts plagued Jenny. Her life with Marcos as his wife had been a sham. Everything about him had been a sham. The man she loved had never existed, and she couldn't love the monster that had been presented in his place.

She couldn't stay here, but she wouldn't go to her father's house. Delia had made her feelings plain before she had stormed out, accusing her of bringing shame to her family, and saying she regretted the day that her father had found her. Yet it was the final, dreadful things she'd said that Jenny couldn't forget, words that had perhaps set off her dream. 'You're Irish trash,' Delia had yelled. 'Just like your mother!'

Jenny's hands trembled as she opened her jewellery box. She hadn't told her father what had been said. Delia would deny it, play her wounded act, and she didn't have the strength or the will to go up against her. Of course she knew what Delia had been inferring – that had her baby lived, she too would have been an unmarried mother.

But I didn't know my marriage was bigamous, Jenny thought. Irish trash . . . no, she refused to think of herself, or her mother, as that. Mary too had probably trusted a man, had been taken in by his lies, but he'd disappeared and left her mother's name in ruins. Was that why Ireland was calling her? Was her mother somehow reaching out from beyond the grave, urging her to go to Ireland, wanting her to uncover the truth?

She looked at her jewellery, hating it now, just as she hated the money in her bank account that Marcos had provided. Despite that, Jenny knew she had to be practical. To do what she wanted to do she had to have money, and if it ran out she could sell the jewels. She stuffed them in a pouch, hesitating as she wondered if her father was right – that the dream had been just an escape from the horrors of reality.

It was an hour later when the entry gate buzzed and Jenny's stomach flipped. She didn't want to open it, couldn't face any more, anyone, and froze. All was quiet and at first she thought that whoever it was had given up . . . but no, the buzzer went off again, this time incessantly. Jenny put her hands over her ears, but it didn't drown out the sound, and at last, stuffing the pouch of jewellery in her pocket, she went downstairs.

'Who is it?' she asked, her voice tremulous.

'It's the police. Let us in.'

Jenny allowed entry, wondering why they were here as she waited at the door. There was a thump of a fist on wood, and she opened it, staring at two very large men. They weren't in uniform and so at first she thought they must be from CID, but then they shoved her aside without a word, leaving her only able to cry out, 'What are you doing? What do you want?'

'What's owed,' one growled.

'I . . . I don't know what you mean.'

'Edna Moon lost her son, and we think she should be compensated.'

'Edna! Edna sent you here?'

'Nah, course not.'

'I don't understand. You're . . . you're not policemen?'

'Do we look like pigs?'

Jenny stared up at the man, shaking, and he answered his own question. 'Nah, but saying that got us in. Now then, down to business. Word's got round about Edna, and in our area we look after our own. It's down to Cane that her son's dead, and as I said, we think she deserves compensation.'

'You . . . you want money?'

'Yeah, that's right.'

'I . . . I think I've got a few pounds in my purse.'

'A few quid! You must be joking,' the man said, swinging around to address the other man. 'Right, AJ, let's look around. If she ain't got cash, we'll take it in kind.'

'No . . . no, you can't do that.'

'Who's gonna stop us?' he said as moving to the telephone, he ripped it from the socket. 'We'll start in there, and you . . . you're coming with us.'

Jenny's arm was grabbed and she was dragged into the drawing room, forced to watch in horror as the other man began to yank open drawers.

'Nothing much here,' he said, throwing things aside, 'but those ornaments and paintings might be worth a few bob.'

'I'll hold on to this one, AJ, while you stick 'em in the van.'

This continued, room by room, Jenny's legs barely able to support her as she ineffectually continued to plead, 'But none of this is mine. It . . . it belongs to Pat now. Pat Cane . . . his . . . his wife.'

'So what! That hard-faced, greedy cow will be sitting in clover now, but she won't do anything for Edna Moon.'

'She . . . she told me not to take anything.'

'If it ain't your stuff, what are you worried about?' he snapped. 'Now shut up! Your whining is getting on me wick.'

Jenny was then pushed upstairs, shoved onto her bed, and then noticing her packed cases the man called AJ asked, 'Going somewhere?'

'Pat . . . Pat Cane told me I've got to move out.'

'Now, why doesn't that surprise me,' he said, opening one of the cases.

'It . . . it's just my clothes.'

'Yeah, I can see that, and as that bitch is going to get the lot, I'll do you a favour and leave your gear alone. Where are you moving to?'

'I . . . I don't know, but a long way from here.'

He nodded, then left her things untouched, instead moving across the room to open a wardrobe and exclaiming, 'Fuck me, look at these suits.'

'I'd rather fuck her, AJ.'

'Let's get this job done first. Do you reckon they'd fit me?'

'Yeah, maybe, but I won't get into them.'

'I thought you said you'd rather get into her.'

Jenny began to shake, her eyes darting frantically round the room, seeking escape, but then AJ swung round, his eyes surprisingly kind. 'He's just joking. Like me, he ain't so hard up that he'd want Cane's leftovers.'

The other man, now rooting in the drawers, paused as he said, 'Well, well, look at this.'

'Jackpot! Rolex, Cartier, and those cufflinks are gold.'

'Yeah, they must be worth hundreds.'

'With all the other stuff, that should do it. Come

on,' AJ urged as they stuffed the valuables into their pockets, 'let's go.'

'What about her? She's bound to call the Old Bill and we don't want any of this put on Edna.'

AJ pursed his lips and then sat down beside Jenny. She scrambled away from him and he laughed. 'Scaredy cat, ain't yer. Now then, we don't like narks where we come from, so be warned. And as anything we get for this lot is going to Edna, you could call us good Samaritans.'

'Why don't we just shut her up permanently?'

'No . . . please, I . . . I won't say anything,' Jenny gasped, fighting for words. 'You . . . you're right. What does it matter? It . . . it isn't mine. None of it is mine and . . . and I'd like to help Edna.'

'Good girl,' he said approvingly, 'and anyway, what could you tell the police? You could give a description of us, but we're pretty average really. Names? We didn't use any and forget about him calling me AJ. It was just something set up for tonight.'

'It's still a bit risky,' the other one warned.

'Nah, she's all right,' said AJ, then looking at Jenny again. 'I'm taking a chance on you, but as I said, be warned. If you open your mouth you'll live to regret it.'

'I . . . I won't say anything,' Jenny said desperately. 'I . . . I promise.'

'Right, come on then, let's go,' he said, rising to his feet.

'Ain't you gonna at least tie her up? It'll give us a bit of time.'

'There's no need. The phone'll be out of commission for a while, and anyway, she's gonna keep her mouth shut.'

'Are you?' the other man asked, his eyes, unlike AJ's, hard on Jenny.

'Ye . . . yes . . .'

'Go,' AJ urged, pushing the other man out of the door.

There was the sound of them thudding downstairs, and then the front door slammed. Jenny heard the sound of an engine, tyres crunching over gravel, but couldn't move. She was still shaking, in shock, and time seemed to stand still.

Slowly, gradually, her limbs stopped shaking and at last Jenny got off the bed. She wanted to run then – run to safety, run to someone. Her father! Her stomach heaved and she dashed to the bathroom.

At last, only bringing up bile now, it was over and Jenny straightened, feeling dizzy and weak. She staggered to the sink, and in the mirror over it saw that her face was bathed in perspiration. She wanted a bath, as though she could wash away all the horrors of what had happened since Marcos's death. More than that, though, she wanted to get away from this house. It was then that the strange feeling engulfed her again, an overwhelming need, and all thoughts of running to her father died. Only he would want her – only he would welcome her.

Jenny quickly sloshed water over her face, cleaned her teeth and gargled, then hurried back to her bedroom. She couldn't spend another night here, wouldn't spend another night here. She took the pouch of jewellery from her pocket, amazed that the man who had held her hadn't realised it was there. Jenny stuffed it into one of her cases and now hurriedly packed an overnight bag in a strange state of automation. She put on a coat and a scarf, flung the bag over her shoulder and heaved the rest of the luggage downstairs.

It had felt like hours and hours had passed, but it was still only ten thirty as Jenny stepped outside. The darkness seemed to cushion her as she loaded the cases into the boot and then got behind the wheel.

She didn't look back at the house as she drove away. Something or someone was calling her, urging her on. Jenny was going to Ireland.

Chapter Forty-Five

The two men were whooping as they drove back to Battersea, pleased with their haul.

'What a mug, Billy. Or should I say "AJ"? She fell for it hook, line and sinker.'

'No need for that AJ crap now,' Billy said, grinning. 'It's thanks to my old woman going to offer her sympathies to Edna that we've got a nice bit of stuff to flog. I might just buy her a bunch of flowers.'

'Why break the habit of a lifetime? The shock might be too much for her, and anyway, if Cane hadn't kicked the bucket, Edna wouldn't have opened her mouth. She was shit-scared of him.'

'A lot were, but good riddance to bad rubbish, that's what I say.'

'Unlike Pat Cane, his bird on the side's a bit tasty.'

'Yeah, she is, but she didn't look much more than a kid and I felt sorry for her. She was frightened out of her wits when you suggested shutting her up permanently.'

'It did the trick though.'

'That, plus the fact that the soppy cow swallowed that shit about the proceeds going to Edna.'

'Like I said, she's a mug. Are we taking the stuff straight to Mickey the fence?'

'We need to get it off our hands, so yeah.'

'Should fetch a nice few bob.'

'Yeah, and it's all going in our pockets.'

'What! We ain't giving it to Edna?'

'Shut up you daft sod,' Billy said, grinning at the mock shock on his mate's face. 'You know perfectly well we're not giving her a brass farthing.'

Jenny had no idea how long it would take her to get to Fishguard, but as the miles passed her mind began to calm. She didn't care about the things those men had taken, or that Pat Cane would find the house ransacked when she turned up on Thursday. She had liked Edna, and now understood why the woman had been so reticent to talk about Marcos. Though money couldn't compensate Edna for the loss of Tommy, her son, at least it would cushion her for a little while financially.

Jenny continued on, feeling cocooned in the car. The further she drove, the safer she felt, but eventually her eyelids began to droop. She realised that if she didn't stop now it would be too late to find somewhere to stay overnight. Nearing Marlborough, she spotted a sign for a hotel, and gratefully pulled in.

It wasn't very large, but Jenny parked up, grabbed her overnight bag and went inside. There was a man sitting behind a small reception desk, and she asked, 'Have you got a single room for the night?'

'Yes. I'll just need a few details. Your name, please.'

'Jennifer Cane,' she said automatically. She hated to use it now, but with all her documents in that name she had no choice until she could get them changed.

'First floor, the number's on the key and the bathroom's further along the landing,' he said, passing it over. 'Will you want breakfast in the morning?'

'Yes, please.'

'It's served between seven thirty and eight thirty.'

'Thank you,' she said, looking around as he pointed to a flight of stairs. She heaved her overnight bag further onto her shoulder and took them.

The room was small and adequate. Though nearly midnight, there was one thing Jenny wanted more than anything now – a bath.

The water was hot, and for a while she just lay and immersed herself as her tension eased. However, Jenny was so tired she was soon back in her room, yawning. She expected to go straight to sleep, but instead, though her body was relaxed, her mind wasn't. If her father was right, that this urge to go to Ireland was nothing but her imagination, there were other places she could go. So many places, and surely in one of them she could make a new life for herself? She'd be alone again and for a moment the thought was unbearable. Memories of her childhood now rose to haunt her. There had been times back then, when she had felt alone, that there was something missing in her life and she felt the same now, an inner yearning, a reaching out for something that wasn't there. At last, with a question still on her mind, Jenny finally drifted off to sleep.

The yearning was leading her to Ireland. Would she find her answers there?

On Wednesday evening, Edward tried to ring Jenny to let her know he was on his way, but found that Delia was right and he couldn't get through.

'I told you, Edward, I tried earlier, but I think Jennifer must have already had it disconnected.'

'Right then, I'm off to collect her,' he said. As he headed for Almond Crescent, Edward was still cursing himself, annoyed that he hadn't paid attention to his instincts. Marcos had played him, played a part. All along Edward had felt that something wasn't quite right about the man, but his desire for them all to be a family again, which had meant including Marcos, had led him to set his doubts to one side.

The crescent was deserted, but then it always was, those living here usually inside, in houses set well back from the road and mostly hidden from view. Jenny's was the same . . . no, not Jenny's now, Edward corrected himself. His daughter had been left with nothing. The house was in darkness as he parked in the drive; feeling puzzled, Edward let himself in.

'Jenny, it's me,' he called, fumbling for the light switch.

No answer, and beginning to feel worried now Edward dashed upstairs to Jenny's bedroom where, after fumbling for a light and turning it on, he stood frozen by what he saw. The room was a mess, with what looked like some of Marcos's clothes thrown all over the place, but there was no sign of Jenny. Edward went to her wardrobe and opened it but found it almost entirely empty. It was then that he knew. His daughter had gone, left, and without any warning. Edward switched off the light and went downstairs. He threw the keys on the hall table, left the house in darkness as he'd found it, slamming the door behind him. He could guess where Jenny had gone and he would go after her.

'*Gone!* Gone where?' Delia asked when Edward returned.

'To Ireland, I think.'

'What on earth for? Surely you didn't tell her?'

'No, of course I didn't. It's just some sort of daft idea Jenny got into her head, but I thought I'd talked her out of it.'

'Obviously not – It's me isn't it? She didn't want to come home because of me.'

'No, Delia, I'm sure it isn't that.'

'Then why run off without a word?'

'I don't know, but I intend to find her. I'll arrange a couple of weeks off and leave for Ireland on Saturday.'

'But we've got a viewing then.'

'The sale of the house will have to be put on hold. We aren't going anywhere until I find Jenny.'

'Edward please, my reputation is already shattered and I can't bear the thought of remaining in this area.'

'The gossip will die down.'

'Edward,' Delia appealed, 'hasn't it occurred to you that if Jennifer wanted us to know where she was going she'd have left word; rung us or left a note. You say you think she's gone to Ireland, but what if you're wrong and you go off on a wild-goose chase?'

'I suppose you're right, but what else can I do?'

'Jennifer has been through so much and it may be that she just needs some time on her own to sort her feelings out. We can give her that, and still sell the house.'

'What if we don't hear from her before a sale goes through?' Edward said.

'We can leave word that we've moved, and if we're in another area, it might encourage her to come back.'

'I suppose that makes sense, but I'm worried sick about her, Delia.'

'So am I, but I suppose we've got to accept that Jennifer is a grown woman now and capable of making her own decisions,' she said, glad that she'd been able to talk Edward round and hoping that she was right. That before long they would hear from Jennifer.

Chapter Forty-Six

With the money in her purse used up to pay for the hotel, Jenny needed to find a bank the following morning. She drew out what she felt would be sufficient to last her for a long time and then continued on her journey. However, what with needing the occasional stop for refreshments, being unused to maps and judging distances, it was dark again by the time she neared Carmarthen in Wales. She had set out blindly, with no idea of the ferry timetable, but having been told at a hotel she'd pulled into that Fishguard was about another hour's drive, Jenny had used their telephone and found that a ferry would be leaving for Rosslare in the morning. That had sealed her decision and she had stopped for the night.

Now though, it was Thursday morning and at last she was crossing the Irish Sea. The water was rough, tossing the ferry as though it wanted to disgorge its passengers into its depths. Many were sick, but Jenny had made her way to the deck, exhilarated as the wind buffeted her face, something still calling her.

On and on, across the sea, hours passing, and when they finally reached Rosslare, Jenny was eager to disembark. She had to take her turn queuing to disembark, and while she was waiting she studied the map of Ireland she had bought on board. She found Dray, which lay on the coast towards Dublin, and at last, as the driver in front of her started his engine, she quickly stowed the map.

Jenny drove down the ramp with no idea how long it would take her to reach Dray, but it didn't matter. She was here, in Ireland, and for now that was enough. As she drove the narrow roads, she was enchanted by the countryside on one side, and occasional views towards the sea on the other. This was where her mother had been born, where she had grown up, and Jenny couldn't wait to see Dray.

She stopped for something to eat in a little village, charmed by the lilting voices around her, by the smiling faces, and the wonderful fish stew which she ate with relish. Marcos would have loved this, she thought, but then tensed. No, no, she didn't want to think about him, the man she had loved only a facade.

'Did you enjoy that?' the woman who had served her asked.

'Yes, it was lovely.'

'I haven't seen your face before. Are you staying around here?'

'No, I'm just passing through, on my way to Dray.'

''Tisn't holiday season, so what's taking you there?'

Jenny paused, but then said, 'I was hoping to find out something about a family who lived there by the name of Murphy.'

'It's a common enough name,' the woman said, her features hardening as she picked up the empty bowl. 'Now can I get you anything else?'

Jenny didn't know what she had said to offend the woman and, puzzled she shook her head. 'No, no, thank you.'

She rose to her feet and paid the bill, noticing as she did so that faces that had been smiling were now straight as she left. Upset, unable to work out why 'a common name', as the woman called it, had caused everyone to react like that, she continued her journey, finding that dusk was falling when she at last reached her destination.

Dray looked to be a fairly large place, a town rather than a village, but all the hotels she saw were closed. One of the roads she took led to a deserted esplanade, the pebbled beach desolate as waves crashed to the shore. Jenny remained in her car, staring out to sea, feeling lost and alone. She hadn't known what to expect, but this place was nothing like the one she'd seen in her dream. Yet this was where her mother had lived, where her family had lived. Giving herself a mental shake, Jenny at last drove off again.

She would find somewhere to stay, and if nothing else, she might at least find where her mother was buried. She would lay flowers, and at least it might make her feel closer to the mother she had never known. It was to become Jenny's mission.

Pat Cane was still fuming on Friday morning, but there was no way she was going to the Old Bill. Where she came from you sorted out things your own way, and Wimbledon or not, she was going to start asking questions. She'd been hampered until now with moving in and sorting out bedrooms, but now she was coiled and ready to act.

'Mum, I'm going next door.'

'Thissa room too big. I'm cold.'

'I'll get you a blanket to wrap round your legs.'

'I don't like it here.'

'Don't tell me you'd rather live in Battersea.'

'It . . . it'sa strange here. Can'ta we go home?'

Pat sat down again, heaved a sigh and said, 'Look, this place is a palace. At least give it a try, perhaps for a month or two. If you really can't settle after that, I'll flog it.'

'You's a gooda girl,' Maria Cane said, patting Pat on the knee.

'You're more a mother to me than mine ever was, and through it all, we've had each other.'

'Yes, but I don'ta deserve you. My husband was a monster and when he died . . . God forgive me, I was glad. I gotta my punishment. Marcos grew up worsa than him; evil, wicked, and now I'ma glad he'sa dead too. I will be punished again, I know I will.'

'No, you won't. You have every right to feel like that, we both do. Now I'll get you that blanket and then I'm off. Don't worry, I won't be long,' Pat said, and after tucking a blanket around her mother-in-law she hurried out.

Gawd, sod this, Pat thought. It wasn't like popping next door in Battersea, the distance from the nearest neighbour bloomin' ridiculous, but at last she was knocking on a door, and the horsey-faced woman who opened it looked her up and down.

'Yes, can I help you?' she asked.

'Me name's Pat and I live next door now,' she said, arm flapping in the general direction.

'The Canes' house?'

'Yeah, that right, but the bitch who was living there has run off with some valuable stuff and I want it back.'

'I beg your pardon. Who are you referring to?'

'Jennifer Cane, as she had the nerve to call herself, but she wasn't his wife. I am.'

'What! But I thought they were married.'

'Nah, she was just my old man's bit on the side. Still, it sounds like you knew her, so do you know where she went?'

392

'We were barely acquainted and I have no idea,' the woman said haughtily.

'Well, if you hear anything let me know, 'cos when I get hold of her I'll wring her bleedin' neck.'

The woman paled at this, her eyes wide in shock as she stammered, 'Yes, well . . . if . . . if you'll excuse me now,' and the door closed.

Pat wasn't about to give up yet. Someone must know something so she set off to knock on more doors.

It didn't do any good, and by the time Pat returned home, she'd already had enough of Almond Crescent.

'Bloody load of stuck-up gits,' she said, flopping onto the sofa, 'and one woman had the nerve to shut her door in me face.'

'They not friendly?'

'You must be kidding,' Pat said, her mind now made up. Rich or not, palace or not, they didn't fit in here and now she didn't want to. She was a Battersea girl, born and bred, and though they wouldn't go back to Mysore Road, she'd find them another house, somewhere perhaps facing good old Clapham Common.

When the doorbell rang late in the afternoon, Delia pulled back the curtain; seeing Penelope Grainger outside, her heart skipped a beat. She patted her hair, went to the door and forced a smile as she opened it.

'Penelope, how nice to see you. Do come in.'

'Mrs Lavender, this is not a social call. Is your daughter here?'

No first names now, Delia thought, but kept up her front. 'No, I'm afraid not. She . . . she's away at the moment.'

'Then I suggest you tell her not to come back.'

'Penelope, please, what happened wasn't Jennifer's fault. She thought her husband was an honest businessman, we all did.'

'Husband! I don't think so, especially as I've just had the dubious pleasure of meeting my new neighbour. His wife.'

'Oh, no . . . no!'

'Yes, well, I rather liked your daughter and suspect she was taken in by that rogue, however, *Mrs* Cane is out for blood. It seems that when Jennifer left, she took valuables that didn't belong to her.'

'But . . . but she wouldn't have done that!'

'I'm only repeating what that awful, common woman told me, and may I add she said something about wringing Jennifer's neck. I felt I should warn her, and as I said, it might be prudent if she didn't come back. Goodbye, Mrs Lavender.'

With that, Penelope swung round and marched off, leaving Delia to call ineffectually, 'Good . . . goodbye.'

Oh God, this is too much, Delia thought as she went back to the living room. Pouring a good measure of brandy, she gulped it down, gasped, and then almost collapsed onto a chair. She felt she had lost everything now, her reputation, her social standing, but like Penelope she didn't blame Jennifer. She had in fact grown fond of her, oh not as a daughter of course, she could never be that, though the fault was not Jennifer's, but Edward's. Anger boiled, anger that had been suppressed for too long. By persuading her to adopt, Edward had been the instigator of her feelings from the moment he had carried Jennifer as an innocent baby into the house.

Yes, Delia admitted, Jennifer had been innocent, but nevertheless she had made the girl's life a misery, driven her out at just sixteen years old.

It wasn't Jennifer she should have driven out, Delia thought, grinding her teeth. It was Edward! She had worried about divorcing him, worried that back in those days she'd be cut dead, but what good had that done? Yes, she'd managed to build a respected reputation, but it had been for nothing, now torn to shreds. Well she had nothing to lose now. She could leave Edward. Divorce him!

Delia poured another brandy, a large one, uncaring if it went to her head, and by the time Edward came home her anger had grown into volcanic proportions that erupted as soon as he walked into the room.

'I hate you! Do you hear me, I hate you!' she screamed, running up to him and pounding his chest.

'Stop it, Delia! What on earth is wrong with you?'

'There's nothing wrong with me! It's you! You caused all this.'

'You're behaving like a mad woman,' Edward said, grasping her arms and pushing them to her sides.

'Yes, I'm mad . . . mad to have stayed with you.'

'Delia, for goodness' sake, what's brought this on?'

'It's you! You've ruined my life!'

Edward pushed her away. 'I've just come home, I'm tired, and in no mood for your hysterics.'

'I'm *not* hysterical! You must have thought I was stupid, blind, but you were wrong. From the moment you placed Jennifer in my arms, I had my suspicions.'

'Oh, for goodness' sake, Delia, not this again.'

'I just wish I could prove it, but proof or not, if Jennifer was here now I'd at last tell her just what sort of man you are, why I was driven to act as I did. I hate myself for the way I treated her now, took it out on her, but I hate *you* more.'

'You're out of your mind.'

'No, Edward, in fact for the first time I feel my mind is clear,' Delia said, a strange calm washing over her. 'I'm leaving you now, going upstairs to pack and then I'll consult a lawyer. I said some dreadful things to Jennifer the last time I saw her, called her mother trash, and though I'd like to apologise I doubt I'll see her again. My only hope is that, however unlikely, while in Ireland she somehow stumbles across the truth. She'll hate you too then, Edward, and I think more than she hates me.'

'Maybe, but it's more likely she'd find what *you* did was worse, unforgivable. You should thank me that I've ensured she will never find out.'

Delia's teeth ground as she stormed from the room. She might not be able to tell Jennifer, but she'd tell Robin – and just in case Edward tried to use it against her, she would tell her son everything, even including the role she'd played in all this.

Chapter Forty-Seven

Edward couldn't believe it. Delia hadn't been bluffing, had actually walked out and, now that the initial shock had worn off, he just hoped she didn't come back. Delia had threatened to tell Jenny, and though there might not be any proof it wasn't something he wanted his daughter to hear. That still left Robin. Had Delia been in touch with their son? If so, what had she told him?

It was a gloomy Saturday morning and Edward was in the garden. Some of the early daffodils were in bloom and tulips were poking their heads through the soil, but the sight failed to cheer him up. He went inside again, about to ring Robin when the doorbell rang.

'Good morning, Mr Lavender.' It was the estate agent. 'I've brought my clients to view the house.'

Edward's first reaction was to say it was no longer for sale, but then realised that, in order to keep Delia away from Jenny, it would be prudent to put as much distance between the two of them as possible.

'Come in, but excuse the mess. I'm afraid my wife is away.'

The agent escorted the couple around, and when they were ready to leave, Edward had a feeling they liked what they'd seen. With the house to himself again, Edward went to the telephone, saying as Robin answered, 'I suppose you've spoken to your mother?'

Edward listened, and then said, 'Robin, I did not lie to her. Mary really was a distant relative, one I hadn't even met. If your mother thinks differently it's all in her head.'

He listened again. 'She told you that too! I'm surprised; after all, what she forced me to do doesn't put her in a very good light. If Jenny found out she would be devastated, and it's kinder to keep her in the dark.'

Robin wasn't so sure, but after a little convincing he agreed.

'Well goodbye for now,' said Edward, 'but before you hang up, let me assure you again that what your mother has accused me of is totally unfounded. I hope you believe that.'

Robin made a murmuring sound, neither saying whether he did or he didn't, but Edward felt his son was almost convinced. Delia could shout all she liked, but there was no proof and never would be. Replacing the receiver, Edward went out to the garden again.

Spring flowers, heralding a new season, and as he began to pull out some emerging weeds the task settled his mind. He didn't want Delia near Jenny now and would go along with the divorce, offer no arguments that might incur a delay. Though it would cost him half of everything he had, it would be worth every penny.

The weekend had passed and early on Monday morning, Jennifer was at the Holy Redeemer Church. It was her last hope in her search to find her mother's grave, or that of any other relative. As Jenny searched the headstones, she thought back over the last day or so. She hadn't meant to but somehow she'd upset people with her questions, any mention of the Murphys meeting with suspicion, as before. Wherever she went now, eyes seemed to be watching her, and even when she'd climbed up to Dray Head, staring out to sea, she had felt a menacing presence.

She'd had a broken night's sleep, waking early, and now her mind was foggy as she tried to make sense of it all. Surely after all these years it wasn't because of her mother? She had been pregnant and unmarried, something that had no doubt been frowned upon, but that didn't explain this level of animosity.

'Can I help you, my child?'

'I . . . I'm looking for my mother's grave. Her name was Mary Ann Murphy.'

'It isn't a name I'm familiar with,' the priest said, 'but I have a little time before the next service. Come inside and I'll look at the church records.'

'Th . . . thank you, Father.'

'Was she born in Dray?'

'I think so, but when I've asked about a family called Murphy it . . . it seems to upset people.'

The priest chuckled. 'That isn't surprising. In these parts any questions from an English outsider would be met with suspicion.'

The penny finally dropped and Jenny gasped.

'Now don't be thinking we're all rebels,' he said, leading her into a small room and removing a large, bound book from a shelf. 'Do you know when she was born?'

'Not exactly, but I'm eighteen and I know she died when I was born.'

He began to turn page after page, finding nothing, then took down another book and looked through that. 'No, I can't find any reference to Mary Ann Murphy. Are you sure she came from these parts?'

'It . . . it's what my father told me, and . . . and that her parents died when their house burned down.'

'Let's see if we can find Sean. He's one of Dray's oldest residents and still takes care of the church grounds.'

Jenny shivered as they went outside again and she followed the priest until he found an old man tending to the grass on the far side of the graveyard.

'Sean, did you know a family that hailed from here some years ago? The Murphys – their house burned down.'

The old man did not look up, simply shaking his head.

'Are you sure? This young lady is looking for the grave of her mother, Mary Ann Murphy, and perhaps the rest of her family who died in the fire.'

'Never heard of any Murphy's house burning down. Doubt they came from here.'

The priest turned to Jenny. 'It seems you may have come to the wrong place.'

'But my father was related to them, came here to visit them when he was a child.'

'I've lived in Dray for over seventy years and I'm telling you, they didn't live around here,' the old man insisted.

'I . . . I must have misheard the name. Is there somewhere similar?'

'Not in this county,' he said, going back to his work now.

'Thank you for your help,' Jenny said, 'and thank you, Father.'

'Good luck, my child. I hope you find what you're looking for.'

With a small wave Jenny walked away. Despite what she'd said, she knew she hadn't misheard her father. He had definitely said Dray, but how could he have been so mistaken? She wanted to talk to him, ask him. As it was a Monday he'd be at his office and she'd be able to avoid having to talk to Delia if she rang him there.

'Jenny, thank God. Where are you?'

'I'm in Ireland, in Dray, but it's been a waste of time. There aren't any records here of a family called Murphy.'

'Darling, it was so many years ago and I was only a child when I travelled there with my parents. I . . . I have so little memory of it . . . I must have got it wrong.'

'Dad, please try to remember.'

There was a moment's silence on the line, but then Edward said, 'I'm sorry, I thought it was Dray and I can't think of anywhere else. Jenny, listen, I felt you had gone to Ireland and was going to come after you, but your mother convinced me to stay here. She's gone now, left me, and we're getting a divorce.'

'What! But why?'

'Things haven't been right between your mother and me for years, Jenny, but it won't make any difference to us. I'm selling the house, had an offer first thing this morning, and once it all goes through, you and I can move away from here.'

'I . . . I'll think about it, but, Dad, you said my real mother was put in a home, gave birth to me there. You must know where it was.'

There was a short silence, but then he said, 'Er . . . yes. It was in, er . . . Limerick.'

'Can you remember the name of the home?'

'Not really, I was just glad to get away from there, to take you away from there. It was a grim place, run by nuns, called something like the Saint someone-or-other's home for fallen women.'

Jenny's thoughts raced. 'Dad, on the adoption certificate you gave me, there's nothing on it about my place of birth, or my real mother's name. There must be records somewhere that I can get hold of.'

'I'm afraid not. As your adoptive parents, our names are shown on your certificate and not that of your mother. I'm afraid you aren't allowed access to your original certificate.'

'Why not? Surely I have the right to see it.'

The sigh down the line was audible. 'It just isn't possible and it's done I think to protect unmarried mothers. They may have kept the birth and adoption a secret, gone on to make a new life for themselves, married, had more children.'

Jenny didn't understand. 'Dad, my mother died and so what harm could it do to just find her grave?'

'I know, but it's the law, darling.'

'It doesn't seem right, but at least I know she died in Limerick. I'll go there, see if I can find the home and where she was buried.'

'But why, Jenny? What good will it do?'

'I . . . I want to put some flowers on her grave.'

'Jenny, please, I'm worried about you and want you to come home.'

'Not yet, Dad. I need to do this, have to do this.'

'At least keep in touch, ring me, and don't stay away for too long.'

'Goodbye, Dad,' Jenny said, replacing the receiver. She'd go back to the pub where she was staying; it had been the only place she'd found open that could offer her a room. She would leave Dray, go to Limerick, she decided and now nervous of bumping into anyone, she almost scuttled up to her room.

With legs stretched out in front of her on the bed, Jenny studied the map, her eyes travelling past Dublin, up along the coastline. She yawned, still tired after a broken night's sleep, and before finding Limerick her eyes were starting to droop and she hardly realised it as she drifted off.

The dream came, the beautiful place, and Jenny was lost in it when the sound of voices intruded, along with the smell of food, woke her. The aroma teased her nostrils again and her stomach growled. She'd missed breakfast and would need to eat something before setting off, and of course she had yet to pay her bill.

Jenny would be glad to leave Dray, but first she had to brave the bar, and she walked in to find the landlord and landlady, along with a few customers, smiling at her.

'Sure, there you are,' Mrs Quinn said from behind the bar. 'Are you after some lunch?'

'Yes . . . yes please.'

'I've a nice stew. How does that sound?'

'Lovely.'

'I'll fetch it,' she said, smiling warmly before bustling away.

'So, you're trying to trace your mammy's grave?' Mr Quinn said, vigorously polishing a glass.

'Yes, that's right, but I didn't have any luck.'

''Tis sorry I am we couldn't help you.'

'Can I buy you a drink, darlin'?' a customer asked as he came to the bar.

'Thank you, but I'm only having a cup of tea.'

'You should try the Guinness.'

'Michael, if she'd wanted Guinness she'd have asked for it,' Mr Quinn told him.

'Maybe some other time,' Jenny said.

'There'll be music tonight,' Michael said. 'Patrick over there on his fiddle. You'll enjoy the craic.'

'I'm afraid I'm leaving shortly.'

'Now that's a shame. Are you going back to England?'

'No, but if you'll excuse me I need to get my map,' Jenny said, hurrying back upstairs to fetch it. It seemed odd, as though she'd gone to sleep in one place and woken up in another. Everyone was so nice now, warm, friendly, and for the first time since arriving she was beginning to like Ireland.

When she went back inside, Mrs Quinn was putting a steaming bowl of stew on a table.

'Lamb,' she said, 'but be careful, 'tis hot.'

Jenny thanked her and, so hungry that she couldn't wait, she blew on each spoonful, finding the stew delicious. Once she'd finished, she spread out her map.

'Can I help you, me darlin'?' Michael asked, sitting down next to her.

'I'm looking for a place called Limerick.'

'Are ye thinking your mammy's from there?'

'I . . . I'm not sure,' Jenny said.

''Tis there,' Patrick said as he came to stand by the table, pointing at the map. 'Over towards the west coast.'

She looked up at Patrick, smiling. 'Thank you.'

He smiled back at her, nodded, and then went back to his own table. Michael gently patted her shoulder, and before going back to the bar he said softly, 'I hope you find what you're looking for there.'

Jenny asked for the final bill, paid it, and with good wishes ringing in her ears, she dashed upstairs to pack her things.

As she left the pub Jenny found herself thinking that somehow Dray looked different now. A weak sun was shining through broken clouds, and she could just imagine it packed with holiday-makers in the summer.

She, however, was going to Limerick.

Chapter Forty-Eight

Jenny was still driving across Ireland when Edward came home from work to walk into a silent house. It didn't bother him and he threw off his coat before going through to the kitchen. It was a mess, would probably have caused Delia to have a fit, but so what? She wasn't here any more and that suited him just fine. In fact, if it hadn't been for Jenny and Robin he'd have left her years ago.

He heard a sound, the front door opening and went into the hall to see Delia standing just inside, her eyes like ice as she glared at him.

'How dare you!' she spat. 'How dare you lie to my son!'

'Lie about what?'

'You know what! You've gone too far now, persuaded Robin that it's all in my head, that I'm losing my mind.'

'What do you expect, Delia? You've always been prone to unreasonable behaviour, hysterics, and

Robin knows that. After all, he's seen enough of it over the years.'

'You . . . you,' she ground out, 'you won't get away with this. Admit it! Go on, admit it!'

'No, Delia, I'll admit nothing. Now I suggest you leave.'

She lost it then, picking up a glass vase from the hall table to throw at him. Edward moved quickly to one side and it smashed into the wall. Shards of glass flew everywhere, but Edward just smiled sardonically. 'As I said, Delia, unreasonable behaviour.'

'That's enough, Dad,' Robin said, suddenly rounding the door and stepping inside.

'What are you doing here?' Edward asked, shocked but recovering quickly. 'Why aren't you at university?'

'Mummy's still upset and I was worried about her. I told them it was an urgent family matter, drove down, and I'm glad I did.'

'I am too. You've seen her state of mind for yourself now.'

'Yes, I've seen it, but understand it too. We've had a good long talk and I can see now that, despite your denials, everything she's accused you of makes sense. I always wondered why Mummy couldn't take to Jenny, why she acted as she did, and just telling me years ago that she didn't want to adopt her didn't really cover it.'

'Robin, your mother may think it, accuse me of it, but it was, and still is, all in her mind. I'm not going to admit to something I didn't do, some mad idea she got into her head from the beginning. What about the role she played, the one that could break Jenny's heart if she found out?'

'I'm not happy about it, but it was a lot to ask of Mummy and in a way I can sympathise.'

Delia nodded. 'No doubt, you thought Robin would turn on me when I told him the truth, *all* of the truth, but he didn't. He's on my side.'

'Is this true, Robin?' asked Edward.

'Dad, I don't want to take sides. I just want you and Mummy to sort this out and get back together.'

'No, Robin,' said Delia. 'Our marriage is over now and I'm seeing a solicitor in the morning to file for divorce.'

'Do that, Delia. I'm sick of these accusations and I'm not putting up with it any more. A divorce suits me too.'

'You think you're clever, don't you, that I can't win, but you won't feel so clever when I take half of everything you've got.'

'It'll be worth it to see the back of you.'

'You . . . you . . .' she ground out again, but as words seemed to fail her, Delia spun round to march out of the house.

'I'll have to go after her,' Robin said.

'I understand, son. We'll talk again, but in the meantime, look after your mother.'

With a quick nod and a wave, Robin was gone, just about managing to get into Delia's car before she sped off. Edward closed the door, puffed his cheeks, and returned to the kitchen.

Delia had been devious, hoping that while Robin had been out of sight, he'd admit the truth. Thank the lord he hadn't, instead managing to turn it all onto her. Robin wouldn't tell Jenny any of it – the last thing he'd want to do would be to hurt his sister. Now all Edward had to do was to keep Jenny and Delia apart.

Jenny had worked out her route and was now nearing Portlaoise. She didn't like driving in the dark, preferring to see the wonderful views and she had stopped several times. Now though, a soft, misty rain was falling.

When she reached the town, Jenny decided to stop overnight. She parked the car, grabbed her overnight bag and stepped out. She looked around, and needing to stretch her legs, light rain or not, she walked for a while. The street she took eventually led her to a square with a grassy island in the centre. There was a pub on the corner, its lights shining in welcome and she headed towards it. Perhaps they'd have a room.

They did, and after being shown it she was

invited warmly to come downstairs again for a drink. Jenny agreed and found a bar of smiling people, including a group who soon drew her into their conversation.

'So, you're on your way to Limerick?' one pretty dark-haired girl said when told her destination. 'What's taking you there?'

'Family,' Jenny said, leaving it at that.

'I thought I could see a trace of Irish in you,' a young man said, smiling warmly.

Jenny sipped her Guinness, trying not to show that she didn't really like the bitter taste, and the conversation turned from her to other things. After an hour, the smoke from cigarettes became too much, her tired eyes stinging. She made her excuses, said goodnight to the group, glad to go up to her room. They had been so nice though and she was starting to feel strangely at home in Ireland as she climbed into bed.

With no memory of falling asleep, Jenny woke the next morning, feeling disorientated as she sat up in bed. Her mind cleared and she smiled sleepily, ready for the next stage or her journey. Would she reach Limerick that day? She hoped so.

After a hearty breakfast Jenny set off, pleased to see as she walked back to her car that it had stopped raining. She placed the map beside her on the passenger seat, but as she drove away she felt a sudden wave of loneliness. It would have been wonderful to have someone with her, someone to share this journey, to pass the time having a good old craic – as the Irish would say.

A long drive stretched ahead, and the roads narrower than those in England, but after leaving Portlaoise, traffic became light. Time passed and she drove by villages – Mountrath, Castletown – and she stopped in Moneygall for a bite to eat before pushing on.

She covered many miles, but there were a lot more still to go, and so Jenny carried on though the light was fading, until, at last, exhausted, she saw the lights of Limerick. Unable to face driving another mile, Jenny pulled up at a tall house on the main road offering bed and breakfast.

Barely taking in her surroundings, Jenny was given a room on the first floor and climbed the stairs, her shoulders slumped with disappointment. With so little information, how was she supposed to find any trace of her mother here? From what she had seen, Limerick was a large city, its illuminations stretching for miles . . . and once again, it was nothing like the place Jenny had seen in her dreams.

In London, Tina was planning her wedding. She'd made friends with a lot of stall holders and all of them would be invited. 'How about pie and mash, along with jellied eels, for the reception,' she asked Paul, hiding a smile.

'Leave it out. I can't see that going down well with my mates in CID, let alone their wives.'

'I was only kidding, though it's cheap grub and would save us a good few bob. Jenny went off to Gretna Green to get married. It must have cost peanuts, but I don't fancy that either.'

'Can't you just forget about her? She's out of your life now and I don't want her coming back into it.'

'Paul, I hardly think about her at all these days,' Tina protested, and it was true. Jenny was well and truly in the past now and she had no intention of ever seeing her again. They had once been good friends, and for a while they had needed each other, but Tina had moved on, found a new life and didn't want to be reminded of the past.

'I'm glad to hear it. Jenny was nothing but trouble and I don't want you involved with her.'

Tina doubted that Jenny had been involved or had any knowledge of what Marcos Cane had been up to. She had tried to warn her at the start, had been right about Marcos, but Jenny had refused to listen to her. Of course Jenny had paid for that now. From what Paul had told her, Marcos had already been married and Jenny had lost everything. Of course she'd be all right. She had well-off parents who were no doubt picking up the pieces.

'Come on, Tina, put that list aside now. It's getting late and I think we should turn in.'

'Yeah, all right,' she agreed, and soon she was snuggled up to Paul in bed. Yes, Jenny had her parents, but she had Paul, her life all set now to be a happy one. She had no idea what would eventually happen to Jenny, but as Tina closed her eyes, she wished her well.

With no idea that Tina had been thinking about her, the morning brought a surprise for Jenny when she went downstairs to find a middle-aged woman lying at the bottom, groaning as she clutched her leg.

'What happened?' Jenny asked, crouching at her side.

'I tripped, twisted my ankle . . . at least I hope that's all it is.'

'Let me help you up.'

The woman groaned in agony, unable to put any weight on her foot, and worriedly Jenny stood supporting her. She didn't know what to do next, but thankfully at that moment a man appeared, rushing over.

'Nuala, are you all right?'

'Does it look like it, Finn?' the woman said, her voice sharp with pain.

The man went to her other side, and Jenny was pleased that between them they were able to help her across the hall and into a room where they lowered her onto a sofa.

Finn lifted Nuala's legs up and then bent to look at her foot. 'It's swellin' up.'

'I can see that, and now what are we supposed to do?' Nuala asked worriedly. 'With Kaitlin having her baby, and it being Bridget's day off, who's going to see to the breakfasts?'

'That can wait. I'll call the doctor.'

'It can't wait, Finn. Our regulars have to eat before they go to work and there's this young lady too. What are we going to do?' she wailed again. 'You're hopeless in the kitchen.'

'I can put out some cereal and the guests will have to make do with that. Now calm down and I'll ring the doctor.'

'Cereal! No, no, get me something, anything to bind this foot and I'll see to it.'

'No, Nuala, that foot might be broken.'

Ignoring him, the woman swung round to put her foot onto the floor, but then yelped.

'It's all right,' said Jenny hastily. 'I'll see to the breakfasts.'

'You . . . you can cook?' Nuala asked.

'Of course I can,' Jenny insisted.

'Did you hear that, Finn? Show this nice young colleen where the kitchen is.'

'All right, but then I'm ringing the doctor,' he said.

Jenny was led down the hall, Finn saying, 'Thanks, it was good of you to offer. We've five guests, including yourself, and you'll find bacon and things in the refrigerator, bread in the bin, with pots for tea over there.'

'I'll manage, you ring the doctor,' Jenny urged, unaware as she set to work that her journey to find her mother's grave was going to be put off for a while.

Chapter Forty-Nine

"Tisn't broken, just badly sprained,' Nuala told Jenny when she returned from hospital. She was now sitting in the kitchen on a chair by the hearth, her foot propped up on a stool. 'Thanks for all you've done. I don't know how we'd have managed without you.'

'It was no trouble,' Jenny told her. 'I was glad to help.'

'I wasn't at the front when you arrived last night so I don't even know your name.'

'It's Jennifer Lavender. Jenny.'

'Nuala, I hate to tell you this, but there's more bad news,' Finn said, walking into the room. 'I rang Bridget to ask her to come in, but she's gone down with bronchitis.'

'What! She was fine yesterday. What about the rooms? They need cleaning.'

'I can at least tackle that.'

'Finn, you can't manage to do everything on your

own, and it's not just today. If Bridget has bronchitis she may not be back for some time.'

Jenny listened, felt sorry for them and her mind turned. Limerick was so large and she could be here for some time. 'I'm going to stay in Limerick for a while. If you like, I could help out until Bridget comes back.'

Nuala brightened. 'If you're sure, that would be great. We'll pay you, and your room will be free of charge, meals included.'

'Yes, especially as Nuala has to stay off that foot and you'll have to cook them,' Finn said, winking at Jenny. 'Our regulars like an evening meal too.'

'That's fine,' Jenny said. 'Now tell me where the cleaning things are and I'll make a start on those rooms.'

'You arrived late last night, a stranger, but I had a feeling you'd become a blessing,' Nuala said. 'You've already seen to the breakfasts, cleared up, and I think before you do anything else you should sit down and have a rest and a cup of tea. Finn can make it.'

'Take no notice of Nuala and her feelings,' smiled Finn. 'I keep telling her she's off with the fairies.'

'Yes, he does, but I usually turn out to be right.'

Finn shook his head and carried on with making the tea, while Nuala asked, 'Jenny, what brought you to Limerick?'

'I . . . I think my mother may have been buried here. I'm looking for her grave.'

'Oh, you poor girl,' Nuala exclaimed, but then her brow furrowed. 'Why do you only *think* she was buried here?'

'It . . . it's a long story.'

'Nuala, leave her alone. It's none of our business,' Finn protested as he handed them both a cup of tea.

Nuala nodded, looked at Jenny and said, 'Sure, you don't have to tell us anything you don't want to.'

'It's not that,' Jenny said. She was worried that they, like Delia, would think badly of her mother. 'It's just that it might shock you.'

'Now how will we know if you don't tell us? And anyway, in return for what you're doing for us, we might be able to help you in some way.'

Jenny knew that it would take her a very long time to search such a large city. She looked at Nuala, seeing the kindness in her eyes, and stuttered, 'She . . . she died in a home for unmarried mothers.'

Instead of looking shocked, Nuala said sympathetically, 'The poor girl, though I can't say I've heard of one of those homes around here.'

'They'd hardly advertise themselves,' said Finn.

'I know that, but I might recognise the name.'

'It has a saint's name, but I don't know which one, followed by saying it's a house for fallen women.'

'Well now, that's hardly keeping it quiet,' Finn said.

Nuala shook her head. 'I've never heard of it and that's hardly a name that would pass me by. Are you sure it's in the city?'

'Well, no, not really.'

'In that case, I think you'll find it's somewhere on the outside, somewhere secluded. But searching the whole county of Limerick will take some doing.'

It wasn't what Jenny had hoped to hear, but she felt she wanted a break from travelling and this seemed the ideal opportunity. She'd ring her father when it was time to leave, to find out where she had to head for outside of the city, and surely with that information the home would be easy enough to find?

'I'm in no hurry, happy to stay for a while,' she said, then drank down her tea. 'I'll get on with those rooms now.'

'Well now, Finn. Unlike Bridget, Jenny is keen to get on with her work. You can show her where the sheets are and anything else she needs.'

'You could have given me a chance to finish me tea, Jenny,' Finn said, but his smile belied any sting in his words as they left the room.

Jenny smiled too; she already felt sure that she was going to like it here.

Over two weeks had now passed and early on a Saturday afternoon close to the end of March, Edward was reading a letter from Delia's solicitor. It ended with the suggestion that he sought his own legal council. He was happy with that, in fact he couldn't wait for the divorce proceedings to begin. He was more worried about Jenny. She still hadn't rung him again, and with the sale of the house in progress, he wanted her back and soon.

He folded the letter. He didn't have to worry about Delia talking to Jenny now. She had moved to Richmond, and as for Robin, his son had agreed that it was better for Jenny if she never found out. The chances of her doing so were unlikely, in fact many, many millions to one, especially as he had sent his daughter on a wild-goose chase. It hadn't been a nice thing to do, but he'd had no choice, and now all he wanted was Jenny safely back under his roof.

His ears pricked at the sound of someone trying to open the front door. He could guess who it was, but Delia had no chance. A minute later the door-bell rang, but he didn't hurry to answer it. Let her wait.

The letterbox rattled and then must have been lifted, for Delia's voice was loud as she shouted, 'Edward, I know you're in there. Open the door!'

He finally did, to be confronted by her red-faced anger, but said calmly. 'What do you want, Delia?'

'How dare you change the locks!'

'You left; we're separated and supposed to communicate through our solicitors. I have every right to stop you just walking in when you feel like it,' he said, his smile sardonic and sure to wind her up, 'after all, I might have been entertaining.'

He was wrong. Instead Delia took a deep breath, her smile matching his as she said, 'Fine, I don't want to come in. I just wanted to see your face when you hear what I have to tell you. I just hope you don't know already or that would spoil my fun.'

'Know what?' he asked.

'You thought you'd always be safe, that the law would always protect you, but you're about to come unstuck.'

He sighed. 'No doubt my solicitor will inform me of any changes to the laws on divorce.'

'No, Edward, I'm talking about adoption laws.'

For a moment Edward stiffened, but then relaxed. He had nothing to worry about. 'Strangely enough, when Jenny rang a couple of weeks ago she asked about her birth certificate. Now you say there are changes. What changes?'

Delia was obviously enjoying this as she said triumphantly, 'Adopted children are going to be given the right to see their official birth certificates! It'll be made official next year.'

Edward shrugged, saying nonchalantly, 'It makes no difference to me. I have nothing to hide.'

'She . . . she isn't . . . ?'

'No, Delia, and now you're going to have to eat your words.'

She slumped, shaking her head. 'I'm sorry, I . . . thought . . .'

'Yes, you've made it perfectly clear what you thought, but it's too late for apologies. Now if you don't mind, I'm busy,' he said, about to close the door.

'Edward . . . wait . . .'

'No, Delia, in future anything you have to say to me must be through our solicitors.' And with that, he firmly closed the door.

Smiling, Edward went back to the kitchen, picking up details of a house. He read through them again. The house was in Chelmsford, Essex, and he was sure that Jenny would like it. It would be a bit of a nuisance changing offices, but his company had a branch there and in fact had told him that an opening was coming up for a new static, regional manager. He smiled . . . it felt like this was meant to be, that everything was going his way. He was safe.

Jenny found that she liked working for Nuala and Finn. The work wasn't overtaxing and after doing the cleaning that followed breakfast, she had time off in the afternoon and again after dinner in the evening. She took the opportunity to explore Limerick, discovering that it was spread over both sides of the River Shannon, the city overlooked by Woodcock Hill to the north, and the Silvermine Mountain in the east.

The countryside around Limerick beckoned, but

Jenny knew that she would have to put off her search for the time being, at least until Bridget came back. In some ways, she found the delay didn't matter, for a sort of contentment had begun to enfold her. She was becoming increasingly fond of Nuala and Finn, and of the regular guests too, all nice men who had come to work in Limerick and who, with no home of their own, had turned the bed and breakfast into some sort of facsimile of one. In fact, she was beginning to feel like she was part of a large family, and was almost sorry to think that, with Nuala's ankle almost better, and Bridget sure to return any day now, her brief sojourn would be soon over.

'Jenny, Jenny,' Nuala said, her eyes shining as Jenny went back to start on the evening meal. 'We've just heard that Kaitlin's had her baby and it's a boy. I had a feeling it would be.'

'That's wonderful,' Jenny enthused. She had learned that Kaitlin was Nuala's daughter, one who had come late in Nuala's life after four sons, who had now grown up and seemed to be scattered everywhere.

'Can you manage on your own?' asked Nuala. 'I can't wait to get to the hospital to see him.'

'Of course,' Jenny said. Seeing Nuala hesitate, she urged, 'Go on, I'll be fine.'

'Jenny, you're still a blessing,' she said. 'Come on, Finn. Let's be off to see our grandson.'

Jenny watched them leave, Nuala barely needing

her stick now, and then she went into the kitchen to see that the potatoes had already been prepared. Nuala was managing to do more and more these days, and though Jenny knew she should be pleased, she wasn't really, only saddened that she wouldn't be needed for much longer.

Dinner was almost ready by the time Nuala and Finn returned, both very excited.

'Oh, wait till you see him, Jenny. He's just perfect. Kaitlin and Donal are so happy.'

'Does he have a name yet?'

'Yes, Aiden.'

'That's nice. I like it.'

'I see you've got everything ready,' Nuala said, smiling.

'You didn't leave me much to do.'

'Get away with you. There was still the gammon to finish off, the cabbage to cook and tables to be laid.'

'Only five.'

'There'll be a lot more in the summer, we're always full then.'

'I won't be here in the summer.'

Nuala sat down, placing her stick beside her, her expression now one of sadness. 'I know, but I'm going to miss you.'

'Jenny's been good to stay as long as she has,' said Finn. 'And you know she wants to be off searching for that home.'

'Yes, but sorry, Jenny, it seems that Bridget still isn't fully recovered,' Nuala said with a smile of satisfaction. 'And as my foot is still paining me, you can't go yet.'

Jenny smiled. She knew that Nuala's foot was almost better, but it was lovely to think that the older woman didn't want her to leave yet. She heard the sound of chairs scraping in the dining room, and quickly began to dish up.

With a new baby to celebrate, the evening meal soon turned into a party and it was much later when Jenny finally went to bed, giggling and decidedly tipsy, but happy. After all she'd been through – a marriage that had been a farce, the loss of her baby, being told to move out and then robbed, she had left England in fear and deeply unhappy. Working for Nuala and Finn had helped to take her mind off it, and Jenny drifted off to sleep, at that moment wanting to stay with them for ever.

Chapter Fifty

'Finn, I dread telling her,' Nuala said nearly a week later.

'I know. You've grown fond of her.'

'I wish she could stay. I mean, my foot...'

'I know what you're doing, but it won't work. Your foot is fine now, and at this time of year we can't afford to pay both of them.'

'Kaitlin won't be back for a while yet.'

'Nuala, she won't be needed until the summer.'

'Shush, she's coming,' Nuala warned, and moments later Jenny walked into the room.

'Did you have a nice walk?' Nuala asked, trying to force brightness into her tone.

She obviously failed as Jenny answered, 'Yes, but what's wrong?'

'Sit down,' Finn said, 'we've got something to tell you.'

As though she sensed what was coming, Jenny said, 'Bridget's coming back.'

'Yes, on Monday.'

'And . . . and your ankle's better.'

'Well . . .'

'Now then,' Finn warned. 'You know it's fine now.'

'Yes, yes, 'tis better,' Nuala reluctantly admitted. 'I'm sorry, Jenny.'

'What for? I said I'd help out for a while and knew it wasn't permanent.'

'You don't have to leave, you could stay here as a guest,' Nuala said hopefully.

'I'd love to, but I can't. I . . . I really do want to find my mother's grave.'

Nuala nodded sadly. Finn was right; she'd grown very fond of Jenny and would miss her. There was something about her, something lost that brought out the mother in her. Perhaps it was that Jenny was on this mission, a sad one, travelling alone, and now she said anxiously, 'Will you keep in touch, Jenny, let me know how you get on?'

'Yes, if you'd like me to.'

'I would, and if you come back to the city, we'll always find a room for you.'

Jenny bent down and Nuala felt soft lips on her cheek. 'Thanks, and I'm going to miss you.'

Nuala took Jenny's hand. 'I'll still want a hand until Monday. Don't be running off yet.'

'I didn't intend to,' she said, a choke in her voice as she went to the sink. 'I . . . I'll get on with dinner. How many have we got to cater for?'

'Just six,' Nuala said, finding that she too was close to tears. In such a short time Jenny had become like a part of their family, and saying goodbye to her would be like saying goodbye to one of their own.

Robin was white-faced on Saturday morning, unable to believe his ears.

'What do you mean, it's over?'

'I'm sorry,' Julia said. 'I've met someone else, and it made me realise that I . . . I don't really love you.'

'Julia, you can't do this. We've made so many plans.'

'I know, but surely it's better to find out now?'

'Don't do this! We're supposed to be leaving here after our final exams, getting married in South Africa.'

'I don't want to marry you now.'

'Who is he? Do I know him?'

'It . . . it's Stuart.'

'What?' Robin exclaimed. Stuart was one of his flatmates, a so-called friend. 'How long has this been going on?'

'A . . . a few months.'

Robin's jaws ground. In all that time he hadn't spotted a thing. Stuart was good looking, often had girls in his room, and to think that one of them had been Julia made his stomach clench as though he'd been punched in the gut.

'You've been sleeping with him?'

She nodded, whispering, 'Yes.'

'Huh, another one he's added to his harem.'

'It's not like that. Stuart isn't seeing anyone else now.'

'I didn't take you for a fool, Julia,' Robin said, hoping to salvage something of his pride before he walked away. 'You're just one of a long list, but he's welcome to you.'

'You're wrong, he loves me . . .'

'Mug,' Robin spat over his shoulder. He stormed away, heading back to his flat, but there was no sign of Stuart there. The bastard had left Julia to tell him and was obviously keeping out of his way. However, as Robin paced the room, it began to sink in that he was more upset by his so-called friend's betrayal than the fact that Julia had broken up with him.

With the wind taken out of his sails, he sat down. He'd thought himself in love with Julia, was looking forward to going to live in South Africa, the job he'd been offered a brilliant one. Was that it? Had he been so blinded by ambition, by the life that was opening up to him, that he hadn't noticed that he was more in love with the concept of the job than the girl?

In no mood now to have it out with Stuart, Robin began stuffing things into an overnight bag. He'd go home for the weekend, cool off, pick up the pieces and make new plans . . . Yes, but where was home now? In his mother's rented flat or in what was, until it was sold, his father's house?

Jenny too was making plans. She would be here for the weekend, but was unable to imagine staying on any longer after that, having to see Bridget doing what for a while had been a job she loved. It was time to move on.

'Nuala, would you mind if I make a call to England? Jenny asked. 'I'll pay the charges.'

'Bless you, of course I don't mind.'

She went out to the small reception desk and rang the number, finding her father excited to hear from her.

'Jenny, at last,' he said. 'Are you on your way home?'

'No, Dad, I'm still in Limerick. It's a huge city and I don't think the home for fallen women is here. Was it somewhere on the outskirts?'

'I . . . I think so,' stammered Edward.

'Then why on earth did you send me to the city?'

'Jenny, it was a long time ago and I couldn't remember exactly where it was.'

'You must have some idea.'

'I, er . . . I think it was close to a village, but can't recall the name.'

'Was it to the north of the city, the east, or what?'

'I'm not sure, perhaps south.'

'All right, I'll head in that direction.'

'Jenny, no, you've been away for a month now. It's time you came home.'

'Dad, I'm not coming back to Wimbledon.'

'But you won't have to, at least not for long. I've found a house in Essex.'

'When are you moving there?'

'I hope in a few weeks. Jenny, I've done this for you, darling, to give you a fresh start.'

Sudden tears flooded Jenny's eyes. A part of her wanted to go home, to run to her father, to live in Essex, away from all the bad memories, but the other part was still desperate to find her mother's grave. She fumbled for a piece of paper and picked up a pen.

'All right, give me the address and I'll come there, but first I have to lay flowers on my mother's grave.'

'What if you don't find it?'

Jenny didn't even want to think about that. 'Dad, I've got to go, just give me the new address.'

Edward continued to argue, but when Jenny insisted that she'd have to hang up he finally gave in and she wrote the address down.

'Thanks, and bye, Dad.'

'Jenny—'

She replaced the receiver, ran up to her room, grabbed her map, and went back to the kitchen to spread it on the table. So many names . . . so many villages.

'It makes me sad to see you looking at that

thing,' Nuala said as she walked in and flopped onto a chair. 'It reminds me that you'll be leaving us soon.'

'Yes, on Monday.'

'Jenny, 'tis a hard task you've set yourself.'

'I know, but though my father couldn't remember the exact place, at least I have a direction now.'

Nuala looked at the map, smiled and pointed. 'Kilkee, I was born and married there. 'Tis a beautiful place, one to soothe your soul.'

'Why did you leave?'

'Finn came from here, and when his parents died we took over the place.'

'You must miss it.'

'I do, sorely, though I go back occasionally to see my family. As I said, 'tis beautiful, next to the sea with a wonderful sandy, horseshoe-shaped beach that stretches for about a mile. It's a very popular place for holidays.'

Jenny frowned. It sounded similar to the place she'd seen in her dream, but then she shook off the thought. It was just a coincidence and she had to head south, not to the coast. She looked at the map again, decided on a route and then folded it, hoping that at last she'd find the place she was looking for. It would be awful saying goodbye to Nuala on Monday, the thought painful, but she had to leave . . . had to find her mother's grave.

*　　*　　*

'Robin, I wasn't expecting you,' Delia said in surprise, though she was happy to see her son.

'Hello, Mummy.'

'Come on in. You look half starved and I'll get you something to eat,' she said, regarding Robin worriedly.

'Probably because of a diet that consists mainly of baked beans.'

'What! Is that all you eat?'

'Only kidding,' Robin said as he flopped onto the sofa. 'I manage on a bit more that that.'

'I'm glad to hear it, but why didn't you let me know you were coming?'

He shrugged. 'Last-minute decision.'

Delia was pleased the meal she had just finished cooking would stretch to two and gave her son the lion's share. By the time they had finished eating, however, she was looking at Robin, frowning.

'What's wrong, darling? You're awfully quiet.'

'It's nothing; just that I've broken up with my girlfriend.'

'You once mentioned a girl called Julia, is that the one?'

'Yes, and she's been the *only* one, until now. I was going to marry her.'

'Marry her! And just when were you going to tell me?'

'It was complicated.'

'What do you mean?'

'She's South African and after my finals I was going to move there and work for her father.'

'You were going to South Africa!' Delia cried, astounded.

'Yes, but you needn't worry. As I said, we've broken up.'

'I suppose I should say I'm sorry, but I . . . I can't. After hearing that, I'm only relieved.'

'It was a good job, one that would have taken me straight to the top and you could have visited us – even stayed if you liked it.'

'Yes, well, it seems it isn't going to happen now,' Delia said as she gathered up the plates.

'How are *you* doing, Mummy? Have you spoken to Dad again?'

'No, and I don't intend to. Last time I rang him, I said I was sorry again, admitted I was wrong, but he doesn't want me back, and that's that. I'm going to move on now, start that business I mentioned ages ago.'

'Do you need any help?'

'Get your exams out of the way first, darling. You never know, you could end up working for me! I'm going to need a good accountant.'

Robin smiled at last. 'Thanks, but even though the job in South Africa has fallen through, I have higher ambitions.'

'I'm glad to hear it. Nevertheless, if I'm really

successful, I might eventually need more than an accountant. I might want you as a partner.'

'Now that sounds more promising.'

'You needn't look so amused. I just might surprise you.'

'I hope you do; in fact I wish you every success.'

'Thank you, darling,' Delia said, kissing her son on the top of his head, though still shocked that Robin had been planning on going to South Africa. She felt full of relief that he wasn't now, and that he'd chosen to stay with her rather than his father this weekend.

Edward might have Jennifer – his *adopted* daughter, as she now accepted the girl was – but Delia still had her son. She knew that she could have lost Robin when she'd told him the truth, but he'd understood, had stood beside her, and for that Delia counted her blessings. Her marriage was over and she had to think about her future now. As long as it included Robin, that was all that mattered to her.

Chapter Fifty-One

Edward was in the new house, waiting in despair for Jenny. Where on earth was she? He'd expected her to turn up ages ago, but instead it was now the middle of May and there was no sign of her. Her search would have proved fruitless and surely there was nothing to keep her in Ireland now. Had she somehow lost his new address, was that it?

He glanced at the clock. Robin should be here soon and it had been a long time since he'd seen his son as well. He knew the boy was annoyed that he'd refused to take Delia back, and that it was a long drive to Essex from Birmingham, but with a week off from university, he'd at last persuaded his son to make the journey.

'Hello, son,' he said, when at last Robin arrived. 'You made it then.'

'I was a bit worried about the car. I thought at one time she was going to give up on me.'

'Car! It's more like a pram, but you're the one who wanted it.'

'It's a Citroën 2CV, not a pram, and she's usually as good as gold.'

'Until now.'

'She still got me here,' Robin said as he looked around the living room. 'This isn't bad.'

'I like it, but sit down and I expect you could do with a drink. Beer?'

'Yes, great.'

Edward poured the drinks, then asked, 'Have you by any chance heard from Jenny?'

'No, not a word, haven't you?'

He shook his head. 'Not since the last time I spoke to her.'

'Has she got your new telephone number?'

'No, but I was expecting her back by now, or failing that she could have dropped me a line. I'm beginning to think she may have lost the address.'

'Could be, but if she wants to find it, I'd have thought she'd ring me. Dad, you don't think she's somehow found out, do you?'

'No, it's impossible.'

'I hope you're right, but Mummy said something about new laws coming into force next year.'

Edward sat down opposite his son. 'It still wouldn't do Jenny any good. For her sake, and you know why, I had the forethought to make sure she doesn't know her mother's real name.'

Robin looked shocked. 'I'm not sure, Dad; the more I think about it, the more I feel Jenny has a right to know.'

'No, son, she's been through enough. Jenny needs to get on with her life now, to make a fresh start and we should help her. If we don't she could spend years on a search that could lead anywhere, and when it ends in failure it could destroy her. It's better this way, you must see that.'

Robin thought about it for a while, but then to Edward's relief he nodded. 'Yes, I suppose you're right. As I once said, what she doesn't know can't hurt her.'

'That's right,' Edward said, hoping that soon there'd be a knock on the door, and he'd find his daughter on his doorstep. Then, at last, he could relax.

Jenny was feeling despondent. She had searched place after place, winding across the south on tiny roads as she went from village to village, her search ever widening. She was so tired of travelling, of sleeping in different beds, some comfortable, some not, and was nearly ready to give up. She was lonely too, meeting people just briefly before moving on, tired of hellos and goodbyes.

She lay in bed that night after another fruitless journey, in yet another stopover, miles from Limerick, and surely too distant from the city to be the right place. If only her father had given her at least a village name – without one her search was proving impossible. She thought about his new house in Essex. He must have moved in by now, and was probably upset that he hadn't heard from her. Maybe it was time to drop him a line, tell him she was coming back. She'd try one last place, one a woman had told her about that day, a convent that took in lost souls. It sounded unlikely, but Jenny felt she had to give it a try. She closed her eyes, fighting despair. She felt like that – a lost soul – but at last she slept.

The dream came, the same beautiful vision, and Jenny awoke very early on Thursday morning with it still in her mind. Why? Why did that place haunt her dreams? She flung back the blankets and went to have a wash before she got dressed, packed her overnight bag and headed downstairs. She'd have breakfast, pay yet another bill, and then head for the convent.

'It's been lovely to meet you,' the owner said. 'Have a good journey.'

'Thank you,' Jenny replied, but found that she had to gulp back her emotions. The woman reminded her of Nuala and she was tempted to return to Limerick, to stay with them for a few days before going back to England. No, she had to try this one last place and, waving goodbye, she left to get into her car.

It was two hours later and yet again Jenny was disappointed, her journey a wasted one. She headed for the nearest village, feeling disheartened as she found somewhere to have a drink. It was a lovely day, the sky blue, sun shining, and the countryside beautiful; yet it failed to cheer her.

'Are you here on holiday?' the woman behind the counter asked as she served her.

'Yes, touring,' Jenny replied, in no mood to give the real explanation. She'd seen it so many times, the look of disapproval on some faces when she asked about a home for fallen women, though there were others who had tried to be helpful.

'You're on the border of County Limerick. Are you going on to Cork?'

'No, I don't think so.'

'You should. It's popular with tourists, and close by is Blarney where you can kiss the famous stone.'

'I'll think about it,' Jenny replied as she took her cup and went to sit down. This wasn't a holiday, but the woman's words triggered thoughts of Nuala. The place she'd been born in sounded perfect for a holiday, somewhere to soothe your soul she'd said and, unhappiness swamping her, Jenny felt she needed somewhere like that.

It was time to give up – she just couldn't go on,

couldn't face this aimless search any longer. For a moment Jenny was temped to go to Kilkee, yet it wasn't a place that could soothe her soul, it was a person. And that person was Nuala.

Her mind made up, Jenny went to find a telephone. Before going back to England on Monday, she'd double back and stay with Nuala and Finn for a few days.

Soon, feeling a little better now that the decision had been made, Jenny was on her way to Limerick.

Back in Limerick, it was very late, and Nuala was yawning, but she was determined to stay up. Jenny had rung to say she was coming here for a few days and she was looking forward to seeing her.

'Go to bed, Finn,' she said, seeing that her husband was yawning too.

'I'll stay up a while longer.'

'I hope this means that Jenny found her mother's grave.'

'Didn't she say?'

'No, just that she was coming back here.'

'You didn't tell her you're going to be away?'

'I thought it could wait. Are you sure you can manage?'

'Nuala, how many times are you going to ask me that? Kaitlin is going to leave Aiden with Donal's mother, then there's Bridget, and her cousin has offered to help out too. I'll be fine.'

'I just need to see for myself that my dada's all right,' Nuala said. Then hearing a knock on the door, she hurried to answer it.

'Hello, I'm here, but I'm sorry it's so late.'

'Jenny, come on in, your room's ready.'

As Jenny picked up her cases and stepped into the light, Nuala saw that she looked exhausted with dark shadows beneath her eyes. 'You look awful.'

'I'm all right, just a bit tired. It was a long way and I still don't like driving in the dark.'

'You should have stopped somewhere for the night.'

'I just wanted to get here, to see you and Finn again.'

'And it's pleased we are to see you,' Nuala said, giving the girl a hug, 'but for now I think a hot drink and then bed for all of us.'

'It's funny, but it feels like I've come home.'

'Hello, Jenny,' Finn said. 'I'll take your cases up to your room.'

'And I'll make you a drink,' Nuala said.

'Don't do that. I've kept you up long enough.'

'It won't take a few minutes, though I expect Finn will be off to bed.'

'Yes, I am. Goodnight, Jenny,' he said, picking up the cases. 'I'll drop these off on the way.'

Nuala beckoned Jenny to the kitchen. The poor girl looked dreadful, so pale, so tired, and talking could wait until the morning.

Chapter Fifty-Two

For the first time in ages Jenny slept like a log and didn't open her eyes until gone nine the next morning. She was glad to have the same room, the same familiar bed. It was as she'd told Nuala last night, it felt like she'd come home.

Lazily she got up and, when dressed, went downstairs to poke her head into the kitchen. 'Good morning.'

'Jenny, you're up at last. Sit yourself down and pour yourself a cup of tea.'

'Are you sure? You don't usually allow guests in the kitchen.'

'You're more than a guest, darlin', you're like part of the family, and as you're the last one up I'll have a cup of tea with you.'

Jenny felt she was right – that it wasn't a place she had needed, it was a person – and seeing Nuala's smiling face had lifted her spirits already. She was glad now that she'd decided to take such a long, circuitous route back to England.

Nuala sat down, poured the drinks, and then said softly, 'Now tell me. How did you get on?'

'I looked everywhere, but I couldn't find it.'

''Tis a shame, but your mammy will be looking down on you and she'll know you did your best.'

'Do you really believe that?'

'Yes, and you should too. You're a lovely girl, one your mother would be proud of.'

Tears came then, tears she'd held in check for so long. She'd failed, but perhaps Nuala was right, perhaps her mother would understand.

'That's it, you have a good cry,' Nuala said as she reached across the table to grasp Jenny's hand.

'That's the last of them,' Bridget said as she walked in with a pile of plates, only to halt in her tracks when she saw Jenny sitting at the table, sobbing. 'Oh . . . oh dear, what's wrong?'

'She's just a bit upset, that's all,' Nuala said. 'Just leave the plates and I'll see to them. You can get on with the rooms.'

Bridget put them by the sink and then placed a light hand on Jenny's shoulder. 'Can I do anything to help?'

'Bridget . . .' Nuala warned.

'No, it's all right,' Jenny said, touched by the girl's concern as she fought her tears. 'Thank you, but I'm fine now.'

Bridget hesitated, but at another warning look from Nuala she went to get on with her work. Jenny managed a watery smile. 'I only saw Bridget briefly before I left, but she seems nice.'

'She is, but needs a bit of pushing to get on with her work. Now then, what would you like for breakfast?'

Unsure that she could eat anything, and knowing it was past the time that Nuala served food, she shook her head. 'Nothing, thanks.'

'You'll at least have a bit of toast,' Nuala insisted as she stood up.

'I've put you behind, and I'll only eat a bit of toast if you let me help with the washing-up.'

'There's no need for that.'

Jenny ignored her and now went to the sink, soon immersing the plates in hot, soapy water. Nuala looked at her and shook her head, but she was smiling as Finn walked in.

'Jenny, what's this? You're a guest.'

'I'm just giving Nuala a hand.'

'The dishes can wait,' Nuala said firmly. 'Now dry your hands, sit down, and eat your toast.'

'It's best to do as she says,' Finn advised. 'She's not one to argue with.'

'Haven't you got light bulbs to change?'

'Yes, Nuala, I'm on me way.'

Jenny ate her toast, finding that she had an

appetite after all, and then took another slice while Nuala stood over her like a sentinel.

'Good girl,' she finally said, sitting down now, 'and before you try to wash up again, I have something to tell you. My sister rang to tell me that my dada isn't too well. He's in his late eighties now, and though Maeve said she doesn't think it's anything to worry about, I feel I have to see that for myself. I'm going to Kilkee in the morning.'

'Oh, Nuala, I'm sorry. I hope he's all right.'

'So do I, but 'tis a shame you're only here for a few days. I'll be away for a week and won't be back before you leave.'

In the circumstances, Jenny knew it couldn't be helped, but felt a surge of disappointment. 'Never mind, at least I've had a chance to see you today and as I don't want to be chased out of the kitchen yet, I'm going to help you with that washing-up.'

And she did, the two of them chatting until at last it was finished. Jenny was about to go to her room to unpack a few things when Finn appeared, frowning.

'Nuala, I've got a bit of bad news.'

She paled. 'Finn, not my father!'

'No, it's the car.'

'You eejit!' Nuala exclaimed. 'Why didn't you say that to start with? I . . . I thought . . .'

'Sorry, I'll start again. The garage just rang. They

haven't got the part yet and the car won't be ready in the morning.'

'I'll just have to go by bus then,' Nuala said.

'There isn't one that goes all the way and you'd have to change buses perhaps two or three times. Can't you leave it until the car's fixed?'

'And how long will that take?'

'I'm not sure.'

'Not sure! What good is that!'

'It won't hurt to wait.'

'No, Finn, I have to go. I . . . I have this feeling on me.'

Without hesitation, Jenny said, 'I'll take you, Nuala.'

'You will? Oh, Jenny, are you sure? It's nearly a two-hour drive.'

'Is that all?' Jenny said nonchalantly to prevent any further protest. 'I could be there and back by lunchtime.'

Nuala hugged her then, her voice a croak. 'I don't know how you do it, Jenny, but you seem to turn up just when I need you. It's like you were sent here to help me again.'

'Now you're off with the fairies again,' Finn said.

'Or the leprechauns,' Jenny said, grinning.

'Oh, you two, you're as bad as each other,' Nuala said, smiling, 'but you've got to admit it's strange.'

Yes, Jenny thought, she had come back just when Nuala needed her again, and though it was just a coincidence, she was glad that she was able to help.

That night, in bed, Nuala couldn't sleep. Since Jenny had arrived she'd had this strange feeling within her, an urgent need to get to Kilkee, but it had eased from the moment Jenny offered to drive her there. She'd had a similar sort of feeling the last time Jenny had stayed with them, when the girl had been looking at her map and for some reason she'd felt compelled to point out Kilkee.

Nuala plumped up her pillow, worried again. Had she been forewarned then that her father was going to be ill, that Maeve shouldn't be dismissing this latest bout of bronchitis so flippantly?

'Nuala, stop fidgeting and let's get some sleep.'

'I can't help it. I'm worried about my dada.'

'Maeve said he was no worse when you rang her earlier.'

'She didn't say he was any better.'

'You'll see for yourself tomorrow.'

'It's a blessing Jenny turned up when she did. It's almost as if she's meant to take me to Kilkee.'

'Now you sound like you're off with the fairies again.'

'You always say that when I get funny feelings, but they're usually right.'

'Not this time. Your dada will be fine. Now

451

go to sleep,' Finn said, this time putting an arm around her.

Nuala found it comforting; her last thought before drifting off that there was more to her funny feelings this time, something she couldn't put her finger on.

Chapter Fifty-Three

It was raining as Jenny and Nuala set off for Kilkee. Finn had shown her the route, across the River Shannon then on into County Clare. The road looked all right at first, but then they would have to leave it and take a minor one to the coast which Jenny knew from experience would slow them down. She knew Nuala was itching to get there and as she drove she asked, 'Are you all right, Nuala?'

'Yes, anxious to see my dada, that's all.'

'Tell me more about Kilkee,' Jenny said, hoping it would take Nuala's mind off her fears.

'I told you, it's beautiful, but it's not just that, the weather can be soft there too. My dada says it's because the rocks of Duggerna Reef guard the bay from the full force of the Atlantic and the beach has lovely soft sand that slopes gently down to the sea.'

'It certainly sounds lovely.'

'It is, and I've seen dolphins in the bay. Now they're a sight to behold.'

'Oh, I'd love to see dolphins.'

'I can't promise that, but you don't have to rush back to Limerick. I know you're disappointed that you didn't find your mother's grave, and perhaps before you go back to England a little holiday in Kilkee is just what you need.'

'I must admit I was upset, though I felt better after talking to you. It . . . it's something else now, something that seems to be pulling at me and . . . oh, this is going to sound silly.'

'I doubt it'll sound any sillier than my feelings, but I've learned to trust them.'

'It's just that I felt drawn to come to Ireland, as if something was calling me, and now when I go back to England I'll feel I've left something unfinished, something just out of reach.'

'You did your best, Jenny, and if this is guilt you're feeling there's no need.'

'No, it isn't that . . . at least I don't think so.'

'Ah well, as I said, maybe a little holiday in Kilkee will do you good. Did I tell you it's a place to soothe your soul?'

'Yes, and perhaps I will stay for a few days,' Jenny said. She didn't tell Nuala that as they continued their journey the feeling she had of being pulled was growing stronger. Maybe Nuala's anxiety about her father was rubbing off, and now she too began to worry about what they'd find.

* * *

Passing through Kilrush, Nuala knew that they'd soon be there. The sky had now cleared and the sun was shining, the sea gleaming both to the front and the side of them. Loop Head was off to the far left of the peninsula and Kilkee just ahead. It was strange, but the closer they got, the more her anxiety lifted. She felt a little foolish that she'd made such a fuss, Jenny driving her all this way for what might turn out to be nothing. As Maeve had said, her father was no worse than usual.

Lacking any sense of urgency now, Nuala directed Jenny to her family home, though only her father and sister still lived there now. When they pulled up outside the stone-fronted, two-storey house, Nuala got out of the car, but Jenny remained behind the wheel.

'Come on, Jenny,' she urged.

'Are you sure? I don't want to intrude.'

'Don't be daft. Now get out of that car.'

As Jenny did so, the front door opened and Maeve stood on the step, waving. Nuala smiled, pleased to see her sister. Maeve had never married, no man able to see past her outward appearance, and as a young woman she had almost entered a convent. Perhaps she should have warned Jenny, but thankfully she acted perfectly normal when Maeve spoke as they walked up the path.

'Hello, Nuala, and you must be Jenny.'

'Yes. It's nice to meet you,' Jenny said.

As they walked inside, Nuala's eyes went straight to her father and she rushed to kneel at his side. 'Dada, how are you?'

''Tis just me chest, that's all, and Maeve told you that.'

'I know, but I wanted to see for myself.'

'Well now you have, so get off your knees and pour me a drop of whiskey.'

'No, Dada,' Maeve warned. 'You can have a cup of tea, but none of the hard stuff.'

'Stop treating me like a child in me own house. If I want a drink I'll have one.'

'It's only half past ten,' Maeve said patiently. 'Can you not wait till lunchtime?'

'I can't see the hands on that clock and thought it was later than that. Yes, all right, I'll have a cup of tea.'

'Dada, this is Jenny. She drove me here to see you,' Nuala said.

The old man's rheumy eyes looked at Jenny and his old Irish charm was evident as he said with a smile, 'Hello, darlin', and welcome to me home.'

'Thank you,' she said.

'Jenny, sit down,' Nuala urged. 'I'll give Maeve a hand with the tea.'

Going into the kitchen, however, she found that Maeve already had it made. 'I'm sorry, you were right – Dada seems fine.'

'He's as tough as old boots, but it's lovely to

see you and I hope you're still going to stay for a week.'

'Yes, of course I am, and, Maeve, I think Jenny would like to stay for a few days too.'

'She'll be welcome,' Maeve said. 'Jenny seems a nice girl and didn't even blink when she first saw me. Did you warn her?'

'No, I didn't think to.'

'There's something familiar about her, as if I've seen her before but can't place where.'

'Jenny's from England so I doubt that. She came here to find her mother's grave, and is sore disappointed that she couldn't.'

'Did her mother come from these parts?'

'No, but it's a long story so I'll save it till later,' Nuala said, the two of them saying no more for the time being as they took the tea through.

Jenny was chatting to Nuala's father, but a part of her mind was elsewhere. From the moment she had driven into Kilkee it had felt as if she'd been there before, had seen it before . . . though of course that was impossible.

Nuala's father was a lovely old man, telling her all about Kilkee, and Jenny listened patiently though she'd heard most of it from Nuala. It had been a bit of a shock when she'd first seen Maeve, but she'd managed to hide it. Maeve was tiny, badly deformed, with one leg shorter than the other and her back humped crookedly. It made her head sit to one side towards her left shoulder, yet when she smiled, it was Maeve's face that arrested you, intelligence shining out of the most beautiful blue eyes that Jenny had ever seen.

'Moore Bay is nice, but there are some lovely cliff walks to explore if you've a mind,' the old man said.

'Yes, I'd love to see more of Kilkee.'

'Well now, as you're staying with us for a few days, you'll be able to do just that,' Maeve said as she placed a teapot on the table.

'I . . . I was going to find a hotel.'

'Sure, there's no need for that. We've got plenty of room, haven't we, Dada?'

'Yes, but if I'm to have three women in my house, I don't want you all fussing over me.'

'Don't worry,' Nuala said. 'We won't do that.'

'Of course you can all take it in turns to pour me a whiskey,' he said, his wizened face crinkling as he smiled cheekily. 'I just hope yous two won't be as mean as Maeve with the measures.'

Jenny found his smile infectious, and the sisters obviously did too.

'Dada, you know that isn't true' said Maeve, though she was smiling.

'Don't you be believing her,' the old man said. 'I think she uses a thimble as a measure.'

Jenny laughed then and they all joined in. As soon as she'd seen Kilkee she'd decided to stay for a while, intending to find a hotel, but was now glad that she'd been invited to stay with Nuala's lovely family. Once again, she didn't think it was the place that would soothe her soul, it was these wonderful people, the fondness they had for each other shining through. Not only that, she would be able to spend more time with Nuala, a woman she'd have loved as her mother – the mother she had never known.

With their father settled for the night, and Jenny in bed too, Nuala and Maeve were still up. They didn't see each other that often and were enjoying catching up, but it was Jenny who was the first subject up for discussion, Maeve saying, 'So, are you going to tell me more about Jenny?'

'She's been quiet all day and hardly opened her mouth when we went out for a walk.'

'She has a look of sadness about her, but as you told me she can't find her mother's grave, I suppose that explains it.'

'Yes, the poor girl was adopted and seems to have this need to find ties to her mother.'

'Why was she adopted?'

'Her mother died giving birth in a home for unmarried mothers. It was run by nuns and Jenny was told it was in Limerick.'

'Why couldn't she find it?'

'I don't know, and 'tis odd. Jenny said the man who adopted her and took her back to England collected her from there, so why couldn't he say exactly where it was?'

'Yes, that is a bit strange. Where was her mother born?'

'That's another odd thing. Jenny was told that her mother came from Dray, but there was no trace of her, or any other family there. I wouldn't say this to Jenny, but I think it's almost as if this man doesn't want her to find any trace of her family.'

'I still think I've seen her somewhere before. You don't think her mother came from these parts, do you, and I'm seeing a family resemblance?'

'I suppose anything's possible, but rather than raise false hope I think it's best not to mention it. Jenny's been searching long enough, and I don't think she could stand any more disappointment.'

'Yes, you're probably right. Now come on, tell me all about Aiden. I hope you've brought some photographs with you.'

'Of course I have,' Nuala said, going to get her handbag, all thoughts of Jenny and her family forgotten for a while now as she proudly showed off her new grandson.

Chapter Fifty-Four

Jenny awoke the next morning, anxious to see more of Kilkee. Nuala had walked her down to the promenade yesterday and, as Jenny's eyes had swept the beach, she'd been overwhelmed by that feeling again. She had seen it before and now knew where. It was the place, the beautiful one she had seen in her dreams. If she hadn't offered to drive Nuala here she'd never have found it, and now the coincidences – Nuala having being born here for one – were piling up until she was utterly confused.

Jenny was the last up and Nuala and her father smiled warmly when they saw her, the delicious smell of bacon cooking wafting from the kitchen.

'Jenny, you're just in time for breakfast,' Nuala said.

'Sorry, I didn't realise it was gone nine.'

'If you're not used to it, 'tis the sea air. I slept in a bit too.'

'As everyone would have the Irish say, top of the morning to you, Jenny,' said Maeve as she came in from the kitchen. 'Now, how about the pair of you giving me a hand?'

'You wouldn't think she's the youngest, would you?' Nuala said as they followed Maeve. 'She sounds just like my mother.'

'I'm only three years younger than you, and 'tis you who mothers everyone if you get the chance. I bet Kaitlin doesn't get a look in with Aiden.'

'Sure she does . . . well, when I'm not around.'

Jenny listened to the banter, feeling almost at home in this cosy house. She took the plates as they were handed to her, and found she couldn't wait to tuck in. The sea air may have made her sleep in, but it had also given her an appetite. When they sat down to eat she found the bacon perfect and crisp, and the egg cooked just right as she dipped thickly buttered bread into the yolk.

Once her plate was clean, Jenny sat sipping a cup of tea and her eyes strayed to the window. It was another lovely day and she couldn't wait to go out.

'Nuala, after we've cleared up, do you mind if I go for a walk?'

'You don't have to ask my permission,' Nuala gently admonished. 'You're on holiday and free to do what you like.'

'That's right, after all, Nuala isn't your mammy,'

Maeve said, then blanched. 'Oh, I'm sorry, I shouldn't have said that.'

'That's it, let Jenny know I've been talking about her,' scolded Nuala.

'It's all right, I don't mind, and as for Nuala being my mother, Maeve, I wish she was.'

'Oh, Jenny, what a lovely thing to say,' Nuala said as her eyes flooded with tears.

'Now don't start blabbing,' Nuala's father admonished. 'I don't know what's the matter with the lot of you. Three women here now and not one of you's poured me another cup of tea.'

The emotional spell broken, they all laughed, and after helping to wash up Jenny was soon on her way down to the sea.

'I'm sorry, Nuala, I spoke without thinking,' Maeve said as the door closed behind Jenny.

'It's all right. Jenny didn't seem to mind that I'd told you about her.'

Maeve grinned. 'She'd have to be desperate to want you for a mother.'

'You cheeky . . .'

'Sure, I'm only joking,' Maeve interrupted hastily.

'I hope you two are not going to keep this up for a week.'

'No, Dada,' they both chorused and then, like two young girls, they giggled.

'Nuala, it's lovely to have you here,' Maeve said,

meaning it. Most of her time was spent with her father, and to see her sister was a treat.

Sometimes she envied the life Nuala had – a husband, children – and cursed that she'd been born with a deformed body. Few knew of her dreams, that one day a man would come into her life, one who would look at her without pity or disgust. She had accepted that it was never going to happen, yet still couldn't help longing even at this age to know what it felt like to be held in a man's arms, to be kissed, to be loved.

'Here, Dada, take a look at my grandson,' Nuala said, placing a photograph in his hands.

He tilted it back and forwards, trying to focus on it, but Maeve knew he could see little now.

'Yes, a fine boy,' he said eventually, handing it back as though he'd taken a good look.

'Talking of boys,' Maeve said, 'have your sons been home lately?'

'No, they're still in England, working, and not one of them shows any sign of getting married.'

'They've plenty of time. They're not in their thirties yet.'

'Dada, one is and the others aren't far off,' Nuala told him.

''Tis a shame they've not seen Jenny,' said Maeve. 'She's a pretty girl and if she married one of them she'd at least have you for a mother-in-law.'

'There's nothing I'd like better, but that's just

wishful thinking. Jenny will be gone soon, and I'm going to miss her.'

'Where does she come from in England?'

'I don't know. She doesn't say much about the family who adopted her, but I have a feeling she's left a lot of unhappiness there.'

'Well then, perhaps you could persuade her to stay.'

'That would be grand, but her home is in England, not here, and as I said, she'll soon be going back to it.'

'Is it time for my whiskey yet?'

'No, Dada, you've only just had your breakfast,' Maeve told him, used to his constant requests, along with Nuala talking of her strange feelings. Still, it was very obvious that her sister was fond of Jenny and no doubt there'd be a few tears when she left.

Jenny saw steps leading down to the beach and decided to walk on the sand. It wasn't the holiday season yet and there weren't that many people about, but Nuala was right, the reef did protect the bay from the force of the Atlantic. She went down to the water's edge, took off her shoes and began to head along the wet sand towards what she'd been told was Donegal Point.

Deep in thought, Jenny continued to walk, the beach becoming almost deserted the further she strolled. She should have written to her father, told him she was coming back, but it hardly seemed worth it now – she'd probably arrive before the letter. As she took in the scenery, though she'd made up her mind to go to Essex, a part of Jenny still wanted to stay in Ireland, even more so now that she had seen Kilkee.

What was it about this place, Jenny wondered. Just then she saw a lone child in the distance who seemed to be searching for something in the sand. There were three people at the top of the beach chatting and the child probably belonged to one of them, Jenny decided as her thoughts now turned back to her father and the prospect of living with him in Essex.

Sand had gathered between her toes and, bending down, Jenny endeavoured to get it out, moving away from the damp sand to dry her feet. She paused to look out to sea, wondering if she would spot dolphins, but could see nothing. She wasn't even sure it was the right time of year. She'd have to ask Nuala's father when she went back, but for now, she continued to walk.

Jenny was close to the little girl now, the child still searching the sand, her hair a mass of dark, wind-blown curls. She had found something and looked up now, smiling with delight when she saw Jenny.

'Erin, Erin,' she cried, holding up a large shell, 'look what I've found.'

'It's lovely,' Jenny said, about to explain that her name wasn't Erin when a young woman came hurtling down the beach towards them.

'Faith, you know you shouldn't talk to . . .' she shouted, skidding a halt.

From that moment everything seemed to happen in slow motion. Their eyes met, and Jenny found that looking at the young woman's face was like seeing her own reflection.

For a moment both stood frozen, neither of them able to believe what they were seeing, but then the little girl's voice broke the spell.

'Erin, I thought she was you. She looks just like you.'

'How can this be?' Erin asked.

'I . . . I don't know,' Jenny said, unable to tear her eyes away from Erin.

'You're so like me you could be my twin.'

Surely it wasn't possible, Jenny thought. They couldn't be twins, but nevertheless she blurted out, 'You . . . you weren't adopted, were you?'

'Yes, I was . . . No, don't tell me you were too?'

Jenny nodded, and now, taking the little girl's hand, Erin stammered, 'I . . . I think we need to talk about this.'

Jenny walked beside her up the beach, finding that her head kept turning to look at Erin. Every time she did so, as though they were in unison, Erin was looking at her too. Was it possible? Jenny thought. Were they twins? Was this the reason that she had always felt that something was missing in her life?

As they approached the two young lads that Erin had been with, their mouths gaped.

'I know,' she said, 'it's strange, but take Faith home, will you? We'll talk about this later.'

Looking as bewildered as Jenny felt, they led the child away, while Jenny still felt she was dreaming. Alone now, the two of them began to compare things, finding many similarities, their shared birthday being the most significant.

'Oh, Jenny, we need to sort this out, but I think you really are my twin sister,' Erin said, and spontaneously they fell into each other's arms.

Jenny clung to Erin. 'Now I've found you, it feels like I've always missed you.'

'And I you.'

Jenny knew there were a lot more questions to be asked – how they had been adopted into different families for one – but for now all she wanted was to hold her sister and never let her go.

Chapter Fifty-Five

Nuala was beginning to get really worried now. It was four in the afternoon and Jenny had been out since just after ten that morning.

'Will you stop fretting?' Maeve chided. 'She's not a little girl, she's a young woman.'

'I know, but what if she's lost?'

'She has our address and only has to ask for directions.'

'Yes, yes, but . . .'

Nuala paused as there was a knock on the door, and hurried to open it, her hand clutching at her heart in shock, while her eyes went from one to the other. This couldn't be. It was only the slightly darker shade of hair and style, along with their clothes that separated them.

'Yes, I know,' Jenny said in understanding. 'I felt the same. This . . . this is Erin, my twin sister.'

'Holy Mother of God,' Nuala gasped. 'Come in, come in. Maeve! Maeve, you've got to see this.'

'Well I never, I thought there was something,' Maeve said, as her eyes finally settled on Erin, 'but I didn't expect a twin. Do you live in Kilkee?'

'No, but my aunt does and I've often been here to visit her.'

'Of course, that's it. Your auntie must be Corinne Feeby.'

'Yes, that's right, though of course she isn't my real aunt. Like Jenny, I was adopted.'

'Nuala, it's like a miracle,' Jenny said as she stood grasping her sister's hand. 'Erin is here on holiday, but she'll be leaving tomorrow. If . . . if I hadn't driven you here, if I hadn't gone for a walk on the beach today, we might never have met.'

'*Now* laugh at my feelings, Maeve,' said Nuala.

'You said it was to do with Dada, not this.'

'I know, I know, but now I think I was meant to bring Jenny here.'

'Will you stop talking daft?' her father said. 'And with four women in me house now I need a drop of whiskey.'

Nuala poured him one, thinking that though her dada might think her daft, she, like Jenny, felt that a miracle had happened – that she had been used as some sort of instrument to bring these two girls together. Tears welled in her eyes. She felt so privileged and, inwardly, Nuala prayed to the Holy Mother in thanks.

*   *   *

The old man had dozed off after a large glass of whiskey, and after telling Nuala and Maeve everything they'd found out and gone through some of the questions that still needed to be answered, Jenny waved goodbye to Erin. She wasn't sad, knowing she'd be seeing her sister again in the morning, when the only sadness then would be in saying goodbye to Nuala.

'I just don't understand why your father sent you off in the wrong direction,' Nuala now said.

'Nor do I, but I intend to find out, and that's the least of it. He told me that my mother was a distant relative and that was why he adopted me, but why leave Erin behind? I've always thought there was something missing in my life, but I never dreamed I had a twin and it seems so cruel that he never told me.'

'Yes, it does, and I still think it's amazing that you bumped into each other,' said Maeve. 'But God is good, and though it took Him some time, He managed to bring you together.'

'Well, will you listen to that,' Nuala snorted. 'So, Maeve, you believe me now?'

'Yes, all right, don't go on about it!'

'Now that's enough!' said their father, waking up. 'A man needs a bit of peace in his home. As for Jenny finding her sister, I just hope they don't bicker all the time like you two.'

'Sorry, Dada,' Maeve and Nuala chorused, and then they both collapsed with laughter.

Jenny found their good humour infectious and joined in, the old man trying to shout above the noise, 'Will one of you get me a whiskey!'

It was some time before he got it. Erin was up early the next morning, all packed and ready to go. She had only known happiness with her adoptive parents, John and Margaret Brown, and she loved her two younger brothers. They had come along after her adoption, surprising her mother who had thought she was unable to have children. It hadn't made any difference to Erin, she had still been treated like their beloved daughter, her home life a happy one. It would be a wrench to leave, but she was also joyful that she and Jenny had found each other. She knew that the boys were rarely up early, so had said her goodbyes last night, telling them that she'd be home again soon.

'Mammy, 'tis strange you didn't know that I had a twin.'

'It isn't really. The nuns didn't tell me.'

'Your Mammy was desperate for children and if she'd known, she'd have adopted the pair of you,' said Erin's Aunt Corinne. 'Yes, that's true. I think it's cruel that you were separated.'

'Mammy, where did you adopt me from?'

'From a place in County Cork, a home for un-married mothers.'

'That's funny. Jenny said she was adopted from a home in the Limerick area.'

'I agree, tis odd.'

'Are you sure you don't mind me going to England?'

'I'll miss you, but I can understand why you want to go.'

'Dada said the same when I rang him last night. It's just that I feel I have to meet this man, the one who adopted Jenny. She said he's some sort of distant relation.'

'Well then, I suppose you have to go.'

'Bye, Mammy,' Erin choked, hugging her mother and then her aunt. She had never been apart from her mother before, but she was also excited at the prospect of seeing Jenny again. 'Make sure you ring me regularly, Erin.'

'Yes, Mammy, I promise I will,' she said, then picked up her case to hurry out. Jenny was expecting her and she didn't want to be late. Erin felt a thrill of excitement. She had a sister. A twin sister and it still felt like a dream.

Jenny felt that her emotions were on a rollercoaster. Tears when saying goodbye to Nuala, and Maeve too, had already touched her heart. Then she had felt pure joy when Erin got into the car beside her and they set off. She had driven to so many places in Ireland, always alone, but she didn't feel alone any more.

The sisters chatted during the drive, finding they had so much in common, not least their sense of humour. Jenny felt complete, that the missing something she had always been aware of was now sitting beside her. Then, during a quiet spell when they were just content in each other's company, the questions arose again in her mind, the ones her father had to answer.

'How did you learn to drive?' Erin asked. 'It's something I've wanted to do, but the lessons have to be paid for and I haven't been able to afford it.'

Jenny told her, Erin gasping as she listened until at last she had heard everything.

'So, you see, I thought I was married but I wasn't.'

Erin was sympathetic, especially about losing the baby, and asked a few more questions about Marcos. 'So you were left with nothing?'

'Oh, I wouldn't say that. I've still money in my bank account and jewellery to sell.'

'Well, Jenny, it seems we are different in two things.'

'Really! I think we're identical.'

'In looks, yes. But one, I'm broke, and two, I'm still a virgin.'

Jenny laughed, Erin too, the two of them so happy in each other's company. It was a long drive though, and they decided to stop en route for the night, settling down in a twin room.

'Jenny?' whispered Erin before they both drifted off to sleep.

'What?'

'I already love you so much.'

'And I you too,' Jenny said, smiling sleepily. It had been a long time since she had felt this happy, her pain at Marcos's betrayal fading to insignificance in the light of finding Erin. How could she mourn a man she had never really known, the one she had thought she loved having been just a shadow? She would always mourn the loss of her baby, but hoped she would one day have others. For now Jenny was just content with this – with having her sister beside her, their connection so strong that she knew it would never be broken again.

Chapter Fifty-Six

Edward opened his door on Thursday evening and blinked. No, no, this wasn't possible!

'You look surprised, Dad,' Jenny said as she stepped inside, her twin sister behind her. 'I don't know why though. You must have known about Erin.'

Edward's mind had frozen, his throat constricted and heart beating like a drum in his chest as he gripped the arm of a chair and sat down. Jenny looked so cool, so composed, her twin identical, both looking at him, both waiting for him to speak. He couldn't, not a word, as the questions continued from Jenny.

'Why didn't you tell me about Erin?'

At last Edward found his voice. 'Your mother would only agree to adopting one of you.'

'Oh, so it's her fault that you left my sister behind?'

'Yes, it is. I'm afraid I had no choice.'

'It would have been kinder to leave us together. At least then a family might have come along who'd adopt both of us, Erin's for instance. The woman who adopted her would never have separated us.'

'Jenny tells me that you're a distant relative,' said Erin.

'Yes, that's right,' Edward said, feeling now as though he was drowning in his own lies.

''Tis strange that she couldn't find any trace of them.'

'I . . . I thought they lived in Dray.'

'Yes, and you thought the home you adopted Jenny from was in the Limerick area. Strange too, when according to my mother it was in County Cork.'

'Dad, I think you lied to me, but why?' Jenny asked.

Edward shook his head, unable to answer Jenny.

'Please, Dad, both Erin and I deserve the truth.'

He looked at his daughters, so alike, so beautiful and saw that their eyes were so like their mother's, a woman he had betrayed. How could he tell them that? Jenny was right though, after all she had been through, she did deserve the truth, but it could mean that he could lose his daughters for ever. After what he had done perhaps it was no more than he deserved, but still he fought to find words to redeem himself if only in some small way. He just hoped he could soften it somehow. 'Please, both of you sit down. I have something to tell you.'

They did so in unison, sitting side by side on a

sofa. 'I . . . I'm more than a distant relative. I . . . I'm your father.'

'*What?* You mean our real father?' This burst of words from Erin, but Jenny remained silent, in total shock.

'I'm not proud of this, but I . . . well, I had an affair with your mother. When she told me she was pregnant, I panicked, and I'm afraid I abandoned her.'

'But why?' Erin asked.

'I was married, with a baby already – Robin, my son – but as the months passed I was plagued with guilt about your mother. I went back, intending to at least offer financial support, but I was too late and she wasn't there. Fortunately she had left me a letter, telling me she had gone back to Ireland, that she was going into a home to have her baby.'

'Yes, one for unmarried mothers,' Jenny said bitterly, recovering enough now to speak.

'I went there to find her, but couldn't get any information until I confessed I was the father. It was only then that I was told your mother had died giving birth to you both.'

'Did she know that you were married?' asked Erin.

'No, she thought I was single.'

'So you lied to her?'

'Yes, I'm afraid so . . . But, believe me, I'm not proud of what I did.'

'So when you found out that she'd died giving

birth, you came back to England and lied to Delia too, fabricated a story about our mother being a distant relative?'

'Yes, but as I said, she would only agree to adopt one of you, leaving me with an agonising choice. You were identical, and it was almost impossible, but in the end a nun picked you up Jenny and the decision was made for me.'

'I can't believe they agreed to separate us.'

'Well they did,' he said, unwilling to admit that he'd had to leave a substantial donation to the home before it was made possible.

Both girls were staring at him, both white-faced. Unable to bear the look on their faces he fled the room, mumbling an excuse that he had to go to the bathroom.

Jenny was staggered and she could see that Erin was too. As the shock subsided, anger rose, anger at what their father had done. She surged to her feet.

'Erin, I can't bear to look at him now. I'm going. Are you coming with me?'

'Yes, let's go.'

Jenny was still so angry that she slammed the door behind them. She had driven only a short distance before she had to pull up, to find that as she looked across at Erin, her twin had tears in her eyes too.

'I . . . I just can't take it in,' Erin said.

'Nor me.'

''Tis dreadful to think about what he did to our mother.'

'I know, and I can't seem to find any excuses for him.'

'Jenny, do you realise that we look a lot like him?'

'Yes, but I always thought it was because we were related, however distantly,' Jenny said. 'I wonder now if Delia guessed and that's why she treated me so badly.'

'She shouldn't have taken it out on you. 'Twasn't your fault that he lied to her.'

'Erin, I still can't take it all in and I'm not sure that I ever want to see our father again.'

'I feel the same at the moment, but he *is* our Dada, Jenny.'

'Yes, and that means that Robin is our half-brother.'

'What is he like?'

'He's nice, you'll like him. I doubt he knows about this and he's in for a shock. We'll have to arrange to meet him.'

'I'd like that, but it'll have to be soon, Jenny. You know I'm going back to Ireland next week, and though I don't like my job in a café I can't afford to take more time off. What about you? What are you going to do and where will you live?'

'I don't know, but I suppose I should start looking for a flat, and eventually a job,' Jenny said. 'For now though, let's find somewhere to eat and to stay for the night.'

It was only later, lying in bed in yet another hotel, that Jenny had an idea. Could it work? Yes, perhaps, but it needed a lot more thought before she put it to Erin.

Chapter Fifty-Seven

When Jenny and Erin met up with Robin, they found out that he already knew the truth.

'I was shocked too when Dad told me. I think he guessed you'd get in touch with me, but he wanted me to hear it from him. I know he's sorry and that he isn't proud of what he did, but it's still a bit hard to swallow. My mother suspected the truth and it's why she made your life a misery – that and perhaps guilt that she would only agree to adopt one of you.'

'It's all so awful, Robin.'

'I know, but I think they are both genuinely sorry.'

'I'm not sure I can forgive either of them,' Jenny said.

'Jenny, but perhaps we should try,' Erin advised. 'If we don't we may become bitter and the past will ruin our future.'

'It seems your twin has a wise head on her shoulders,' Robin said. 'Don't forget that Dad made a fool of my mother, but she's managed to move on. She's made a new life for herself and has started a business, one that already looks as if it's going to be successful.'

'Well, bully for her,' Jenny snapped.

'See what I mean,' said Erin.

At last Jenny smiled. 'All right, point taken.'

'Robin, you just have to know how to handle her,' Erin said. 'Now tell me, how does it feel to have two sisters?'

'I suppose I'll just have to put up with it,' Robin said, grinning widely. 'Now tell me, what are your plans?'

'I have to go back to Ireland soon,' Erin said.

'How about keeping in touch? We could ring each other or write.'

'Yes, I'd like that.'

'What about you, Jenny?' Robin asked.

'I'm not sure what I'll be doing yet, but I'll let you know.'

'And Dad?'

'I'd like to talk to him again before I go back to Ireland,' Erin said.

Jenny pulled a face. 'I'm not sure that I want to see him again just yet, but you can ring him if you want to. I haven't got his telephone number, but no doubt Robin can give it to you.'

He did, and an hour later they parted, hugging and agreeing to keep in touch. 'He's nice. I like him,' Erin said as Jenny drove back to the hotel that they had stayed in close to Richmond where they had met up with Robin.

'Yes, he is,' Jenny agreed. Robin had asked her about her plans, but she hadn't revealed what she had in mind.

That night, Jenny lay in bed going over her idea again. 'Erin, are you still awake?'

'Yes, I am. I've been laying here dreading the thought of going back to Ireland without you. I'm going to miss you so much.'

'I've been feeling the same about you, but I've had an idea. I still have quite a bit of money in the bank, and along with the sale of my jewellery, it may be enough for us to start something up a little business together. In Ireland of course.'

'Oh, Jenny, that sounds great, but what sort of business?'

'At first I considered a bookshop, but as I haven't had any experience in running one, it's not something I feel confident about. However, we've both worked in a cafe so how about something like that, perhaps a nice little tea room.'

'Yes, I like the sound of that.'

'To make a decent profit it would have to be somewhere that's popular with tourists.'

Erin sat up, switched her bedside light on, her grin wide. 'How about in the place that brought us together?'

Kilkee! Oh, yes, that would be perfect,' Jenny cried.

'I can't wait to get started, and as we'll be together, I'm sure my Mammy won't mind if I leave home, especially with my Aunt Corinne on the doorstep to keep an eye on me.'

'I'll be able to see Maeve and her father too, and even better, Nuala when she comes to visit them,' Jenny enthused.

'In that case it seems to me that Kilkee is going to be the perfect place for us,' Erin said, then yawning.

'Yes, I think so too, but I think we both need to get some sleep now.'

'All right, but though I'm tired I think I might be too excited to sleep.'

Jenny felt the same, but as Erin turned off the light, she closed her eyes, at last drifting off to sleep, content in the knowledge that she and Erin were going to remain together. She just hoped it would be for a long, long time.

Had Jenny been able to see into the future, she would have seen that many, many years of happiness stretched ahead for both her and Erin. The tea room would be successful, and even when they both married, they would continue to run it together, the sisters now that they had found each other, inseparable.

THE END

In Conversation with Kitty Neale

1. If you were stranded on a desert island, which book would you take with you?
I'd be hopeless in that situation, so perhaps a book giving tips on how to survive.

2. Where does your inspiration come from?
It usually comes when I imagine a character and a situation they are in, but there have been occasions when the memory of a place triggers off a story, such as Drapers Alley in *Family Betrayal*.

3. Have you always wanted to become a writer?
With my childhood background and education, it wouldn't have been mentioned or encouraged so no, I'm afraid not. I loved reading, but it would never have occurred to me that I could become a writer.

4. What's the strangest job you've ever had?

Goodness, now you've stumped me. I've had a variety of jobs, but I can't say that any of them were strange. I met some strange people along the way though which has made the journey fascinating.

5. When you're not writing, what are your favourite things to do?

I love meeting friends for lunch, swimming and lazing by the pool in the summer with a good book, and of course . . . SHOPPING!

6. What is a typical working day like for you? Have you ever had writer's block? If so, how did you cope with it?

I start work at around 10am and my first job is to edit the previous day's writing. I then carry on, and if the story is flowing well I usually lose all sense of time. There have been occasions when my hubby will stick his head in the door to ask if we are eating today. As for writer's block, if I'm not having a particularly good day, I find it best to stop for what I call thinking time. I take a break, relax for a while, do something else, and then I find the story begins to unfold in my mind again.

7. Do you have any secret ambitions?

I'd love to see one of my books made into a TV drama or into a film, but as most writers probably want the same thing, I don't suppose it can be called a secret ambition.

8. What can't you live without?

My family and friends – a bathroom (I'd be no good in a tent) – my computer or at least a type-writer (my handwriting is dreadful and after a few sentences illegible).

9. When you were a child, what did you want to be when you grew up?

From the first time I saw one, I wanted to be a ballet dancer.

10. Which five people, living or dead, would you invite to a dinner party?

Billy Connolly
Stephen Fry
Princess Di
Bill Clinton
Gloria Hunniford

What's next?

Tell us the name of an author you love

Kitty Neale | Go ▶

and we'll find your next great book.